Fiona Harris and Mike McLeish are a talented husband-and-wife writing and performing team. They have carved out impressive and unique careers in the arts, both as individuals and as a creative duo.

Fiona has written and co-written fifteen books, for both children and adults. Her extensive work in prime-time TV includes sketch comedy shows like *Flipside*, *Skithouse* and *Comedy Inc.*, as well as marquee television dramas like *The Beautiful Lie*, *Tangle* and *Offspring*.

Mike has worked in mainstage musicals – including *Keating! The Musical*, *Shane Warne the Musical*, *Georgy Girl: The Seekers Musical* and *Beautiful: The Carole King Musical* – and television, in shows such as *Utopia*, *Mustangs*, *Wentworth* and *The Time of Our Lives*.

In 2019, Mike and Fiona released their internationally award-winning comedy web series *The Drop Off*, which to date has won a dozen international 'Best Web Series' awards. Channel 9 screened a telemovie version of the show in 2021.

THE DROP-OFF

FIONA HARRIS &
MIKE McLEISH

echo
PUBLISHING

echo
PUBLISHING

An imprint of Bonnier Books UK
4th Floor, Victoria House, Bloomsbury Square
London WC1B 4DA
www.echopublishing.com.au
www.bonnierbooks.co.uk

Echo Publishing acknowledges the traditional custodians of Country throughout Australia. We recognise their continuing connection to land, sea and waters. We pay our respects to Elders past and present.

First published 2020
This edition published 2023

Printed and bound in Australia by Pegasus Media and Logistics

The paper in this book is FSC® certified. FSC® promotes environmentally responsible, socially beneficial and economically viable management of the world's forests.

Cover design: Design by Committee
Page design and typesetting by Shaun Jury

A catalogue entry for this book is available from the National Library of Australia

ISBN: 9781760688011 (paperback)
ISBN: 9781760686246 (ebook)

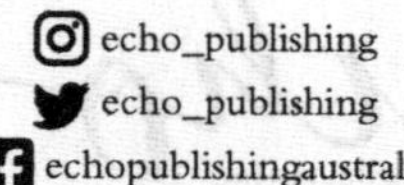

For Finn and Abbie, who have taught us how to be grown-ups, but still let us act like kids.

It's not right that someone so pretty should have to be around idiots like us but it's kind of like she's got a force field around her. Like the stink can't touch her. I watched her again today. She's amazing. I didn't know a girl could be that strong and that pretty at the same time. It's like she's breaking the rules.

And I'll say it. I'll say it to her if I get the chance. I'll say it to her after the first time we're together. I'll kiss her and I'll say, 'You're amazing.' And she'll smile and kiss me back and I'll say, 'Will you be mine?' And she will. And then everyone will know.

And I'll hold her hand and bring her sausage rolls with sauce on the side because she likes to pick up her sausage roll and wipe it in the sauce in a circle around her plate. And I'll learn heaps more things about her like that so I can do more things like that for her so I can be a good husband for her.

Lizzie

Hey buddy, so maybe I should start at the beginning like most good stories do …

Nope. Delete delete delete.

Dear Greg, I have a story to tell you …

Worse. Am I Hans Christian Andersen now? Delete delete delete.

Hey Greg, so yesterday I was at school drop-off when I saw …

Too sudden. Gotta ease him into it.

Shit. This was hard. Clearly it had been a while since I'd written anything more challenging than the labour ward register.

Dear Greg, I have to tell you something. And it's probably best if I tell you in chronological order. Well, yesterday, when I was –

'Mum, someone stole my hoodie!'

Dammit.

'I'll call Interpol!' I yelled back. 'Unless it's still in your bag from last term!'

'I already looked there!' The volume of Zara's voice was escalating. I saved my few measly words as 'Lizzie's Xmas Presents' and closed it. Greg would rather commit hara-kiri than peek at his wife's secret gift ideas. His ruddy face grinned out at me from the framed photo beside the computer, as if saying, *Yep, I'm an honourable bugger, all right!*

The photo was taken on the beach last summer, and the six laughing faces in the photo, including my own, were all mashed into each other. It looked like someone had squished us into a fishbowl. Zara was missing her right arm and the bottom half of Max's face was cut off. Not my husband's forte, the art of the selfie. After a series of epic fails, Greg had finally managed to take this single half-decent shot before we'd all collapsed backwards onto a bed of wet sandy towels.

There was a distinct twang in my chest, like someone had just reached in and plucked the top of my ribcage with a plectrum. Greg deserved to know the truth, which meant I had to make time to finish the letter; in hindsight, 8.25 a.m. on a school morning hadn't been the wisest choice. Had I honestly expected to get through the opening sentence, let alone a paragraph, without one of my four offspring demanding my attention? I was lucky to get through my first wee without interruption, let alone write a life-changing letter to my husband. If I wasn't so gutless, I'd have an actual conversation with the man. We did live in the same house, after all. But Greg had never been one for 'scenes' – a word Zara used to describe any conversation that escalated beyond a quiet chat over a cup of Milo – and the chat I needed to have with Greg could well grow from a 'scene' into a full-blown 'drama'.

The man I'd married twelve years ago was an unassuming six-foot-two brick-shithouse Aussie, wary of any man who confessed to no interest in footy or hard work, and with a deep love for his family, beer and shepherd's pie. The order of the latter two were interchangeable, depending on his mood, but they were always a distant runner-up to his family. Us. A lot of people take in Greg Barrett's stubbled face and paint-spattered overalls and make the assumption that there isn't a whole lot going on upstairs. But not only was my husband a born workhorse and naturally kind-hearted, he was also full-lurch-forward funny, loyal and cluey as hell.

However, not cluey enough to know that his wife had been keeping a secret from him for the past fifteen years, so I'd mapped out my ingenious plan in bed last night.

1. *Finish letter before next early shift*
2. *Get up extra early and leave letter on front seat of Greg's work van*
3. *Make quick escape to early shift so Greg could read letter while I was safe at work.*

No man I knew (except maybe Sam) would be foolish enough to confront his wife in a place full of women who are in the worst pain they're ever likely to experience. Greg would be torn to shreds in seconds. A pack of hungry wolves would be more merciful.

'Mum!'

'*WHAT?*'

Zara, half-dressed and bursting with pre-teen rage, stood in the doorway. At eleven, she was already as tall as me, had her dad's white-blonde hair and green eyes, and was whippet-thin. Obsessed with comics, CGI and coding, Zara planned to work for Pixar when she grew up. Aside from her impatience, my eldest daughter was prone to hyper-sensitivity and could be moodier than the hottest, most tormented teenage vampire. But she was also a brilliant mimic who made me laugh more than any of my other kids.

'My hoodie?' Zara's head was at a 45-degree angle, her hands on her bony hips.

'Have you looked in your wardrobe?'

'Yes!'

'Did you find Harold Holt in there while you were at it?'

After two weeks of school holidays, Zara's bedroom had reached a level of chaos that a black hole would applaud.

'What?' She shook her head like she was addressing a malfunctioning printer.

'Even if your hoodie *was* in that wardrobe, you'd need the full Beaconsfield team to get it out!'

'What are you *talking* about?' Zara said. 'I just need my hoodie! I'm meeting Amy on the corner in five minutes!'

I marched through the house with an almost hyperventilating Zara close behind. Along the way, I hollered instructions to my other children, only some of whom were visible.

'*Max*, Lego! In its box or in the bin! *Stella*, you know there's no TV on school mornings! *Archie*, why are your runners on the toaster? That's just ...'

At the doorway to Zara's room, I was struck dumb with astonishment. It looked like it had been ransacked by small-time mobsters who most definitely did not find what they were looking for. Clothes, shoes, comics, graphic novels, necklaces, various lip balms, books and earrings covered every square inch of every available space. Zara had always been a slob, but this was some next-level shit.

'Can you find it?'

'Are you kidding me?' I spun around to face her. 'Zara, I can't find your *bed*!'

'It's not that bad,' she said sulkily. 'I just pulled a few things out.'

'Ozzy Osbourne is neater than you.'

'Okay, seriously, Mum,' she said, patting me on the arm. 'Enough with the old people references.'

Stella pushed past me and stared in horror at the apocalypse that was also her bedroom.

'I cleaned this room *last night*!' She flung her skinny arms around like Kermit the Frog being operated by the work-experience kid. 'You have *no respect* for my space!'

'Oh, don't be such a drama queen,' Zara said, rolling her eyes. 'It's just a few clothes.'

Stella tugged at her long golden plaits in despair, huge eyes almost popping out of their sockets. As long as she continued to live in our three-bedroom house (the office doubled as the dining room), poor Stella had to share a room with Zara. It was the old Felix Unger and Oscar Madison story, but with two cantankerous pre-pubescent sisters instead of two grumpy fifty-something men.

Sometimes it seemed to me that Stella was a 45-year-old tax accountant trapped in the body of an eight year old. She wanted to be a Corporate Social Responsibility Events Manager when she grew up. I had no idea what uni course she needed to enrol in for that. It was best to intervene before my youngest daughter self-combusted.

'Zara, this room is to be spotless by the time you go to bed tonight or no Bounce with Cara on Saturday.' I took an almost catatonic Stella by the shoulders and turned her away from the scene of devastation. 'And you can borrow Archie's spare hoodie for today,' I called back as I continued steering Stella down the hallway.

'Archie's hoodie smells like feet!'

'Your *bum* smells like feet!' Archie yelled as we passed his bedroom.

Honestly, a sea sponge had a sharper wit than my son.

'Good comeback,' I said, popping my head into Archie and Max's room.

Archie was sprawled across his green rug, drawing a character I could only assume was Spider-Man. He'd recently seen the Tom Holland version and was now obsessed. Spider-Man drawings of all shapes and sizes were pinned in meandering rows on the cork board above his wooden desk, covering faded sketches of Han Solo and Darth Vader.

'Take your manky shoes off my toaster, please,' I told him, releasing Stella to continue stumbling down the hallway like a baby giraffe. 'Archie, now!'

'What?' Archie said without raising his head. 'Who's having toast?'

Archie couldn't have been more different from his twin, Zara. Greg and I secretly called him the Absent-Minded Professor. Archie was academically gifted, but his lack of social skills was matched only by his inability to conjure up a decent comeback to his sister's sass. He also did things like pop his runners on top of a kitchen appliance. And the poor kid did stink. No matter how many times I washed that damn hoodie it still smelt, as Zara said, like feet. His runners reeked like blue cheese. I detested blue cheese, hence my outrage at the sight of those runners propped on my toaster like a wanky art exhibit.

'He put them there while he was brushing his teeth with *my* electric toothbrush!' Max announced, running into the room he shared with Archie, carrying what looked like his entire collection of Lego. Max dumped what remained in his arms into the huge box in the corner of their room, dropping at least half the pieces as he went. 'There!'

Max, my baby, was only six, so rarely moved slower than a power walk and bore the remnants of one condiment or another on his face at all times.

'Let's just be grateful he didn't pop the electric toothbrush into the toaster, or we'd all be stuffed,' I said, picking up a Lego fuselage.

'*Swear jar!*'

'*Stuffed* is not a swear word!' I called back to Stella. 'Now turn that TV off or you'll hear a real one!'

'I'm going!' a hoodie-less Zara announced, opening the front door. 'And you're gonna be *wrecked* with guilt for the rest of your life when I die of hypothermia!'

'*Wracked*, sweetie,' I said, plucking a tiny policeman's helmet from between my bare toes. 'I'll be *wracked* with guilt.'

I loved my kids, but Jesus they gave me the shits.

After ordering Max, Stella and Archie to complete the morning routine of teeth, shoes and lunchbox in schoolbags for the eighty-eighth time, I decided to get dressed myself. Our bedroom wasn't much tidier than Zara and Stella's, but I was the parent, so y'know, 'do as I say, not as I do'. Housework had been dropping down the priority list for a while now, with school holidays and my hours at the hospital ramping up before my long service leave in a few months. And now Rick Cooke – Rick fucking *Cooke* – had appeared out of nowhere like a giant, painful pimple that you really wanted to squeeze but knew you shouldn't for fear it would only double in size and life-expectancy. Thank God Sam had stolen that stupid bloody hat, or I might never have spotted Rick when I did and got the hell out of there before he spotted *me*. That was twenty-four hours ago but I was still shaking.

It had started out like any other Tuesday morning drop-off, with Megan, Sam and I convening on 'our' bench in the Baytree Primary schoolyard to share whatever was on our minds. Sam and Megan were my drop-off mates, and together we drank coffee and talked shit for a few precious minutes each day.

Sam had just handed us our coffees when Megan glanced over at something and frowned. 'Hey Sam, did Lola get caught eating her lunch in the toilets again?'

'No, why?'

She nodded towards the playground where kids were doing death-drops off the monkey bars, swinging upside down from the top of the flying fox and wobbling across the chain bridge. Some younger siblings – dragged along to drop-off with no choice in the matter – were chewing bark chips, maybe as a form of protest. In the middle of this bedlam stood Penny Guthrie, principal of Baytree Primary, talking intently to Sam's daughter, Lola, who was looking up at Penny and shaking her head.

'Oooo!' I crowed. 'Lola's in trouble with the principaaaal!'

It was strange to see Sam's well-behaved, if slightly odd, daughter being told off. Lola had always stood out from the rest of Stella's grade-three class. She wore her school dress long (at least six inches below her knees), piled her long dark hair into a high-top bun and used words no one expected to hear coming out of an eight year old's mouth, like 'objectionable' and 'ne'er-do-well'. Lola Hatfield was kooky. I liked her.

'I hope she hasn't been quoting Jane Austen to her classmates again,' Sam said, fiddling nervously with the lid of his coffee. 'At her last Lit Circles session, she told Charlie Briggs he was "illiterate and coarse".'

'Guthrie creeps me out,' Megan said, looking down at her phone.

'I wouldn't call her creepy,' Sam said. 'Thatcher-esque, maybe.'

Penny Guthrie dressed exactly the way you'd imagine a school principal would, if it was 1955: knitted turtleneck, blazer, slacks and black pumps. She wore minimal makeup on her pale skin and her blonde hair was in a low ponytail, held in place with more hairspray than necessary. Behind her sharp eyes was an unnerving calm that had undoubtedly developed from years spent dealing with young children and – more to the point – their parents. She'd replaced the previous principal, who'd been at the school for over a decade, at the start of this year. It couldn't have been easy, starting from scratch with all the teachers, kids and parents, especially parents as disinterested as Baytree parents. So, we weren't exactly qualified to judge how creepy or not creepy she was, considering none of us had engaged her in conversation.

'Oh shit,' Sam said, squeezing his takeaway cup so hard that the lid popped off. 'She's coming over.'

Sure enough, Penny Guthrie was on the move, hands behind her back, crunching her way across a carpet of bark chips.

'Relax, chicken little,' I said. 'She's heading back to her office.'

But Penny suddenly veered left and headed straight towards us.

'Oh shit!' Megan hissed. 'She *is* coming over here! You're fucked! And you've got coffee on your jeans.'

'Good morning!' Penny said, approaching us with a smile that didn't reach her eyes.

'Hi Penny,' Megan and I chorused cheerily.

'Hello ...?'

'Megan, Oscar Wylie's mum.'

'Lizzie, many kids' mum.'

'Good morning,' she said before turning to address Sam. 'You're Sam, Lola's dad?'

He gave the tiniest, most reluctant nod an adult could give a principal.

'I noticed you going through the lost-property bin yesterday at pick-up,' Penny said, her frozen smile faltering slightly.

'Yeah, it's like a bottomless pit, that thing.' Sam chuckled, perhaps in some misguided attempt to invite Penny to join him in the obvious amusement of the lost-property bin. She didn't.

Megan's finger dug into my right thigh, and suddenly I was back in year nine when Melissa Morton and I tried to suppress our giggles as Mr Winter leant over our desks and roared, '*What the hell is so funny?*'

'Yes, lost property remains a work in progress,' Penny replied. 'Did you find what you were looking for?'

'Uh, no, I didn't unfortunately.' Sam was rattled.

'But you did find this?' Penny said, pulling out a school hat from behind her back.

'Lola's hat!' Sam reached for it, but Penny held it back.

'Is it?' she asked.

'Yeah. I mean, I think it ... it was ...' Sam glanced at us in desperation. He'd gone too far with the whole 'that's Lola's hat' facade to turn back now. It was hard watching our mate being tortured like this, but we couldn't take our eyes off the slow-motion car crash playing out in front of us. Brilliant stuff for a Tuesday morning.

'All right, it's not hers,' he confessed, crumbling like stale bread, 'but it's her size and there was no name on it and, look, I'm sure the karma of the lost-property bin will make sure ...'

Megan turned to me, her eyebrows raised. 'The karma ...?'

'... of the lost-property bin?' I repeated back to her.

Sam ignored us. 'It's just that I've lost count of how many times Lola's lost her fuck ... funky ... school hat this year and there's still two terms to go!'

'I understand,' Penny said. 'Kids lose hats. But I would've thought it best for Lola to learn about responsibility and consequences rather than having you steal her a hat, wouldn't you think, Sam?'

She was good.

'It's July,' Megan said, frowning. 'Do they really need hats?'

'Yes, they do, Megan. School policy.'

'I'll make sure Lola has a good look for it at home,' Sam said.

'In the meantime,' Penny continued, 'she must stay in the shaded Italian garden during recess.'

'Fair enough.' Sam was trying to fold in on himself to the point of invisibility.

The principal released Sam from her stare and took in all of us. 'Are you all coming to Careers Day?' she asked in a bright new tone. 'The children are very excited.'

Sam half-nodded and mumbled something incoherent.

Megan grinned. 'Yep, I'll be there.'

'I'll have to check my roster,' I said. 'But I'm really hoping I can make it.'

I was lying. Standing in front of a room full of six year

olds and talking about extracting babies from vaginas wasn't my idea of time well spent.

'Yes, well, I *hope* we'll see you all there,' Penny said. 'Have a lovely day.'

Megan turned to Sam the moment Penny was out of earshot. 'Still don't think she's creepy?'

'You're full of shit.' I flicked Megan on the thigh. '*Yep, I'll be there!*' I mimicked Megan's response to Penny. 'Since when have you *ever* gone to something like that?'

'I know why she's going,' Sam said. 'She wants to get the kids to go home and beg mummy and daddy to buy clothes from Chill.'

Chill was Megan's online kids' clothing and accessories business. If it was 'Lit', 'Dope' or 'Legit' (I knew these words thanks to Zara), Chill stocked it. The business had over forty thousand followers on Instagram and had won the Kids Fashion Boutique Awards three years running. In other words, when it came to kids' fashion, Megan Wylie was legit lit.

'I resent that,' Megan sniffed. 'I'm doing it for the children, Sam. The *children*.'

'All right, Angelina,' Sam said. 'You gonna adopt them too?'

'You've lost the moral high ground, hat thief,' I said.

'It was probably some poor little redhead's precious hat,' Megan said.

'Redheads never lose their hats,' Sam said. 'That's life or death for them.'

'I'd start by looking in the girls' toilets,' I said, nodding towards a glum Lola, now sitting alone in the Italian garden like a loser. 'Stella said Lola always takes her hat off to wash her hands. Something about nineteenth-century etiquette.'

Sam jumped up and ran towards the girls' bathroom.

'He'll be back when he realises he can't go in there,' Megan said, going back to her Instagram feed.

I grinned, turning my head to watch Sam sprint across the yard, and that's when I saw him. Rick Cooke. He was just standing there on the other side of the yard, chatting with students. Just standing there. In my school! No one expects someone from their past to crash-land in their present like a meteor, and Rick had no right being in my present. He was something I'd left behind. Something I'd had to get on the other side of, to get here. And Baytree Primary was my turf; it was where I felt comfortable, drank good takeaway coffee and had banal morning chats with my mates. To them, I was Mum Lizzie: honest, good, dependable Lizzie; tough but fair Lizzie. Seeing Rick on my turf had twisted and tested my sense of identity. Because he knew a different Lizzie. A long-gone Lizzie.

Shaken, I'd made some lame excuse to Megan about having to take the dog to the vet and got the hell out of there. As I'd walked home, my heart racing, it dawned on me that after all these years I had no choice but to finally tell my husband the truth. He was bound to bump into Rick at some point and I just couldn't have Greg find out what I'd done all those years ago from a stranger. It was unthinkable. But then, so was the idea of Greg finding out who his wife really was.

'Mum?' Stella said, dragging me back to the present.

'Huh?'

She was standing next to me, schoolbag on and eyebrows raised. 'We have to GO!'

I pulled my duffel coat tighter around me and glanced at the school building. I didn't know if it was Melbourne's wind chill factor or fearing that Rick Cooke might be around somewhere that was giving me shivers. I scoped out my surroundings like a canny fugitive. The back gate was in the opposite direction to the building, so if Rick did appear, I had my exit strategy worked out. I shouldn't have come into the school at all, but it was my turn to bring coffee. And apart from the caffeine hit, I really needed a Megan and Sam hit this morning.

Megan was a single mum to six-year-old Oscar, and also happened to be unfairly beautiful. When I'd first spotted her at Max's kindergarten concert, I'd immediately assumed that the tall, skinny, thirty-something with perfect skin and cascading brown-blonde locks was a bimbo. As my friend Aileen said, 'It's perfectly fair not to like attractive people. They're guilty until proven innocent.' But Megan had a ferocious mind with a mouth to match. And she was funny.

Sam was a full-time house husband and dad to Lola and Tyler. He had a kind face, was a SNAG in the truest sense of the acronym, and one of the good guys. His wife, Bridget, was a big corporate something-or-other who was away a lot. Megan and I had never met her, and Sam got a bit weird whenever we brought her up, so we stopped. Fine with us. We loved the Sam we hung out with at drop-off and had little interest in his marriage. The first time I noticed him (not hard; he's six foot three) he was trying to choose between a Kingston and a Monte Carlo at the Prep orientation morning. As our offspring sat at tiny tables, literally trying to shove square pegs into round holes, we were banished to the stale-smelling, airless staffroom, out of our clingy kids' sight. I knew Sam and I would get along when I clocked him rolling his eyes behind the back of a mum who 'just hoped her Sebastian would be able to relate to the less mature kids'.

The location of choice for our daily drop-off chats was a bench in the far corner of the schoolyard. It wasn't that we didn't like other parents, we just weren't particularly interested in finding out whether we liked them or not. But today I'd moved to a different bench. One even further away from the school building and near the netball courts.

'Wrong bench.'

'Huh?'

'Why are you over here? There are *children* over here.'

Megan may as well have said there was a pungent smell of dog shit over here.

'Less sun.' I wasn't ready to tell Megan the truth about Rick yet. If ever. Anyway, it wouldn't be fair to Greg if my friends knew before him.

Megan frowned. 'It's winter.'

I handed Megan her coffee, hoping to distract her. It worked.

'Yay!' she beamed, grabbing the takeaway cup and sitting beside me.

'Good morning, ladies!'

I turned, and Megan tilted her torso to look past my shoulder. 'Hi Henry!'

Henry beamed and shuffled a few feet away from the crossing, an invisible tether preventing him from straying too far from his post. Bald, bespectacled and with a deeply wrinkled face that never surrendered its smile, Henry must have been at least seventy, but had the energy of a fifty year old. He'd been the crossing guard outside Baytree Primary for as long as I could remember. 'Bit warm for July!' he called out.

Henry's daily commentary on the weather was as inevitable as the tide. In the six and a half years I'd been at the school, I'd never heard him voice an opinion on anything else. He and my dad would get along. Old men and the elements seem to have a very special relationship.

'Yeah,' I called back.

'Supposed to rain later today!' Henry shuffled closer, but Megan gave him a cursory nod and turned her back on him, shutting the conversation down like a disgruntled guest on *60 Minutes*.

'I ... uh ... wanted to keep an eye on Max.' I nodded towards my son who was careening backwards down the slide.

'Since when?'

'Since he's been having issues with a kid in his class.' This was crap. If anyone's kid was going to be causing issues it would have been mine, but it was all I could come up with on the spot.

'Which kid?'

'He won't tell me.' No point naming and shaming some innocent kid. I was a lying lowlife, but I had standards.

'I bet it's that little fucker Charlie,' Megan said, curling her lip. 'That kid needs a slap.'

'Who needs a slap?'

I looked up to see Sam standing beside the bench.

'You,' Megan said without missing a beat.

Sam turned and poked his bum out towards Megan who ignored him and went back to her phone. I handed him his coffee.

'Zara looks cold,' Sam said, wrapping his hands around the warm cardboard cup.

On the other side of the schoolyard, my daughter was shivering like a junkie. Her friend, Amy, was furiously rubbing Zara's arms, as if trying to start a fire in a snowstorm.

'How could you let her out like that?' Sam asked. 'It's freezing. Poor thing.'

'It's July,' Megan said. 'S'posed to be cold.'

'You wouldn't be saying "poor thing" if you'd seen her bedroom,' I said to Sam. 'That kid is going to end up on *Hoarders*.'

Megan laughed, and for the first time in twenty-four hours I relaxed.

Megan

Megan always opened Oscar's lunchbox as if she were unzipping a body bag. Sometimes she'd find something perfectly manageable, like a half-eaten banana or a discarded LeSnak wrapper, but other times it was mashed pieces of strangely shaped cheese, liquefied apple cores, a bread crust that could cut diamonds, or plain old dirt.

Dirt!

Megan was fairly certain she hadn't packed dirt for her son's recess snack, but there it was, a hefty handful of dirt with a smattering of tan bark. But it was still early in the term and the lunchbox was yet to develop that complex aroma of mould, sugar syrup and six-year-old boy.

She had *not* missed this after-school routine over the break. Lunchboxes and mystery tan bark were a distant memory at their Barwon Heads Airbnb over the school holidays. 'Jesus!'

'You said a naughty word, man!' Oscar appeared in the doorway, pointing a skinny finger at her.

'Man' was the new big thing in Oscar's vocabulary. *Probably picked it up from bloody Adam,* Megan thought.

'Max says *his* mum has a swear jar.' His tone solemn and tiny brow furrowed. 'And he says it's always full.'

'I'm sure it is,' Megan said, smiling. 'Who told you Jesus was a naughty word?'

Baytree Primary wasn't a religious school. At least, she couldn't remember seeing any documentation saying it was.

Then again, Megan rarely read school correspondence. They could have started lessons on how to join a cult and she wouldn't have had a clue.

'Nana Clara.' Oscar dropped to his belly and wriggled under the counter to retrieve a stray piece of Lego. 'She said you shouldn't say it so much like you do cos it's bas … bast … basfam …'

'Blasphemous.' Jesus Christ! *Of course*. Who else but Clara Campbell would chastise a 35-year-old woman through a child? Oscar had spent two nights with his paternal grandmother on the final weekend of the holidays, and she'd obviously taken the opportunity to further indoctrinate him. Megan wouldn't have been surprised if her son had returned wearing a crucifix around his neck. Her chest burned. She'd become adept at deflecting her ex-mother-in-law's jibes, corrections and withering judgements, but when Clara started lecturing Megan through her kid, it cut through.

'I don't care what Nana Clara told you,' Megan said. 'Jesus is only a naughty word if you believe in God and I don't.'

'But Nana Clara says it's *bad* not to believe in God.' Oscar's voice trembled and his caramel-coloured eyes, so like his dad's, filled with tears.

Megan sat on one of her recently purchased – and totally worth the money – Matt Blatt bar stools and pulled Oscar on to her knee. She threaded her fingers through his sweaty honey-coloured fringe and gently brushed it back off his face. 'Did Nana say something bad might happen to me if I don't believe in God?'

Oscar nodded and Megan took a deep breath. It wasn't the first time she'd heard of her wretched post-mortem fate.

It had been a weekly warning during the Tuesday night dinners Megan had been forced to endure throughout her two-year marriage to Bryce. Clara would sit at the head of her polished-teak dining-room table and, over lukewarm plates of shiny, over-cooked silverside and soggy vegetables, assure her there would be no free pass at the Pearly Gates for non-believers like Megan when she departed this world. The instant Megan Wylie carked it, she was on a one-way express to the fiery pits of hell. The main perk of Megan's divorce three years ago was never having to listen to Clara's religious bullshit ever again. Or so Megan had thought.

'Nothing is going to happen to me just because I don't believe what Nana Clara believes, okay?'

'But God is always watching us, like Santa!' Oscar was sounding more panicked by the second. 'He gets angry if you don't believe in him, man!'

'How does Nana Clara know?' Megan asked. 'Has she met God?'

'Don't think so.' Oscar frowned. 'But you haven't met Santa and he's real.'

'Who says I haven't met Santa?'

Oscar's eyes bugged. 'Have you?'

Megan scoffed. 'We go waaaay back!'

'What's he like?'

'White beard, fat, red suit, twinkle in his eye ... y'know, pretty much what you'd expect.'

'Have you met *God*?'

'No,' Megan confessed. 'But I don't believe in him, so that might make it a bit hard.'

'But isn't that a sin?'

Megan felt as though she was trapped in a purgatorial loop. When she and Bryce had first started dating, Megan had smiled and nodded whenever Clara got going on one of her Heaven and Hell rants. There were many times Bryce had left his mother's house with tiny purple and yellow bruises on his upper thigh, because discreetly pinching her boyfriend under the table was Megan's only outlet during Clara's dinner sermons. Bryce found his mother's ravings amusing, which infuriated Megan even more. Years spent living with a religious zealot had made Bryce impervious to her diatribes. Clara's words seemed to bypass him altogether and – like heat-seeking missiles – plough deep into Megan's flaming eardrums instead. She managed to hold her tongue for a couple of years, until one night when Megan was six months pregnant, tired and hormonal. When Clara raised the subject of her future grandchild's christening, Megan had snapped.

'We're not going to christen our baby!' she shouted at a shocked Clara. 'Religion and all of its bullshit, including dunking babies in God water, are about as relevant as witch-burnings or Kodak shops.'

Megan could feel Bryce's knee gently pressing against hers under the table, but she was on a roll. 'It's not going to happen, Clara.' Megan threw her hands up, launching overcooked peas off the end of her fork and onto Clara's glistening floor tiles. 'There's more chance of me dunking my baby in your soggy mashed potato.'

Clara turned a disturbing shade of crimson. Seconds passed, and as quickly as Megan's blood pressure had soared, it began to subside.

'I … it's the pregnancy … the hormones. Sometimes I …'

But she was drowned out by the sound of metal legs scraping across the tiles as Clara slowly pushed her chair back. 'I'll just check on the apple pie.'

Clara had refused to make eye contact with either of them for the remainder of the meal and they left soon after. Bryce had nicknamed Megan 'Linda Blair' after that, throwing his hands up and shouting, '*The power of Christ compels you!*' whenever she waddled into the room for weeks afterwards, sending her into fits of laughter. But Clara's fanaticism wasn't so amusing when it was poisoning Megan's beautiful boy's mind.

'Nothing bad is going to happen to me just because I say a word some people don't like,' Megan said. 'Nana Clara believes different things to us but that doesn't mean she's right, okay?'

As Oscar nodded and nuzzled into the side of her neck, Megan decided she needed to talk to Bryce about this. They might not be married any more but they still shared a belief system when it came to Clara's underhanded schemes to save her grandson's soul. Besides, Megan had assumed Clara had more pressing matters to contend with these days. Like saving her own son from those fiery pits. Oh, how Megan wished she could have been there to witness Clara's reaction to the news that her perfect son was leaving his wife for a man.

The toilet flushed down the hall and Megan remembered that she'd actually brought two boys home from school.

'Where's Toby?' Megan hadn't seen him since they'd arrived back half an hour ago and she'd stuffed them both with berries and crackers.

'In my room playing Lego.' Oscar shrugged. 'He's *obsessed*, man!'

'Well, his mum's coming soon.' Megan lifted Oscar off her knee and gave his bum a tap. 'So, go play.'

Oscar ran off and Megan looked at her phone. Just

enough time to check Chill emails and put in the new stock order – two hundred T-shirts emblazoned with Robin Williams in full Mork costume with the words *NA-NU NA-NU* underneath. No kid would ever have heard of *Mork & Mindy*, but the kids weren't the ones buying the clothes. Megan was extremely skilled at tapping into parents' nostalgia and knew most of them were less concerned about practicality, and more focused on their little ones wearing useful conversation starters.

Managing the Instagram, the stock and the designers kept Megan busy, and the constant demands of running a business on your own was definitely stressful, but she stayed on top of it all for the most part. Chill's office was the front room of Megan's three-bedroom terrace house, a house that displayed all the signs that one of its inhabitants was a small boy. Her sense of style meant their house could get away with a certain level of mess. The furnishings were so chic that anything that was on top of them – a lunchbox on the stove, a toy dinosaur on the couch, a frayed book and a banana peel on the coffee table – looked deliberate, like they had been carefully placed there by an interior designer staging a photo shoot.

Megan opened her laptop and rolled her eyes when she saw an email requesting donations to some kids' charity. She knew if she donated to one, the Internet's sneaky algorithms would kick into gear and the rest would come a knockin'. It was no way to run a business. Sure, she believed refugees deserved more humane treatment, and that doctors who land in war zones should be protected, it was just easier to take care of her own world.

Delete.

The second email wasn't much better; a reminder from

Oscar's school that they were looking for volunteers for the end-of-year school concert. Megan scoffed. *Yeah, not likely,* she thought. *As if I don't have enough on my plate already.*

Delete.

An hour later, Megan was composing a lengthy email to a new wholesaler who was trying to convince her that his prices *weren't* retail (nice try, mate) when the doorbell rang.

'Shit!' Damned punctual parents. Well, that was the end of her working day, at least until Oscar was in bed.

A short, frazzled-looking mum in loose tracksuit pants and a striped threadbare T-shirt smiled as Megan opened the door. 'Hieee,' she trilled. 'I'm Janey, Toby's mum.'

'Hey,' Megan said, turning to head down the hallway. 'I'll get Toby.'

'Oh, okay ...' she heard the woman say. 'I'll just ... uh ... wait here, then.'

'Okay,' Megan called back. The last thing she needed was this woman hinting for a friendly cup of tea. Megan had nothing personal against Toby's mum – except for the fact that she was wearing Kmart tracksuit pants with Crocs – but she wasn't open to a potential new friendship just because their sons were mates. Lizzie and Sam were all Megan needed. Just smile, nod and keep moving down the hallway.

The boys were sprawled on Oscar's blue shag rug, assembling some kind of monstrous green Lego dinosaur.

'Toby, your mum's here.'

'Awwww,' Toby whined.

'Toby! Come on, please, sweetieeeee?!' Janey took a tentative step into the house but stopped when Megan shot her a look. A vampire who knew she couldn't cross the threshold without an invitation.

Megan pulled Oscar to his feet. 'Come and say goodbye like a good host, please.'

Once, Megan would have *asked* Oscar if he *wanted* to come and say goodbye, but Lizzie had taught her that the less questions asked of young kids the better.

'You're the boss, not them!' Lizzie said one day when she overheard Megan asking Oscar if he wanted to 'get off the swing and let someone else have a go?'. 'Of course, he's gonna say no if you *ask* him! What kid *wants* to get off a swing and give someone else a go?'

Oscar obediently put down a piece of claw and stood up, but Toby didn't move.

'You can take the racing driver man home if you want?' Oscar said.

'Serious?' Toby immediately jumped to his feet. 'Thanks, man!' He bolted down the hallway towards his bewildered-looking mum, clutching a tiny Lego figure in his hand, eager to escape before Oscar changed his mind.

'Oh, um … thank you!' Toby's mum looked blindsided, as if her kid had never left anyone's house with so little fuss.

Closing the door behind them, Megan turned to Oscar. 'Three scoops of chocolate ice-cream for you tonight!'

'But it isn't even Friday!'

Megan squeezed his cheeks together. 'Let's live dangerously, huh?' She planted a kiss square on his puckered lips.

'Muuuum!' Oscar wiped his mouth, smiling. 'I'm too big to kiss now!'

'Is that right?' Megan reached out towards him again with zombie arms.

Oscar squealed and turned to run but Megan was toc

quick. She threw him down on the hallway runner and proceeded to cover his face with sloppy, loud kisses.

★★★

Something was wrong. Megan lifted her eyes from her phone screen, saw two activewear mums she didn't know heading towards her and quickly brought the phone to her ear.

'Yeah, I'll have to have a look at our stock and see if we have enough for that order ...'

Megan nodded, listened to no one and kept her eyes fixed squarely on the grey asphalt at her feet. The two mums hesitated, then swerved away and walked in the opposite direction. Megan kept the phone to her ear, waiting until they were safely across the other side of the yard. She had zero interest in small talk, signing up for school events or discussing her previous incarnation as the Sleek Briefs girl; a hugely successful ad campaign Megan had starred in at the age of nineteen. She hated that she was still recognised for that stupid ad.

When Oscar had first started at Baytree Primary, a few parents had tried to talk to Megan about how their friend/brother/uncle/dad had a huge crush on her, but soon got the hint that the ex-model had zero interest in that, or any other conversation, and left her alone. Luckily, it wasn't hard keeping to yourself at Baytree Primary. Most mums and dads opted to dump their kids in the Kiss & Go Zone, which was basically one step away from kidnap victims being kicked out of a moving car outside their house before their captors sped away, the passenger door still swinging wildly, so there were rarely more than a handful of grown-ups in the schoolyard on any given morning.

'Pretending to be on the phone again?'

Megan looked up to see Lizzie standing in front of her. 'Yep.' Megan looked her up and down. 'You in your pyjama pants again?'

'Having a fat day.'

Megan knew this wasn't Lizzie fishing for a compliment. Lizzie wasn't particularly crazy about her body, but she didn't make a big song and dance about it, believing there were far more important things to obsess about. As far as Megan was concerned, Lizzie had it all; classic curves combined with an equally attractive self-confidence, although apparently it had been so long since Lizzie had waxed her nether regions that Greg had started humming seventies' porn bass lines whenever she got out of the shower. Luckily, according to Lizzie, Greg preferred the natural bushy look to the baby rodent look and was a 45-year-old horny teenager.

But there was something slightly off about Lizzie this morning. Most people might assume it had something to do with her turning up to school in pyjama pants, but wearing half her sleepwear to drop-off was a Lizzie Barrett special, especially on a fat day. Megan noticed that she kept looking around the schoolyard with a strange unreadable expression on her face. She was about to ask if her friend was okay when Lizzie pointed to Megan's nether regions.

'How's the thrush?'

'Yeah, better.'

'Yoghurt?'

Megan had no idea how someone who hadn't had sex in over a year had contracted thrush, but thanks to Lizzie's home remedy – fresh Greek yoghurt on a pad – the yeasty curse was now a distant memory. 'So gross, but so good.'

Despite her limited experience with female friendship,

Megan truly believed she'd struck gold with Lizzie, who was honest, funny and possessed an unassuming, natural air of authority, as well as the ability to not give a shit at all the right times, about all the right things. Lizzie's zero-bullshit vibe was what had first attracted Megan to her two years ago at the end of year kindergarten concert.

In the spirit of political correctness, the kinder had abolished the traditional Christian nativity play, replacing it with an all-inclusive, interfaith celebration, which were very de rigueur in Melbourne's inner suburbs.

For someone who embraced the idea that every religion was as full of shit as the next, Megan found the whole spectacle hilarious. The kids had been asked to represent a variety of cultures, so there was a Vietnamese Jesus, a ginger Allah, a skinny Sri Lankan Buddha and Oscar was the Hindu god Ganesha. Most parents were on board with this religious mish-mash, and there were lots of approving expressions, then Megan spotted a pretty mum standing at the back of the room, with a look on her face that could only be described as bemused delight. The woman caught Megan's look and widened her eyes as if to say, '*What the hell?*'

Megan widened her eyes back. As soon as the Christmas Chaos Show was over, she headed outside and found the woman standing by a trestle table laden with cold sausage rolls and gluten-free mini-muffins.

'What a fucking dog's breakfast,' she muttered to Megan. 'I mean, I'm all for freedom of religion, but for fuck's sake. Which politically correct character belongs to you?'

'Ganesha.' Megan pointed to Oscar who was filling his elephant head with sand. 'Otherwise known as Oscar. Yours?'

The woman pointed to a small boy who kept tripping over the long orange sheet draped around him as he tried to kick a soccer ball. 'Max,' she said. 'One of the three wise Buddhas.'

'Amazing.'

'Best Christmas concert ever.' Lizzie smothered her sausage roll in sauce. 'I'm Lizzie.'

Megan was thrilled to learn that Lizzie was a Baytree Primary parent and, soon after that, found herself with her first real female friend. Making friends had never been Megan's specialty. Half the girls at her all-female girls' grammar had been jealous of Megan's looks, and the other half misinterpreted her shyness for self-importance. When she was nine, Megan's mum, Ellie, had signed her beautiful daughter up with a modelling agency in an effort to distract herself from her own recent separation. Megan scored a few catalogue gigs and TV ads, which quickly led to a celebrity status at her school she'd never sought out. It got harder to make friends when Megan started senior school and was constantly being pulled out of class for casting calls and jobs. Her classmates made snide comments about 'Megan the Model' and once, Megan arrived at her locker to find a page of the catalogue ripped out and stuck to the front of it – her eyes blackened, a curly moustache above her lip and a speech bubble saying, '*Look at me! I'm a slut!*'

Then there was Kaatje, the girl Megan had worked the modelling circuit with during her early twenties. The two of them spent hours hanging out in waiting rooms and dark airless studios doing long boring shoots together and Megan thought she'd finally found a real friend. She soon discovered it was a one-sided affair, as paper-thin as most of the models they worked alongside. Kaatje expected Megan to pander to her diva meltdowns, drive her all over town for castings and lend her endless amounts of money that she never paid back. When a younger, hotter version of Megan appeared on the modelling scene, Kaatje dropped Megan like a carb-laden hotcake. Megan heard on the ex-model rumour mill years later that Kaatje had developed a cocaine habit, blew all her money, moved back in with her parents, and was working part-time as a checkout chick.

When Megan enrolled Oscar at Baytree Primary, she'd sworn she wouldn't engage with anyone but Lizzie. In her experience, making friends was hard and painful, and the last thing she needed was nosy mums in the schoolyard asking why Bryce sometimes came to pick-up with a man. Then Lizzie introduced Megan to Sam, and Megan felt, at the age of thirty-five, as though she'd finally found her tribe.

Lizzie now peered over Megan's shoulder.

'Hey, what's happening on The Gram?'

'No one calls it that.'

'Yet.'

'Never.'

'Good morning, ladies!'

Henry was leaning on the fence behind them, the lollipop stick in his hand and his huge dentures gleaming in the morning sun.

Megan smiled politely. 'Oh … hi …'

'How's it going?' Lizzie said, giving him a polite wave.

They went to turn back around but Henry was in the mood for a chat.

'Lovely morning!' He gestured to the blue sky. 'They said it might rain later but it's perfect now.'

'Yeah,' Megan said shortly. 'Anyway, have a good day.'

'You too, ladies!' Henry grinned, tipping his wide-brimmed lollipop-man hat at them. 'Take care now!'

They turned back before Henry extended the chat any further.

'Oh, Jesus, he does not stop.'

Megan followed Lizzie's eyeline to the bike-shed area where one of the school dads, Dave Podanski, was talking to a pretty school mum. At forty years old, Dave still dressed like a university student.

Megan had only met Dave a few times through Sam, but had quickly pegged him as an ageing nerd who'd managed to maintain a childlike enthusiasm for everyone and everything. The awkward dad had an unfortunate habit of planting his foot deep into his mouth, but there was something undeniably likeable about him.

'This is better than *The Bachelor*.'

'And harder to watch.'

'So, what are we staring at today, with absolutely no discretion whatsoever?' Sam stood at the end of the bench holding a tray of takeaway coffees.

'Oooo!' Megan squealed. 'Gimme!'

They nodded towards the schoolyard *Bachelor* action as Sam handed Megan her soy chai latte and Lizzie her flat white.

'Jesus, she's gonna file an injunction or something.' Sam plonked down on the end of the bench.

'Is Dave married?' Megan asked.

'Yep,' Lizzie said confidently. 'And I am extremely proud of myself for knowing that.'

'How the hell *do* you know that?'

'His kid was Zara's buddy last year,' Lizzie said. 'She insisted on telling me every detail about his life.'

'Aaah.'

'Which one's his kid?' Sam asked.

'Jack.'

'Which Jack?' asked Megan.

'Jack in 1/2C?' Sam said.

Megan rolled her eyes. 'There are four Jacks in 1/2C.'

'No that's 1/2D. There's only three Jacks in 1/2C.'

'Oh, Jack B from 1/2D?' Megan asked, squinting as she tried to picture Dave's son.

'1/2C.'

'Yeah, but which one?'

'I think it's Jack D,' Sam said.

'In 1/2C?'

'Jack D from 1/2C?'

'Oh my GOD!' Lizzie threw up her hands. 'I'm going to stab you both in the face if you don't shut the fuck up.'

Some kids nearby playing four-square turned to stare at them and Megan pointed at Lizzie.

'So, what'd you make this morning?' Lizzie asked Sam, waving at the kids apologetically.

Before becoming a dad, Sam had been a sous chef at a fancy-pants restaurant. These days his culinary creations were limited to lunchboxes and home-cooked meals, but he still took immense pride in his cooking. The most creative Megan got was using tortillas instead of bread.

'Sourdough loaf with olives, feta and thyme,' Sam said. 'And I got a beef rendang on the go in the crockpot before we left, so that's dinner sorted.'

Megan shook her head. 'Freak.'

Lizzie shrugged. 'I'm planning a Nando's feast for tonight's dinner.'

'Did you think about what to bring for Careers Day?'

Megan asked, trying to sound as casual as possible.

'That would imply that we're going,' Lizzie said.

'Oh, come on, please?' Megan gave them both her best puppy dog eyes. 'Do it for Max and Tyler.'

She just *had* to convince them to go. Business hadn't been good lately – mid-year slump – and this was just the opportunity she'd been looking for. She needed this more than she wanted to admit out loud, but she didn't want to go on her own.

'As we've already established, your prime motivation is to drum up business,' Sam said. 'What's in it for us?'

Lizzie rolled her eyes. 'Nothing, that's what.'

It was time to bring out the big guns.

'Tell you what,' Megan said, 'if you both come, I'll bring coffees for the next month.'

Lizzie and Sam considered Megan's offer for a few seconds before looking at each other and nodding.

'You're on,' Lizzie said.

'Shit!'

Sam and Lizzie followed Megan's eyeline to the two activewear mums making their way back towards them.

The three friends immediately lifted their phones to their ears and began simultaneous pretend conversations.

Sam

To: jack_woz_here@hotmail.com
From: samhatfieldchef@bigpond.com
Subject: FaceTime can suck the big one

Hey dickhead,

Thanks for the tip on the mini-tarts for Careers Day, but I'm not sure Lola's teacher would approve of the coffee liqueur. Caffeine, booze and eight year olds is a volatile combination at the best of times, let alone in a classroom. We don't want to cause a rebellion. At least not until high school.

Not much else to report. Lola's reminding me more and more of Maggie Smith every day. Tyler is still head-butting. I'm thinking about enrolling him in one of those schools for the gifted. He was sitting cross-legged on the bathroom floor brushing his teeth last night and made the obvious choice to head-butt the door of the bathroom cabinet as a full stop to the tooth-brushing. Split the door down the middle, like he was the star attraction of a martial arts demonstration – a martial art where you're only allowed to use your head. I'm pretty sure those doors are solid oak.

I didn't notice until this morning when I went in there to vacuum. I mean, I heard the sound of the impact last night, but I was just happy he'd brushed his teeth. And it didn't sound too big. Not like over the weekend when he head-butted that bronze statue in the entrance hall. You know the one Bridget shipped back from Italy? The nude woman wrapped around the nude dude and he's holding a really big fork or something and you can see the dimples above the nude woman's bum? Yeah, Tyler head-butted *that* as soon as we walked in the door from footy. They won, so no logic, as if I might still be searching for some.

I winced at that one. It sounded like someone was announcing an emperor.

He snaps oak and dents bronze. He might be Thor.

So, I took the broken door off and managed to seamlessly Tarzan grip the doors. There's no way Bridget will notice.

Then, because I'd wiped down the doors of the sink cabinet, everything else looked dirty, so I worked outwards and wiped down the whole bathroom. I used enough Windex to power a small tractor.

I also found what looked very much like a pube.

Bridg and I don't use that bathroom. And Lola is *eight*! Say it ain't so.

Bridget's in Malta, not Mauritius, but easy mistake to make, particularly for someone as geographically challenged as yourself. We organised a FaceTime with Bridg so the kids could say hi. I had to wake them up at 5.30 for a 5.45 call. The only thing I hate more than FaceTime is a ute with P plates. The entirety of the call sounded like a bunch of sad, angry, tired people playing a weird version of Marco Polo:

'Mum?'

'Sweetie?'

'Can you hear me?'

'Mum?'

'Sam, is the Wi-Fi playing up?'

'Mummy?'

'Sweetie?'

'Sam, just stay in one place for God's sake!'

Quality time.

And look, I don't know what made you think I'd be the best person to give you advice about recreational drug use. As far as I'm concerned, it's not a drug, it's pot, and everyone should do it all the time. Kids should sprinkle it on their mini-tarts, world leaders should pass a pipe and fix the world, etc. If you feel like you should take a break, you're wrong. Go to your nearest bong shop and buy a three-chamber Pyrex monster with a cone the size of a keep cup.

I'm also available for free relationship advice.

Hope you're okay, mate. You always fight the good fight and your emails make me laugh.

What I'm trying to say is, your pain provides me with great mirth, so don't go finding a miracle cure. That'd be totes selfish.

S x

PS: Stop asking me to send pics of Megan and Lizzie. They belong to me.

PPS: When we text, you need to ease off on the GIFs. It's getting out of hand.

Lizzie

'You look like shit.'

'Always a pleasure to see you too.'

'What's going on?' Aileen frowned and pointed a freckled finger at my face. 'Is it Greg? The kids? Has Nicole the admin bitch been at you again? I'll *fecking* slap her!'

A couple of people at other tables turned to stare at the loud Irish woman.

'Someone's going to report you.'

Aileen Doyle; kind, loyal, generous, vile temper. She was the most popular midwife at the hospital, but also the most feared; not by new mothers – they adored and trusted her with their lives, their babies and their vaginas – but by other midwives and nurses. God forbid Aileen got wind of a midwife telling a labouring woman to 'keep it down a bit', or a nurse who gave a new mum grief for requesting uterus contraction pain meds. Aileen would track down the culprit, bail her up and ball the poor girl out for being an 'insensitive eejit'. A few staff members had complained about Aileen Doyle over the years, but she was still working at St Vincent's hospital because she was damn good at her job. I was lucky enough to be her best mate, a title I wore like a badge of honour. We first met at college on orientation day, seventeen years ago. As the Bachelor of Midwifery course coordinator droned on about the correct use of a timetable, I heard an exasperated sigh.

'Ah Jaysus. Is he *fecking* serious?'

Behind me was a woman about my age with black wavy shoulder-length hair and alabaster skin, cradling her chin in white freckled hands, staring at the course coordinator in amazement. His name escapes me, so I'll call him Dweeby McDweebface.

She saw me looking. 'I suspect your man there assumes our IQs are as low as the bebbies we'll be helping bring into the world,' she whispered, while pointing at Dweeby.

Over morning tea that day, Aileen told me she'd wanted to work with 'bebbies' since she was a kid. Unlike me, she was on the hunt for an Aussie doctor to marry while she was at it. 'Or a male nurse.' She shrugged. 'I'm not fussy, like.'

We were inseparable in college and both landed jobs at St Vinnie's after graduating. Other than when we each took maternity leave, and the time Aileen went back to Albury-Wodonga to look after her mum for six months, we'd been working alongside each other for fourteen years.

Today was my half-shift, so the two of us had ducked to the café across the road for a quick coffee before Aileen headed back to work.

She narrowed her eyes at me. 'What is it then? Don't think you can hide something from me.'

Obviously I *was* hiding something from my best friend, but I just didn't have the energy for an Aileen Apocalypse today. So I lied.

'Feeling nervous about my long service leave.'

Brilliant. Stroke of genius.

'Nervous?' Aileen stuffed half a coffee scroll in her mouth. 'You should be DELIGHTED! I'd give my left tit for another ten weeks off! Both tits!'

Aileen had spent the majority of her long service leave

lying on the couch and bingeing Netflix in her pyjamas. She'd drag herself off it long enough for basic household duties, but otherwise, Tim Tams and TV were her constant companions.

Aileen's husband, Daniel – not a doctor, alas, but an Italian plumber – eventually told her that if she didn't change out of her flannel PJs he'd file for divorce on the grounds of 'passion fatigue'.

'I'm not the binge-watching type,' I said. 'I like being busy. I'll go mad at home on my own all day. I'm used to people and noise ... and feeling useful.'

Whoa. Where had that come from? I thought I was looking forward to ten weeks off, but there were obviously a few nagging doubts submerged in the shallow end of my subconscious. Looking after a husband, four kids and a dog, and working multiple twelve-hour shifts a week, forces you into a groove. If the music suddenly stops, you're probably gonna fall over and smash your head on the kitchen floor.

'You've got ages to figure it out.' Aileen crammed some almond croissant into her mouth. 'Well, some of us have to go back to work. What are you up to on your Wednesday night off? Shagging?'

'Auntie Carmen's birthday dinner.' Just the thought of it was exhausting.

'Say happy birthday from me,' Aileen said, brushing buttery flakes from her fingers. 'How old?'

'Sixty-eight.'

'Christ.' Aileen shook her head as if the number was too big to comprehend. 'We'll still be working here at sixty-eight, for our sins. And you and Greg will be those sickening pensioners who still hold hands and help each other in and out of the car.'

The invisible plectrum twanged my ribcage again. Would we be that couple? Or would Greg be long gone by then? Too horrified to have stayed married to a dirty liar.

That night, the six of us piled into our second-hand Toyota Kluger to head over the bridge to Abelas – the restaurant my family had owned and run for almost fifty years. It was only a twenty-minute drive from Ripponlea to Williamstown, but I may as well have been living in the Amazon as far as Dad was concerned. He'd never forgiven me for leaving the western suburbs to live in Melbourne's south-east with 'all those stuck-up bastards', even though he'd never known anyone from our side of town. Dad once saw a story on *A Current Affair* about some rich south-east suburban arsehole ripping off poor working-class second-generation immigrant Aussies and had made up his mind then and there.

He wasn't too thrilled that I'd chosen midwifery over the family business either, but since my brother Joey stepped up a few years ago, I was officially off the hook.

The Abela family restaurant was right next door to the Abela family home: the house I grew up in, and the house Dad and Auntie Carmen still lived in today. My grandparents helped Mum and Dad buy the run-down, three-bedroom red-brick house soon after the young couple announced their engagement. The café next door had recently gone out of business, so my grandparents – ever the business-savvy wogs – forked out a few extra bucks to buy the café too.

'And we turned that shithole café into the best pastizzi bar and restaurant in the southern hemisphere!'

Modest fellow, my dad. But Abelas did develop a reputation among the local skips as the 'pretty little wog place' that made the best pastizzis in the west. Dad painted the brick walls white, and the window shutters red, replicating his favourite local restaurant back in Malta, and exposed wooden beams lined the ceiling. Wooden chairs, and tables covered in the requisite red-and-white checked cloths scattered around the white-tiled floor gave the place a warm cosy atmosphere, and the walls were covered in framed black-and-white photos of Dad's family across generations. To my eternal shame, Dad refused to take down the photos of me as a metal-mouthed twelve year old in a lilac velvet pantsuit.

I resented Abelas as a kid, and constantly dreamt of a different life – a better life. In my childhood fantasies, we lived in a white weatherboard house with native trees out the front, exactly like my best friend Melissa's house. Dad worked in a skyscraper in the city, which meant we only went to restaurants for special family occasions, not because I had to fold thousands of red napkins. Also, my mum was alive and baked scones, not pastizzis.

It's embarrassing to think how ashamed I was of my family's business back then. As a slightly less bratty adult, I was now proud of Abelas and its legacy in the community, but that didn't mean I was in the mood for it tonight.

As I pulled into a space across the road, we looked over to observe the scene playing out through the restaurant's front window, which was like an Old Testament painting of chaos and carnage come to life. My eldest brother, Chris, was swinging three-year-old Marcus around by his feet, as Rosa, his wife, waved her arms around, shouting at him from behind the counter. Dad was bellowing at Chris, as

Marcus's dad, my youngest brother Lucas, egged Chris on to go faster. The rest of Dad's ten grandchildren were either kicking a soccer ball, chasing each other around the tables, or staring at their phones. Joey, my other brother, was carrying a tray of soft drinks that were in danger of being upended by one of the kids. Poor Dad sat in the midst of the chaos looking like he was about to have a nervous breakdown. He loved his family, and he loved his restaurant, but the former was trashing the latter. Auntie Carmen and Lucas's wife, Shelley, were nowhere in sight. Probably preparing tonight's birthday feast out back in the kitchen. As usual, we were the last to arrive.

'I don't have the energy,' I said.

'Whaddya mean?' Greg said, undoing his belt. 'Looks pretty low-key by Abela standards.'

'I've got a new teacher,' Zara announced from the backseat, apropos of nothing. 'His name's Rick Cooke and he's really cool and he said he knows you, Mum.'

My stomach plummeted into my black leather ankle boots. *Rick knew I was a mum at the school.* He must have seen me that day in the schoolyard. *Fuck!*

'Really?' I said, finding the contents of my handbag suddenly fascinating.

'He said you were at the same soccer club when you were teenagers.' Zara had unclipped her belt and leant forward to stick her head between the seats. 'I bet he was good. He looks as fit as Higgsy.'

This was high praise. With his floppy brown hair, chiselled jaw and athletic frame, Baytree Primary's sports teacher, Rohan 'Higgsy' Higgs, looked as if he belonged on the cover of GQ magazine, or in the latest AFL draft.

'No way he was as good as your mum,' Greg said proudly.

'Nannu reckons Mum could have played for the Matildas.'

'See!' Max bounced up and down like a deranged chimp, shaking the whole car. 'Mum played soccer, so I should too!'

'I don't remember a Rick Cooke,' I repeated, staring into my bag, heart pounding.

Why was I lying? Stupid!

'He remembers you,' Zara said.

What would Zara think of her mother if she knew the truth? What would any of my kids think?

'Course he does,' Greg said, whacking me affectionately on the leg. 'Your mum's a babe.'

'Don't say "babe", Dad!' Archie glanced up from his *Spider-Man* comic. 'It's embarrassing for you, and us.'

'Ugh,' Stella groaned. 'Nessa's wearing that faux fur jacket again.'

Thank you, judgemental daughter, for redirecting everyone's attention back to the restaurant, just as my heart was about to burst out of my chest, *Alien*-style.

'What a punish,' Zara groaned.

'I think it makes her look sophisticated,' said Greg, ever the diplomat.

'Are you serious?' Zara cried. 'It makes her look like a wanker!'

Greg frowned. 'Wait, I thought it was Scarlett we didn't like?'

My two daughters sighed with enough force to propel a hovercraft.

'No, Dad, Scarlett *used* to be annoying but she's better now,' Stella explained. 'Nessa's the annoying one.'

Greg glanced at me. 'Can't keep up.'

'Maybe they think *you two* are annoying,' I said. 'Ever thought of that?' They were right, though. Joey's only child, twelve-year-old Nessa, was a pretentious little shit and the jacket did make her look like a wanker.

'All right, manners everyone,' I said, hoping I didn't sound as shaky as I felt. 'Max, bring the Lego tub for the little boys.'

A 'Closed for Private Function' sign hung askew off the large gold doorknob beneath the red Abelas sign, and the moment we opened the door we were bombarded with a cacophony of voices.

'*Christopher! Put him down!*' Dad waved his hands in the air as if swatting at invisible bugs. 'This is a place of business not Luna bloody Park!'

Chris set Marcus down, who immediately zig-zagged towards the tub of Lego in Max's hands.

'Here she is!' Dad came over to grab my face between his hands and plant kisses on my cheeks. 'My princess of the south-east. How's the weather over there?'

'Same as here.' My father was obsessed with the weather. Tracking it, reading about it and regularly announcing updates on it. 'You look good, Dad.'

'Pah!' More hand waving. 'I look old! I'm old man now, Lizzie.'

'Bullshit,' I said, kissing him on his scratchy stubbled cheek. 'You're only as old as you feel.'

At the age of sixty-nine, Dad's thick hair was still mostly black. He'd managed to stay trim despite working in a restaurant that served some of the fattiest food going. It had only been a few weeks since I'd seen him, but I'd missed him and suddenly wanted to be five years old again so I could lay my head on his chest and ask him to fix my problems the way he fixed my dolls when Christopher tore their heads off.

'*Zara!*' Chris's youngest daughter, Poppy, would have been desperate for her favourite cousin to arrive. 'You're *here*!' The tiny girl torpedoed herself across the room and launched herself into Zara's arms.

After hugging their nannu, Max and Archie disappeared under a nearby table with Marcus, while Alex, the cutest Abela at fourteen months old, wriggled out of Stella's arms and tottered across the floor to join the big boys.

As the rest of us spent the next five minutes greeting various members of the clan, I could feel my heart rate beginning to slow. My family was the perfect distraction from the Rick conversation in the car. Thank God we were here tonight and not around the dinner table at home. The only distraction there would have been Max's trick of blowing a pea out through his nostril.

'Hey little sis!' Joey was only one year my senior but had lorded that fact over me since we were kids. I noticed he looked tired as I hugged him. The poor thing had been married to Psycho-From-Hell Deanna, who'd finally left him two years ago for her personal trainer. Their daughter, Nessa, was following in her superficial mother's footsteps, but Joey adored her and spoiled her rotten, which was doing her no favours as a human being.

'How ya doing, Joey?'

'We're all right,' Joey said with shrug. 'Had to put up a fight to bring Nessa tonight. It's Deanna's week but she eventually said yes.'

I glanced at Nessa, who was sitting in the far corner looking at her phone with her cousin Scarlett, and wanted to say he could have saved himself the bother since she didn't seem the least bit interested in being here.

'Hey girls!'

'Hey Auntie Lizzie!'

They didn't even bother raising their eyes from their feeds, their faces tinted alien pale.

I felt a thump on my arm and turned to find Chris grinning at me. Forty-seven and still nailing the annoying big brother thing.

'G'day dickhead.'

We then proceeded to go through the traditional Lizzie/Chris greeting ritual:

Chris gives Lizzie a hug so tight it borders on painful; Chris digs his fingers into Lizzie's armpits; Lizzie screams and pushes him away.

Classic forty-something brother–sister stuff.

Chris's black wavy hair, like Dad's, was speckled with grey and starting to thin out, and there were a few more wrinkles around his eyes, but other than that, he was still the robust Maltese man he'd transformed into at the age of eleven.

'You made it!' Rosa expertly navigated the throng, a fake smile plastered on her Botoxed face. 'We were worried you'd forgotten!'

Chris had also married a passive-aggressive pain in the arse.

'Wouldn't be much of a human if I forgot the birthday of the woman who raised me,' I said cheerily.

Rosa's left eye twitched and her smile flickered. 'I was only *joking*!' she said.

The mantra of the passive aggressive.

'Where's the birthday girl?' I asked Lucas, who managed a quick hug before running off to prevent Alex choking on a Lego brick.

'Kitchen!' he shouted over his shoulder.

Auntie Carmen stuck her head through the kitchen hatch. 'Shut the door!' she yelled. 'The flies!'

My aunt was obsessed with flies and letting them in or out. Same went for air conditioning.

'It's July!' Dad shouted back. 'Too cold for flies.'

Auntie Carmen walked out of the kitchen, wiping her hands on a tea towel.

'Here's my *ftit qattus*!' she said, holding her arms out.

Auntie Carmen has called me her 'little cat' ever since I can remember. Something to do with my independent streak and being light on my feet, apparently.

'Happy birthday!' I said, wrapping my arms around her large body and kissing her on both cheeks. 'You're looking as beautiful as ever.'

Everything about Auntie Carmen was big. Her personality, her makeup, her voice, her colour-scheme and her body. Today her short blonde spiky hair was wrapped in her trademark blue-green scarf and a chunky multi-coloured necklace dangled over the enormous breasts that had been the perfect pillow throughout my childhood. Her pink shift dress perfectly matched her bright pink eyeshadow, pink-rimmed glasses, purple stockings and pink running shoes. In short, Carmen Abela resembled a diner waitress from the 1950s who'd been raised by drag queens.

She grabbed my face. 'What's up your bum?'

'What?'

Green-grey eyes flashed behind her pink glasses. 'What is it? Huh?'

'Nothing!' I removed her hands from my cheeks. 'Just tired. Getting my period.'

'Still! Thought that well would have dried up by now.'

'I'm forty-two!'

'Could happen any day.' She wagged a bejewelled finger at me. 'Don't believe those stupid magazines that say forty is the new thirty. Bullshit!'

'Auntie Carmen!' Stella cried from behind her, where she was trying to wriggle out of Chris's headlock. 'Don't swear!'

'Jesus, child!' she cried. 'I'm sixty-eight years old for fuck's sake. If I want to swear, I'll bloody swear! Fuck. There, I did it again.'

Stella's mouth hung open and Chris laughed so hard that he loosened his hold on her.

'Now, come and give your Auntie Carmen a big birthday kiss!'

Stella pursed her lips defiantly, crossed her arms and sat on a bar stool. Auntie Carmen was over to her in a split second – she was very sprightly for a woman her age – and covered Stella's face in sloppy kisses. Stella wriggled and screamed, then dissolved into giggles.

Marcus crawled out from under the table. 'Me next! Me next!'

Good to see the Abela tradition of 'Death by Physical Affection' was still going strong. In the days, months and years after Mum died, I received my fair share of sloppy kisses and hugs from the Maltese community. I was only four, so it was a kind of torture being forced to inhale various scents, ranging from mothballs to mustiness, from the men and women who played bocce with Dad every Saturday. These days an uncle or aunt could be in danger of being chastised on the spot for 'unwanted physical contact' towards a child, but I think that's bullshit. Kids are *supposed* to feel uncomfortable and awkward when fat Auntie Margaret with the moustache pulls you in for a big wet kiss on the cheek. Siblings *should* tease each other and fart on one another's heads. Life *is* awkward and uncomfortable!

'Okay, everyone!' Rosa shouted over the noise. 'We can serve up now that the Barretts have finally arrived!'

Subtle.

After we'd scoffed down our fair share of pastizzis, timpana, rabbit stew and torta tal-irkotta, Dad was on his feet.

'If only my Angela was here.' Dad took out a crusty hanky to wipe the tear that appeared at the mention of Mum's name. 'It would make her so happy to see us all together celebrating my big sister Carmen tonight.'

The kids weren't remotely affected by the mention of their long-dead grandmother. They'd heard the same speech from Dad at every family gathering since they could understand the spoken word.

I squeezed Dad's hand to let him know that every Abela over the age of fourteen was thinking about Mum too, even though I didn't remember her at all, to be honest. I have a faint memory of Mum showing me how to make pastizzis, but aside from that it's a blur.

We'd all heard the story of how Mum and Dad met. Joseph Abela and Angela Caruana were seventeen, fresh off the boat with their respective families, when they headed to the Maltese club one night. It was love at first sight, they danced all night and fell madly in love, so the story goes, and 'Angela had a ring on her finger within six weeks'. Auntie Carmen says it was more like a year, but Dad never lets facts get in the way of his stories. They worked hard after they were married, but when the four of us came along, Mum gave up the long hours at Abelas, although she still made pastizzis in the home kitchen. Dad, however, spent twelve to fourteen hours a day in the restaurant. Then Mum was diagnosed with ovarian cancer and, three months later, she was gone. After twelve years with his beloved, Joseph Abela suddenly found himself alone and a single father to four young kids. He was a mess. If it wasn't for Auntie Carmen helping out at Abelas and at home – making sure we were all fed and washed on a daily basis – the five of us may well have ended up on the streets.

Dad now turned to his life-saving sister and lifted his glass of Shiraz towards the wooden beams. 'Everyone, raise a glass!'

'*... to freedom!*' Stella sang at the top of her voice. Her current obsession was the Broadway musical *Hamilton*, which she quoted at every given opportunity.

'No!' Dad snapped. 'To Carmen!'

'*To Carmen!*' we all chorused.

'Thank you, thank you,' Auntie Carmen said, sweeping her hands in front of her regally. 'All hail the old cow for managing not to die for another year.'

'Pah!' Dad spat, covering a mortified Stella in tiny drops of spittle. 'You will never die! God put you here to torment me all my days.'

'Ungrateful old bastard,' Carmen said, grinning.

'Crazy old bitch,' Dad replied, grinning back.

Ain't sibling love grand?

'Auntie Carmen, we love you!' I said, raising my fourth glass of house Merlot – Greg was driving. 'Here's to another sixty-eight years.'

'Please God, no!' She looked horrified at the thought.

'Can we have kannoli now?' Chris's stomach was still his topmost priority at every family occasion.

'Wait!' Greg pushed his chair back and stood up.

Every head whipped towards my husband, as though it were the first time he'd uttered a sound at an Abela family event, which probably wasn't that far from the truth. The poor man could hardly get a word in most of the time.

What the fuck? Greg was going to give a *speech*? The man who'd rather saw off his own testicles with a blunt butter knife than bring attention to himself? And he was nervous, which meant that whatever this was must be important, especially if he was prepared to announce it in front of my family.

'I wanted to say happy birthday to Auntie Carmen too,' he began, nodding and raising his glass to her, 'but also to acknowledge another special event today.'

'You finally got rid of the Toyota!' Lucas shouted.

'You're pregnant!' Dad cried in delight.

'Piss off!' I said. 'I am not!'

'*Mum!*'

'Sorry, Stella,' I said. 'Swear jar when we get home. Promise.'

'Excuse my wife's potty mouth,' Greg said. 'But actually, I know something Lizzie doesn't think I know ...'

The timpana began making its way back up my throat. He'd found out about Rick and was going to make some weird kind of Poirot-esque announcement! I felt light and unstable, as if I might become two-dimensional and slip to the floor. I could tell by Auntie Carmen's expression that she had no clue what was going on. The Rick and Lizzie story was all ancient history as far as my family was concerned, and I had to stop Greg reminding everyone of the Abelas' dark day.

I touched his arm. 'Greg, how about we ...?'

'On this night, fifteen years ago, I met Lizzie Abela at a shithole ...'

'Dad!'

'Sorry, Stella.'

Stella threw up her hands as if to say, 'can you believe this family?'

'... at a dubious Melbourne venue known as Inflation,' Greg continued. 'Now, I'm not usually one for remembering dates ...'

'Or deodorant,' Archie mumbled beside me.

'... so I thought I'd take the opportunity, in front of her entire family, to say, ha ha, I remembered, and you didn't!'

Everyone cheered except Rosa, who looked as though she'd swallowed an un-pitted olive. I grinned up at my beautiful idiot of a husband. He looked so handsome in his denim shirt and jeans with his freshly washed short blond hair. As he rubbed his hand back and forth across his stubble. I felt as full of love for him as I was with relief that the subject of Rick Cooke wouldn't come up tonight. Not *tonight*.

'Happy anniversary, Lizzie Barrett,' Greg said, tipping his Asahi bottle towards me. 'You are the emotional rock and the beating heart of the Barrett family, the driving force behind us all, and we'd be lost without you.'

Oh God. Why did he have to go and ruin a perfectly acceptable smart-arse moment with genuine love and affection. I blinked back tears as everyone roared their approval, apart from my brothers who booed Greg's sentimentality.

Greg leant down and pecked me on the cheek. 'Love you, buddy.'

'Love you too.'

Stella held out a tissue. 'I'll let you both off the swear-jar penalty because Dad was sweet, and you got all weepy.'

'Very generous,' I said, taking the tissue and dabbing at my eyes.

'Right, now that the soppy Greg and Lizzie crap is over, can we have the kannoli?'

'Yes, Christopher,' Auntie Carmen sighed. 'Go bring it out.'

Chris ran for the kitchen and everyone resumed chatting, yelling and laughing. I stared at my husband, in awe of his unexpected display of bravery, honesty and love, and realised I was distinctly lacking in two out of those three right now.

Megan

Megan parked her BMW in front of Applewood Retirement Village and took a deep breath. She hated this place, but this was where her mum, Ellie Wylie, had chosen to see out her remaining years, so here she came twice a week. Megan always hoped to find Ellie in her villa, but more often than not she could be found hanging out in the communal lounge area, social butterfly that she was.

Ellie Wylie was seventy-eight, sharp as a tack and still as politically incorrect as ever, and Megan adored her. She'd gotten used to having an older mum, even though it was harder when she was a kid. The kids at Megan's school often mistook Ellie for Megan's nana, and some of the nastier ones teased her about it. Megan was always fiercely defensive of her mother, but secretly felt embarrassed about how old her mum looked compared to the other kids' mums.

Ellie was thirty-nine and running a successful homewares business when she met Megan's father, Dean Wylie. One of her regular suppliers, Dean was very handsome and ten years younger but had assured Ellie the age gap wasn't a problem. They married not long after, and when Ellie became pregnant at the age of forty-two, she was ecstatic, having long accepted that her child-bearing days were behind her. Megan's brother, Matt, was born two years later, and the Wylie family was complete.

Megan and her mum had always been close, and it was just the two of them for the most part these days. Matt fell in love with a guy he met in a nightclub and moved to Sydney when he was nineteen. Although the relationship didn't last, Matt's love affair with Sydney had. Megan and her mum only saw him a couple of times a year, usually when he needed money or at Christmas when he needed a place to stay in between parties. And Megan's dad was long gone, having run off to Queensland with a woman half his age when Megan was eight. His departure hadn't had a huge impact on Megan's day-to-day existence, as he'd always been a distant, distracted father who was away for work a lot. And when Dean had been home, he was moody. Radios and TVs were turned off and there were no games because 'Dad needs to work in peace'.

Megan's memories of her father were of him being an imposing figure: tall, bearded and broad-shouldered with huge, soft hands. He wasn't an affectionate man, and Megan couldn't remember ever seeing her parents hold hands or hug, let alone kiss. The most tender moment Megan ever shared with her father was the day he left. Dean sat her and Matt down on their brown leather sofa and informed them that he and Mummy 'didn't love each other any more' and that he was going away to 'give Mummy some space'.

Six-year-old Matt had one eye on the TV and hadn't heard the first part of their father's brief speech. He was thrilled. 'Mummy's going to space!'

'Do you still love *us*?' Megan had asked.

Her father had put those huge hands on either side of her small face and nodded. 'Of course, sweetie.'

She hadn't believed him but saw the tears in his eyes as he leant forward to give her a hug – the most affection she'd ever received from this huge, quiet stranger who happened to be her dad.

'I'll just be gone a little while.' He gave Matt an awkward one-armed hug and walked out the door without looking back.

A 'little while' turned into three years, when he showed up unexpectedly at Megan's twelfth birthday, gave her another awkward hug, said, 'Happy birthday, sweetie,' and left. Again. Megan hadn't seen him since. He'd tried to reach out once or twice when she was a teenager, but she'd refused to have anything to do with him.

'He's your father, Megsy,' Ellie had said at the time. 'I don't want you to have regrets.'

'I won't, Mum,' Megan said defiantly. 'As far as I'm concerned, I only have one parent.'

Ellie was the one who'd given Megan the money to start Chill five years ago. 'One of the benefits of having a wealthy mum who'd had kids later in life,' Megan had told Lizzie. Then, two years ago, Ellie had announced to her shocked children that she was selling the five-bedroom family home they'd grown up in and moving into a swish local retirement village for a 'better social life'.

Ellie had never strayed very far from the affluent inner-city suburb where she'd raised her kids, so Megan wasn't surprised that she'd chosen the expensive Brighton retirement village Applewood, over an apartment on the Gold Coast.

This morning, Megan was walking across the manicured lawn, heading for her mum's villa, when she passed a group of dripping wet residents who'd just been for a swim.

'Morning! Lovely day!' they chorused.

'Yep,' Megan said, averting her eyes from the stray pubic hairs escaping from one of the women's bathers and hurrying towards her mother's building.

Another cheery male resident beamed at Megan as the lift doors opened. 'Here to visit someone, are we, love?'

No, I'm here for a Tinder hook-up.

'Yes,' Megan said, looking at her phone, hoping to cut the conversation short.

'Who's that then?'

'Ellie Wylie.'

'Oh, she's in the lounge, love,' he said. 'Just saw her.'

Bugger! The doors opened at her mother's floor and Megan stayed put, waiting for him to get out so she could head back down to the foyer, but he wasn't moving.

'I'll take you there if you like!'

'I know where it is, thanks.'

Just get out.

'Righto, then!' He tipped his flat cap at her and shuffled out. 'Have a good day, love.'

Megan looked at the time. It was just after eleven, so her mother was probably having morning tea with 'The Applewood Gang'. Great. More inane conversation was on the horizon.

Megan crinkled her nose at the overpowering scent of lavender and must as she entered the spacious Applewood lounge. It was dotted with worn, bright yellow couches, low metal tables and plastic chairs. A large flat-screen TV in the corner played an episode of *Home and Away.* She spotted her mum and a group of residents at a table in the kitchenette on the far side of the brightly lit room. Megan recognised one or two of them but didn't know the others. Ellie was the opposite of her daughter and had built up quite the collection of friends since arriving at Applewood. People were drawn to the sprightly senior's forthright manner and biting humour. Ellie was never mean, but she could be shocking at times, like the time she introduced Megan to a fellow resident the day she moved in.

'Joan and I went to school together!' Ellie said, throwing her arm around the tiny elderly lady beside her. 'She was a big-time judge back in her day!'

Joan had badly dyed black hair, large red designer frames with thick lenses, a matching red shirt and black tailored pants, reminding Megan of an oversized ladybird.

'Joan used to tell everyone she hadn't seen a penis until she got married,' Ellie said, winking at Megan, 'but I was the witness at her shotgun marriage so she's a damn liar!'

Horrified, Megan had been about to apologise to the ladybird woman, when Joan giggled and swatted at Ellie's hand.

'Oh, fuck off, El!' she chortled.

They love it! Megan thought then. The oldies loved Ellie's naughtiness. They'd lived long enough to not give a shit about too much and it took a lot to embarrass them. Her mother's mischievous nature was an asset at Applewood.

'Megsy!' Ellie jumped to her feet and threw her arms around Megan. 'Hello love!'

Despite her age, Ellie was fighting fit thanks to her daily walks and swims. With her grey pixie cut, tanned skin and green eyes – inherited by both her children – Ellie resembled a twinkly eyed elf from an Enid Blyton book and was considered a bit of a fox among the male contingent at Applewood.

'Hey Mum.' Megan returned her mother's fierce embrace.

Ellie gestured towards the woman and man at the end of the table. 'You remember Helen and Bob?'

'Hi.' Megan wouldn't have been able to name them if she was being held at gunpoint.

'And these old farts are Lucy, Carol and Bert!' Ellie pointed to a frail bird-like woman to her left, a large woman wearing a floral dress opposite her, and a shrunken bespectacled man.

'Hello,' Megan said.

'Your mother never stops talking about you!' The fatter woman threw her hands up and almost knocked a cup of tea out of the man's hand, startling him. 'It's "Megan this" and "Megan that" twenty-four seven!'

The others chuckled and nodded in agreement.

'Bullshit!' Ellie said. 'She's exaggerating! It's eighteen five, tops!'

'How have you been, dear?' Helen asked.

'Good. Busy.'

'Oh yes, busy, busy!' the fat lady said, nudging the man next to her. 'Remember busy, Bert?'

Bert let out an emphysemic chuckle and Megan wondered if the poor man had uttered a single word in fifty years.

'You were right about her being a beauty, El,' the skinny woman said, looking Megan up and down as if she were a prize heifer. 'You're gorgeous, dear!'

'Thank you.' Megan cocked her head modestly. After years of receiving compliments, Megan had her response down to a fine art.

'I bet the lads are lining up around the block for a date with you, ay?' Bob said in a thick Scottish accent. 'Beautiful lass like you!'

The dirty old perve gave her a salacious wink and Megan had to hold back from throwing his milky lukewarm tea in his face.

'Dirty old perve!' Ellie scolded, echoing her daughter's

thoughts. 'Keep it in your pants, Bob, she's forty years younger than you!'

Bob grinned as the others tittered and chuckled.

'And don't mention the word "date" around this one,' Ellie continued. 'Won't have a bar of a men, will you?'

'Gay, is she?' Helen perked up. 'My granddaughter just climbed out too.'

'It's *came* out, Helen, not climbed,' the fat lady corrected her and mimed what Megan could only assume was pushing doors of a closet wide open.

Helen waved her hand dismissively. 'Came ... climbed ... they're still *out*, aren't they?'

'I'm not gay,' Megan said quickly.

'No, she's just fussy,' Ellie agreed. 'My *son's* the gay one.'

'Hey Mum, can we go to your villa?' Megan asked before the gay conversation could continue. 'I need to put some Oscar dates on your calendar.'

'Where is Oscar?' Helen looked around as if the child might materialise behind her. 'He's so adorable.'

'At school, you nitwit,' Ellie cried. 'Where else would a six-year-old boy be on a Thursday morning? At a board meeting?'

They all chuckled again. *Honestly*, Megan thought, *with an audience like this, Mum could start her own Applewood Comedy Night*.

'Come back and visit us again, love!' Bob called out as Ellie and Megan began heading out of the room, earning himself a death stare from Helen.

'Our singing group performs next week!' Lucy shouted. 'We'd love to see you there!'

I'll pass, thanks, Megan thought, throwing them a cursory wave.

'What was the big rush?' Ellie asked as they stepped into the lift.

'I don't come here to see them, Mum. I come to see you.'

'Still, might be nice next time.'

Megan followed Ellie into her one-bedroom villa. It was a nice apartment but could have been much nicer if Eleanor Wylie had a clue about décor. Although Ellie grew up with money and was wealthy throughout her adult life, there was no accounting for taste. From the floral-patterned lounge suite to the zebra-print rug, her mother's apartment was an explosion of clashing colour schemes, patterns and mismatched trinkets. A flat-screen TV and framed photos of Megan and her brother sat atop a bright-blue TV unit in the corner of the room. A huge print of the twelve apostles hung on the wall opposite. Knick-knacks and souvenirs from Ellie's extensive travels cluttered the shelves of a tall glass display unit, and a Moroccan-style yellow and orange poof sullied the appearance of a Memphis velvet armchair that Megan had bought as a housewarming gift. Megan found it ironic that her mum had spent her entire working life running a business that specialised in making homes beautiful, yet her own taste was so bad.

'So, what's going on with Oscar?' Ellie took her Underwater Dogs calendar off the wall and grabbed a biro from her Yummy Grandmummy mug.

Megan flopped into the armchair. 'Nothing, why?'

'You said you had to give me some dates.'

'Oh, that was just an excuse.'

'Oh,' Ellie said, frowning. 'Right. So, you well?'

'Fine.'

'How's my beautiful boy?' Ellie took a packet of biscuits from the cupboard and laid them out on a plate. 'Still playing footy?'

'Yeah, Bryce is picking him up for training tonight.' Megan took out her phone to tap in a reminder to make sure Bryce had ordered Oscar's new footy shorts.

Ellie held out the biscuits. 'And how are you two getting along these days?'

'Fine, why?' Megan asked, taking a Monte Carlo.

'Just asking,' Ellie said, sitting on the couch and pulling her legs up under her. 'Is he still with that man?'

'His name's Adam, Mum.' Megan slow-blinked. 'You know that.'

'Rather not say it.' Ellie crossed her arms like a stubborn child. 'He's the reason my grandson's parents aren't together.'

'If it hadn't been Adam it would have been someone else,' Megan said, 'with Bryce being gay and all.'

'Doesn't it make *you* want to meet someone?' Ellie asked. 'Seeing the "happy couple"?'

Megan smiled at her mother's attempt at air quotes, which looked like she was pulling handgun triggers.

'I'm not interested in a relationship,' Megan said. 'I'm happy on my own.'

She meant it too. She'd done the Tinder thing, been on a few dates, had a few shags, but no one came close to ... anything. Megan had once told Lizzie that she might like to be a nun.

'Those chicks are never alone,' Megan had said. 'Always walking around in pairs. It might not be too bad. Do the obligatory prayer thing a few times a day, hang out, talk about how ace Jesus was and spend the rest of the time in my cell on Insta.'

Lizzie winked. 'And how hard would you rock that habit?'

'Harder than Whoopi,' Megan replied.

She'd been joking about the nun thing but was dead serious about not wanting a relationship.

'What about when you're older and Oscar's moved out?' Ellie asked. 'I'll be dead and you won't have anybody.'

'Cheery thought, Mum.' Megan raised her half-eaten biscuit in salute. 'Thanks.'

Megan glanced down as her phone lit up with a stream of Instagram notifications. She'd posted an '80s Atari joystick T-shirt that morning, and it was getting a lot of love from her forty-two thousand Chill followers.

'Actually, I wanted to ask you a favour,' Ellie said, brushing biscuit crumbs off her grey leggings.

'Hmm?' Megan said, staring at her screen.

'Helen's son is moving back from Adelaide and needs to find a school for his kids,' Ellie said. 'I said maybe you'd talk to him and his wife about Baytree Primary?'

'I'm not really the best person to ask, Mum.'

Ellie frowned. 'Oscar goes there, doesn't he?'

Megan sighed. 'I'm busy, Mum.'

'It wouldn't take much time to just ...'

'Shit!' An email from a bohemian beach label popped up on her screen, demanding that all orders be in ASAP or she'd miss out on this season's collection, which was the last thing she needed this month. 'Dammit!'

'What?'

'An order I need to put in, or I'm screwed,' Megan said, standing up. 'Sorry, Mum, gotta go.'

'But I didn't even tell you about Harriet and the bus trip!' Ellie cried. 'People kept asking for unscheduled toilet stops, which made us ten minutes late to the gardens, and

Harriet suggested everyone wear pads on the next trip, so Susie told her she could stick her pad up her ...'

'Save it for next week,' Megan said, heading for the door. 'You know I love a Harriet story. Come for dinner Monday night. Okay?'

The flat-capped old guy from earlier was waiting outside the lift, staring in Megan's direction, a lewd grin straining to lift the sagging skin on his face. Had he spent this entire time riding the lifts, or had he just been hovering in the hallway, waiting for Megan to come back? She considered retreating to the safety of Ellie's room, but knew she had to get past this libidinous senior citizen eventually. He had nowhere else to be.

'Why the rush, love? Places to be and all that, I s'pose.'

Megan jabbed at the lift button then turned to address the flirty fossil.

'Yeah, my girlfriend just called,' Megan said sweetly. 'She's really horny so I'm off to her place for some serious sex.'

The lift doors opened nearly as wide as the old dude's mouth as Megan stepped inside. As the doors closed, she threw the dumbstruck man a final, friendly wave.

'Dad's here!'

Oscar almost knocked the laptop out of Megan's hands as he jumped from the couch to the window ledge.

'Oscar!' she cried. 'Careful!'

She'd spent the last two hours madly trying to get her orders into the beach label, breaking her 'no TV after school' rule but Oscar had incessantly nagged her to 'get off your computer' so she'd finally compromised by doing her work beside him on the couch while he watched *The LEGO Movie* for the hundredth time.

Oscar leapt off the couch and yanked the door open for Bryce, whose hand was poised like ET, ready to ring the bell.

'Dad!' Oscar leapt into his father's arms.

Megan closed the computer and stood up, feeling that familiar flutter in her belly as she watched her ex-husband's muscular arms encircle her son's small body and lift him up. As per usual, Bryce had achieved his 'I look totally stylish and gorgeous without making an effort' look in blue jeans and a white T-shirt that showed off his pecs.

'Hey dude,' Bryce said. 'Ready for training?'

Bryce and Adam had enrolled Oscar in the local under-7s football team at the start of the year, and despite Megan's initial reservations about her baby playing such a rough sport, it had been great. Oscar looked adorable in his white shorts and blue-and-white-striped guernsey, and even though Megan knew nothing about the game, she enjoyed watching him running around the oval, chasing and tumbling and kicking. Bryce took him to training and they both attended the games; Bryce with Adam, and Megan with Ellie. They never sat together, of course.

'Yeah!' Oscar cried. 'Are you gonna watch me?'

'You bet,' Bryce said, lowering Oscar back to the floor.

'No phone, okay?'

Bryce put his hand on his heart. 'No phone.'

Oscar's footy games were the only times Megan wouldn't dare touch her phone. Her son constantly checked to make sure she was watching and still talked about the time she'd made the mistake of replying to an email during a game and had missed him kicking a goal. He'd refused to speak to her in the car, and for a full hour once they got home – a new record.

'Let's go!' Oscar said, tugging on Bryce's hand. 'Bye, Mum! See you after.'

'Hold your horses, mate,' Bryce said. 'Gotta talk to your mum. You go hop in the car.'

'But I don't wanna be late! And the coach ...'

'We won't be late, promise!'

Oscar didn't look convinced but ran off to jump in the backseat of Bryce's brand-new Jeep Wrangler – a ridiculous car for a man who'd never been off-road in his life. The closest Megan's ex-husband had ever come to camping was once when they were first married and he'd fallen asleep at sunset, in a hammock ... in their backyard.

'What's up?'

Megan assumed Bryce wanted her to have Oscar over the coming weekend because he and Adam were off on one of their weekend Hobart trips. Apparently, the pretty town was one of the hippest places to visit these days, and Bryce loved telling anyone who would listen about the MONA Pavilions and how the experience was always so 'spiritually enriching'.

'Um ... well ...' he said, fidgeting with his car keys. 'I have some news.'

'Right.' Megan felt a shiver on the back of her neck. There was no way this was *good* news. Not for her, anyway.

'*AdamproposedandIsaidyes.*'

'You're getting married?' Her heart was thumping so hard, she was sure Bryce would notice it through her jumper.

'Yeah,' Bryce said with a sheepish grin. 'You're invited, of course ...'

Megan slapped a hand to her heart in mock gratitude. 'Thank you for thinking of me.'

'Megs, I didn't want this to turn into a thing, I just …'

'Congratulations,' she said, cutting him off before he said anything else or before she broke down in front of him. 'You'd better go, Oscar's about to melt down.' Megan could see Oscar's face pressed up against the car window and he was frantically pointing at his *Star Wars* watch.

'Can we just …'

But Megan had already stepped back inside and closed the door. She heard the car start up and drive away and that's when she finally allowed the tears to fall. Fucking Bryce. Fucking *Adam*. She swiped angrily at the traitorous tears on her cheeks, took a deep breath and looked at her phone. She had an hour before Oscar got back. More than enough time to go pay Michael a visit at the bottle shop.

Michael, a fifty-something man who lived in flannel shirts tucked into his jeans, always wore an expression of intense interest as Megan described what she was in the mood to imbibe, as if she were telling him something crucial and urgent. He'd listen and nod, bouncing the knuckle of his hairy forefinger off his lips as his eyes scanned the shelves, and she was always grateful for the attention he paid her. Once when Lizzie and Sam had asked her what she'd done on the weekend, Megan had responded, 'Oh, not much, caught up with my friend, Michael. Bottle of wine. It was nice.' If Megan had to fill in an emergency contact on a school form, Michael would be on her shortlist.

The way things were looking, she should probably get his contact details.

Sam

To: jack_woz_here@hotmail.com

From: samhatfieldchef@bigpond.com

Subject: An incident at the market

Oh mate.

I just made a monumental dick of myself. I'm sitting in the car, sweating. I was at the market (I'm making those mini-tarts for Lola's class) scrutinising the raspberries (because I care deeply about my mini-tarts) when I think I hear someone talking to me, except I assume they're not, because I'm at the market and I'm blocking out the existence of other humans. But this woman is next to me, pointing at my raspberries, saying, 'You gonna interrogate those berries?'

So straight away I'm thinking, *That's a line! This woman's trying to pick me up. At the market!* Of course, it doesn't occur to me that I haven't been on the singles' scene for eons and how the hell would I know if it was a pick-up line? So, as if to prove just how rusty I am, I respond: 'Well, these berries have been seen loitering around my daughter's primary school, so I'm gonna let 'em know what's what.' I made the raspberries into paedophiles. But wait, there's more. This woman's response to my response was to stare and smile strangely, so I decide to *keep talking*!

'Yeah, um, I'm thinking some basic waterboarding and sleep deprivation until I break them.' I'm planning to torture paedophile berries now.

Then she says, 'You could always threaten them with a NutriBullet.'

She's on board with the berry torture! Which makes me laugh. Really loudly. It got a fair bit of attention. The Vietnamese woman who runs my favourite fruit stall looked over and shook her head. But Sassypants throws me a bone, because she's nice. I would've walked away from me by this point.

'What school does your daughter go to?'

'Baytree.'

Then something struck me: I'm wearing Ugg boots, my mankiest trackies and a T-shirt Lola got me last year that says *Bad Puns. That's How Eye Roll*. Abort! So, I say I better get home and make a start on these mini-tarts. But then I start this ramble about not being against plus-sized tarts and I embrace tarts of all sizes.

The last thing she said was, 'Okay, well, maybe I'll see you around.'

And what did I say, Jack? What was my parting conversational gift? I know you know. But I will type the words so you can confirm that I am a bigger dickhead even than you.

Her: 'Okay, well, maybe I'll see you around.'

Me: '*Not if I see you first*.'

I just head-butted the steering wheel upon reliving that. Her name was Sasha and I saw her head over to the second-hand book stall and walk behind the counter. So now I know where she works. But I don't even know if I told her my name.

That was bad. I mean, I hope my haplessness is giving you some joy, but man, with the benefit of a few minutes' hindsight, that was humiliating. Should I go back? Say it'd been a weird morning and I was in shopping mode or something? It's the sort of thing I should tell Bridg, but there'd be the whole explaining about why I was talking to some woman at the market and I'd say she started talking to me and Bridg would say something like 'I'm sure she did' and then we'd fight. So, I'm telling you instead; my other wife. Gotta get home now. Thanks for listening, dickhead. Speak soon.

S x

I've called twice now but nobody's home. Their machine isn't even on. I really wanted to hear her voice right now but she might still be at training.

Dad's off his face and just told me he's glad Mum's dead because I'd drive her fucking insane if she was still around. If Mum was still around, she'd break his nose with a crockpot and tell him to get the fuck away from me. The crockpot hasn't been touched since she died. Should probably dust it off and put it to good use. But he's not worth it.

She strokes my hair and says, 'He's not worth it. He's not even worth your time.' Then she says she loves me and then nothing that drunk fuckwit says matters in the slightest.

It's like she clicks her fingers or waves her wand (or however she makes her magic happen) and makes me know, with such fierce certainty, that everything's going to be okay because we have each other and we're always going to be together and nothing – nothing – is stronger than us. I'll just sit in my room and leave my chest of drawers up against the door until Dad runs out of steam. He's still yelling, but I can't tell what now. The words 'fucking useless' pop up a lot. I can't wait to take my love away, as far away from Dad and all this shit as possible, and then it will just be us.

Dad's banging on my door now but he's wobbly. He won't get through tonight. He'll punch the door too hard and swear and then go back to the lounge and fall asleep in front of Halifax FP*.*

Maybe I'll go and find that crockpot when he does.

Lizzie

I yawned and Megan recoiled.

'Jesus, you could eat an antelope with that mouth.'

'Sorry. Early morning.'

I'd been up since 5.30 a.m., thanks to Zara's pre-dawn meltdown about an unfinished science project that was – of course – due today. No better way to start the day than working out how to take cotton balls and a piece of raffia and make a respectable molecular model. After that crisis, I had to deal with the fallout from Max's 'I'll make my own breakfast' adventure, and in the midst of that clean-up, the great hunt for Archie's hat began. We discovered it under the barbecue just as Max started on at me about Careers Day.

'Did you remember it's today?' he asked, looking both hopeful and panicked. 'What work thing are you gonna bring?'

I was all over it. I'd hit up George, the theatre tech, for forceps and an amnihook at my last shift, both of which were in my bag, ready for their close-up. Once Max was satisfied his mother wasn't the worst parent at the school (today), I made four lunches, stacked the dishwasher, fed the dog, put a load of washing on, told each child in the house to put their shoes on eight times each, got myself dressed and the whole lot of us out the door by 8.30 a.m. Greg left for work at 6 a.m. every day, so was spared the morning chaos. Lucky bastard.

Apart from the early mornings, I wasn't sleeping particularly well either. Tomorrow would be a week since I'd spotted Rick, right here in this schoolyard, and yet I had done precisely nothing about finishing the letter to Greg and giving it to him. Thank God he was flat out with work this week. Greg usually did school pick-up on Mondays, but I'd 'kindly' offered to do it today. The look of gratitude on his face was enough to make me feel like even more of a duplicitous cow than I already did. The time bomb ticking over my head was getting louder with every minute that passed.

'Lost someone, Lizzie?' Sam approached us holding a Tupperware container.

'What?'

'You look like a meerkat on the lookout for a pack of jackals.'

Shit. Was I that obvious?

'Just, uh, checking if Archie found his bike helmet.'

'That's a lovely pink container you have there, Sam,' Megan said.

'Tarts,' Sam said.

'Rude,' Megan said.

'No,' Sam said, holding up the container. 'Raspberry tarts. For the ... bring-something-into-class-to-show-what-your-parents-do thingy.'

'Careers Day?' Megan asked, still looking at her phone.

'That's snappier,' Sam said, gesturing at us to make room for him on the bench.

'Are you pretending you're a chef?' I bumped Megan's hip with mine, shuffling her along, and tried to get into drop-off banter mode, rather than scanning the yard like a possessed meerkat.

'I *am* a chef!'

'*Was* a chef,' Megan corrected, glancing up from her morning Insta fix. 'You *used to* work at Attica.'

'The only difference between then and now is that I don't get paid to cook any more,' Sam argued, plonking down on the bench.

'Give us a look then!' I reached over and peeled back the corner of Sam's Tupperware lid to reveal at least a dozen picture-perfect tarts, topped with fresh cream and plump juicy raspberries.

'We should check them ...' Megan's hand was stretching towards the tub.

'... for nuts,' I added, slipping my fingers under the lid.

'Back away from the tarts, tarts!' Sam snapped the lid down, almost catching my fingers. 'What did you bring, Lizzie?'

Megan and Sam recoiled as I brought out my show-and-tell items.

'What the hell, Lizzie?' Megan squealed.

'It's forceps and an amnihook.'

'I know all too well what they are!' Megan said. 'Why would you bring them *here*?'

'Lizzie,' Sam said, 'I'm shaking. How do you think kids will react?'

'They need to know.'

'Know what?' Megan asked. 'That they were dragged into the world with a pair of horror-movie tongs?'

Even before becoming a parent, I was never one who believed in sheltering kids from reality. Apart from the requisite Santa Claus and Tooth Fairy ruses, I've always tried to answer my kids' questions as honestly as possible. Max once heard two teenagers oversharing in a café and asked me, at full volume, 'Mum, what's *anal*?' So, I told him. I waited until we were in the car, but I told him.

'Why couldn't you have brought, I don't know, a teddy bear or a blankie or something?'

'I don't work in the dementia ward, Megs,' I replied. 'I work in the part of the hospital that drags miracles into the world with horror-movie tongs. What'd you bring?'

Megan reached into her Burberry bag and produced a fluffy kid-sized jacket that looked like it had been made at the cost of many Ewoks and a small skateboard emblazoned with *Spongebob Squarepants* artwork.

'Fuck *off*!' I scoffed in disgust.

'What?' Megan blinked. 'It's my job!'

It was apparent to all of us that Megan was already the undisputed winner of Careers Day.

'I'll give you *three* tarts if you go home,' Sam begged. 'Please?'

Sometimes I couldn't help feeling jealous of Megan's life. She looked unreasonably good at unreasonable hours, had an effortless style and sophistication I'd never possessed, and had two nights a week, and every second weekend, to herself. But deep down I knew that I wouldn't trade my crazy Barrett bunch or trackie daks for all the Burberry bags and sleep-ins in the world.

A man laughed behind us and my stomach contracted. I glanced around nervously to see a school dad talking to his kid. Not Rick. Jesus, this was stressful. I felt like a criminal waiting for a crack team of Ricks to abseil down from Black Hawk helicopters and bundle me into a windowless van.

'So, Sammy, big day coming up,' Megan said.

Sam didn't answer. He was in denial about turning forty

next week, so of course we made sure to raise the topic as often as possible.

'You gonna have a party?' I asked.

'Yeah, where are our invites?' Megan said, nudging him.

'No party,' Sam said. 'Too much hassle.'

'Maybe Bridget has organised something?'

'Doubt it,' Sam said. 'She's been in Seattle for two weeks; doesn't get back till tomorrow night. She's flat out on this new project so …' His voice trailed off.

Banter between the three of us flowed easily at school drop-off, but it always hit a block whenever Bridget came up. We could usually tell when she'd arrived home from a work trip, as Sam was a lot quieter than his usually blithe self. He even looked smaller.

The school bell rang, reinforcing its reputation as the unwitting saviour.

'All righty!' I said with forced cheeriness. 'Let's go!'

Five minutes later the three of us were squeezed into small blue plastic chairs at the back of the classroom, as grade-one and -two kids spilled noisily into the room and sat cross-legged on the carpet in front of us. There were only five other parents in the room.

'Huge turnout,' Sam muttered.

'So much for Penny Guthrie's "please make an effort to attend" email,' I whispered back.

Max was sitting in the front row (nerd) and turned around to give me an enthusiastic wave. I grinned and waved back. Poor kid. Having his mum attend a class event could possibly rank among one of the best days of his short life. Mr Hiney and Mrs Godfrey stood at the front of the classroom talking softly to each other, using their faces to keep some of the naughtier kids in line, all eyes, eyebrows and jutted chins. Penny Guthrie sat to the side of the room in front of a poster that read 'We Love Our Local Community'.

'Hey gang!' Dave appeared beside us, a sheen of sweat covering his brow. 'Made it!' Dave looked genuinely excited to be here as he pulled up a blue plastic chair. 'I'm showing some early sketches from my graphic novel. What about you, Megan? What did you bring?'

'Wait a few minutes and you'll find out,' Megan said, not looking up from her phone. 'Wouldn't want to ruin the surprise.'

'Oh, yeah ... right!'

Dave wasn't technically part of our 'gang' but we tolerated him in the same way you'd tolerate a puppy who is sweet, but who also chews your shoes and pisses on the rug.

'Hey, I've got some invites for you guys,' Dave said. 'It's the launch of my graphic novel.'

'Cool.' Sam couldn't have sounded less interested.

Megan, still engrossed in her newsfeed, didn't answer him at all.

'HANDS ON TOP!' Mrs Godfrey shouted over the din.

'THAT MEANS STOP!' the kids chanted, placing their hands on their heads.

Mr Hiney stepped forward, reminding me of Hector the Cat in his orange and dark blue striped polo shirt. 'Thank you, ones and twos.'

Sam stifled a giggle. Forty going on fourteen.

'Before we get started with Careers Day,' Mr Hiney continued, 'Miss Guthrie has a quick announcement for the grown-ups.'

Penny stood up and stepped forward. 'Firstly, welcome to term three!' she began, looking pointedly at us seven adults up the back. 'We have some very special events planned for the remainder of the year and really need your support and help to make them as good as they can be.'

As school communities went, Baytree Primary parents were lazy and useless. Most of us didn't volunteer at the school, myself included. We were busy twenty-first-century mums and dads with zero interest in point-scoring over who spent the most hours manning the barbecue or who made the best brownies for the fete. Most of us had little to no awareness of school events and apparently not a single parent had showed up for the working bee last year. We were lucky to know our kids' teachers' names, let alone when or where the annual Art Attack night was held.

'Our most exciting event is the end-of-year Christmas concert,' Penny continued. 'This year we will have *two* concerts, over *two* separate nights! One is to be performed by the Prep to grade-four students, and the other by grades five and six. Our drama teacher, Miss Mitchell, has her hands full, so it would be great if we could have some parents helping out with the planning and execution of the junior school concert.'

Execution? Who used a word like that talking about a school concert?

'This is a very important event for *your* children,' Penny said deliberately, 'and any assistance – *any* assistance at *all* – that we can get from within our school community would be greatly appreciated.' Her steely blue eyes bored into us, sending a clear message: lift your game, get involved, or she'd hunt us down, one by one.

I glanced over to see if Megan and Sam were as amused by these thinly veiled threats as I was. Sam looked paralysed with fear, but Megan was on her phone and obviously hadn't heard a word.

'So, do any parents here think they could get involved with the junior school concert?'

Megan was still swiping, tapping, swiping, tapping.

'She's asking if any parents here have over thirty thousand Instagram followers?' I whispered in her ear.

Megan's head shot up and she waved her hand in the air. 'Oh! I do!'

Penny, probably resigned to the fact that no one would volunteer, couldn't have looked more shocked if Megan had just confessed to murder.

'Ahh, well, that's ... excellent!' Penny reverted back to her self-assured tone. 'Thank you, uh, Megan. I'm sure Oscar will be thrilled to have his mum helping out with his concert!'

It took Megan about 1.2 seconds to realise she'd been well and truly hoodwinked, and her expression changed to one of distress.

'Oh, I can't ...'

Oscar, beaming, gave his mum the thumbs-up and Megan had no choice but to return it with a forced smile. And there it was. With that single gesture, Megan had promised her son, his friends, the teachers and the principal that she'd help out on a school event. I couldn't have been happier with my work. Apparently, dobbing your mate in for something you wouldn't want to do in a million years felt pretty damn good and was a great distraction from your own tangled web of deceit.

As Penny handed back over to the teachers, Megan's

head rotated towards me, the smile frozen on her face. 'What. The. Fuck?' she growled.

'You're an inspiration to the parents of Baytree,' I said, patting her perfect thigh. 'Your community thanks you.'

'You. Are. Dead.'

'Should have been paying attention,' I said with a shrug. 'You snooze, you lose.'

Sam's shoulders shook with silent laughter and Megan gave him his second violent nudge for the morning.

'What did I do?' Sam demanded.

'Probably put her up to it!' Megan muttered. 'Arseholes.'

'Dave?' Miss Godfrey said. 'Could you come up and tell us about your work as a graphic artist?'

'Love to!' Dave jumped out of his seat and headed to the front of the class, surveying his audience as if he were about to reveal the secrets of a new *Star Wars* movie. 'I have here some sketches from my early work on my forthcoming graphic novel, *Codename: Code*!'

The children gazed at Dave with vacant expressions as he plugged his laptop into the electronic whiteboard. A pencil-drawn image of a man trying desperately to climb out from inside a computer monitor appeared, and the kids oohed and aahed.

'Could this day get any worse?' Megan muttered.

I grinned, even as I was thinking that it could definitely get much worse, for me anyway. Especially if Rick was roaming the school corridors when I left Max's classroom. As Dave banged on about the vagaries of ink technology, I thought about how I'd need to be on constant alert from now on if I wanted to keep hanging out with my mates at drop-off. At least until I'd given Greg that damn letter.

Careers Day was a huge success. Sam's tarts were

devoured by the entire class, although he was visibly distraught when most kids shoved the tarts into their mouths without taking the time to appreciate the textures and balance of flavours. Megan wowed the kids with her affordable designer children's wear and accessories and then handed out Chill business cards.

'Give these to Mum and Dad and make sure you tell them how much you love Chill's clothes,' she said. 'And these cards are magnets too, so you can just whack 'em on the fridge.' She flicked one from her hand, and it stuck smack in the middle of the interactive whiteboard. The kids applauded. The teachers scowled.

My forceps and amnihook demonstration on the classroom doll, Trixie, went down a treat. Lots of squeals and eye-covering and even a few tears. Kids love that gory shit. Max couldn't have been prouder. Despite my performance high, I still felt jumpy as we walked out of the classroom. Down any corridor, around any corner, from any door, Rick might appear.

'I'm gonna go this way,' I said, gesturing towards the door at the far end of the corridor, furthest from the classrooms.

Sam frowned. 'The long way?'

'She wants to get as far away from me as possible.' Megan's eyes glinted dangerously. 'Because I'm going to kill her.'

'Too many witnesses!' I called, walking away.

'This isn't over!' I heard Megan call as I walked out into the cold.

Sam

To: jack_woz_here@hotmail.com

From: samhatfieldchef@bigpond.com

Subject: You asked for it!

Hiya Jack,

I love that you always want to find the fix. That's why you were such a great drummer. Just wanted to serve the song. But my marriage ain't a song. If it was, it'd be unlistenable.

I understand that my marriage is a broken thing. Not like a porcelain mug that falls a short distance and breaks into two perfect pieces. You pick up the two perfect pieces and they fit together so well that you just carefully place the broken thing back on the shelf, safe in the knowledge that nobody else will reach for it and discover that it's now unusable. To everyone else it still looks like a perfectly good mug.

My marriage didn't break like that. My marriage broke like one of those bog-standard latte glasses found all around Melbourne (before our coffee was served to us in recycled vegemite jars or petrified passionfruit shells). I've made my share of coffees for Melbourne's heaving masses. I've seen how those latte glasses break. They explode, and the tiny crystal hail stones somehow cover about a 300-metre radius. It's quite spectacular, but the clean-up's a bitch. No combination of broom and vacuum will find all the pieces. The explosion is too violent, almost cosmic.

Every inspirational video on the interwebs tells the story of a bad situation, followed by a realisation, followed by some royalty-free inspirational music, followed by some footage of the ocean and hands clasping and graduation hats being thrown in the air and a boxer skipping and suddenly – within the 104 seconds it took for the music to swell to its climax – what started as a realisation has ended as a better life. Your best life.

Suck a bag of dicks.

The understanding is a culmination of years of experiences, both colossal and minuscule. The realisation can be nothing more than some casually raised eyebrows and a small nod for no one's benefit but your own. The realisation isn't the thing to be reckoned with. The understanding is the dragon.

I think folks assume that having the understanding that something is over leads to epiphanies, action and enlightenment. Not for me. I've understood where me and Bridg have been for years, but it hasn't spurred me on to make a seismic shift. It's paralysing (sorry). And I'm glad. I won't run away from my kids. They are everything. Sorry to get all thingy, but without those kids, I don't know how or why I'd get up in the morning.

So, I'll happily stay in this arctic marriage if it means I get to see my kids every day.

Love you, mate.

Thanks again for going all Dr Phil. But our marriage doesn't need a doctor. It needs a coroner.

S x

Megan

'Mum!' Oscar pulled Megan along the street towards the school gate. 'We're *so* late!'

Sleeping in on a weekday was a rare occurrence, but Megan had stayed up late answering emails and ordering new Chill stock the night before, finally falling into bed sometime after 2 a.m. She woke to a sleepy-eyed Oscar standing beside her bed, holding her phone up to her face.

'Mummy,' he'd whispered, 'I think it's late.'

Megan scanned the schoolyard as they hurried along the footpath, but Lizzie and Sam were gone and would be furious at missing out on their morning coffees, as per Megan's Careers Day deal.

'Mum, they're all in assembly!' Oscar said, tugging on Megan's arm in alarm and pointing at the school hall. 'I'm late for Monday *assembly*!'

Megan could hear the students' off-key warbling of the national anthem coming from the hall, which meant Penny Guthrie wasn't in her office, which meant Megan would have to wait until assembly to tell her, 'So sorry, but I can't help with the concert after all.'

Dammit.

Sometime after midnight and before 2 a.m. Megan had decided there was just no way she could help out on the stupid school play. She was a single, working mother and things were tight right now. Penny would have to find some other sap to source costumes and paint sets.

'Go on, then,' Megan said, leaning down to give Oscar a kiss.

'Aren't you coming?' Oscar's face fell. 'Parents are invited too.'

It was hard to say no when Oscar had a look of such pathetic hope on his face and knew she had nowhere to be that morning.

'Okay,' she said, turning towards the hall. 'Come on.'

Megan couldn't remember the last time she was inside the Baytree Primary school hall. Probably last year's Christmas concert when Oscar's class had sung 'Santa Wear your Shorts', dressed in Aussie cork hats. The hall was a decent size for a small school, with an in-built stage at the far end. It even had a small kitchen where the older kids had served parents pre-show gingerbread biscuits. Megan looked over to see Penny Guthrie on the stage, addressing the two hundred and forty or so students sitting cross-legged on the parquet floor. The crackly microphone was attached to a small amp that looked as if it belonged in the corner of a thirteen-year-old boy's room. Black metal folding chairs were set up behind the children, and Oscar joined his classmates as Megan quietly slipped into one of the many vacant chairs. Standard poor parent attendance at a Baytree assembly.

'... and I know we will all miss Henry's smiling face as he greeted us every day, just as he's done every morning for the past fifteen years,' Penny Guthrie was saying. 'But we can feel comforted in the knowledge that he lived a long, happy life.'

Megan noticed some of the older students crying and hugging. One of the other mothers sitting nearby caught Megan's confused expression.

'Henry, the lollipop man, died,' she whispered. 'They found him in his flat around the corner. Been dead for three days. But Guthrie didn't tell them that. Trying to keep it nice for the kids.'

'Three days!' Megan whispered back. 'Didn't anyone report him missing?'

'Shh!' hissed another mother.

Megan watched the school captain read out the house points but didn't hear a word the kid said. She couldn't shake the image of Henry's lifeless body lying on the floor, or in his bed or in the bath ... or maybe his favourite armchair. No one had missed him enough to go and knock on his door and see if he was okay. Henry, the sweet old man who'd smiled at her every day as he escorted them across the road, was dead. Henry, who some mornings seemed to need his stop sign more as a support than a signal. Henry, who never tired of applying the appropriate superlatives to the day's weather, had died. Alone. How did someone end up so alone that no one knew he was dead for three whole days? It didn't bear thinking about. Megan felt a crushing sadness and gripped the edge of the chair beneath her to shift her attention from the searing heat behind her ribcage. But why? She hardly knew the old guy.

As the school band butchered 'Another One Bites The Dust' (they may have been shit, but their song choice couldn't have been more morbidly apt), Megan mentally ran through her weekly routine, trying to figure out the most obvious moment in any given week when someone – anyone – would find her body. The thought of Bryce finding it made her eyes shut. The thought of Oscar ... she gritted her teeth behind closed lips. Stop it. He'd be long gone. As her mother predicted, Oscar might move to Tokyo, or Vancouver, or Perth after school. He might never call or visit his old mum. As for friends, Megan's social life was non-existent. When Bryce played daddy every second weekend, she spent the weekend watching Netflix in her trackies. She had Lizzie and Sam on weekday mornings, but once primary school was done and their kids caught the bus to their respective high schools, her two mates would no longer be part of her daily life. As for her work life, 90 per cent of Megan's business involved being on the computer, so there wasn't a lot of human interaction, aside from the odd face-to-face meeting with a new supplier or social-media strategist. She doubted a single one of her thousands of Instagram followers would be checking on her when she was seventy and living in a one-bedder in the 'burbs. Her mum wouldn't be around forever, and Matt didn't want kids so there'd be no nieces or nephews to make sure old Auntie Megsy was getting by. Megan's future wasn't looking particularly well populated.

Megan suddenly felt unstable, as if she might tip sideways and fall off her chair. The credible vision of solitude and loneliness that could be her future settled on her shoulders like a stone gargoyle.

'Megan?'

She snapped out of it to find Penny Guthrie standing over her, staring at her curiously. Assembly was over and kids around her were heading back to their classrooms or packing up chairs. A flushed blonde girl with braces glared at Megan, impatient for her to get up so she could fold her chair and get back to the important business of being a ten year old. Megan stood up and the chair was whipped out from under her like a magician's tablecloth.

'Hi Penny,' Megan said, feeling exposed. 'Sorry, miles away.'

'Nice to see you at assembly.'

'Yeah,' Megan said. 'I wanted to talk to you about the school play.'

'Of course,' Penny said. 'I was going to email you today to ask for your Working with Children details?'

Through the window, Megan could see some of the older girls placing flowers outside the gate, the spot where Henry had chatted to the kids as they entered the school.

'Also, Miss Mitchell has just had some upsetting news about her father's health,' Penny interrupted, 'so she might need to take time off here and there.'

'Oh, well ...'

'So, do you think you could maybe help out a *bit* more than expected?' Penny sounded desperate. 'Maybe help come up with an idea for the junior school concert? It only needs to be an hour long, and Miss Mitchell has a lot on her plate with the grade-five and -six kids and their play, *The Bunyip Who Slept Through Christmas*.'

Megan frowned. 'The what now?'

'It's a Christmas play she bought off the internet,' Penny said, looking unimpressed. 'A bunyip sleeps in on Christmas morning, and his emu and kangaroo friends have to wake him up.'

'Gripping stuff.'

'Indeed. So, it would be nice to have something with a different ... feel for the younger kids' show.'

Megan could see Henry's lollipop hat hanging off the side of the whiteboard over Penny's shoulder. Someone had drawn a bunch of red, blue and yellow flowers beside it.

Fuck it.

'That's what I was going to talk to you about actually,' she said. 'I've got a few ideas, but I'll narrow them down and get back to you.'

Penny's face broke into a relieved smile. 'Excellent!' She clapped her hands together. 'I can't wait to hear what you've come up with. Thank you, Megan. Thank you very much.'

What is wrong with me? Megan thought, walking back to her car. How had news of a lollipop man's death turned her into a person who was 'going to get back to the principal with concert ideas'? Maybe she was getting her period. That must be it.

She'd revisit backing out of this stupid concert once her body had sorted itself out.

'Keep still, please!'

'How much longer?'

'The more you move, the longer it will take!'

Megan raised the camera to her eye again and Oscar sighed, making Megan feel like the worst mother in the world. She knew he hated posing for Chill photos, but she had no choice. The stock had arrived two days late and she needed to get images of the new Westie kids jeans out to her subscribers and on to the socials before end of business.

'Sorry, mate,' Megan said, snapping photos of Oscar with his hands in his pockets and a wistful look on that face that was so like Bryce's. 'Just a couple more ...' She checked the viewfinder and gave him a thumbs-up. 'You're free! Off you go!'

But Oscar didn't move. 'Hey Mum, why didn't Daddy come to Careers Day?'

Wow. The smack in the face that was a little kid's non sequiturs.

'He was away.'

'With Adam?'

'Yeah, with Adam.'

Oscar crinkled his nose, imitating the action he'd seen from Ellie when this topic of conversation came up. 'Was Daddy working?'

Bryce worked in PR, and often travelled interstate. Last week, he'd gone to Sydney and taken Adam with him so they could celebrate their three-year anniversary and impending nuptials. They'd overloaded Instagram's servers with the number of photos they shared. Megan's personal favourite was a selfie of the two of them at a bar, lurid cocktails held up to their chins, the Opera House in the background, the two equally gorgeous-looking men beaming into each other's faces, flushed and happy.

The caption read: *When in Rome, do as the divas do. Am I right? 3 perfect years with this 10. Looking forward to 100 more.* It was typical of the nonsensical bullshit Bryce posted most days. Another was a pic of the two of them in full Spanish dance pose, roses between their teeth. His caption for this glorious moment read: *When the passion takes you, you must dance the FLAMINGO!*

Not a deliberate mistake. He'd suggested he and Megan take 'Flamingo' lessons many years earlier. If Bryce was Melbourne's answer to Ryan Gosling, Adam was his gay Chris Hemsworth. Tall, like Bryce, Adam had the same chiselled jaw, floppy hair and abs to die for. He was a personal trainer, after all. But Adam also wore glasses, which made him even hotter.

'It was a kind of working holiday.'

Oscar looked at his mum the way you'd expect a six year old to when faced with such a glaring oxymoron.

'He wanted to be there,' she added.

'But that's not the same as being there.'

'Hey, have you thought about where you want to go for your birthday this year?'

Oscar's face brightened and Megan congratulated herself for the genius move of changing the subject. It didn't matter that Oscar's birthday was over three months away, he forgot most topics when the B-word was mentioned.

'The zoo!'

'The zoo?' Megan immediately regretted her decision to let Oscar choose his own birthday destination. 'You don't just want to go to Tweedledums?'

Megan had assumed he'd pick the local play centre for his birthday outing in November. He and his friends could run themselves ragged in the safe confines of Tweedledum's walls, while Megan sat in the play centre café with a latte and her laptop.

'Uh-uh.' Oscar firmly shook his head. 'The zoo, please.'

'Okay.'

At least she'd have Lizzie to help; Oscar and Max were good mates.

'And I want Daddy to come too,' Oscar said quietly, looking nervous. 'Is that okay?'

Megan's heart broke. The poor kid was scared to ask if his own dad could attend his birthday party. 'Of course!' She forced a smile onto her face. 'I'll let him know.'

'Yay!' Oscar cried. 'Can I play on your phone?'

'No,' Megan said. 'But you can do some drawing. There's blank paper on my desk.'

Oscar raced out and Megan sat down, opened her laptop and connected her camera.

'Come on,' she muttered as her laptop took an age to start up. She had so much work to do, so many emails, and still had to get dinner sorted before taking Oscar to footy training because Bryce was in Sydney again. She felt exhausted just thinking about the next few hours.

'Muuuum ... can you come here?'

Megan closed her eyes briefly and exhaled. 'Where are you?' she called, getting up.

'In your office.'

'What are you ...?' Megan's voice faded away as she entered the front room to the sight of Oscar at her desktop computer.

'Why are you still in here?' she said. 'You were supposed to get some paper and draw.'

Megan clocked the panicked look on her son's face and a cold tingling ran all the way from her forehead down to her stomach. She walked over to look at the screen.

Blank. The cursor blinked at her dumbly.

'I just wanted to do the eggs game ...'

'Oscar,' Megan tried to keep her voice calm as she pressed Ctrl Z. Undo. Oh God, *undo*. Nothing. 'Where are the words that were on the screen?'

'They went away,' Oscar said softly, his lip trembling. 'I didn't mean to. I'm sorry ...'

Half a day's work. Two thousand words of copy for her subscribers that were supposed to go out tonight. Gone.

'Shit!'

A trembling lip gave way to wailing as tears spilled from Oscar's eyes and Megan was torn between the impulse to cuddle him to her chest or throw him out the window. In the end, she did neither.

'Go to your room,' she said quietly. 'I've told you not to touch the computer when I'm not with you. Now, you need to think about what you've done. I'm very disappointed.'

Oscar ran out of the office and she heard his wails move through an impressive crescendo.

Megan flopped down into her desk chair and pulled the keyboard towards her. *Looks like it's takeaway tonight*, she thought, beginning to type.

Sam

10.07 a.m.

S – Where you now? x

B – bne

S – ?

B – brisbane

S – Oh yeah of course. Ha! X

11.17 a.m.

S – You still landing 7ish? x

B – far as I know.

S – Yay! Missing you. Xxoo

1.48 p.m.

S – I'll let the kids stay up a bit so you can give 'em a cuddle. x

B – no don't do that they need sleep.

S – Fair enough good point. x

S – If they're asleep, maybe we could have a cuddle? Xx

1.52 p.m.

S – Sorry. Airports aren't sexy, are they?

1.56 p.m.

S – Bridg?

B – need to get report done before boarding.

S – No worries. Sorry. Safe flight. X

Lizzie

Babies have always fascinated me. I was the clucky kid who asked people – usually Abelas' customers – if I could hold their baby. I loved their tiny fingernails and wrinkly hands, their smooth skin and chubby legs. And their smell. Divine. When I had my own, I'd spend hours gazing at them. During college, a dickhead stoner bailed me up at a party one night and spent a solid hour informing me that losing my mother at four had created feelings of abandonment that had subconsciously steered me towards midwifery. Who knows? Maybe Dickhead Stoner was right. Regardless, I love being around babies and births and that's my job, so happy days. And walking into St Vincent's for my Monday afternoon shift, I was happier still because, for the next ten hours, I'd be flat out soothing screaming almost-mothers, mopping up amniotic fluid and gasbagging at the midwife station, which was the perfect diversion from my worrying thoughts.

'Hey girl!' Aileen was filling out cards at the midwife station.

'How was your morning?' I asked, throwing my bag under the desk.

'Bedlam,' she said, rolling her eyes. 'First delivery was a proper cone head and the mum was convinced she'd birthed an alien. Then I had to confiscate a selfie stick off some fecking "influencer" mum who was trying to live stream her own labour. I had to up her pethidine to get the stupid thing off her.'

The perfect diversion.

The only one left awake to greet me in our dark, silent house that night was our Labrador, Bailey, and she jumped up and down like a lunatic. *Look! It's her! I don't believe it! She came back! Again!* Once Bailey had recovered from the excitement and was back on her bed. I headed for the kitchen. A cup of tea and Vegemite on toast were my post-work sustenance after a long shift, and my God it had been long. Three Caesars, two breech and one teenager who was dropped off and left on her own. After she'd popped out a perfect nine-pound boy in under three hours, she asked if she could move in with me. As I sat munching toast and sipping tea, I could see my laptop through the open door of the office, displaying a random selection of family photos. There was no reason I couldn't have another crack at finishing the letter now. I was wide awake and there would be no interruptions. But even when presented with such a rare and ideal working environment, I had no clue how to start.

I thought back to when Rick Cooke and I had first met – a thousand years ago when we were both playing under-17s soccer. I'd been playing soccer for almost ten years by then. After losing Mum, Dad had retreated into himself, and it was Auntie Carmen to the rescue when she volunteered him to coach the under-10s at the Williamstown Soccer Club. Dad told her he didn't have 'time for that bullshit!' but Auntie Carmen was unfazed. He loved it, of course, and his scout's eye soon turned towards his two eldest sons, then seven and nine, dreaming of lucrative contracts and endorsement deals. Dad's dreams died a quick death when he saw the boys play. Soccer balls and Christopher's feet were like magnets with the same polarity, and Joey was scared of the ball, running behind his teammates, or the opposition, if it came near him. And Lucas was only three, so any chance he had at world glory was still a way off. Dad was describing this epic family tragedy to a customer at the restaurant one day when the man turned and nodded at me. I was six at the time, and my best friend Melissa and I were drawing at a table. I was probably drawing babies.

'What about her?' the man said.

'She's a girl.'

Members of the Maltese community who inhabited the western suburbs of Melbourne in the 1980s found the idea of a girl playing soccer both insane and hilarious.

'So?'

'Football too rough,' Dad said, wagging his hairy knuckles in the guy's face. 'My Lizzie get hurt. No good for girls.'

'Rubbish,' the guy laughed. 'Look at Martina Navratilova and Chris Evert!'

'Pah!' Dad spat. 'That *tennis*! Girls' game.'

'Don't say that to John McEnroe,' the guy said. 'He'd crack his racquet across your head. Navratilova too!'

'They can both bloody *ilaqli l-bajd*!'

'You should think about it, Joseph,' the guy said before walking out.

Auntie Carmen overheard this whole conversation and relayed it to me a few years later, although I'm not sure an eight year old needed to know that her father said John

McEnroe and Martina Navratilova could lick his balls, but that's Auntie Carmen. Loves details. The customer must've made an impact, because soon after Dad announced that I was going to training with him. I wasn't sure I wanted to go, but a wink and nod from Auntie Carmen told me I should. Chris and Joey thought it was the funniest thing they'd ever heard and made lots of hilarious comments like 'Don't break a nail!' and 'The round thing is the ball and you're supposed to kick it'. I don't remember that first training session, all I know is that soccer always felt effortless. Running, connecting with the ball and weaving around other players all came very easily.

After that, I was Dad's great sporting hope. It took a while for the community to get behind Dad's all-girl soccer team, but when the Felines started winning games, we soon built up a decent following. I could have filled a small shipping container with the 'best player' trophies I collected over the years, which probably would have meant more if I'd loved the game. Soccer was okay, but it wasn't a passion for me. Dad was no Damir Dokić and I was never forced to keep playing, but he couldn't have been prouder or happier, which was my main motivation to do so. I eventually convinced Melissa to join the club, and soon after that I met Rick. Suddenly my life became a whole lot more entrenched in the soccer scene.

The last place I ever expected to meet my first boyfriend was the soccer club. Most of the boys I met there were stupid, obnoxious or arrogant. I wasn't such a great catch myself in my early teens, with my poofy brown hair, gappy teeth and no boobs. Young Lizzie Abela was usually dressed in a poncho of some sort, with brown velvet cords and desert boots – basically your stock standard, unattractive child. By fifteen, I'd developed C-cup boobs and ditched the ponchos and velvet cords, but still felt the pressure to disprove my classmates' theory that I was a permanent resident of Lesbos. The fact that I lived and breathed soccer didn't exactly help dispel the rumours.

While the other girls at school were donning eyeliner and lip gloss or putting blonde tips in their carefully blow-dried hair, I had zero interest in that 'girlie shit'. My thick Maltese mop was usually pulled back into a low ponytail and only washed once a week. I wore no makeup (Dad would have killed me) and whichever pair of jeans and T-shirt was closest to my bed in the morning. Still, by the end of year eight, my fair-haired-green-eyed-extremely-Anglo best mate Melissa and I somehow found ourselves part of a 'group'. Unfortunately, I soon made the mistake of announcing that I was bored with the 'Who is the cutest surfie?' conversation and suggested we play down-ball instead. The girls looked at me like I'd just dropped my pants and shat on the oval.

That afternoon, as Melissa and I sat at our corner table in Abelas drinking blue heaven milkshakes and doing algebra worksheets, my best friend informed me that unless I changed my attitude towards boys, the other girls wanted me out of the group. The thought of wandering the playground alone like a social pariah with BO for the next three years was horrifying.

'Chrissie Alfonsi told everyone you must be a lezzo if you don't like talking about boys,' Melissa whispered across the table. 'She said that she didn't want to invite a big lez like you to her slumber party because you'd probably try to finger her in her sleep!'

'*Ugh!*' I cried. 'As *if*!'

'*Lizzie!*' Dad shouted from the kitchen. 'This is a place of workplace!'

Dad was prepping for another busy Friday night – his least favourite job – so I decided not to point out that: the restaurant was empty; his yelling was ten times louder than mine; 'This is a place of workplace' was the worst sentence ever.

'Sorry, Mr Abela!' Melissa said, giving Dad her sweetest smile.

'Ah, you good girls,' Dad said, polishing a soup spoon as if the queen herself might use it.

'Suck up,' I whispered.

'So?' Melissa whispered, returning to our important agenda item. 'What are you going to do?'

I tapped my pen on my teeth. 'I guess I could *pretend* that I like talking about boys.'

Melissa nodded her approval. 'You should make up a story about meeting a cute boy at training!'

'There *are* no cute boys at training.'

'I said *make up* a story.'

'Okay,' I said, pissed off with the whole situation.

Unfortunately, I made the monumental error of not running the story by Melissa before relaying it to the rest of the group the following morning. The scenario began with me strolling around the soccer ground when, out of the nearby bushes, I was grabbed and thrown on to the grass.

'I was shitting myself,' I told the wide-eyed girls gathered around me. 'But I yielded to his firm embrace as he kissed me tenderly, and the sweet-tasting kiss lasted for hours before the stranger – who I'm almost positive was a surfie – jumped up and ran away leaving me weak with desire.' I'd memorised most of this from a passage in one of Auntie

Carmen's Mills & Boon books. Melissa gawked as if she was watching rhinoceroses mating as I relayed this tale of passion and what was basically sexual assault.

'What was a gorgeous surfie doing in the bushes at some soccer ground?'

Chrissie Alfonsi. Trust that smug little bitch to apply logic to my deeply flawed fantasy.

'Prob'ly, um ... having a nap.'

Chrissie smirked before flicking her hair and walking away, closely followed by the rest of the group.

'I said make up a story about *meeting* a cute boy!' Melissa hissed once they were gone. 'Not being *attacked* by one!'

But despite the reputation I developed around school as the 'Bush-Rape Girl', I refused to back-pedal on my tale of the Soccer Ground Kiss Bandit. A few months later I managed to attract the attention of a greasy-haired, pimply faced St Mark's college boy at the brother–sister schools' annual disco. It proved to be an all-round disappointing experience. It was all tongues, saliva and bad breath and lasted a whopping thirty seconds. I never heard from the nameless Catholic boy (with the kissing technique of an epileptic lizard) again, but I could finally say – without a hint of an overblown lie – that I'd been kissed. Chrissie Alfonsi and the rest of my classmates had witnessed our thirty seconds of teenage glory, and finally the Soccer Ground Kiss Bandit became a distant memory.

Rick Cooke came into my life soon after this triumph. Melissa and I were sharing a Gatorade after a particularly exhausting under-17s game, when a pack of boys stampeded into the clubhouse and arranged themselves around a table like a fake gang in a school play. If you squinted, they resembled a group of orangutans, beating on the table, hopping up and down in their chairs and screeching. Melissa and I were not impressed.

Rick stood out from the buffoonery. As his mates ricocheted around the table trying to prove chaos theory, Rick sat still, only moving his head to engage with his teammates. A large, crumpled sports bag sat on the floor between his feet. Sticking out of the zip pocket was Stephen King's *The Shining*, which I had devoured earlier that year. I was intrigued by this teenage soccer-playing boy who *read books,* and kept sneaking glances at him, gradually giving him the full once over: a shock of thick brown-blond hair that stuck up in front, tanned legs, flushed cheeks and huge brown eyes. I was in the midst of studying those tanned legs when he looked up and smiled a 'sorry my mates are such fuckwits' smile at me. I blushed. Not only was he considerate, mature and cute, he was also the first boy who'd ever paid a single jot of attention to me at the club.

At training that night, I could feel Rick's eyes on me from the opposite pitch and ramped up my fancy footwork. A week later, kicking at the grass and fumbling his words, Rick asked me to go to the video arcade with him after Saturday's game. Melissa covered for me and over hot chips and cola, I learnt that Rick had also lost his mum when he was younger. I don't know if it was the mother hen in me or teenage lust, but I was smitten. We shared a quick, surprisingly tender kiss behind the *Warriors of Fate* machine before Dad picked me up, and the next day Rick asked me to 'go with him' over the phone. I said yes. Melissa, Chrissie Alfonsi and the whole world rejoiced.

Auntie Carmen helped me construct a plan for Rick to slowly win Dad over before we shared the news with him.

Rick spent weekends helping Dad pack up equipment, hand out raffle tickets and man the barbecue for a whole season. It worked. Rick could be very charming when he wanted to be, and Dad liked him. Melissa started dating Rick's mate Lachy, and soon we'd expanded into a core group of eight. We were a tight bunch, going to the arcade or bowling on Friday nights, playing soccer matches on Saturdays, then staying at the clubhouse for barbecues and discos. We lived and breathed soccer, the club and each other.

Rick was always the quietest of the pack. The other boys were raucous and loved making comments on which soccer chick was the hottest, but Rick always stayed close to me and didn't say much. The boys nicknamed him Mouse, but when we were alone, he spoke about books, dead mothers and his feelings – things he'd never discuss around our friends. He made me feel beautiful, clever and adored, and found everything I said fascinating. Rick's intense, loving focus gave me a new confidence and I began to see myself the way he saw me. Suddenly my poofy hair, gappy teeth and curvy figure were sexy and unique. He made me endless mixtapes, most of which included at least two Phil Collins and/or Bryan Adams songs. No sixteen year old could have asked for more.

The first time we had sex it was suitably awkward and painful, but Rick was a patient lover, and we soon got the hang of it. It would be a few years before I experienced my first orgasm, but back then foreplay was way more enjoyable than the main event, so I didn't mind. Location was obviously an issue. My house wasn't an option, so we'd usually go to Rick's house on Saturday nights and wait for his dad to pass out in front on the TV before sneaking into Rick's room. The Cookes lived in a rundown weatherboard near the club, and Rick's dad, Brett, lived off benefits after an injury at the Toyota factory. They had very little money, and Brett drank a lot of what they did have. Rick was super skinny when I met him, but we thickened him up with pastizzis and milkshakes over the years. He was ashamed of his poverty and as we lay in his single bed together, he'd tell me how he was going to make something of himself and buy a house as nice as mine one day.

Throughout those formative years, Rick was there, facing and surviving all the milestones of adolescence alongside me. I sometimes had a nagging sensation that maybe I didn't love him as much as I should – that some vital part of me was being overlooked or fazed out – but he was a good man and I didn't want to break his heart, so for a long time I chose to ignore those feelings.

'Hey, you coming to bed?'

Greg was standing in the doorway in his boxers, rubbing one hand back and forth over the top of his bed hair and reaching for the fridge door with the other.

My cup of tea sat on the kitchen bench, now stone cold. How long had I been sitting there?

'Yeah, coming now.'

In bed, Greg snuggled into my back and rested his arm on my thigh. 'How was work?'

'Fine. Busy.'

'So ... Max brought it up at dinner again ...'

'No.'

'Why not just let him try out?' Greg murmured, patting my hip.

Max had been begging to play soccer for the past few

months. I said we couldn't afford it, which was a lie. I had no desire to return to the world of soccer.

'Talk tomorrow,' I said, reaching back to put my hand over his. 'I'm shattered.'

But I wasn't shattered. I was very much awake. Greg was snoring in less than a minute – an infuriating ability possessed by every man I'd ever known – while I lay on my side, staring at him in the darkness and trying to imagine how he would react when he knew the truth about his wife. About Rick and his wife. Would he hate me? Would he decide he couldn't stay in a marriage with someone he didn't trust?

And really, if he did decide that, who could blame him?

Megan

Cody Fletcher @cfletcher58blog

Baytree Primary parents and teachers should be ashamed! How could everyone in that community fail to notice the absence of their lollipop man for three whole days? A man who has worked the school crossing for over 15 years. It's disgraceful. This is an uncaring and selfish community that needs to take a long hard look at itself!

'What the fuck?'

The tweet on Megan's phone was slightly blurry (thanks to three glasses of wine and the late hour) but there was no mistaking the tone. A quick Google search told Megan that Cody Fletcher was '*Proud mum of two beautiful children*' and author of the mummy blog, Mother Unfolding. Had she been sober, Megan might simply have grimaced, acknowledged that Cody Fletcher wasn't exactly wrong, and scrolled down to the next post on her Twitter feed.

But Megan wasn't sober. She was drunk and still feeling fragile after the social-media wormhole she'd descended into hours earlier when she'd tortured herself by scrolling through Bryce's Instagram feed. If the images of Bryce and Adam's blinding happiness weren't enough mental torture for her, Megan had then decided it would be an excellent idea to scroll through comments on Bryce's Mindfulness Facebook page:

wasent this guy marryed to the chick from that ad

yea shes hot!!

musent of been hot enough! ;-)

Memories of *that* night had then rampaged through Megan's drunken mind as she reached for the bottle again and thought for the millionth time how she hadn't even seen the end of her marriage coming. Back then, Megan had been so busy with Chill and a gorgeous toddler that she hadn't noticed the growing distance between her and her husband, so when Bryce told her he'd joined a gym, Megan was encouraging, and maybe a little insensitive.

'Good idea, babe,' she'd said. 'Don't want to end up with a dad bod.'

Gym started as a once-a-week thing, then twice, and soon Bryce was heading off every night. Sometimes he'd be gone for over three hours. Looking back, Megan couldn't believe her stupidity, but then she was usually fast asleep by 9 p.m., exhausted by the business and from chasing Oscar around all day. Sex had been great in the beginning; Bryce was a gentle and attentive lover, but was definitely a lights-off kinda guy. Once Oscar was born, their sex life came to a screeching halt and she didn't even hear Bryce getting home late at night. If she had been awake, she'd have noticed that his gym clothes usually smelt as fresh and clean as when he'd left.

Very late one night, a few months after he'd joined the gym, Bryce stepped on one of Oscar's toys as he crept through the front door. It was one of those annoying Wiggles dolls that sang the whole chorus of 'Big Red Car' at full volume when you pushed its stomach (whoever programmed those things had a deep hatred of parents). In a demented way, she still blamed the stupid smiley Yellow Wiggle for shattering her ignorant bliss.

The sound of The Wiggles' tinny voices echoing down the hallway woke Megan and her first thought was that it was morning and Oscar was playing with that stupid bloody doll again. Then she noticed the time and saw that Bryce wasn't in bed beside her. When she opened the bedroom door she saw Bryce standing in the hallway, desperately attempting to muffle the sound of the noisy doll.

'What are you doing?' Megan whispered. 'It's almost two o'clock!'

She gestured for Bryce to move away from Oscar's bedroom and into the lounge. He followed, the doll finally falling silent as Megan shut the door behind them.

'What the fuck, Bryce?'

Bryce stared, his eyes too wide, and an icy sensation crept across Megan's chest. Wherever he'd been, whatever he'd been doing, it wasn't good. She nodded at the gym bag slung over his shoulder.

'And please don't tell me you've been at the gym.' Her voice was already starting to crack.

'Some of us went for drinks after ...'

'Don't lie to me, Bryce!' Megan hissed, trembling.

Bryce slumped onto the couch, cradling his head in his hands.

'Who is she?'

'No, Megs.'

'Bullshit!' Megan collapsed onto the armchair before her legs went out from under her. 'Who is she?'

Bryce looked up with a pained expression. 'It's a him.'

Megan felt as though an entire layer of herself turned to ash in that moment and fell on the floor. Her first reaction was to laugh. It seemed so ridiculous, like something from a bad Aussie soap opera. It was *fucking ridiculous*. Thoughts swirled through her brain as Bryce divulged all. He'd met Adam in his first week at the gym. They'd made small talk over elliptical training machines, but soon it was a pressed juice at the gym café after a workout, where they swapped life stories and secrets. Bryce had suspected Adam was gay but had never expected to fall in love with him.

'Why would you,' Megan finally exploded, 'when you're *straight*!'

'That's the thing,' Bryce said, starting to cry. 'I've always suspected … that I might not be one hundred per cent straight, but then I met you and, well, I blocked it out. I still noticed guys, but you made me happy …'

'Oh, well, that's good to know.'

'… then Oscar came along, and I accepted this was my life now,' Bryce continued. 'A straight man with a kid, a wife and a mortgage.'

'Jesus, you make it sound so ordinary,' Megan said, tears running down her cheeks.

'Once I met Adam,' Bryce's face brightened at the mention of his name, 'I knew it was right.'

Megan decided she was dreaming. Yes, that was it. She was actually fast asleep, with Bryce beside her in bed. He would be mock outraged when she told him about it in the morning.

'Gee, thanks, babe,' he'd say. 'Next thing you'll be dreaming I'm a Catholic priest.'

But Megan couldn't make herself wake up, and when the sun began streaming through the window a few hours later, and Oscar called out from his cot, she knew it was real. She and Bryce had stayed up all night – talking, crying, shouting and hugging – but at the end of it all, she'd lost her husband.

Megan rubbed her eyes, surprised to find her cheeks wet. She took another swig of the wine and picked up her phone to reread the tweet.

'Fuck you, Cody Fletcher,' she muttered.

And that's when a more-than-slightly drunk Megan began typing a response at 12.35 a.m., her tolerance, self-esteem and self-control at an all-time low, but her cross hairs in sharp, sharp focus.

Sam

To: jack_woz_here@hotmail.com
From: samhatfieldchef@bigpond.com
Subject: Updates galore

Hey dickhead,

Bridget got back last night. Multiple stops in South East Asia. Lucky thing had two free nights in Hong Kong. She works like a mad person, so she deserves the down time.

All your suggestions for increasing staying power after a period of celibacy were much appreciated ... and disturbingly inventive. Didn't matter in the end. Bridg was exhausted. As per your advice, I still tried it on. And I was pretty smooth. I acknowledged her obvious fatigue, then told her how much I'd missed her and said she deserved some relaxation and that I'd give her a massage before bed. And for the record, I would've happily left it at a massage if that's all she wanted. If it led to something slightly more amorous, happy days! But when I suggested the massage, Bridg's immediate response was, 'Oh Jesus, Sam, just have a wank.' Pretty definitive, huh? Bridget went to bed, leaving her suitcase smack in the middle of the hallway. I moved it so the kids wouldn't come a cropper in the middle of the night going to the toilet. I polished off about a pint of Finlandia then fell asleep on the couch watching a doco about some nut-job free climber.

This morning was a hoot! I was still asleep on the couch, cradling the vodka bottle, when Tyler sat on my chest and patted my cheek. I asked where Mum was, and he told me she was in the study. So, I dragged myself off the couch, put the bottle back in the cupboard and went to the study. I made the mistake of making a question sound like a statement.

'You haven't done the lunches.'

Bridg doesn't respond well to statements from me any more. She's come to expect a certain level of subservience. She shrugged like a mob boss and said she had work to do. She asked if I remembered what work was. I left her alone and made the lunches.

Getting out of the house and into the schoolyard is always a nice feeling. Fresh air and fresh people and a few minutes of freedom. Drop-off is like a little oasis.

At one point this morning, Megan said something about me not shaving, then reached out and rubbed my stubble with the back of her fingers. It was hardly a tender moment, but it made me realise it's been a while since I've been touched.

And no, dickhead, I'm not including myself in that. I hear you, you filthy animal.

But do you know what I mean? It was nice. Affectionate.

If Lizzie was there, she would've made it into a thing and we all would've laughed about it, but I'm glad it was let be this morning.

S x

Reruns of Stingers. *Fucking perfect. It's no fun watching shit TV on your own. If we were watching something bad together, we could laugh about it and revel in how shit it was. But on my own, it's just me staring at an average television show because I'd rather do this than sit here in silence. The quiet in this place is like an enemy now. Whenever it's really quiet, I get scared of moving around too much. Silence paralyses me. I find myself standing in one spot for I don't even know how long, looking around the apartment and trying to figure out where the attack will come from. The attack of what? No idea. But I know it's coming. And I always imagine that she's still here somewhere. That whatever's about to crash through the windows or break down the door will be met with the invincible wrath of me, the protector. I mutter to myself the things I'd say to the intruders, clenching my fists and starting to sweat from the fear and excitement of it. Because if I could show her how courageous I am, she'd never leave. She'd understand how much I love her, and she'd want to come back.*

But it's fiction. I'm using hypothetical, imaginary scenarios to try to win her back. She's gone. My rational brain has processed that and filed it away in Understood.

But I don't care if it's impossible or hopeless, because I don't believe in those things any more. I can't believe in the finality of this, because it isn't over. Even if nobody else understands – even if she doesn't – I do. If it's not meant to be, why is she the thing that my mind jumps to whenever it has a moment to itself? Why is she the connective tissue that makes everything I think about make sense? Because she's the one. Even sitting here watching Stingers, *it's her that makes me smile because every time Peter Phelps comes on the screen, she quotes his immortal line from* Point Break*: 'Death on a stick out there, mate.'*

She's the reason I'm sitting here surrounded by filth and scared of going outside and smiling all at the same time. She's the reason I know I'm going to be okay. Because she's the one. And one day she'll realise that too.

Lizzie

'But *why* can't I go?'

'Because you're eleven, not seventeen!'

'What if Amy's mum goes with us?'

'Is she?'

'I think ... yeah, she is ...'

'Okay, I'll call and ask her today.'

'Don't call her! Why can't you just *trust me*?' Zara stomped out of the kitchen and slammed the bathroom door.

What had started as a rational discussion over breakfast had rapidly descended into a full-blown mother-daughter battle. Zara calmly informed me that she'd be attending an outdoor music festival with her friend, Amy, in a couple of weeks, which is when I calmly informed her that no such thing would be happening. Cue descent into shouting, stomping and slamming.

I was assembling the third lunchbox sandwich when Zara swept back in.

'Look out, she's back,' I said.

'What have I *done*?' Zara demanded, arms folded and a face like thunder.

'Well, hopefully you've brushed your teeth and put your shoes on.' I looked down. 'Nope. Still barefoot.'

'You know what I mean,' she snapped. 'Why are you so *angry* with me all the time?'

'I have no idea what you're talking about.' I snapped

Max's lunchbox lid shut. 'Now can you please go and ...'

'You won't let me have a phone ...'

'Because you don't need one,' I said for the three thousandth time that week. 'Not until you start high school and get the bus.'

'... and I bet that even when I *do* get a phone,' Zara continued as if I hadn't spoken, 'you won't let me get Instagram!'

'Correct!' I said, smothering Stella's sandwich in tomato sauce as per her specific instructions. 'Eleven-year-old girls pulling duck-face selfies are a symbol of a crumbling society. Future historians will project holograms of today's social-media teens into their lecture halls and everyone will laugh and marvel at just how unbelievably narcissistic a race we were. They'll look at it like sexism or smoking in public: something completely ridiculous and wrong that is impossible to imagine being real or acceptable.'

Zara stared, briefly shocked into silence, then threw her hands in the air. 'You've *practised that*!' she shouted. 'You are so *old* and you have *no idea* how the world works!'

She visibly shrank as I slammed the knife down on the bench top, knowing she'd gone too far. 'You do *not* speak to me like that,' I growled. 'You, my young friend, just lost your allowance for a week. Now, go outside and bring in that washing like I asked you half an hour ago!'

'I shouldn't have to do chores if I'm not getting an allowance.'

You had to admire her bravery. Determined to get the last word in, even if it meant certain death. As Dad would say, '*arnda blallen gbir*'. (She's got big balls.)

'This is a family,' I said in a tone I usually saved for fathers who asked if they could 'just slip out to make a work call' while their wife was in the final stages of labour. 'We all help out regardless of whether we are paid to do so. Now go outside and bring in that washing, or it will be *two* weeks.'

'Fine, but you have been really grumpy lately!' She made a dash for the laundry before I could respond, or throw the knife.

Max bounded in kicking his soccer ball.

'Out!' I ordered. 'No balls inside!'

'Did you think about it?' he asked, picking up his beloved inanimate, bouncing pet.

'Think about what?' I sighed, knowing full well what was coming.

'Soccer!' Max held the ball above his head as if about to break into 'The Circle of Life'. 'Can I play next season?'

'I told you we can't afford it, Max, now please ...'

'*Pleeeeeeeeease*, Mum!'

'Max Barrett!' I shouted. 'Do *not* start with me this morning! I've had enough from your sister! Now go tell Stella and Archie we're leaving in ten minutes.'

'But ...'

'GO!'

'You're cranky.' He dropped the ball and turned to kick it towards Stella's room. 'You've been cranky all week!'

I sagged. Two out of four kids had now inferred that I'd been acting like the bitch mother from hell. They were used to me saying no to things that their friends' parents *always say yes to* but I wasn't usually so cranky and shouty. It had been over a week since I'd first spotted Rick and it was clearly taking a toll. As Zara would say, I needed *closure*. I absolutely had to finish that letter and give it to Greg, regardless of the consequences. Time for that pesky Sword of Damocles to fuck right off.

★★★

A small, excited crowd was gathered around our bench when I arrived at school. The mini-throng was made up of the activewear clique, the Botox brigade and the let's-get-wasted-on-pills-and-booze-every-weekend mums. A mixed bunch indeed. But even more astonishing was the sight of Megan sitting right at the centre of all the hullabaloo.

'What's that about?' Sam was behind me, looking just as confused.

'No idea.'

One of the mums from the activewear clique sat down and clasped Megan's hands between her own.

'Christ, Megsy's gone all Mother Teresa.'

I nudged Sam. 'Go see what's happening.'

'You go!' Sam said. 'I'm not walking into that pack of wolves.'

'Look, she's doing the "I've gotta make a call" bit,' I said, watching Megan gesturing to her phone and shaking her head apologetically. 'Come on.'

The crowd around Megan dispersed as Sam and I headed for the bench.

'If you want to order five thousand of those hoodies it's going to cost you ...'

'Stop the fake conversation bullshit and tell us what that was about,' I demanded as Sam and I sat on either side of her.

'Did you win the lottery?' Sam asked. 'Cure cancer? Hit a million followers?'

'It's nothing!' Megan rolled her eyes. 'I may or may not have had a few too many wines last night ... and I may or may not have written a post about Henry and our community, which everyone is losing their collective shit over.'

'Show me!' This was one of the few downsides of not being on social media. Every now and then I missed out on something like this. Maybe Zara was right.

Megan tapped, swiped, tapped again then handed me her phone. Sam leant over and we read together.

Dear Cody,
We are a grieving community and you are calling us disgraceful based on an unfounded accusation. For the record, Henry would often not be at the crossing for a day or two. He has family and personal commitments like anyone else. We missed him every time he wasn't there, because he was as much a part of Baytree Primary as the students or the teachers or the families or the classrooms. But this time he will not be coming back, and all of us are dealing with that as best we can. Parents are explaining what's happened to their kids, who are upset and confused. The Baytree teaching staff are offering all the support they can. The kids are laying flowers at the crossing. We will never be ashamed of our community, Cody, because we know what it's made of. Next time you decide to drag someone across the coals for clickbait, maybe talk to them first. You're welcome to visit us at Baytree. There's good coffee nearby and we love a chat.

'Wow!' I said. 'That's beautiful, Megs. Most of it is completely untrue, but still beautiful.'

'Thanks.'

'Fake news,' Sam said. 'But awesome sentiment!'

'I was drunk and feeling sentimental.'

'Jesus, that's gotta be a first for you,' I said. 'The sentimentality part, I mean. Look, even Guthrie's coming over to join the "All Praise Megan Wylie" celebrations.'

'Wouldn't have picked Guthrie for a social-media type,' Sam said. 'What does she post pictures of? Her latest polo-neck skivvy?'

'Shh!' I hissed as the principal approached.

'Good morning!' With her dark hair loose around her shoulders and a smile that actually reached her eyes, Penny looked less severe than usual. 'I just wanted to say how impressed I was with your post, Megan. It's exactly the kind of publicity we need at the moment.'

'Uh, thanks.' Megan looked equal parts chuffed and dazed.

I felt a bit jealous. Megan had never shown an ounce of interest in the school, and here she was receiving praise for her 'community spirit', which was actually all thanks to me dobbing her in, plus a few too many wines on a school night.

'It's given me an idea.' Penny sat down beside Sam and he froze, clearly uncomfortable being in such close proximity to our principal. 'What if we dedicate the end-of-year concert to Henry? It seems fitting, especially in light of your post.'

'That's a great idea, Penny!' Sam said.

I narrowed my eyes at him. Suck up.

'Thanks, Sam,' Penny said, her eyes still on Megan. 'What do you think, Megan?'

'Well, yeah, that would be lovely.'

'A show that reflects Henry's community spirit,' Penny continued. 'You can probably find something like that online. Or you could write something?'

'Me?' Megan looked horrified. 'I'm not a writer.'

'Well, you obviously have a talent with words,' Penny said. 'I'm sure whatever you come up with will be great.

You only need think about the script component of the junior school concert. The teachers will be organising the songs.'

Generous of them, I thought, *since that's their job and all.*

'Anyway, I have a school tour in a few minutes so best I get back to it!' Penny stood then turned back to Megan to deliver one final bombshell. 'It would be wonderful if you could represent the school at Henry's funeral tomorrow to lay the wreath I've ordered. I've emailed you the details. I'd go myself, but I have a PD course all day. Bye now.'

Megan looked as though her phone had fallen in a toilet as she watched Penny stride away.

'You okay?' I asked Megan.

'No!' she snapped. 'Not only do I have to work on this stupid fucking school concert, but apparently I have to come up with the concept for it and *write* it. What? Suddenly I'm Baytree Primary's special envoy to the fucking UN? And I have to go to the funeral of a man I didn't even really know. I hate funerals! I mean, I've never been to one but I'm pretty sure I hate them.'

'You'll be fine,' I said, trying to sound convincing. 'Just pop your head in, lay the wreath and get out.'

'Can you come with me? Please?'

'I'm working.'

'Sam?'

'Can't.'

'Why not?'

Sam squirmed on the bench. 'Just ... can't.'

'Arseholes,' Megan muttered. 'The least you can do is help me with the show.'

'No way!' The idea of it was laughable. 'I don't have time for that.'

'Neither do I!' Megan shrieked. 'But you dumped me in this shit, so now you can help me shovel it.'

A familiar shape appeared in my peripheral vision and I knew – I just knew – it was Rick.

'Lizzie?' I'd let my guard down and now he was standing less than six feet away from me. I felt sick.

Everything felt as if it were moving in slow motion as I turned my head to look at him. He'd barely changed. Still thin but fit, with tight muscles that showed through his dark-blue jumper. A full head of that familiar strawberry-blond mop, although greys were vying for top spot, and a few more lines etched into the corners of his Jersey cow eyes, now framed behind black-rimmed glasses. Still handsome too, the shine and glow of his youth hadn't been dulled. He was staring at me expectantly. As were Megan and Sam who had instantly forgotten our argument and were far more intrigued by the appearance of this stranger who knew my name.

I had to say something.

Just act normal.

'*Rick!*' My voice sounded high and squeaky. 'Oh my God!'

I stood up on jelly legs and leant in for an awkward hug. His arms tightened around my back for a second before releasing me.

'How *are* you?' I asked a bit too loudly, nervously waving my hands around like a Backstreet Boy.

'Great!' he said, grinning. 'How are you?'

'I'm Megan.' Fed up with waiting for an introduction, Megan was on her feet with her hand out. Rick smiled and shook it but didn't seem as discombobulated as most men when first meeting Megan.

'Sam.'

Rick reached down to shake Sam's outstretched hand. 'G'day.'

'So, how do you know Lizzie?' Megan asked.

'Played soccer at the same club as kids,' Rick said cheerily. 'Even went on a couple of dates when we were teenagers. Seems like a thousand years ago.'

Dates? He made it sound as though we split a thickshake. I was momentarily thrown but quickly decided if that was the story he was telling, I'd happily go along with it, at least in front of these guys. If the man whose heart I'd stomped on wanted to protect me from the truth of my terrible behaviour in front of my friends then who was I to stop him.

'Who have you got here?' he asked me. 'Any in grades five or six?'

'Zara and Archie Barrett.'

I'm talking to Rick Cooke!

'Zara's in my class,' Rick said, nodding. 'Seems like a good kid.'

'I've also got Stella in grade three and Max in grade one.'

'Wow,' Rick laughed, shaking his head. 'You've been busy.'

'How about you?' I said, desperate to steer the conversation away from the mental image of me getting 'busy'. 'Kids?'

'Two.' He opened his wallet to reveal a photo of two gorgeous dark-haired girls. 'Kristy and Layla.'

'They're beautiful!' Megan gushed. 'Have you ever thought about getting them into modelling? I run a children's online fashion business and we're always looking for fresh kids.'

'Unbelievable,' Sam muttered.

'Thanks, but I think we'll pass.' Rick smiled, shoving the wallet back in his pocket. 'I should get back to class. Lovely to meet you, Megan and Sam. And great to see you, Lizzie.'

'Uh, yeah ... you too.'

I watched him walk away and felt as though I was no longer made of anything solid.

'Ex-boyfriend, huh?' Megan elbowed me. 'At Baytree! What are the odds?'

She had no idea.

Late that night, when the kids were all asleep and Greg was in bed, flat on his back and snoring like a freight train, I crept into the office. The swivel chair creaked as I sat down and I winced, terrified that the slightest noise would wake my husband, when in actual fact a brass band could parade through our room most nights and he wouldn't stir. I pushed my shoulders back, took a labour-worthy breath and opened the 'Lizzie's Xmas Presents' document. But I still didn't know what to write.

How could I tell Greg about everything Rick and I had been through? The love I'd felt for him never quite grew into the I'd-die-for-you kind of love, but I'd had a lot of the 'perfect teen life' boxes ticked: handsome, loving boyfriend; great mates; good family life; local soccer star status. But, at seventeen, I was nurturing a restlessness that was blossoming into something that felt dangerous. Every now and then, as we all lay around Lachy's lounge room watching *Ace Ventura: Pet Detective* for the umpteenth time or drinking Scotch and Cokes at the club on a Saturday night, I'd have the weird sensation that I was suffocating.

I'd suddenly run to the bathroom and splash cold water on my face, forcing deep breaths into my tight lungs and exhaling through pursed, dry lips, as if trying to blow out a stubborn candle.

By the time I finished school it seemed that the course my life would take had been planned and set in stone by everyone but me:

1. Work full-time in the restaurant and save for deposit on house.
2. Get married.
3. Buy house in western suburbs (Items 2 and 3 are interchangeable).
4. Pay off mortgage slowly but consistently.
5. Continue playing soccer socially until pregnant.
6. Produce between two and five children.
7. Allow room in budget for one holiday a year because it's nice to do something spontaneous.

Rick began working in the mailroom at the local Toyota plant the day after his final exam and transformed into an adult overnight. I flicked the switch to autopilot for those first few years after finishing school. I still lived at home, worked full-time at the restaurant, played soccer on weekends and ate at Taco Bill's with our gang every Sunday night. I wasn't exactly filled with *joie de vivre*, but I'd accepted that this was my life.

Rick proposed on the night of my twenty-first. A bunch of us spent the day decorating the clubhouse with purple and white helium balloons, a big silver banner that read 'Happy 21st Birthday!' and purple crepe paper. Auntie Carmen and a few other soccer mums cooked up a finger food feast, there was a full bar (thanks, Dad) and we'd hired a local DJ who we soon discovered had a questionable passion for Hootie & the Blowfish.

I had fun that night. There was the requisite amount of daggy dancing to 'Barbie Girl' and 'Tubthumping', as well as a boozy singalong to Hootie's 'Let Her Cry' later in the night. My mates working the bar got me pissed by making my Scotch and Cokes at a ratio of 80 per cent Scotch, 20 per cent Coke. All in all, it was a standard Saturday night, except that I was an adult ... and by the end of the night, a fiancée. Dad made a beautiful speech that made everyone cry, including him, and Melissa spoke about my humiliating teen years, including the bush-rape-girl story, which dried Dad's tears up quick smart. Just when I was preparing to jump back on the parquet dance floor, Rick took the gold bedazzled microphone from the DJ, got down on one knee in front of the hundred or so people jammed into the room and gazed up at me.

'Lizzie Abela,' he said, 'will you marry me?'

Cheers, whistles and catcalls swarmed around the room as I stared down at him, drunk and speechless. The word 'NO!' roared through my brain right as I heard myself say 'Yes', and then Rick was lifting me off the ground and whirling me around, which was not a great idea considering my inebriated state. I raced to the bathroom and vomited straight into the toilet while Melissa held my hair back with well-practised care. I'm still not sure if it was a reaction to the alcohol and the subsequent spinning, or because I'd just agreed to marry a man I loved but wasn't *in* love with. Even at twenty-one, I knew the difference.

The next year was a flurry of pre-wedding activity. Auntie Carmen was beyond thrilled to be organising a wedding for her 'little cat', and I proceeded to spend the next year distracting myself with Dean Koontz novels, long hours working at the restaurant ... and Scotch. Lots of Scotch. Dad insisted on paying for the whole wedding – although he didn't have much choice since Rick's dad didn't have two cents to rub together – and I begged him not to go overboard.

'My only daughter is getting married!' Dad shouted to the full restaurant when I told him that the horse-drawn carriage was probably a bridge too far. 'You only marry once in this life, and you should do it properly! Like the royals!'

Finally, the church, local function centre and priest were booked, the dress was bought and paid for, and all two hundred people had ticked the 'Yes, I will be attending' box on the garish, embossed RSVP cards. Auntie Carmen loved opening them and announcing the confirmed attendees with wonderfully exaggerated grandeur. 'His Lordship and Lady Gianchino are thrilled to be attending the wedding of Princess Elizabeth and Prince Richard!' The first time Auntie Carmen saw me in the enormous white meringue dress she'd picked out, she wept and told me how proud my mother would be. Rick and my brothers had rented their monkey suits, Melissa and three other friends from our gang had their lilac taffeta dresses ready to go, and the priest was locked in. Every single item on the to-do list had been crossed off, except the one in my head that read, 'Lizzie is *thrilled* to be attending the wedding of Princess Elizabeth and Prince Richard'.

'You are going to be the spunkiest bride Williamstown has ever seen!' Melissa squealed the day before the wedding. She'd come to meet me on my lunch break at the restaurant to go over some last-minute bridesmaids' business. 'Nervous?'

'I *really* am.' I silently pleaded with her to understand what I was telling her: *I don't want to do this. Please help me.*

'Totally normal,' Melissa said, waving her hand at me. 'Once you see him standing in front of that altar, you'll be fine.'

But I couldn't picture Rick standing on that altar. Worse than that, I couldn't picture myself walking up the aisle in that ridiculous dress. Nothing about any of it felt right.

'I love you so much,' Rick said to me on the phone that night. We'd agreed not to see each other the day before the wedding. 'I can't wait to spend the rest of my life with you, Lizzie Abela ... soon to be Lizzie Cooke!'

The moment I heard my new name – *Lizzie Cooke* – it was like waking up. I began to hatch my escape plan as soon as I got off the phone. I knew it would hurt my family and friends in a way they'd never forget, or possibly forgive, and that it would break Rick's heart, but I couldn't marry him. I was too much of a chicken shit to go straight to his house and tell him that I'd changed my mind, so late that night I packed a bag and my passport and left a note on my bed that read:

Dear Dad and Auntie Carmen, I'm so very sorry but I can't go through with it. Please tell Rick how very very sorry I am. I'm going away for a while, but I'll be in touch and pay back every cent you've spent on the wedding. I promise. I love you both. L x

Then I walked to the depot, got a late bus to the airport and caught the first flight to Sydney. I felt ashamed. Ashamed and selfish. On the plane, I slowly absorbed the enormity of what I'd just done, and it hit me like a tonne of bricks. I actually jerked my head back in my seat, scaring the man next to me, while my ex-fiancé slept at home in his bed, most likely dreaming about our magical day. I was a selfish coward, but on that night, in that moment, my only thoughts were of escape. Running from the life I'd allowed to happen, and everything in it. I wanted to start again. So, I did.

Megan

Megan couldn't help but imagine a ghostly Henry floating around the huge bluestone church, surveying the turnout with great satisfaction. It was packed! Who knew the sweet old lollipop man could pull such a huge crowd? As she slid into a half-empty pew at the back, it occurred to her that she'd never draw a crowd like this to her own funeral. She instinctively went to pull out her phone, then stopped. Scrolling through photos of healthy, living humans while Henry's dead body lay encased in wood less than thirty metres away probably wasn't appropriate. She glanced at the polished timber coffin in front of the altar, then looked away. She wasn't all that comfortable with death staring her in the face like that. Although, she couldn't help wondering what Henry was wearing. A suit? Or the grey woolly jumper, khaki pants, and high-vis vest he was wearing when Megan last saw him?

If she did find herself floating around at her own funeral, she was sure she'd hate whatever Best & Less or Target outfit Ellie chose. She made a mental note to provide her mum with explicit instructions on her funeral attire. She assumed Ellie would hold her daughter's funeral in a church, despite Megan's atheism. It would be a small affair. Ellie, Matt, Oscar, Lizzie and Sam would be there, and a few Applewood residents who would show up to support their heartbroken friend.

'Such a shame,' the old ladies would say. 'So young.'

'Such a shame,' the old men would say. 'So pretty.'

The bitchiest girls from school, Janice Waters and Natalie Brady, might make an appearance, just so they could pretend they were besties with the girl from the Sleek Briefs ad. Megan could see them updating their statuses with posts like: *Just makes me realise how fragile life is and how precious every moment really is. Feeling very lucky today. RIP beautiful lady.*

An old man with a hearing aid gestured for Megan to move down the pew. She shuffled along, wondering why a guy who was so deaf would sit so far back. Surely an octogenerian like him got the VIP treatment at funerals?

Megan glanced to her left, reviewing her escape route out of the church. She'd give this funeral ten minutes, tops. She'd kept her promise by showing up and laying a wreath with a card that read: *We will all miss you, Henry. Thank you for everything you've done for us and our school. Love from the kids, teachers and parents of Baytree Primary School.*

No one would know if she didn't stay for the whole service. Megan looked at the time on her phone and sighed, drawing a dirty look from the hearing-aid dude beside her. *Not so deaf, after all, are you*? Megan thought. She scrolled through her mental to-do list: visit Mum, schedule the week's social posts, update website with new stock and accompanying images, school pick-up. Megan's fingers, unaccustomed to being device-free, twitched in her lap, so she distracted herself with some good old-fashioned people-watching. She assumed the people comforting one another in the front row must be Henry's immediate family. *Where were you?* Megan thought sharply, watching a middle-aged woman dab at her eyes with a tissue. If you were his daughter, why weren't you checking on him? She suddenly hated the eye-dabbing lady, despite the fact that she knew nothing about the circumstances of Henry's death and shouldn't be such a 'judgey cow', as Lizzie would say. Just when it seemed as if the church would need a quick renovation to fit in all the mourners, the priest took his place at the pulpit.

'Welcome, everyone, to this very special celebration of Henry Northcott's life,' he said, a huge smile on his face. 'Please stand for the first hymn.'

The organ started and the entire congregation stood and lifted their voices. It sounded amazing. *Is this what happens at funerals?* Megan wondered. *Do priests smile?* She'd assumed it would be all tears and misery. She certainly hadn't expected a smiling priest and a congregation singing 'Morning Has Broken' with the gusto of a gospel choir.

At the end of the hymn, the priest invited the eye-dabbing woman to speak about her father. *Ha!* Megan thought. *I was right!*

The black-clad woman walked up to the lectern, laid out some notes and began to speak in a shaky voice. 'For those of you who don't know me,' she began, 'I'm Henry's daughter, Margaret. In one way, none of us are surprised that Dad left us while his entire family were on the other side of the world for his grandson's wedding.'

Megan shrank in the pew. *I'm a bad person.*

'Dad hated making a fuss, and never wanted to spend his last days in a hospital bed,' Margaret continued. 'Stubborn old goat.'

The entire congregation chuckled and Megan suddenly felt like a callous intruder.

'Dad refused to come on the family trip,' Margaret continued. 'We pleaded with him, but he insisted he didn't want to be a burden. That was Dad to a T: thoughtful, considerate and so kind ...' Margaret broke down, leaning on the lectern for support. A tall man with shaggy brown hair and a kind face immediately jumped up from his spot in the front pew and went to her. He put his arm around the woman and whispered in her ear, and Margaret nodded, gave him the paper and lay her head on his shoulder. Megan suddenly felt her eyes fill with tears.

'I'm Eddie, Henry's grandson,' he said in a clear, confident voice. 'This is obviously very difficult for Mum, so I'm going to help her out.' He began to read and Megan listened as the life of Henry Northcott played out in her mind like a movie montage, all narrated in the soothing deep tones of his handsome grandson. Margaret had written with great affection about the man who had grown up in England, married his teenage sweetheart and emigrated to Australia in the sixties. Henry had worked as a handyman, a tram driver, a metal worker, a builder, had maintained the church gardens and the adjoining community centre, and founded the local DIY Kids' Club. He and his beloved wife Lucille had three children, and when Lucille died a few years ago, the community had rallied around Henry. He was a much-loved and respected figure in the community, volunteering for everything from fostering dogs to lollipop-man duty, and chipping in at various community working bees, always turning up with a car full of ancient tools that he used expertly and with unwavering vigour. Henry's three children and eight grandchildren were all overseas when he died.

'It gives us small comfort to know that he and Grandma are together again,' Eddie concluded. 'He missed her so much but is now able to spend the rest of eternity with his beloved Lucille, until the rest of us get up there and ruin their peace and quiet.' Everyone, including Megan, laughed through their tears.

A man from Henry's bowling club got up to speak next. 'When he didn't show up for bowls on Monday, we thought he'd nicked down the coast to stay with Jeff.' He turned to Henry's family, tears streaming down his face. 'He told us he might do that. You know the old bugger refused to have a mobile phone so we just ... we thought ...' He trailed off and Margaret and another woman rushed to hug him, assuring him that it was no one's fault.

The service went for almost an hour and a half, and Megan stayed until the end. A stream of people got up to speak about Henry Northcott, including three teenagers who Henry had helped reclaim their skate park from aggressive drunks, apparently with the aid of a large wrench and some very colourful language. These kids spoke affectionately about how Henry had given them their park back and the impact he'd had on their lives. There were so many sides to this man that Megan found it hard to keep up.

There was a slideshow too, accompanied by Rod Stewart's 'Forever Young'. Grainy black-and-white shots of a grinning child in rural England, adult Henry on his wedding day, Henry nursing babies, Henry playing with his kids, Henry surrounded by loving family, friends and colleagues. There was even a photo of him smiling proudly in his lollipop-man uniform. Henry had been doing volunteer work with the Salvation Army since his twenties, dishing out soup to the homeless at a local shelter two nights a week. In her twenties, Megan had been living off the royalties from her ad and handouts from her mum, and spending most of her time partying and travelling, until she'd ended up in Berlin where she'd done an anti-Bowie and delved into a lifestyle very much dictated by recreational drugs. What would a slideshow montage of Megan's life look like? What photos would they use? Babyco catalogues from the toddler years, Target catalogues from the teen years, her wedding day, holding Oscar when he was first born ... then what?

Megan was overwhelmed by a mixture of emotions as she sat in the back of the church. Shame was definitely in the mix – shame that she'd been fobbing Henry off day after day, assuming he was just another pervy old bloke who was only friendly because Megan was a bit of a hottie. The old man she'd dismissed as an insignificant senior citizen had lived this life – this enormous life – and was so very loved. There was also deep admiration, as well as a kind of envy, which immediately brought shame back to the forefront. But she couldn't help it. Who would speak about her in this way when she died? Henry was good. He *did* good things. He was selfless. What had Megan done? As they stood for the final hymn, Megan wondered what constituted a 'good' eulogy? Maybe something along the lines of ...

Thank you and welcome to the several thousands of you who have crammed into St Patrick's Cathedral, and to the masses outside watching on the big screen, for Megan Wylie's memorial service. Megan travelled the world six times during her life, forged a successful career as a foreign correspondent and UN Peace Ambassador and made stacks of cash. She had a string of exotic lovers, eventually settling down with acclaimed actor Chris Hemsworth. This amazing, courageous woman with hundreds of friends and truckloads of money, definitely did not die a nobody.

The reality would be more like ...

Welcome to the handful of you who have attended Megan

Wylie's funeral today. Megan was born into a semi-dysfunctional family in the south-eastern suburbs. She could sing all the words to 'No Scrubs' by the time she was fourteen, and although she didn't know who the first prime minister of Australia was, she did know the names of every member of Destiny's Child. From an early age, Megan was obsessed with clothes. She loved to dance and liked a drink or three from an illegal age. Her body could definitely be described as stereotypically good. Megan had a few unfulfilling relationships, including her marriage to a closeted gay man who waited until they had a young son before deciding to embrace his true self and fuck right off.

The priest called on the pallbearers to take their positions around Henry's casket and Megan suddenly felt breathless. She wouldn't be able to cope with watching Henry's coffin being lifted and carried out by his sons, grandsons and friends, weeping as they escorted this extraordinary man out.

As she fumbled for her bag, choking back sobs, the hearing-aid dude gave her a comforting pat on the shoulder. 'We'll all miss the old boy,' he said, wiping away tears.

Megan stumbled out of the pew, almost running for the door as hundreds of voices began singing 'Abide With Me' in perfect unison behind her.

Sam

To: jack_woz_here@hotmail.com
From: samhatfieldchef@bigpond.com
Subject: The case of Sam's missing balls

Hey dickhead,

Just got back from pick-up where I had a good chat to Lizzie's hubby, Greg. He seems like a solid bloke, y'know? Not a bogan, but a man who is embraced by bogans. I've told you Lizzie's a midwife, yeah? She does insane shifts sometimes, but never says boo. Just does her thing and then tells us awesome stories about bodily fluids and screaming women.

You sent me that last email at 2:43 a.m. You on the crank again? I hear what you're saying but talking to Bridg won't help. The travelling mum situation has gone unaddressed for too long. I've adapted. Bridg goes away, I run a tight ship and there's more laughter in the house. I drink more than I should, watch what I want after the kids go to bed, then drink more, chuckle to myself and fall asleep on the couch. I don't really get hangovers any more, so the mornings are fine. Then Bridg comes home and brings her stress back with her. Stress like radiant heat.

The kids annoy her. They long for her attention, because she's their mum and they've missed her, but she's with adults when she's away, so kids – even hers – just give her the shits. They're loud and irrational.

I too shit her. It doesn't matter what I've achieved around the house, Bridg has a radar that can seek out whatever hasn't been done. And *that's* the thing she'll ask about when she gets home at the end of her work day.

'Did you follow up with the heating people?'

Nope. Cleaned the house, vacuumed, mopped, did two loads of washing (including drying, folding and putting away), did a food shop, prepared three nights' worth of meals and sorted out Lola's camp excursion forms, which involved logging in to and/or creating accounts for no less than three different 'vitally important' school apps – it's the modern version of triplicate, but heaps less effective. I also researched and reconfigured all our Wi-Fi settings to make sure coverage is even around the house. That one wasn't even on my list, but I did it anyway because good Wi-Fi is a source of great tension in the modern Aussie household, and our family is no exception.

But no, I didn't follow up with the heating guys.

Mainly because we own clothes and live in a house with walls and a roof, and an oversupply of doonas, blankets, throw rugs and oversized towels that could probably see us through the next ice age.

But I didn't do the thing Bridg wanted me to do, so she does that little exhale through her nose and purses her lips, and looks at me with an expression that literally translates to, 'What the hell did you *do* all day?'

I digress.

If I sat Bridg down and said, 'Look, I think we need to talk about the familial upheaval caused by your constant travel,' my feeling is that she'd blast a hole in my torso, like what the Predator did to Jesse 'The Body' Ventura.

And what you said is right; it's 100 per cent right and rational and WISE! But I can't.

There was one particular FaceTime while she was away last week when I was thinking about what you said. I was thinking, 'Say it. Say it now. She can't reach through the phone and throttle you.'

I'd dropped the kids off and had this really cool chat with Lizzie and Megan about the benefits of owning a really good-quality iron, and I'd come home feeling good and happy, so I went straight to the kitchen.

I hit the radio and that awesome Staple Singers song starts – starts at the very beginning of the song as if someone had been waiting to press play for me. 'I'll Take You There'. I *love* that song. So, I'm cooking and dancing and singing. House is clean. Shopping done. Washing done. Kids safely delivered to school. I'm thinking after I cook whatever this masterpiece turns out to be, I might even get the guitar out of the garage.

My mobile rings, and I shouldn't have looked. I shouldn't have even had the fucking thing on. The school have the home phone if anything happens. This is what phones do. They yank you out of whatever moment you might be in, or about to find, or even start to look for, and the phone barks at you, reminding you that your moment isn't important. Your moment doesn't mean shit compared to what the phone has in store. That's where it's all happening; on the phone. I'm projecting onto the phone. Sorry phone.

It wasn't the phone's fault that 'Bridget wants to FaceTime' popped up on it. She was in Manchester and it was night there and we'd missed each other at the designated time because Lola forgot she had netball trials this morning.

I answer, because I'd rather sacrifice my current mood than deal with the repercussions of not answering. So, the Staple Singers are abruptly faded out, the stove is turned to a low simmer (I was toasting mustard seed and Cassia bark – masterpiece), I take a gallows breath and answer the phone. As I'm answering I'm thinking there's nothing in the frame that she'll see that she won't like. Washing baskets in the background tip her over the edge.

She's a bit pissed. Outside some bar, drinking something that looks fluorescent orange, like it could change her molecular structure, and I remember it's the last day of her conference. It was all about exploring how best to create an atmosphere of initiative-based outcomes and find fresh new meanings for their customer experience. How to effectively jizz in each other's faces.

But I learnt years ago not to in any way mock the corporate wankery that Bridg has to wade through daily. That wankery pays the bills and keeps me in the life to which I have become accustomed. We used to laugh about it together, but it hasn't amused her for a while.

She asked to talk to the kids. I reminded her they were at school. She said, 'What?' implying that I had deliberately altered global time zones. I asked how the conference finished up. She said it was energising to be surrounded by brilliant people. Then a man called her name and her voice jumped half an octave when she responded, but I couldn't hear what she said cos she lowered the phone or put it against her chest or something. I heard laughing. A man laughing. Bridg laughing. I hadn't heard that laugh for a long time. As her face came back into view, she was finishing a sentence, '. . . no one, I'm coming now. I'm coming!' She looked back at the phone and said she had to go because these were the nights when the real business happened. I said it'd probably be easier just to wait until she's home to see the kids. She agreed and said she'd better go, again.

Then, due to the joys of latency, I said 'Love you' at the same time that she said 'Bye' and hung up, but I heard one more little burst of laughter before she hit the red button.

Sending you love double-dipped in sadness, as always.

S x

Lizzie

'What the HELL is going on in here?'

It looked as if Stella, Myabi and Skye had set small explosive devices in all my dry baking ingredients, ducked behind the kitchen bench to avoid the blast zone and pushed the detonator. Brown powder and white gooey splodges covered every square inch of the kitchen benchtop and floor. Dirty mixing bowls, wooden spoons and plates spilled out of the sink. Bailey was up on his hind legs, licking icing sugar out of a bowl on the counter, and the moment he heard my voice, he jumped down, bringing the bowl with him, which smashed into pieces.

Three eight-year-old, chocolate-covered faces looked up at me with fear in their eyes.

'We're making fudge,' Stella squeaked. 'We're going to clean up and ...'

'*I can see that!*' I squatted down to pick up broken pieces of crockery. 'This kitchen looks like a bloody war zone! Who said you could make fudge?'

'Actually, we asked ...'

Something in my brain snapped.

'*Jesus Christ!*' I threw the broken pieces into the bin. 'I finally get time to clean the house this morning and then I have to come home from work to this! I said you could have friends over after school, Stella, not destroy the house!'

All right, that's enough. Come on, now, a voice at the back of my brain was saying. *Calm down. You're scaring the shit out of them.*

But I couldn't stop.

'Nobody in this house has any appreciation for what I do!' I was ranting and raving and stomping around the girls, who seemed to have frozen on the spot, picking up dirty bowls and flinging them into the sink one after another. 'I am sick of cleaning up everyone's *shit*!'

Stella burst into tears and ran out. Myabi and Skye stared after her, then back at me, their mouths opening and closing like goldfish. I sighed, pulled a ten-dollar note out of my pocket and squashed it into the almost full jar on top of the fridge. 'Swear jar.'

The girls nodded slowly, like twin perpetual-motion toys.

I found Stella lying on her bed, clutching Moomoo and crying her eyes out. I sat on the bed and placed my hand on the small of her back. 'I'm so sorry, baby,' I said, my heart breaking. 'I really am. I completely overreacted.'

'Dad said last night that we could make fudge!' Stella cried into the pillow. 'We were starting to clean up when you got home. You know I always clean up!'

'I know, honey.' I was feeling worse by the second.

'That was so embarrassing!' Stella flipped over to reveal a face streaked with tears and her usually fair complexion dotted with red blotches.

'Maybe you could tell Myabi and Skye your mother is having a mental breakdown?'

'It's not funny!'

'No, it's not,' I said. 'I'll apologise, I promise. What else can I do to make it up to you?

Stella wiped her face and stared at me solemnly. 'I was

actually going to ask you about something.'

'Anything.'

'If you could help out on the junior school concert with Oscar's mum?'

Anything else, please!

'Well, um, it's a bit hard because ...'

'You've never volunteered for any school stuff,' Stella said, fixing me with a bleary-eyed stare. 'And Mr B said we should ask our parents to help.'

'But I work, Stell,' I said. 'Oscar's mum works from home, so she has more free time.'

'But your long service thingie is coming up.'

Crap.

'And if you were helping on the concert,' Stella said, wiping her eyes with one of Moomoo's hind legs, 'you could show Myabi and Skye that you aren't as mental as they think you are now.'

She had me there. 'Let me think about it.'

Stella flopped back and stared up at the *Hamilton* poster on her wall. 'That means no.'

I looked at that crown of golden hair and my heart almost burst out of my chest. That crown that had grown out of a soft fontanelle that I'd loved to press my nose to and inhale my beautiful baby's scent. My Stella was so smart and forthright, but she was also fragile. There was a time last year when I was making her an after-school snack, and she was telling me about a kid in her class whose parents were divorcing. Stella was very focused on which of the parents was the 'bad one' and which was the 'good one', so I explained that it wasn't a case of good or bad, just that grown-ups sometimes stopped loving each other and weren't happy together any more.

She went quiet, and when I turned back from the fridge, she was staring straight at me.

'You and Dad had better not ever get divorced.'

'Well, y'know, if he keeps leaving his filthy boots outside the back door for me to trip over ...'

I was trying to be funny, but Stella wasn't having it.

'It would break me,' she said, without a hint of humour. 'It would break me, Mum.'

She was so serious that I didn't make light of it, even though the thought of Greg and me separating was ludicrous to me back then.

Back then. Now it actually seemed like a distant possibility.

'Okay. I'll help.'

She looked up, delighted. 'Really? Oh, thanks, Mum!' She frowned. 'But you can't have a meltdown at school like just then.'

'Promise.' We shook on it. 'Should I apologise to Myabi and Skye for my *Mommie Dearest* moment?'

'Wha ...?'

It was a long shot. 'Should I go say sorry?'

'I think it's probably for the best, Mum.'

'Done.' I hugged her and mumbled into her sweaty, chocolate-smelling hair, 'Then I'll get us all fish and chips.'

'And calamari rings?'

'Yep.'

Stella didn't hold on to her anger like Zara did. The conflict would burn fiercely, but briefly. That could well change as she grew older, but for now I was happy to achieve forgiveness through a few calamari rings and volunteer work at her school.

★★★

The smell of our local fish and chippy was an emotional salve, giving me the chance to reflect on recent events with a relatively peaceful perspective; the guilt and shame I felt about Rick, deceiving Greg, losing it with Stella. All these things feeding the other and perpetuating a litany of less-than-ideal behaviour as a mother, partner and friend. Enough was enough. Once the kids were in bed, asleep in a greasy food coma, I'd give Greg the letter that I'd finally managed to finish and face whatever questions he wanted to throw at me. We'd talk it through until it was no longer a thing that could do our marriage the slightest bit of damage. I tried to imagine my husband's expression, but I had absolutely no idea how he'd react to my dirty secret. This was new territory for us. As low-key as Greg was, this situation didn't guarantee a low-key reaction and my breath caught in my chest as I considered the terrible possibility of losing him.

Greg had always been my great leveller and could placate me with nothing more than an understanding smile and a hand on my waist. It was never patronising, pat-on-the-head type reassurance, Greg just understood me better than anyone ever had, and knew how to make me feel as if everything would be okay. The sex was still very good, and we'd proven to each other time and again that our sexual compatibility had never waned. But more than anything else, Greg understood that I was more fragile than the front I presented to the world; the strong, unflappable, no-nonsense woman that I'd expertly crafted myself into while living in London for three years.

Two days after doing a runner from the wedding, I walked out into the teeming Heathrow terminal and headed straight for the nearest pay phone. I knew Dad and Auntie Carmen would be at the restaurant by then, so I left a message apologising again and telling them I'd arrived safely in London. Going to the other side of the world was a big deal for me. Aside from a holiday in Bali with the soccer gang when I was nineteen, I'd never ventured far from the Western suburbs of Melbourne, and certainly never on my own. I'd purchased a *Lonely Planet London* book at Sydney airport, and mapped out a rough plan on the flight. I got the Tube into the city, checked into a backpacker hostel in Covent Garden, met a 23-year-old singer/dancer/actor from Adelaide named Rita and got a job working in an Aussie-themed pub called the Walkabout. So began an extremely highbrow chapter of my life that involved dying my hair blonde, spending most of my waking hours either working or drinking at the Walkabout with Rita and my new gang of Antipodean mates, and a brief foray into line-dancing. None of my London mates knew anything about my life back home, and that suited me just fine.

There were a few short-lived romances, followed by a drama-packed relationship with a cheeky blond boy from Durham with green eyes, a deep husky laugh and a gorgeous accent. He took me to comedy clubs, called me Abela, made me fall in love with him and then cheated on me with anything that had legs and a vagina for the next two years. After Durham boy broke my heart one too many times, I finally ended it. It took longer than it should have to ditch him, but the pain and suffering I experienced over that time felt karmic. I felt as though I deserved the betrayal and heartbreak after what I'd done to Rick. Alanis Morissette was my constant companion in the wake of Durham boy. I'd walk around London, Alanis screeching through my headphones as I sob-sang the entirety of *Jagged Little Pill*. (These days I still went to Alanis for a dose of fortitude whenever I was feeling brittle.) Up until Durham boy, I'd only heard songs – or seen movies – about people's hearts breaking, unable to think about anyone or anything else. When it became my story – my very own rom-com gone wrong – I decided that I wouldn't risk myself like that again. Self-preservation would henceforth prevail. Greg recognised that in me from the get-go.

I returned to Australia three years after my disappearing act, and two years later I met Greg. Aileen and I were out celebrating the end of exams in a city pub when a tall, scruffy-haired stubbly bloke wearing a blue-and-white checked flannel shirt walked straight up to us and asked if I had a light. Three drinks later, Greg admitted he didn't smoke – he just wasn't very original when it came to pick-up lines. I fell for the straight-talking, open-book, non-judgemental Greg Barrett straight off the bat, and it wasn't just his ruggedly handsome looks. It felt as if something chemical – and entirely mutual – was happening between me and another human being. When we kissed later that night I was sure every lightbulb in Melbourne must have surged with uncommon brightness. We were both so sure, so quickly, that we were *it* for each other and talked about the feeling as though we'd discovered magic was real.

'I'll tell you when I fall in love with you, Lizzie Abela,' he'd said after that first kiss, 'which will be in about two minutes.'

Neither of us wanted to search any more; there was no need because we'd found each other. Job done. Tick. When the subject of ex-boyfriends first came up early in our relationship, I went into detail about Durham boy, but glossed over my teenage years and early twenties. 'The usual awkward pash and grope sessions at bluelight discos,' I'd said, avoiding eye contact, 'a couple of boyfriends after school, but nothing much.'

I couldn't tell him about Rick, because really, who could love a heartless bitch who'd left a man the night before their wedding? Jeff Buckley was the soundtrack of our relationship. Greg and I would make love to 'Everybody Here Wants You' and 'Morning Theft', then sit in the lumpy double bed in his St Kilda share house, talking, smoking (me, not Greg), drinking red wine and eating chocolate ice-cream until the sun came up. I'd walk around in a daze for the next week, as though coming down off a drug, until the following weekend when we'd do it all again. Greg would send me texts like: *My one and only Lizzie. You push my buttons in every possible way. I am yours always. I couldn't live without you, my love.*

It took me a long time to say 'I love you' back to Greg. There was a lot of self-protection going on, but eventually he won me over. The fact that he never questioned, fought against or resented my self-preservation in the early days – not even when I'd deliberately step back from our burgeoning love – only made me fall harder. By accepting my fortress walls, he'd managed to scale them. One night, about six months after we'd started going out, we were lying in Greg's bed listening to 'Mr Brightside' blasting through the wall he shared with his bong-head housemate, Tim, when I sat up and looked straight at him. 'I can't remember ever being this happy,' I said. 'God, I love you.'

Greg stared at me for a moment. 'That's the first time you've said it first,' he said, his voice cracking.

I still loved Greg as much now as I did then, even more if possible. But now I was scared of all the unknowns that would be unleashed once I gave him the letter. I feared this great big thing that was hanging over our heads, ready to crash down and smash everything we had.

I could hear Stella and her friends playing outside as I entered the house, the steaming hot fish-and-chips package in my arms. 'Wash your hands, girls,' I called out, heading towards the kitchen to grab the tomato sauce. I stopped when I saw Greg sitting at the kitchen bench holding a piece of paper, an eerie expression on his face. I was too late. He looked at me and held it up. I saw the words at the top of the page.

Dear Greg, I have something I need to tell you and I think it would be best if I did so in chronological order. That's how these things …

'So,' Greg said, his eyes cloudy, 'This is an interesting read.'

Invisible hands were pressing down on my chest. 'I was going to give it to you tonight.'

'Max was printing soccer images for his wall.' Still that eerie expression. 'He saw the "Xmas Presents" document. Being six and all, he couldn't help himself, could he? When he saw my name, he thought he'd print it and give it to me.'

I was vaguely aware of the fish and chips burning my forearms. 'I was going to give it to you.'

'But you didn't.'

Megan

Megan was relieved to find Ellie sitting on her balcony, flicking through a *Woman's Day*. She wasn't in any mood for the *Cocoon* gang today.

'What the hell happened to you?' Ellie shrieked. 'You look like you've seen a ghost.'

Megan did look a fright. She'd caught sight of herself in the lift mirror on the way up and shocked herself. Her hair was lank and dry, her complexion pale and yesterday's mascara was smudged under both eyes.

'I didn't sleep well last night.'

Ellie jumped up and went to her. 'Everything okay, hon?'

Megan collapsed onto the yellow couch, exhausted. 'I went to a funeral yesterday and it was a bit sad, that's all.'

'A funeral?' Ellie looked startled. 'Whose?'

'The school's lollipop man,' Megan explained. 'I was representing the school.'

'Henry Northcott?' Ellie asked.

'You knew him?'

'I didn't, but quite a few here did,' Ellie said, sitting back down and picking up the magazine again. 'Apparently he was lovely.'

'Yeah,' Megan said. 'He was.'

'Sorry, did you say the school sent *you* as a representative?'

'Yes, why?' Megan said defensively.

Ellie's eyebrows shot up as the corners of her mouth went down. 'Just surprised, that's all.'

'Why?' Megan knew this wouldn't end well but didn't care.

Ellie looked down, flicking through pages of long-lens shots of celebrities with red arrows pointing out various areas of their bodies that were grossly lacking.

'I've never even heard you mention Henry,' Ellie said. 'And it's not like you're ...'

'Like I'm what?' Megan was baiting her mother now.

'You're not exactly the most community-minded individual, that's all,' Ellie said, looking up. 'You've never had any interest in the school, let alone its lollipop man.'

Megan knew Ellie was right but was incensed nonetheless. 'For your information, I'm in charge of the junior school Christmas show this year.'

'You?' Ellie's hand froze mid-page turn. 'Volunteering at the school?'

'That's right!' Megan was now in full, self-righteous flight. 'They asked for volunteers and I stepped up.'

This wasn't true, of course, but Megan was suddenly enjoying her new 'selfless' identity. She also didn't want to give her mother the satisfaction of being right.

'Well, that's fantastic, love,' Ellie said, looking genuinely impressed. 'What play are you doing?'

'No idea yet,' Megan replied with total confidence.

'Do they want a traditional kind of thing?' Ellie closed the magazine, excited by the topic. 'You could do *A Christmas Carol.* That's always an audience favourite.'

'What's that?'

Ellie recoiled as if Megan had burped into her face. '*A Christmas Carol*,' she repeated, hoping her daughter hadn't heard her properly. 'Scrooge.'

'The Bill Murray film?' Megan vaguely remembered

seeing it as a kid. 'That wasn't very good, was it?'

'Are you fucking *serious*?' Ellie's face turned purple and her eyes bugged out of her head. 'Bill Murray? Jesus *wept*!' Ellie looked as if she were about to self-combust. 'Charles Dickens' Scrooge!' she yelled. 'You do know who Charles Dickens is?'

'Yes, I know who Charles Dickens is!' Megan had definitely heard the name but wouldn't be able to hum any of his stuff.

'It's my own fault,' Ellie said, shaking her head. 'If I'd left you in school instead of dragging you off to stupid castings, you'd be more cultured.'

'Sorry for being such a dumb arse,' Megan sulked.

'Oh, shut up.' Ellie went to sit beside her. 'You know I couldn't be prouder of you.' Ellie kissed Megan's cheek. 'You're extremely smart and successful, not to mention a wonderful mother, and I love you to bits, you silly chook,' she said. 'You can't help it if you're an uncultured swine when it comes to literature.'

Megan laughed. 'So, where do I find this *Christmas Carol* show? Would it be online?'

'Oh no, you're going old school research for this one, my love.' Ellie opened her purse and handed Megan a card. 'The Applewood Library has a copy.'

There was a new email waiting for Megan when she checked her phone later that day. She frowned. Why was the new teacher (a.k.a. Lizzie's ex-shag) emailing her?

Hey Megan,

Hope you don't mind me getting in touch. First off, great post!

Really brave. Anyway, I spoke to Penny today and she said you'd be needing help from teachers to organise the junior school concert, so I'm putting my hand up! I've had loads of experience with drama, so let me know when we can get together for a brainstorm. I'll try to rally a few other teachers to get involved, and maybe you could get a few more parents on the team too? You're friends with Sam and Lizzie yeah? How about roping them in too? You guys make a good team.

Chat soon

Rick

Ha! Lizzie and Sam would be more likely to put their hand up to clean the school toilets.

The Applewood Library's hardback copy of *A Christmas Carol* lay beside her laptop. Megan kept glancing at it as she replied to work emails and liked a few posts over the next hour. When the ancient Applewood librarian had slid the tattered book across the counter towards her, Megan instantly knew that the likelihood of getting Prep to grade-four kids excited about a story as old as Christmas itself was slim. As she waited for the chatty librarian to fire up her ancient PC, Megan had even considered legging it out of there and leaving the book on the counter, but she knew Ellie would find out and give her hell.

After reading the description on the back of the book, Megan vaguely remembered the story of the old miser being visited by three ghosts, but didn't see how it could work as a school play. She'd have to modernise it somehow or the kids would be falling asleep mid-sentence, not to mention the parents forced to watch it. Scrolling absent-mindedly through her Insta feed, Megan's mind replayed moments from Henry's funeral the day before: the old man beside Megan singing 'Jerusalem' at the top of his voice as tears streamed down his face; Henry's seven grandchildren reading a poem they'd written for their beloved Poppy; Margaret leaning over the coffin to kiss it gently; Henry's *This is your Life* video, where he walked into his local bowls club to cheers, claps and whistles for his surprise seventieth birthday party.

She glanced over at the book again. Now that she'd told Penny and her mum that she was going to do this, the least she could do was read the bloody thing. Besides, it was Bryce's weekend with Oscar, and she didn't exactly have anything else lined up this Saturday night. Megan closed the laptop, picked up the book and headed over to the couch.

She turned to the first page.

> *Marley was dead: to begin with. There is no doubt whatever about that. The register of his burial was signed by the clergyman, the clerk, the undertaker, and the chief mourner. Scrooge signed it. And Scrooge's name was good upon 'Change, for anything he chose to put his hand to.*

Megan sighed. *Fuck me, it's gonna be a long night.*

Sam

To: jack_woz_here@hotmail.com

From: samhatfieldchef@bigpond.com

Subject: sick and tired

Hey mate,

I just got back from walking the dog. Saw a bulldog that weighed more than me. I get nostalgic at the dog park. Bridg and I did a lot of courting at that park. Courtship? We'd smoke a joint and play with other people's dogs. Bridg was a canine magnet.

Then we'd lie under a tree and talk about whatever: why dogs are better than people, about music or art or her job. Free and easy talk. Pre-kids. Then post miscarriages too. That park was where we'd go to cry. No talking. Just tears. You've seen me here before. You've told me it isn't useful to think about how Bridg used to be, but I have to. I have to remind myself that *this* woman is still *that* woman.

She's been through the wringer, Jack. The miscarriages. The fucking IVF. The all-consuming relationship anaesthetic that is IVF. Yes, it worked, and we have two beautiful kids, and it's a miracle. But that shitstorm of emotional and physical upheaval took Bridg away. I got kids – we got our kids – but I had to lose my wife.

I wasn't going to tell you – not until tonight after pouring another pint of vodka on top of it – but straight after my introspective trip to the dog park, I decided to surprise Bridg at work with her favourite apricot Danish and a long black and tell her to come and sit on the grass with her husband because he loves her, and she deserves a goddamn Danish. So, I did.

And I felt like I did when my mum gave me ten bucks to go to the Fun Factory in 1989. I was floaty and grinning like an idiot. I apologised to her receptionist for not bringing a Danish for her as well, explained that she wasn't the mother of my kids, so she had a ways to go before surprise pastries.

She laughed and told me she'd call Bridg. She was still smiling as she spoke into the phone, eyes on me, sitting with my paper bag and coffee tray. Then the smile faded.

She stood up and walked through one of two glass doors that flanked the rear of her reception desk, so it was just me sitting there. Then the other door opened and there was Bridg. She looked at me sympathetically, as if she was about to sit down, put a hand on my knee and say, 'Sorry for your loss.' But she didn't sit down. She stopped in front of me, her hands clasped in front of her. I held up the paper bag and said, 'Snacks.'

Bridg smiled at me like I was a child. Then she said very quickly and evenly, 'Sam, this last trip gave me lots of time to think and I think you'd agree that it's not working any more, so I've decided to leave.'

I can't explain exactly what happened next, or even how I'm feeling now, so soon after. I remember standing and letting the coffees fall to the floor and not caring. I think I handed her the Danishes.

I should've given them to the receptionist.

S x

Lizzie

Aileen stared across the Laminex staff room table, her mouth open and her fair Irish complexion looking almost waxen under the harsh fluorescent lighting. I'd just finished relaying the Rick story to her, even though I'd had no intention of doing so when I started my shift five hours ago. I'd been writing out a care plan for a new admission when Aileen had marched into the midwife's station and demanded to know why 'I'd been walking around with a face like a cat's arse'.

'What?'

'Tell me, right now, what's going on with you?' She snatched the pen out of my hand and slammed it down on the desk. 'And don't give me this "nothing, I'm just tired" bullshit!'

So it was that over the next five hours, in between monitoring foetuses, administering internal examinations and reassuring labouring women that they absolutely *could* keep pushing, I told Aileen the whole story. It was a relief. I could feel the invisible hands that had been pressing down on my chest for days easing their pressure as the story poured out of me. It was past midnight by the time we staggered into the staffroom for a break at the tail end of a stupidly busy shift, and I brought Aileen up to speed on the last week.

'You fecking dark horse!' she said, finally finding her voice. 'I had no idea my best friend was a Julia Roberts!'

'Huh?'

'The Julia Roberts movie with Richard Gere?' Aileen said.

'*Pretty Woman?*' I asked. 'Are you calling me a prostitute?'

'No!' Aileen roared laughing. '*Runaway Bride!* Different movie with Julia Roberts and Richard Gere! My point is, how could I not have known that my best friend left a man at the altar?'

She didn't seem annoyed that I'd kept this from her, just stunned and amused. This was one of the many reasons I loved her. No judgement.

'Not proud of it either.'

'The night before the wedding!' Aileen said, still trying to process it. 'Fuck!'

'Shhh!'

For the first time all night the ward was silent. The last thing we needed was a new mum waking up and crying out for more Tramadol. I wasn't usually a graveyard-shift kind of girl, but I'd put my hand up for extra shifts this week. I just couldn't deal with the tension that seemed to seep out of the walls of our house every night once the kids were in bed.

'And you and Greg haven't even talked about it yet?' Aileen asked. 'Christ, Daniel would have gone *spare*! We would have been up all night thrashing it out.' She grinned. 'Italians, see? That lot get riled up over a soggy lasagne, let alone a wife's secret past. Didn't Greg have, like, a gazillion questions?'

'Well ...' My gut twisted as I replayed that night in my mind. 'The kids ran in screaming for fish and chips, Greg got the plates out and I made sure everyone had an even amount of potato cakes so we didn't get to talk.'

'Yeah, but after that?'

'Stella's friends were over,' I said. 'I drove them home and when I got back, Greg had gone to bed. He left before I woke up the next morning.'

Okay, so that was a lie. I'd been wide awake when I felt Greg stir just before dawn the next morning. My husband was one of those people who didn't need an alarm clock – he'd been getting up at the same time for so many years that his body clock was Swiss. I'd been facing away from him, staring at the burnt-orange spine of a chick-lit book on the bedside table when I felt Greg climb out of bed. It would have been so easy to turn and stop him with a soft, 'Hey' or 'Greg?', but I just lay there, paralysed with indecision and fear, listening to him opening cupboards and drawers in the semi-darkness, as he put on his daily uniform of shorts, black T-shirt and steel-toed boots. When the bedroom door closed behind him, I exhaled loudly and realised I'd been holding my breath.

'But what about *since* then?' Aileen said.

'We were very polite to each other all weekend,' I said, getting up to open the biscuit tin on the counter, 'which I fucking *hate*, but we were flat out driving the kids all over the place for sport. And did I mention the fact that I'm too gutless to bring it up?' I offered Aileen a stale lamington.

'You're not gutless,' Aileen said, taking it. 'You're a bit of a dolt, but you're not gutless.'

I sat back down and shook my head.

'Ah, Lizzie,' Aileen said, putting her hand over mine. 'I've known you and Greg for years, like. Ye adore each other.'

'This feels different.' I tore my stale lamington in half, revealing the red line of I-can't-believe-it's-not-jam inside.

'Bad different. We haven't been here before and I know he's waiting for me to say something.'

'So why don't you?'

'I'm scared. And I don't know what to say.' Hot tears pricked at the corners of my eyes. 'Apart from "Hey, I'm really sorry for not telling you that I was engaged to another bloke once and left him at the altar!"'

'Start with that,' Aileen said. 'It's better than saying nothing.'

'But what if one of us says something that changes things forever.' The tears were falling freely now. 'What if he says he can't trust me again? Or that he can't love me any more?'

'Ah, ya silly mare.' Aileen pushed her chair back and came round to give me a hug. 'That's never gonna happen.'

But I could hear the uncertainty in her voice. Not even Aileen could guarantee that Greg's feelings towards me hadn't changed.

'I've picked the play!'

Megan's excited voice jolted me out of the half-comatose state I'd drifted into moments after lowering my tired body onto the bench. It felt as if I was nursing the mother of all hangovers, even though I hadn't had a drop of alcohol the night before. My head ached and my eyes, stinging with fatigue, felt so heavy that it was taking every ounce of willpower to keep them open. I'd grabbed Greg's spare pair of crappy sunglasses out of the key basket to spare the world the sight of my bloodshot, baggy eyes. If only I could hide the rest of me behind something equally as effective like a body-sized pair of sunnies or some basic invisibility powers.

I'd made even less effort with my drop-off attire than usual this Tuesday morning; a pair of grey tracksuit pants and an oversized black Bonds windcheater that I'd picked out of a pile of dirty clothes on the bedroom floor. This glamorous look was topped off with my well-worn black Ugg boots.

The only bright spark in this dark day was that Rick wouldn't be making an appearance. Zara had told me yesterday that her new favourite teacher was doing a PD course all week.

'He won't be back until next week.' Zara was devastated. 'And the fill-in teacher is so boring compared to Mr Cooke!'

'So, you like Mr Cooke?' I'd asked, doing my best impression of a normal mum having a normal conversation with her daughter about her normal teacher.

'He's awesome,' Zara said dreamily. 'And he's really good at soccer too.'

I prayed Zara hadn't waxed lyrical to Greg about her 'awesome teacher' while I was at work. It might just send the poor man over the edge. This was what I'd been thinking about when Megan's excited voice shook me out of my reverie. Megan was looking as gorgeous as ever in skinny black jeans and an off-the-shoulder top. Her shiny beauty was a bit too much to bear this morning. She handed me one of the three coffees from the cardboard tray in her lap and I cradled it to my chest like the magical nectar it was.

'What play?' I inhaled the beautiful bitter smell and took a long sip.

'The school Christmas play!' Even in my bleary-eyed state I could see that Megan was peaking. 'The one you dobbed me into helping with, remember?'

I didn't know if it was lack of sleep or lack of brain cells, but something wasn't computing. The last I heard Megan was furious about being roped into this school concert fiasco. But her bright shiny eyes told a different story this morning. She seemed happy about it. Had I missed something?

'I thought you were getting out of that?'

'Me too,' Megan said, waving her hand airily. 'But then I thought, why not just do it, y'know?'

'Who are you and what have you done with my friend, Megan?'

'Nice sunglasses,' she said dryly. 'You doing some welding later or …?'

I delivered a one-finger salute as I took another sip of the sweet, sweet coffee.

'So, you wanna know what show I picked?'

This new incarnation of Megan Wylie was unnerving to say the least.

'Umm … sure?'

'*A Christmas Carol!*' Megan pulled a hardback book from her bag and held it out as though displaying a precious artefact. 'It's perfect, don't you think? I was up half the night reading it, and it's actually really good once you get past the ye olde language.'

The only time I'd ever seen Megan so passionate about something was when a Chill Instagram post had cracked twenty thousand likes.

'Scrooge?' I took the dog-eared copy from her. The sticker on the front read *Property of Applewood Retirement Village Library*. 'Did your mum give you this?'

'I borrowed it from her library, yeah.' Megan grabbed the book back.

'Makes sense, I guess,' I said with a shrug. 'Scrooge hates Christmas, *you* hate Christmas ...'

'Are you comparing me to Scrooge?' Red blotches appeared on Megan's cheeks.

'No.' I was too tired to pander this morning. 'Relax. I'm just saying that's one thing you have in common.'

Megan's dad had left them the week before Christmas, so I could understand why she hated it. I'd probably boycott the entire season.

'Well, I don't *love* Christmas,' Megan said defensively, 'but that's not why I chose it. Have you read it?'

'Yeah, at school,' I said. 'Isn't Dickens a bit ... ambitious for Prep to grade-four kids? Why don't you just buy a play online? That's what they did last year. No one expects it to be *Hamilton*, for God's sake.'

'Those online plays are shit,' Megan said, frowning. 'There's no meaning behind them. We're dedicating this play to Henry, and *A Christmas Carol* has a great message about community, which was Henry to a T. The kids will get a lot out of it.'

Since when had Megan given a crap about *the kids*?

'You'll help, won't you?' Megan clutched my arm excitedly, as if asking me to help her shop for the perfect party outfit. 'With costumes and props and stuff?'

I was about to say there was more chance of me playing 'Stairway to Heaven' on the recorder at the next school assembly, when I remembered my promise to Stella. 'Sure, whatever.' I pushed the sunglasses up to rub my twitching left eye.

Megan gasped. 'Christ, you look like you could eat brains!'

'Shut up,' I scowled. 'I've had a few night shifts in a row.'

'Doesn't Greg usually do drop-off after night shift?'

He did, but I was wide awake this morning and decided I may as well get up, despite not getting in until after 2 a.m.

'I'll take them,' Greg had said, first thing.

I froze, mid-leg swing over the side of the bed.

'That's okay.' I'd used the same tone of voice on a stranger who'd offered to let me order ahead of him at the café the other morning. 'I'm awake so you can go straight to work.'

I hated this polite bullshit between us: apologising as we squeezed past each other in our tiny kitchen and cross-referencing the kids' extra-curricular calendar dates like office co-workers, instead of two people who'd seen each other on the toilet more times than we'd care to admit. The kids had noticed, of course.

'Why are you talking like that?' Max asked when I'd asked Greg if he could please pass me the sauce at dinner on Sunday night and he'd passed it with a robotic, 'Here you go.'

'Like what?' I could feel my cheeks heating up.

'Like weirdos,' Max said, picking up a sausage with his fingers. 'You're talking to each other like weirdos.'

'You are,' Archie agreed.

'We are not,' I said sharply. 'We're using our manners. Remember those, Max? Use your fork!'

'Yeah, nah, that's a different kind of manners,' Zara chimed in. 'This is like people from those body-snatcher movies.'

'Are you fighting?' said Stella. Straight to the point as ever.

'No!' we both said too quickly.

The kids stared but before they could make any further

awkward observations, I asked Stella about Lin Manuel-Miranda's latest gig. As she droned on about something to do with a *Hamilton* tour in Cambodia, I clocked Greg sighing the kind of sigh that would usually be reserved for the end of a particularly disappointing footy game. We'd never gone this long without addressing an issue, and the worst part was that the responsibility lay with me.

Megan was staring at me now, waiting for my explanation.

'Yeah, he does but ...'

'Heeeey, ladies!' Dave stood in front of us in his crumpled purple shirt, dark-blue jeans and ancient Converse.

God bless you and your impeccable timing, Dave Podanski.

'Hey Dave!' I beamed at him. 'How's it going?'

He pulled a bunch of envelopes out of his Crumpler bag. 'It is my greatest of pleasures to cordially invite you to a rather special event.' He was speaking as if he knew we'd been discussing Dickens. He handed us each a black envelope, looking as excited as a kid giving out invitations to a birthday party hosted by the actual Iron Man. He bounced on his toes as we opened them and pulled out the invites, which were printed on what looked like cardboard from the future.

'Three ten GSM metallic,' Dave said, answering a question nobody asked.

'Wow,' Megan and I intoned in sync.

The invite read: *You are invited to the official launch for the debut graphic novel from Dave Podanski,* Codename: Code. *Please join Dave and the team at Bar 404, Thursday July 30th at 1900 hours for drinks, nibbles and identity theft.*

'So, you'll come, yeah?'

Megan and I glanced at each other.

'Dave, that's this Thursday,' Megan said.

'Yeah.'

'It's Tuesday,' I said. 'A bit more notice would've been good.'

'Yeah, I know, but the first run of invites just looked ... shit,' he said, clearly traumatised at the memory, 'and it's a graphic novel, so it had to be right.'

I smiled apologetically. 'I'm sorry but ...'

'You got plans?' Dave stared at us in despair and his shoulders slumped to the point of double dislocation.

'Well, no,' I said, 'but I mean, that's the night after... Wednesday. Which is tomorrow, so it's just a bit ...'

'Are three coffees too much before nine o'clock? Because I'm on my fourth and it feels right.'

Sam. Dave had saved me from Megan. Now Sam had saved me from Dave. Thank Christ.

'I think three is a good limit up until midday at least.' Megan looked as grateful as me for the diversion.

Sam sat down, tapping his fists together as if he'd just discovered he had hooves. 'What are these?' He grabbed Megan's invitation.

'Just a thing that's on,' Dave said and shrugged sadly, his tone well and truly in the doldrums.

'Oh shit!' Sam examined the invitation with the intensity of a young Indiana Jones. 'Your graphic novel. Dude, this is huge!'

'I've got one for you too,' Dave said, brightening slightly.

'This Thursday?' Sam yelled loud enough for Megan to shush him.

'Yeah,' Dave said, 'short notice, so it's fine if ...'

'So what about notice?' Sam threw his hands out and

only narrowly avoided giving me a paper cut on my face. 'We're coming!' Sam looked drunk. Seemed drunk. He was manic in a way I hadn't seen before and it was a bit disconcerting.

'Great!' Dave was thrilled.

'Isn't Friday your birthday?' Megan asked Sam.

'Oh yeah,' Sam said, looking as if he'd genuinely forgotten. 'Even better. We can have a drink to celebrate my impending decrepitude!'

'Awesome!' said Dave, seemingly high off Sam's fumes. 'Here's your cordial invitation to the launch of *Codename: Code*!'

He handed Sam a black envelope and Sam snatched it and held it aloft like a golden ticket. 'I'll be there, man. Can't wait. We're all going, yeah?'

Megan and I mumbled various non-committal noises but Sam wasn't having a bar of it.

'Whatever.' He shooed his hands at us as if we were annoying flies. 'We're all going and we're gonna make some memories and it's gonna be the best night ever!'

'Ooookaaaaay.' Megan patted Sam gently on the thigh, as if he were a religious nut who had accidentally wandered into the school and announced that Jesus was coming.

Sam turned to me and did a double take. 'Jesus, Lizzie, looks like *you* were pushed out of a vagina this morning!'

Megan

Bar 404 was cosy and warm after the crisp night air of Carlisle Street, and Megan's face and hands begin to thaw within seconds of closing the heavy glass door behind her. She took off her scarf and scanned the room. The venue for Dave's *Codename: Code* launch was a typically hip inner-city bar: ratty antique sofas, walls of exposed brick, hardback books and black-and-white framed photographs lining the wall. Huge speakers on either side of the small makeshift stage in the corner were pumping out the kind of music you'd hear in a seventies sci-fi flick, and the scene before Megan was a kaleidoscope of beards, checked flannel shirts and vintage dresses: wall-to-wall hipsters, geeks and artists of all descriptions.

She screwed up her nose as the pungent scent of patchouli drifted into her nostrils but couldn't help being impressed by the number of people who'd turned up for Dave's Geekfest. Dave, the awkward, socially inept school dad, had drawn quite a crowd, and for the second time in a week, Megan was reminded of how few friends she had.

She quickly spotted one of the few mates she *did* have sitting at the long polished wooden bar. Sam wasn't looking his sharpest tonight; a four-day growth, crumpled blue denim shirt (didn't he own an iron?) and blue jeans that had some kind of food stain down the front. His tall lanky frame was hunched over a bottle of Peroni, which he was staring at like a hypnotist. Megan wondered if he'd had a fight with that Ice Queen wife of his. *He'll be right*, she thought, watching him take a big swig of his beer, *Lizzie and I will make sure he has fun on his birthday eve.*

Weaving her way through the noisy crowd, Megan suddenly felt grateful to her bossy mother for forcing her to come. She, Sam and Lizzie rarely, if ever, socialised together outside of their morning schoolyard chats. Hanging with her drop-off mates after dark would be fun.

Until half an hour ago, Megan had had no intention of venturing out on a cold Thursday night for Dave's event. Her evening had been well and truly mapped out. Once Oscar was asleep, she planned to read *A Christmas Carol* again and make notes on costumes, props and staging ideas. She'd actually been looking forward to it. Ever since Henry's funeral, the lollipop man had been popping up in Megan's dreams more frequently, and she was determined to do him justice with this concert. In fact, she'd been having lots of weird dreams since the funeral; dreams she'd rather forget in the light of day. Last night she'd dreamt that the ghost of Christmas future and Henry had taken her on a tour of Henry's graveyard, recommending good spots for Megan to be buried where she wouldn't be too lonely. Dave's launch had been the last thing on her mind, but then Ellie had popped over unannounced and spotted the invite on the fridge.

'You going to this?'

'Nah,' Megan said, flicking on the kettle to make them a cup of tea. She'd only stuck the invite on the fridge to feel popular since she couldn't remember the last time she'd received an invitation to anything.

'Why not?' Ellie frowned. 'I'll look after Oscar. Go have some fun. You're not dead yet!'

'I've got too much work to do.'

'Work can wait!' Ellie took Megan firmly by the shoulders and steered her towards the bedroom. 'Get changed. I will not be deprived of a night alone with my grandson.'

Megan had first texted Lizzie and Sam. There was no way she'd go unless one or both of them were going too. After receiving answers in the affirmative from both, Megan had thrown on her Nobody jeans, brown heeled boots and sparkly black peasant blouse, before her mum literally pushed her out into the cold night air.

'Hey,' Megan said, squeezing in next to Sam at the bar. 'Where's Dark Horse Dave?'

'Huh?' Sam's eyes were slightly unfocused as he turned towards her. Megan wondered how long he'd been here.

'Dave?' Megan repeated slowly. 'The guy who invited us, and who apparently has more friends than Oprah.'

'Yeah, popular prick,' Sam agreed. 'You wanna drink?'

'Gin and tonic, thanks.' Megan grabbed the only empty stool left at the bar. 'I'll get the next round. Where's Lizzie?'

Sam gestured towards the other side of the room where Megan saw Lizzie talking to Dave and a couple of other beardy people. She was looking gorgeous in black pants, a red silk shirt and ankle boots. It was rare to see Lizzie out of a hoodie and jeans, or pyjamas – basically anything you could throw in a quick-wash cycle – so Megan was thrilled to see her friend dressed up. Lizzie caught her eye, waved and said something to Dave, whose face lit up. He immediately excused himself from his bearded friends, and the two of them began battling their way across the room. Dave received high-fives, fist bumps or handshakes from everyone he passed, and Megan felt a surge of affection towards the man-child she'd only ever regarded with mild amusement.

'You came!' Dave couldn't have been more excited if Megan had come dressed as Wonder Woman.

'Wouldn't have missed it!'

Lizzie made a gagging motion over Dave's shoulder.

'Thanks so much,' Dave gushed, nervously running his hands through his thin spiky hair. 'Can I get you a drink?'

'On it,' Sam said, handing Megan her G&T.

'I'm so happy you're all here!' Dave clinked his glass against each of their drinks in turn. Sam hit Dave's glass with his beer bottle a bit too hard.

'Congrats, mate,' Lizzie said. 'Fantastic turnout.'

'I know, right?' Dave looked almost embarrassed. 'It's a bit overwhelming.'

'You deserve it,' Sam said. 'Following your dream and making shit happen. Fucking awesome.'

Megan detected a bitter tone in Sam's voice and looked at Lizzie to see if she'd noticed it too, but her friend was busy taking a healthy swig of her Scotch and dry. Christ. Lizzie and Sam were obviously up for a big one.

'Thanks, mate,' Dave said.

Sam shrugged. 'It's no Marvel Universe but I'm sure there's a couple of people out there who'll dig your style ...'

Megan and Lizzie frowned at each other. *Was Sam deliberately being an arsehole?*

'Uh, yeah, hope so,' Dave said with a half-hearted chuckle. 'And hey, happy birthday for tomorrow! The big four O!'

'Yup,' Sam said, with all the enthusiasm of a ticket inspector. 'Sure is.'

Dave raised his glass again. 'To Sam!'

'To Sam!' Megan and Lizzie chorused, and they all clinked glasses again before Sam chugged the rest of his nearly full beer.

'Whoa, easy tiger,' Dave laughed. 'The night is young!'

'I fucking hope so,' Sam said, raising one hand to get the bartender's attention. 'I've only booked the babysitter till eleven.'

'Dave!'

A slim dark woman in an emerald-green shift dress beckoned to Dave. She was striking, with long wavy black hair, smoky eyes and red lipstick. From the lotus pendant around her neck, Megan guessed she was Sri Lankan.

'Sorry, guys,' Dave said, waving back. 'The missus wants to introduce me to some animation company peeps she invited.'

'That's your *wife*?' Megan stared in amazement.

'Animation peeps?' Sam crowed. 'You're shitting me!'

'Yeah, that's Keshini,' Dave said, ignoring Sam's outburst. 'Back soon!'

He was instantly swallowed up by the small throng, leaving Megan, Lizzie and Sam staring after him, open-mouthed.

'What the actual fuck?' Lizzie said.

Megan couldn't help but laugh. 'Dave's missus is a stunner!'

'That'd be right,' Sam muttered. 'He gets the career *and* the hot wife ...'

'Sam?' Lizzie frowned. 'You okay, mate?'

'Shweet as, mate,' Sam slurred.

Lizzie looked down at her empty glass and moved towards the bar to order another. Megan decided to hit them up before they both got too blotto.

'Get your phones out,' she ordered.

'What for?' Lizzie said, turning back.

'Date for your calendars.'

Lizzie pushed the blue scarf draped across her handbag aside and pulled out her phone. Sam was having trouble retrieving his from inside his jacket pocket so Megan reached in and took it out for him.

'So, what's this then?' Lizzie asked, opening up her calendar. 'You having a launch too? What will the cool kids be wearing next season?'

'Christmas play auditions,' Megan said. 'Wednesday twelfth of August. In the hall at lunchtime.'

'Why the fuck are *you* running auditions?' Sam frowned. 'Isn't that, y'know, the *drama teacher's* job?'

'Miss Mitchell's got some personal stuff going on,' Megan explained, 'so Penny asked me to help.'

'Hang on,' Lizzie said, dropping the phone back into her bag, 'I said I'd help with props and crap like that. You didn't say anything about watching grade-three and -four kids mumble their way through Dickens!'

'*Dickens?*' Sam shouted. A few heads turned in their direction. 'Why the fuck would they be doing *Dickens*?'

Megan noticed that Sam swore a lot more when he was drunk. 'Because that's what I've chosen,' she said, trying to keep her tone calm. '*A Christmas Carol.*' She pulled the Applewood copy out of her bag to show him.

Sam threw his head back and roared. 'Fuck *off*!'

A few more heads turned.

'You brought it to the bar?' Lizzie stared at Megan in disbelief.

'So?' Megan suddenly wondered if that was a bit weird and shoved it back in her bag.

'Tiny Tim and shit?' Sam scoffed. 'That's hilarious.'

'Why is it hilarious?' Any traces of calm in Megan's voice had vanished. 'I've run it by Penny, and she thinks it's a great idea. It's a Christmas play, isn't it?'

'From five hundred years ago!' Sam chortled.

'Two hundred, actually.' Megan had been doing her research on The Life and Work of Charles Dickens website. 'It was written in 1843.'

'Well, excuuuuuuuuse me!' Sam mock bowed to Megan and almost toppled off the stool. 'Didn't know I was speaking with a Dickens afissshhhhionado!'

'Shut up, Sam!' Lizzie pulled her phone back out and entered the date in her calendar. 'I'll be there, Megs.'

'Thanks,' Megan said, glaring at Sam. 'And I'll talk to *you* about it when you're not being a drunk arsehole.'

'I'm not drunk!' Sam said indignantly. 'An arsehole, yes ... drunk, no.'

'I want one of those chairs from *The Voice*,' Lizzie said, turning towards the bar. 'If a kid is really bad, I'll just ...'

Lizzie trailed off and Megan turned to see what had caught Lizzie's eye. Rick Cooke was standing in the doorway, unravelling a grey scarf from around his neck and looking very handsome in dark jeans and a blue checked shirt. He caught Megan's eye and gave her friendly wave.

'Your boyfriend's heeeeere ...' Sam teased in a sing-song voice.

Lizzie turned. 'I swear to God, Sam,' she hissed, 'if you say anything, I will knock you out.'

'Jesus, calm down,' Sam said, looking genuinely scared.

'Hey Rick!' Megan said as the he walked up to join them. 'How's it going?'

'Good thanks, Megan,' Rick said. 'Hey guys!'

'G'day mate,' Sam said, smiling too hard.

'Hey, hi Rick.'

Lizzie was flushed and Megan wondered if she still had a crush on her old flame. The dude was super skinny – like Stephen Merchant skinny – but the messy hair and Buddy Holly glasses were sexy in a nerdy way. It must be unbelievably weird to have a guy you dated as a teenager show up as your kid's teacher.

'Didn't know you knew Dave,' Sam said, still smiling like a maniac.

'I don't really,' Rick said. 'But we got chatting at school the other morning and he told me about his book. I've always been interested in comics, so he invited me along.'

Megan clocked Lizzie frowning at this.

'Didn't bring your partners tonight?' Rick asked. 'I was looking forward to meeting some more Baytree parents.'

'I could try 'er on FaceTime cos thass always fun,' Sam mumbled.

'I'm solo tonight, and every night,' Megan said. 'Divorced.'

'Greg's babysitting … I'm gonna get another drink,' Lizzie said. 'Anyone else want one?'

Before Sam could say 'beer', Lizzie disappeared into a group of people waiting at the other end of the bar.

'Think I'll get one too,' Rick said. 'How about you guys?'

'My birthday tomorrow,' Sam muttered to no one in particular.

'Happy birthday, mate,' Rick said, clapping him on the shoulder. 'You'll definitely have another one then. Megan?'

'I'm fine, thanks.' As Rick headed down to the other end of the bar, Megan turned to Sam. 'You sure you're okay?'

Sam shrugged.

'Forty isn't old.'

'S'easy for you to say,' Sam slurred, waving his hand at her. 'You and your mid-thirties.'

'Henry didn't start painting or writing short stories until he was fifty-five,' Megan said, this random fact from the funeral popping into her head.

'Henry?'

'The lollipop man!' Megan couldn't believe Sam had forgotten already. They really were the shittiest community. 'The one who died?'

'Oh, yeah yeah yeah,' Sam said. 'Poor dude.'

'Sam, what's ...?'

'HEY GUYS!'

Everyone jumped about three feet in the air as Dave's over-amplified voice boomed through the room. Megan turned to see a sheepish Dave on stage.

'Oop! Sorry, folks,' Dave said, tapping the microphone. 'Forgot I don't need to shout into one of these.'

Sam laughed way too loudly, and Megan prayed he wasn't going to be one of those obnoxious tools who shouted stupid shit out during speeches. She looked around for Lizzie. If anyone could keep Sam under control it would be her, but she noticed that Lizzie was still down the other end of the bar, deep in conversation with Rick. Probably reminiscing about their date to *Basic Instinct* or *Pulp Fiction* ... or whatever blockbuster was playing at the *Sun Theatre* in the mid-nineties. There did seem to be a fair amount of hair flicking and giggling going on, as a very animated Lizzie chatted with Rick. Megan frowned. *What was she doing?*

'Welcome to the launch of *Codename: Code*,' Dave announced. 'It means so much to have you all here for something that's, y'know, a pretty big deal for me. So, I wanted to say a huge thank you to everyone, but to one person in particular.'

He pointed into the crowd, pride and love written all over his face. 'That woman there.' His voice broke. 'My beautiful, amazing wife, Kesh, is the only reason I'm standing here. She's supported me and believed in me, and I couldn't have done any of this without her. I love you, babe!'

They blew kisses to each other as the crowd aaawed and ooohed. Megan felt strangely sad as she watched this genuine display of love and may even have gotten a bit emotional if an excited Sam hadn't chosen that moment to rush the stage and crash tackle Dave to the floor.

Sam

To: jack_woz_here@hotmail.com
From: samhatfieldchef@bigpond.com
Subject: sHTUFF

Maaaaaasssaaaaaaassaaate

I just made the biggest dick of measles even kore than the marek with sassy sasha ladt

Home now spinning out and truing really hard to quitett btu I bumped into every wall and puss of furtiture in the hose just getting my iPad form the kitchens

Drinking alone is mych btter than public. Publivs bad. And I'm already nit surw what I dod . I wad shoutinh ugh] and get kicked out and Lizzie and Mefan wre there and ts fucked]s

birtthdaay tomrro but donnevn care

Shit I need autocoorect

Need to chat ssonn pleade im not okay

Lizzie

Davidoff fucking Cool Water.

The musky, tart scent had hit me square in the face the moment Rick arrived at the bar. It was like a sensory portal, sending me back into a quagmire of emotions, fears and first-love butterflies. Unwanted adolescent feelings flooded in as I breathed in that fucking aftershave. He'd been wearing Davidoff Cool Water the night we first kissed at the arcade, and I told him how much I loved the smell. It was his signature scent after that, and smelling it tonight brought back too many memories. *For fuck's sake*, I thought. *Almost thirty years later and he's still wearing the same bloody aftershave!*

My natural response to Rick's appearance, and scent, was to get another drink, but I hadn't counted on him following me.

'Scotch and dry?' He was behind me, pointing at my empty glass.

'Uh ... yep.'

Rick looked handsome tonight. Blue suited him, and there was a bit more colour in his cheeks than when I'd seen him at school.

'Good to see some things never change,' he said, smiling. 'Let me get this one.'

'Thanks.' I'd never been one to argue with the offer of a free drink.

He squeezed in beside me to order and the bar was

so crowded that his arm pressed up against mine as he leant over to get the bartender's attention. My heartbeat quickened, my mouth went dry and then the shame set in. What was wrong with me? My ex-fiancé of a million years ago scrubbed up well and made the vaguest of physical contact with me and I turned into a blushing, babbling teenager. I pulled my arm away, pretending to check my phone, and wondered for the tenth time in the past three minutes why the hell I'd come tonight. I wasn't planning on it, but Greg must have seen the invite on the kitchen bench, and when Archie and I arrived home from after-school art class he'd held it up without making eye contact. Something I was unfortunately used to by now.

'You going to that launch thing tonight?'

'Probably not,' I said. 'Archie, unpack your schoolbag, please.'

Greg put his head down to continue chopping capsicum for a stir-fry. 'You should go.' *Chop chop chop.* No eye contact.

Rage surged through me. The least he could do was fucking *look* at me when he was giving me the hint to leave him alone.

'Okay, maybe I will,' I said, flinging my bag down onto the bench with more force than was necessary.

'Great,' Greg mumbled.

'Yeah, *great*!'

It was the least polite we'd been to each other since Greg found the letter. The cracks were starting to appear, and a full-blown implosion was imminent.

When Rick handed me my drink I immediately turned to head back over to Sam and Megan.

'Hey, do you remember when Vinnie stole that bottle of Scotch from the club?'

'Oh my God, he was a wreck,' I laughed. 'Every time a cop car drove past the park, he scurried up the tree faster than a monkey!'

We cracked up at the memory of poor Vinnie clinging to the branches and glancing around furtively as the rest of us huddled in the playground fort, taking turns swigging out of the bottle and pissing ourselves at our paranoid friend.

Two hours later, I had downed maybe five more Scotches, watched Sam make a total dick of himself, helped Megan get Sam into a taxi and waved them both goodbye. Then I headed back into the bar and had two more Scotches with Rick. And it was FUN! I couldn't remember the last time I'd had fun like this. No kids, no placentas, no terrified mothers or fathers-to-be to placate, no tense conversations in the kitchen ... just alcohol, reminiscing and easy conversation.

But as Rick and I laughed and drank, a nagging thought persisted. *Apologise. Tell him you're sorry. SAY SORRY! Now is your chance! Do it!* But I just couldn't. Besides, Rick was happily married with a family now and we were having such a good time, so why dredge up past hurts and betrayals and ruin it? We were talking about the night Phil stole a Stop sign and put it in Vinnie's bed when the bartender called last drinks. I looked around and noticed that we were the last ones left. I remembered Megan and Sam leaving (Sam was *sooo* drunk ... he was gonna be mortified tomorrow) but I had no memory of Dave going, or anyone else for that matter. I looked back at Rick and realised I was having trouble focusing on his face.

'I'll drive you home,' Rick said. 'I've only had a couple.'

Had he? Actually yeah, when I thought about it, he'd

been buying me Scotches but had only been drinking water. He was very sober. It was annoying.

'S'okay, I can do the Uber!' I said, as the bartender wiped down the empty tables and started stacking chairs around us.

'Don't be silly,' he said. 'You only live around the corner.'

'Yeah, K.' I was too tired to argue. Also, the room was starting to spin, and my tongue was stuck to the top of my mouth. Easier to just let him drive me home.

Once we were in his car, which I think was red ... or maybe it was purple ... in an enclosed space with the heater turned up to high, my level of intoxication was undisputable and the pervading smell of Davidoff, inescapable. Rick pulled up in front of my house and I stepped out of the car only to discover that the nature strip was moving. Or maybe that was me. Either way it was very disconcerting ... and a bit funny. I started giggling as I stood beside the car.

'I'll walk you up ...'

'No!' I must have used my scary mum voice because Rick immediately sat back. I felt bad for being grumpy with him, but there was no way Greg could see Rick. 'I mean, noooo thank yooouuu.' I was trying to sound polite and sober but think I sounded more like Dory doing her whale impersonation.

'You sure?'

I nodded so violently that I almost toppled over. 'Assolootley. Night night!'

I faced the front gate, determined as a drunk can be, formulating a plan to reach the front door without making a sound. *I would walk through the open gate (excellent that it was open ... no squeaks to wake The Husband) then up the path and onto those two wooden steps, avoiding the dodgy one that creaked, and get out my keys and open the door, like, with no sound at all. Like, none. Cos I'd be like a ninja. A fucking NINJA! YES!*

'Go!' I waved my hands and hissed at Rick, who was still sitting there watching me through his open window. He didn't seem happy about leaving me on the moving nature strip, but after another moment he waved and drove off.

I put my fingers to my lips. 'Sssshhhhhh!' I was reminding myself to be *very quiet and not wake Greg*! I turned towards my first obstacle – the gate – and saw something behind it that hadn't been there before: a blurry Greg-shaped figure in his undies on the front porch.

'Uh-oh,' I said out loud. This struck me as hilarious and I doubled over with laughter, grabbing onto the small tree on our nature strip for support. Unfortunately, it wasn't as supportive as I'd hoped. The thin branch bent towards the ground and I went with it.

'Ooh shit!' I shouted, before landing face-down in the overgrown grass.

'Classy.'

I squinted up at a grinning Greg. Sadistic bastard.

'Needs to be mowed,' I said in as stern a wife voice as I could muster.

'Least of your problems right now, buddy.' He put his hands under my armpits and lifted me onto my feet in one swift movement. The nature strip, house, footpath – the whole *street* – spun.

'Whoa!'

'Let's get you inside.'

And then I was moving ... as if I was on one of those travelators at the airport, where the whats-it-called thing moves underneath you. I looked down to the ground and decided that Greg must be carrying me.

'You called me buddy,' I said as he lowered me onto the couch. 'I heard you.'

'I'll get you some water,' Greg said, walking into the kitchen.

'You haven't called me buddy for *such* a long time.' This struck me as so sad, and I dropped my head to my chest, which made the spinning room tip off its axis.

'Here.'

Greg handed me water and I took a big gulp. My empty stomach rumbled, and I felt the Vomit Dread. 'Fuck off.'

'That's nice.'

'Not you. Vomit Dread.'

'Shit, I'll get a bucket.'

He started to get up, but I flung my arm out, grabbed the band of his boxer shorts and pulled him back down.

'Ow.'

'Sorry, listen ...' It was hugely important that I say this now. 'I was gonna tell you, y'know, about the wedding thing.'

'Lizzie ...'

'No, shut up ... not shut up cos that's rude ... but *listen*!' Now that I'd started, I had to finish... before the vomit came. 'I was gonna tell you, but I was SO scared that you'd ...'

'I don't think now is the best time for this conversation,' Greg said, smiling at me, which was so nice I can't even explain. 'How did you get home anyway?'

'Rick drove me.' The words fell out before I could stop them. Stupid mouth.

Greg stopped smiling. Now he just looked so sad that I wanted to cry.

'You've been with Rick?' he asked. 'I thought you were at Dave's launch thing?'

'Esssactly! YES! He was *there*!'

'Shhh!'

I didn't think I was shouting but judging by Greg's expression and glance towards the kids' rooms, I must have been.

'He was there,' I whispered as my stomach rumbled again. 'He said I was just around the corner. Easy to drive me.' Actually, I couldn't remember telling Rick my address. Did I tell him? I must have ...

'What's going on, Lizzie?' Greg was using the *I'm-trying-to-stay-calm-but-my-head-is-about-to-explode* voice I'd heard him use on Zara when she scratched his brand-new ute with her bike when she was nine. 'First, you don't tell me about your not insignificant history with this guy, and now you're getting drunk together at social events?'

'Him not drunk. Just me,' I mumbled. 'Didn't know he'd be there. Promise.'

Speaking was getting harder.

'I mean, would you ever have told me what happened all those years ago if he hadn't shown up in your life again?' He sounded angry now. 'How do I know you were even going to give me that letter? You sure didn't tell me you were gonna be seeing him tonight. How do you think it looks from where I'm standing, Liz?'

'You're sitting.'

'I find out this huge thing about your life,' Greg said, his voice trembling now, 'then you don't speak to me for over a week and ...'

'You didn't not speak to ME!'

'SHHH!'

Oh shit. I was shouting again.

'What's going on?'

The sound of Zara's voice made me jerk my head around so quickly that the room lurched sideways, and my rumbling stomach contracted.

'The bucket,' I croaked.

Greg raced for the laundry.

'Are you drunk?'

I smiled at my beautiful frowning daughter in her Billie Eilish T-shirt and polka-dot pyjama pants, her skinny arms crossed across her chest and tried to shake my head, but nothing happened. I tried again, but my stupid drunk brain wouldn't let my head move. Maybe it knew that would be a bad idea. I had to sit still ... very still, until Greg returned with the bucket.

'Oh my God, you are!' Zara cried, looking both delighted and horrified.

'Sick,' I managed to whisper.

Where the fuck was the bucket?

'Yeah, sick from alcohol poisoning,' she sneered.

Greg ran in carrying the large plastic tub I washed the dog in. Jesus Christ, could the man not find a normal-sized bucket for his wife to spew into?

'Zara!' he said firmly. 'Go to bed! Your mother's not well.' He handed me the tub with one hand, and shooed Zara out with the other, who shot me one final sneer before leaving.

I pulled the tub towards my face and inhaled a big old whiff of dog shampoo and wet Bailey. It was all over after that. The Vomit Dread became plain old vomit. Greg held my hair back as I leant forward, my stomach heaving over and over, as I unleashed hell into that stinky tub.

★★★

'Excuse me, do you have Ditali pasta?'

The kid in the Coles apron looked at me as if I'd asked if he had nits. 'What?'

'Ditali pasta,' I repeated. 'I can't see it on the shelf.' I said it as nicely as I could, but if this kid spoke to me in that 'what the fuck do you want, old woman?' tone again he was gonna know about it. I was not in the mood. Go on, kid. I fucking dare you.

'Um, no, sorry,' he said, looking around for someone to palm me off onto. 'But I'll go and find someone.'

I felt slightly disappointed as he scurried off to find someone with a pasta knowledge that stretched beyond spaghetti. I'd mentally pumped myself up to give this Gen Z Ning-Nong of a shelf stacker a dressing-down, when he almost definitely didn't deserve it. It wasn't his fault he was a Gen Z Ning-Nong. Nevertheless, I felt cheated out of a grumpy old woman rant at the 'useless youth', which seemed to be my permanent state these days. Less sleep due to night shifts, housework piling up and a husband who couldn't look me in the eye was slowly but surely turning me into a banshee. That Greg hadn't already moved out after his plastered wife announced she'd been driven home by the man she'd kept secret for fifteen years – not to mention the vomiting marathon – was hopefully a good sign. I'd spent all day Friday in bed and Greg was very sweet when he got home that afternoon; bringing me coffee and ordering the saltiest fish and chips ever – perfect hangover food. The six of us watched *The Princess Bride* again, and it had almost seemed like a normal Friday night, although Zara had given me grief when she got home from school and found me watching Dr Phil and nibbling Saladas.

'How you feeling, Mum?' she'd asked smugly. 'Still *sick*?'

If there's anything more revolting than a sanctimonious pre-teen, I'm yet to discover it.

'How kind of you to ask,' I'd said, matching her tone. 'I'm feeling much better, thank you.'

'Need anything?' She was enjoying her role so much she could barely contain her delight. 'A wine, maybe?'

'No, thanks, sweetie.' My tone shifted slightly, a warning that she was in the danger zone. 'I'm actually feeling quite irrational right now, to the point where I might cancel your sleepover with Madi if you don't go and clean your room right now.'

She was gone from that lounge room quicker than you could say 'Don't fuck with me, kid' and the rest of the weekend had been the usual hectic palaver of netball (Zara, Archie and Stella), hip-hop (Stella), football (Max) and two birthday parties (Max and Zara). The only interactions Greg and I had were along the lines of 'I'll pick up (insert kid's name) at (insert time of day)' and 'If you take (insert kid's name), I'll drop (insert kid's name) off to (insert activity)' but at least we'd *started* interacting. Now that the seal had been broken, maybe we could keep talking about Rick, when the time was right, and ideally when I was sober.

By the time Sunday afternoon rolled around and I had two hours free before the last birthday party pick-up, I decided to head across the bridge to have a cup of tea with Auntie Carmen. We had just sat down for our first sips when Dad ran in, shouting and waving his arms around because he'd run out of flour to make pasta for the Ghagin Grieg special. Before he and Auntie Carmen could start arguing about who had or hadn't filled in the stock order form, I offered to head to Coles and buy pasta and flour.

As I got back into the car – I'd spent so much time

driving that weekend, I must've single-handedly destroyed the ozone layer – I wondered if I should tell Auntie Carmen about Rick's reappearance in my life. I was more than a little apprehensive about the shame and pain it would dredge up, as the Abela family had come to an unspoken agreement years ago to never again speak of Lizzie's 'monumental wedding fuck-up'. We were like a group of teenagers who'd accidentally committed murder and made a pact to deny it ever happened so we could all get on with our lives.

I was twenty-five when I came back to Melbourne and my homecoming had been as weird, disjointed and difficult as I'd expected it to be. I hadn't given anyone a heads-up that I was returning and simply walked into Abelas one Wednesday and almost gave my poor father a heart attack. I'd been sending money home, paying back what I owed them for the wedding, but had only spoken to Dad every few months. This was mainly because I was in a toxic relationship with Durham boy and was worried Dad would figure out that his daughter had turned into a broken fool and insist on coming over to rescue her.

The second I saw Dad, I ran into his arms and we held each other for what felt like an eternity, tears streaming down our cheeks. Dad took turns berating me and telling me how much he loved me and it was quite the dramatic scene. Christopher, however, barely spoke to me for the first three months. He was a week away from marrying Rosa when I arrived back (the reason for my surprise appearance) and made it clear I wasn't exactly a welcome guest.

'The only reason you're invited is because Dad made me,' he said over the phone.

I understood. He was head over heels in love, and about to get married, so he found the whole idea of running out on a wedding – not to mention your family and friends – completely despicable and pretty unforgiveable. Joey, on the other hand, was single and working in the restaurant, and had greeted me as if we'd seen each other every day for the past three years. Lucas was doing a marketing degree and working his way through a plethora of straight-haired skinny blonde girls, and had no interest in, or understanding of, commitment, so I was his hero.

'You're a fucking rebel, dude!' he announced when he found me sitting in the kitchen having a wine with Dad that night.

Auntie Carmen took the longest to come around. I'd written her a long letter soon after arriving in London, trying to explain why I'd kept everything from her, but over the whole three years she never once wrote back. On the rare occasions I rang home she'd refuse to speak to me, and although I understood her feelings of hurt, betrayal and humiliation, it was still heart-breaking. I was more terrified about seeing her than anyone else when I got home and expected that she'd have a hard time forgiving me. I was right. When Auntie Carmen walked into the restaurant that day and found my weeping father and me in each other's arms, she'd stared at me wordlessly, her complexion growing whiter by the second. Seeing her in the flesh was like a punch in the gut. I'd missed her so much.

'Look, Carmen!' Dad had shouted through his tears. 'Our Lizzie has come back!'

I couldn't speak, silenced by fear and a skerrick of hope. Auntie Carmen walked over, pecked me on the cheek and walked out again. She didn't speak to me for the next two months, until one night when the whole Abela clan went to our favourite Mexican restaurant for Joey's birthday dinner.

Auntie Carmen and I both had a few too many happy hour Margaritas, and once Dad went to bed later that night, we had it out. Shouting, weeping, raging, laughing ... the full Maltese kitchen melodrama that lasted well into the wee hours of the morning.

'You broke my heart!' she screamed.

'I'm sorry!' I wept.

'I'd never have let you marry Rick if you'd told me!' she shouted, knocking a pepper grinder off the bench and onto the floor. 'I would have called the wedding off weeks before!'

'I know, and I'm so sorry,' I cried, trying to grab her rough, warm hands between mine but failing miserably due to the amount of tequila in my system. 'I should have told you.'

Sometime around dawn, we'd collapsed into her bed together, exhausted, drunk and relieved. We never spoke of it again. We'd made our peace and there was nothing left to say.

One of Dad's more profound sayings was, 'If you're always looking back at the things you've done, you'll miss what's coming towards you ... and maybe walk into a pole.'

And, so it was. No looking back for the Abela family. I'd tried to contact Rick when I got back too, to apologise in person, but his dad told me he'd moved interstate and slammed the door in my face. Fair enough. Who could blame the man? I was scum as far as he was concerned.

Now, all these years later, here was Lizzie Barrett, a fine upstanding citizen in the eyes of the world – married, kids, good job and heading down to Williamstown Coles to buy pasta for Abelas' Ghagin Grieg special.

A woman about my age helped me locate the elusive

Ditali pasta, and after buying the flour and some items for the Barrett household, I rushed out into the car park to get back to my panicked father. Dogs were barking in the park nearby and I glanced over at the small playground that consisted of a yellow slide, a set of monkey bars, a small wooden fort and two swings. It had been there for as long as I could remember, and I had a sudden flashback to a bunch of us sitting under the wooden fort getting drunk on Lambrusco cask wine after a soccer presentation one night. That was the same night Melissa lost her virginity to Lachy under the huge gum tree at the far end of the park, the tree where two women were now chatting as their dogs ran circles around them.

I looked away, reached into my bag for my keys, then frowned and turned back to look over at the two women again. There was something familiar about the way the one on the left flicked her hair over her shoulder, and her voice as she shouted at her dog to get away from the puddle. Was that …? *Melissa Morton.* The woman calling to the dog was my old best friend. The best friend who helped me shave my calves and toes when I was a hairy ten year old. The best friend who explained what 'Do you want a root?' meant when two boys shouted it at us on our way home from school one day. The best friend who shaped my pubic hair into a love heart to surprise Rick after way too many West Coast Coolers one night. The best friend who saved me from catastrophic levels of humiliation when I pulled a tampon out of my handbag instead of a cigarette in front of the entire boys' soccer team. The best friend who cried when I asked her to be my maid of honour. The best friend I hadn't seen in twenty years. She was a bit thicker around the middle (weren't we all) and her hair was shorter, but it was definitely her. My heart beat faster and my stomach twisted as I ducked behind a huge SUV that would have looked more at home in a Presidential Motorcade than a suburban car park.

The last time I'd spoken to Melissa was the day I returned from the UK. After my family, she was the first person I tried to contact, but like Auntie Carmen, Melissa hadn't replied to a single letter I sent her from London. My old soccer gang had scattered to the winds and none of them wanted a bar of me, but that hadn't bothered me in the slightest. I'd changed a lot in three years and was ready to start a new chapter of my life. Melissa was the only one I cared about. Even before going to Rick's house, I rang her, desperate to reconnect and make amends.

'Hello?'

'Melissa?'

'Speaking.'

'It's Lizzie.'

Silence.

'Can we please meet up? I really want to ...'

'Don't call me again. Ever.'

There was a sharp twang in my chest as I remembered how Melissa's voice had sounded like ice over the phone. I peeked out from behind the car and watched my old best friend put the leash on her dog then walk out of the park and out of my sight.

Sam

To: jack_woz_here@hotmail.com

From: samhatfieldchef@bigpond.com

Subject: Happy Birthday to Me!

Hey dickhead,

Thanks for the personalised Michael Bolton e-card. Can't unsee that.

Apologies for last Thursday night's gibberish. I've been drinking a lot, but that night I outdid myself. One of my drop-off mates – Nerdy Dave – is releasing this graphic novel and Thursday night was the launch. Megan and Lizzie were there too, and Dave was beyond rapt. There were a bunch of other people there who were important; important to Dave's career. But he looked really happy to see his friends.

And I made a fuckwit of myself and probably ruined his night.

I spent almost all of my birthday in bed, wondering if there was a way to measure the magnitude of a hangover, because I think I should be touching base with Guinness about that one (the records people, not the Irish food group). It could well have been the greatest hangover of all time. I felt fine when I woke up Friday morning but I've been drinking long enough to know that I still had enough booze in my blood to keep me cruising until early afternoon. I felt like all of my internal organs had been swapped for rusty car parts, but I was okay. Luckily, Megan arrived at the door, wishing me a happy birthday and offering to drive the kids to school for me, I couldn't have been more grateful, or ashamed. It was around 11 a.m. when I began to feel uneasy, unsteady and sick. Strobe-like fragments of the night before started smacking me in the face. I grimaced and groaned for a good two hours as I contended with my hulking hangover and the puzzle-piece memories that kept peppering my swampy brain.

As best I can remember, Dave was giving a speech, something really nice about his super-hot wife, and I made a horrible joke about him punching above his weight. Then I remember rushing that little stage and hugging Dave, taking the microphone and shouting at everyone to clap because Dave's following his dreams and not everyone has the guts to do that and we should all be more like Dave, and then I'm pretty sure I made up a song called 'I Wanna Be Like Dave' and sang it to him until I was escorted from the stage.

At bedtime Friday night, the kids asked if Mum had gone away again without telling them, and when would she be back, and would she be able to read them bedtime stories when she's back? I said Mummy's really busy at the moment, but of course she'll read you bedtime stories soon. After everything she went through to have kids, it's like she resents their existence.

Once the kids finally passed out, my birthday got even better, because Bridg rocked up unannounced (no Danish or coffee, FYI) to collect some stuff. She announced that we should talk 'separation logistics', like it was some tedious extension of her usual work day.

She informed me that she has a bunch of travel over the next three months and it'll be easier if she just stays OS in between conferences. In a nutshell, 'Hi nearly ex-husband, I'm going away for three months because I can, so you all good with the kids? Great. I'll send money. Bye.'

Treated me like a servant.

But that's the way it's been for yonks. It's only now that I don't hold the mantle of Husband any more that I'm noticing it. I asked her what I should tell the kids. Her response?

'You know them better than me.'

There was no flicker of guilt, or even jealousy, that I know them better. Again, just facts. So now that's something else that's my responsibility: to frame my marriage breakdown in a way that's not completely crushing to my beautiful kids.

I took a shot in the dark and asked, 'Will I tell them about Mummy's new special friend?'

You must've thought it too, dickhead. All that travel. All those Alpha fuckwits with their great hair and great clothes and great apps. They're Bridget's people, those fuckwits. And she's a hottie. She would've been sought after.

She went all 'Don't be fucking ridiculous' on me, but I felt like shit and was giving zero fucks. I told her I'm not an idiot and to tell me his name.

'Whose name?'

'Oh, for fuck's sake, Bridget! It's not like you're trying to salvage anything here.'

She looked at me with what I think may've been respect. Then for the first time in years, she looked uncertain. This wasn't part of her exit strategy, but she could tell I wasn't fucking around. So, she took a deep breath, raised her chin and looked me in the eye.

'Conrad.'

Fucking Conrad. She's been travelling with Fucking Conrad for nearly two years. Premium airport lounges, sitting next to each other in business class, being driven from hotels to conferences and meetings and boardrooms and restaurants and bars and back. And then they'd fuck, safe in the knowledge that their lives are more than ten thousand kilometres away. I can easily imagine Conrad lying next to Bridg, all buff and sweaty and post-coital, pretending to listen to her complain about me.

'How long?' I asked.

'A year. More.'

Fucking Conrad.

I stepped out of the way, and she left.

Happy birthday to me.

I always knew we were a mess but cheating never blipped on my radar. I thought I had a good radar.

I can't believe you're the one I whinge to. You. The dude whose life got flipped like a pancake that landed on the floor. You know all this. I'm sorry, mate. I'm sorry that happened to you and that I was the one who told you that we could make it by morning, and it was a really sweet gig and it could make a real difference. But now I feel like *I'm* the pancake tumbling in mid-air.

So, I come to you – I always come to you though, don't I? – for wisdom and patience and your stupid fucking sense of humour.

Am I gonna be okay?

I really wanna know this one, so try not to crack wise.

Cos I have no answer.

S x

Megan

'Quick, here he comes!'

Megan and Lizzie stood up on the bench and launched into off-key singing. *'Happy birthday to you! Happy birthday to you! Happy birthday, dear SAAAAM! Happy birthday to you!'*

Sam stopped dead in the middle of the schoolyard, mortified, which was exactly what Megan and Lizzie had been hoping for.

'Hip hip ... !' Megan cried.

'HOORAY!' Lizzie shouted.

'All right, you've had your fun,' Sam said, rushing over and glancing at the handful of parents and kids staring at them. 'Get down!'

Despite his surly tone, Megan could tell that Sam was chuffed.

'Happy birthday for Friday, mate!' Lizzie said, hopping down to give him a hug. 'Sorry I only managed a birthday text and wasn't here to embarrass you on the actual day. I was sick.'

'Sick? Ha!' Megan scoffed.

'Shut up.'

'Yeah, Sam the boozehound was a no-show on his birthday too,' Megan said, handing Sam his coffee.

'Here's the present we were going to give you on Friday!' Lizzie handed Sam the large, heavy, exquisitely wrapped gift she and Megan had bought at the homewares shop on Glenhuntly Road.

'Oh my God!' Sam's arms physically drooped with the weight of it. 'What is this? A warhead?'

'Open it!' Megan cajoled.

Sam began to carefully unstick and peel off the multiple layers of coloured paper, eventually revealing the Chasseur stock pot in all its glory.

'Wow!' He beamed. 'Guys, these things cost a bomb.'

'More like a warhead.'

Sam looked as if he might cry.

'I've wanted one of these for ages,' he said.

'Yeah, we know,' Megan said. 'You've been banging on about it for months.'

'Thank you so much!' Sam hugged them both. 'This is the best present ... besides the deformed, ceramic pencil holder from Lola and the picture Tyler drew me of Spider-Man pulling a web out of his nose.'

Lizzie nodded. 'Of course.'

'Hey, umm, listen,' Sam said, looking flustered. 'I'm sorry again. About my behaviour at Dave's thing.'

'You're apologising to *me*?' Lizzie said in disbelief. 'I'm the one who dumped you both to get plastered with my ex.'

'Yeah, but you didn't ruin Dave's night and make a dick of yourself in front of the entire bar, did you?'

'No, but I think my daughter and husband have lost all respect for me,' Lizzie muttered.

'Are you going to tell us what's going on with you, Sam?' Megan said gently. 'And don't give us some shit about being "tired". You've been miserable for days!'

She'd been worried about Sam ever since depositing him in the taxi on Thursday night. He'd been babbling about hiring a private detective to find his balls and making no sense whatsoever but she got the distinct impression it had something to do with Bridget. He clearly hadn't shaved in over a week and his clothes were crumpled and stunk.

'Yeah, you okay, mate?' Lizzie asked.

'Yeah, look, it's just … Bridget left and …'

'Again?' Megan exclaimed. 'She only just got back! Jesus, no wonder you're shattered. You must be …'

'No, she left.' Sam looked at his friends, pained. 'She left me. A week ago.'

Megan couldn't speak. It was awful. She leant over and gave him another, longer, hug and as his arms tightened around her, she felt furious with herself for not noticing her friend's sadness sooner.

'I'm so sorry,' Lizzie said, joining the hug.

'She's fallen in love with a guy at work.' Sam pulled away and picked up his coffee. 'She told me that extra bit of info while I was still dealing with my Hemingway-sized hangover on Friday.'

'On your *birthday*?' Lizzie cried, outraged. 'She told you that on your fucking birthday?'

What a heinous bitch! Megan thought. *Jesus, he was better off without her!*

'She's always had a good sense of occasion,' Sam said with a rueful grin.

'What about the kids?' Megan asked. 'Are they okay?'

'She wants me to tell them,' Sam said. 'She's gone overseas for three months, so I'll have to find a way to deal with it.'

Megan had always known Bridget was an absent mum, but this was some next-level shit. She put her arm around him again. 'I'm trying really hard *not* to say what I *want* to say right now,' she said, sounding calmer than she felt.

Sam gave a short laugh. 'There's nothing you could think that I haven't already,' he said. 'All I care about now is this not breaking my kids.'

'Is there anything we can do?' Lizzie asked.

'Nah, I'm good thanks,' Sam said, smiling. 'Shit, there's Dave. I've got to apologise for… everything. Keep an eye on my fancy pot, okay?' He got up and headed over to Dave, who was talking to a couple of mums on the other side of the playground.

'Fucking hell!' Lizzie exclaimed when Sam was out of earshot. 'What a monster! Who does that?'

'And to *Sam*!' Megan said. 'How could anyone be cruel to Sam? It's like hurting a Care Bear.'

'I can't even imagine the looks on my kids' faces if Greg told them we were separating, but Mummy couldn't be here to talk about it as a family because she'd fucked off overseas for three months,' Lizzie said. 'Those poor kids.'

Megan noticed that Lizzie's usual fiery tone had a strangely introspective sting to it.

'Are you okay?' Megan asked. 'You seem…'

'I'm fine,' Lizzie said. 'Just worried about Sam.'

'We have to help him,' Megan said, watching him approach Dave and hug him. 'These are the moments we have to put our own problems aside and help our fellow man.'

'Did Ebenezer teach you that?' Lizzie joked.

'Yes, actually,' Megan said, defensively. 'He says, "Mankind was my business. The common welfare was my business; charity, mercy, forbearance, benevolence, were all my business."'

'He also says "Bah Humbug", so y'know, grain of salt.'

'I'm serious.'

'You know bits off by heart now?' Lizzie laughed. 'Soon you'll be God Blessing Us, Everyone.'

'You can make fun, I don't care,' Megan said. 'But I know what it means to be a good person now, and I'm going to help Sam through this, whether you wanna help or not.'

'Of course I'm going to help Sam, you fucking lunatic,' Lizzie said. 'But I am seriously concerned about your obsession with that book.'

'I'm not obsessed I just ...'

'Lizzie!'

Megan looked up to see Rick standing in front of them.

'Hey Rick!'

Lizzie's voice sounded strained, as though she'd been karate-chopped in the neck.

'Just wanted to return this,' Rick said, handing Lizzie a scarf. 'You left it in my car the other night.'

Lizzie stiffened beside Megan as she took it. 'Oh, uh, thanks.'

Megan frowned. What the hell was going on with these two? She glanced at her blushing friend and remembered that Lizzie had gone back to the bar when she and Sam left on Thursday night. But surely she hadn't ... no. Not Lizzie. She'd never do that to Greg, would she? Not the Lizzie Megan knew.

'Thanks for driving me home too,' Lizzie said, as if reading Megan's thoughts. 'I *do* remember that ... despite the amount of Scotch in my system.'

'No problem,' he said. 'You have fun, Megan?'

'Not as much fun as this one and Sam,' Megan said, still sensing that weird vibe between Lizzie and Rick, 'but it was a great night.'

'Yeah,' Rick said. 'Great night.'

Did Megan imagine it, or had Rick given Lizzie a meaningful look as he said that?

'Anyway, gotta get to class,' he said, backing away. 'See you both later.'

'Bye.'

The moment he was gone, Megan turned to Lizzie.

'Lizzie ...?'

'Shut up,' she said firmly. 'I drank too much, he drove me home. End of story. I've gotta go to work.'

She stood up and Megan felt bad. '"No space of regret can make amends for one life's opportunity misused",' she said, trying to lighten the mood.

'Yeah yeah, bah humbug, mole,' Lizzie said with a smile, then hurried from the schoolyard as if she were being chased by a rogue magpie.

Megan turned to see Rick standing near the bike sheds, watching Lizzie a bit too intently. The smile faded from her face.

In the week leading up to the auditions, Megan was revelling in her various 'Good' roles. Megan the Good Community Member prepared for the play auditions, telling the grade fours to prepare a short poem (no longer than four lines!) or a few lines from their favourite movie. No one expected, or wanted, more than that from an eight year old. And really, all Megan needed to see was if they could read, string a sentence together and speak above a whisper.

Megan the Good Daughter took cupcakes to the Applewood residents, and listened as ninety-year-old Maggie complained about a recent outing to the city where their excursion leader, Harriet, had told them all to put their hands out the window before they left to see if they'd need a cardigan.

'Like we're a bunch of bloody drongos!' she'd ranted to Megan, before taking her teeth out to suck the pink icing off a tiny cake.

Megan the Good Mother turned off her phone between 3.30 p.m. and 7.30 p.m. every night to build abstract Lego structures and play countless games of UNO with Oscar. Megan the Good Friend took Lola and Tyler home from school all week so Sam could stay at home doing housework, or cooking, or whatever he did. And Megan the Good Ex-Wife had agreed to Bryce and Adam hosting Oscar's mini-sleepover on the night of his birthday. Although, when Megan had asked how Bryce's Mindfulness sessions were going (Good Ex-Wife), and he'd shown her a photo of himself standing in front of a hundred or so students, his hands clasped together, the tops of his fingers resting against his lips, Megan had laughed and said, 'You look like a wanker.' (Bad Ex-Wife.)

But otherwise, Megan felt generally good about being Good, even if she had dropped the ball a bit with work. She'd received a slightly passive-aggressive email from one of her customers who asked, 'if you meant to send me the corduroy overalls instead of the three pairs of jeggings I ordered?' *She'll get over it*, Megan thought. It wasn't as if leggings and overalls were life and death. Not like poor Bert, who had fallen down the front steps of Applewood over the weekend and was now in hospital with severe concussion. Megan had taken his wife, Lucy, a bunch of flowers and a box of her favourite dark chocolates. Henry would be proud.

'You hit your head like silly old Bert?' Ellie asked when

Megan walked into the apartment and found her mother bouncing on a fit ball in front of the TV, doing her daily workout.

'What?'

'Lucy said you took flowers and chocolates round yesterday.'

'So?'

'Sooo …' Ellie paused the DVD, dabbed at a slight sheen of sweat on her chest and turned to her daughter. 'In all the time you've been visiting me here, you couldn't get me up to my room and away from the "Cocoon Gang" fast enough,' she said. 'Now you're bringing them cupcakes and staying for Sunday chats.'

'I brought you chocolate too,' Megan snapped, 'but you're not getting it now.'

'You know I love you.' Ellie wrapped her brown, sweaty arms around Megan. 'And I'll admit that sometimes I was worried you'd inherited your father's selfish streak, but I'm happy to be proven wrong.'

Megan felt as if she'd been slapped. 'You thought I was like him?'

The thought of sharing a single personality trait with that man was galling. Dean Wylie's own happiness was more important than the wife and children he left to fend for themselves. Megan remembered the look on Sam's face when he told them Bridget had left. She knew that look. She'd seen it on her mum's face, and her own every time she looked in the mirror in the weeks, months and years after her dad did his disappearing act. And now, Mum was saying she'd worried Megan was like him?

'You think I could do what Dad did?' she croaked. 'To Oscar?'

'No!' Ellie was horrified. 'Of course not! I only meant he had a tendency at times to… oh fucking hell, I'm sorry.' She lifted Megan's chin to look her in the eye. 'You are a wonderful, caring mother. You would never do that to Oscar, or me, or anyone you love.'

Megan assured Ellie that she believed her, but as they drank tea and ate chocolate – Ellie insisted she deserved a morning treat after her workout – she couldn't get her mother's words out of her mind. *Inherited your father's selfish streak*. She was still thinking about it as she pulled up outside the school an hour later for the auditions. *I'll just have to prove Mum wrong and give this school the best damn Christmas show they've ever seen*, she thought determinedly.

'Okay, quiet now, please … HANDS ON TOP!'

'THAT MEANS STOP!'

The thirty or so kids scattered around the school hall stopped talking and put their hands on their heads.

'That's better.' Miss Mitchell looked as though she was on the verge of a nervous breakdown already. 'If we are going to get through all of you before the end of lunch, you're going to have to listen, okay?' Most students nodded obediently, while the handful of Preps and grade ones who'd shown up, Oscar included, simply gave her their usual vacant stares. 'Good. Now I want you to sit quietly while I chat with Oscar's mum.'

Oscar puffed out his chest and looked as if he might levitate with pride at the mention of his name. Megan grinned. That reaction alone made this all worth it.

Miss Mitchell was a short, older woman with wispy blonde-grey hair and a permanently stressed expression on her face. She didn't dress like the drama teacher from Megan's school days – colourful skirts, tights and chunky jewellery. Lisa Mitchell wore sensible slacks, pearl-buttoned blouses and cardigans. Today Miss Mitchell's ensemble consisted of a soft blue cardigan, a grey ribbed long-sleeved top and patterned silk pants, and she was looking more stressed than usual. This was understandable for a woman who spent her days wrangling feral kids and her nights tending to her sick elderly father.

'Another teacher should be here to help out with behavioural management in a minute,' Miss Mitchell said, leading Megan towards the stage. 'The quicker we can get them to ...' She frowned and pulled her buzzing phone out of her pocket.

'Take it,' Megan said, assuming it was a family-related call. 'My friends will be here soon. They can help out.'

'Are you sure ...?'

'Absolutely,' Megan interrupted. 'Take the call.'

Miss Mitchell answered it and headed for the door. 'Dad? Everything okay?'

The noise level of impatient kids was rising, and Megan was about to give them the old 'Hands on Top' when Rick Cooke appeared.

'Hey Megan,' he said. 'Sorry I'm late. I'm on crowd-control duty.'

'Oh, thanks, I was just ...'

'Okay, you lot!' Rick jogged around to stand in front of the kids. 'Who wants to hear me do a song?'

Half shouted an emphatic '*NO!*', while the other half cheered excitedly, then rolled around laughing as Rick launched into an extremely off-key rendition of Taylor Swift's 'Shake it Off'.

'What the hell is he doing?'

Megan turned to find Lizzie and Sam behind her.

'Stalling till you got here,' Megan said.

'Where's Miss Mitchell?' Sam asked.

Megan noticed Lizzie laughing at Rick as he flung his arms around and swung his hips. 'Family crisis,' she said. 'So, we're on our own. Well, us and Taylor Swift over there.' She caught Rick's eye and gave him a thumbs-up. He stopped singing, but not before shooting Lizzie a goofy grin, who shook her head and mouthed the word 'loser' at him.

What the hell was going on with these two? Megan thought. Was Lizzie *flirting* with this guy? But that was absurd. Lizzie wasn't a flirt. Megan made a mental note to pin Lizzie down after the auditions and talk to her. After all, wasn't it Megan's responsibility as a Good Friend to check in with Lizzie and make sure she wasn't on the verge of doing something she'd regret later?

'Okay, kids,' Rick said. 'I'm going to leave you to your auditions with these awesome parent volunteers.' He pointed to a black chair against the wall. 'But I'll be sitting right there, watching!' He swung two fingers from his eyes back to the kids. 'So best behaviour, please.'

'Come on,' Megan said, steeling herself. She led Sam and Lizzie around to stand in front of the kids as their respective children waved madly, as though they were pop stars walking the red carpet.

'Hey kids!' Megan said, hoping they couldn't tell how nervous she was. 'Miss Mitchell had to do some work, so the three of us are going to run the auditions. Who's excited about the Christmas play?'

The younger kids cheered, while the older ones just shrugged or rolled their eyes.

'Me too!' Megan cried. 'Lizzie and Sam are too, aren't you?'

'Yes, Megan!' they chorused like background Wiggles.

'Okay, let's get started!'

As expected, most of the kids were terrible, and Megan, Lizzie and Sam spent the next fifty minutes watching an endless procession of mumbling, stumbling, uncharismatic children strut their stuff on the hall stage. Megan included her own offspring in the 'shit' category as soon as she saw Oscar and his best mate, Toby, perform a short scene from their favourite film, *The Lego Movie*. Megan's son mumbled his way through a scene, comprised of only four lines of dialogue, with all the stage presence of a broom.

'Okay, who's next?' Sam looked as if he was enjoying himself way more than he should, considering the talent on show.

'Well, that was *Oscar*-worthy,' Lizzie muttered as Oscar and Toby high-fived each other, thrilled with their work.

'Fuck off,' Megan muttered back, 'wait till your kids are up.'

'It's just Stella,' Lizzie said. 'Max is here as Tyler's moral support.'

'You're in for a treat with Tyler's audition,' Sam whispered as two giggling grade-four girls stood up. 'Knock-knock joke.'

'Classic.' Lizzie nodded her approval.

'And Lola, well, you'll see ...'

Tyler's knock-knock joke proved as lame as expected; something about an interrupting walrus, while Lola performed a short scene from *Pride and Prejudice*. Her Elizabeth Bennet rant to an invisible Mr Darcy was enthusiastic, and mercifully short. Sam looked fit to burst with pride and even Megan had to admit that the girl could act and could be a perfect ghost of Christmas past or present. But apart from Lola, Megan was starting to lose hope of there being enough kids to fill out the main roles. One after another, they jumped up to showcase their limited skills as Megan, Lizzie and Sam scribbled comments like, 'Not terrible' (Megan), 'Atrocious' (Lizzie), 'Dear God' (Sam) and 'Kill me now' (Sam's directive to Lizzie after they sat through a seven-minute re-enactment of Mufasa's death scene from *The Lion King*). The grade-four girl played all the roles, including the stampeding wildebeest. Thankfully, the best saved themselves for last and the final stream of grade-four kids, Stella included, restored Megan's faith that the show could work.

'That was fun!' Sam said, passing his notes to Megan.

'Should've gone to my pap smear appointment instead,' Lizzie said, slapping her notes down in front of Megan. 'Would've been more entertaining.'

Megan frowned as she read one of Lizzie's notes: *A table has more personality.*

'Bit harsh.'

'Nope,' Lizzie said. 'True.'

Sam grabbed his Crumpler and stood up. 'I've gotta go make a crème brûlée for my mum's birthday dinner tonight.'

'Show off,' Lizzie said, rolling her eyes.

'Wanna get a coffee?' Megan asked Lizzie before she could do another runner.

'Can't, sorry,' Lizzie said, her eyes darting over to Rick who was escorting kids out of the hall. 'I'm working tonight, so gotta get dinner sorted.'

'Okay, no worries.'

'See ya!'

Megan watched Lizzie walk out into the schoolyard and noticed Rick hang back to talk to her. Lizzie shook her head and laughed at something he said before the two of them stopped in the middle of the yard, talking and laughing. Megan frowned, the pit of worry in her stomach growing deeper by the second.

I broke up with Natalie tonight.

She's great but doesn't compare. None of them have or will. I've known that from the start.

Claudette was exciting and different and French. She was the best distraction so far, but that's a dreadful way to think about a woman you're seeing. Reaffirms for me that I should just focus on uni and make sure I set myself up for a solid teaching job as soon as I'm done. Such grand plans. Jesus. I roll my eyes at my own aspirations these days.

Everything I do is undercut by feeling sad about Lizzie. Or angry at Lizzie. Or still fucking longing for Lizzie.

I swear, I don't even know if she's a real person any more or just this mythical creature I concocted to torture myself. I polished off a bottle of red last night and spent too much time searching for her online. Nothing. No social media, no LinkedIn, nothing. All I found was stuff about Abelas restaurant, and one archived photo from the local rag where I could just make her out, surrounded by her family, pixelated to the point of anonymity.

Sam

To: jack_woz_here@hotmail.com

From: samhatfieldchef@bigpond.com

Subject: CCB

You know what makes me angry, dickhead?

Light cream. Cream without the point. It wouldn't do for Mum. You know Mum. She'd take a mouthful and look down at her favourite recipe of mine – a basic coffee crème brûlée – and furrow her brow slightly as her chewing slowed. She'd ask if I'd used full cream and I'd want to flip her dinner table.

But it's her birthday, so she deserves for her dinner table not to be flipped. Her birthday dinner is tonight and, as always, she will cook five kinds of meat to the point of extinction and serve a range of vegetables that look like they've been the subject of cruel experiments. These delicacies will be served with a loaf of buttered white bread on the side and plenty of tomato sauce on the table to unify the flavours. And I'll take my coffee crème brûlée because I always do.

Bridg used to thank her lucky stars for my crème brûlée because it meant she could avoid eating too much of the main meal. 'Saving myself for Sam's famous CCB,' as it's become known. Bridg knew Mum would never argue with that. She'd just nod and say something like, 'If I had a figure like yours, dear, I'd make sure to watch it too.'

But I couldn't make my CCB without full cream, so I did something I'm not proud of. I left the kids alone at home and went to the shops. Holster that righteous indignation, dickhead. They're big (enough) kids and this was an emergency. Lola knows my phone number off by heart and I made her say it to me before I left. I'm a good parent. The alternative was flipping a dinner table.

There is a heightened sense of urgency when your kids are home alone. Every hindrance seems like it was sent just for you. By the time I got to the shops, Lola had already called once, which made my heart fall out of my arse, but she just wanted to know the Netflix passcode. I told her without thinking. She could've been watching *Deliverance*, but she was alive. By the time I wrapped my fist around a container of full cream, I felt a bit like Odysseus, although my quest had only lasted eleven minutes by that point.

I marched to the checkout where there was one couple in front of me. A couple who'd witnessed the invention of the wheel. Dickhead, they were so old, the woman was trying to pay with a goat. Not true, but a vivid image. She was counting out coins that she was extracting *so slowly* from a purse probably made of mammoth hide. She examined each coin as if it were a lost artefact. Her beloved husband would then confirm which denomination she was holding. I wasn't coping. I was jiggling around like a small child busting for a wee, willing these fossils to obey nature's law and dissolve into dust.

Then I heard a hello and felt a tap on my shoulder. I almost dropped my precious full cream as I turned on my tap-tapper like a viper. Sasha recoiled and laughed. I was not prepared for this. Dickhead, I fear I behaved badly. Sasha asked if I was okay and I spewed out something about crème brûlées and Mum's birthday dinner and old people and light fucking cream. She looked at me with sympathetic bemusement and assured me it would be fine. I informed her that there was a lot more on my plate than a simple dessert and that this had thrown me. She asked what specifically had thrown me. I took umbrage and said, 'Just everything and everyone.'

She nodded and said, 'Okay.' We stood in silence. She took a half step backwards, creating a safer distance. I turned away, blinking hard.

Why did I offload on this woman?

Finally, I stepped up to hand over my cream, brandishing my credit card. The checkout chick scanned the cream and asked if I needed a bag. I said I was sure I'd be able to handle the cream sans bag, and it came out narky. She asked if tap payment was all right. I said, 'When is tap not all right?' She looked at me with such potent disdain that I felt myself blushing, knowing I was being a total twat and that Sasha was right there. I tapped my card, picked up my cream and looked back at Sasha to apologise, but her eyes were on the floor. She was stoic.

I left with the cream, but no dignity.

I got home to find the kids safe and well. Tyler was playing *Minecraft*, and Lola was watching *Tea with the Dames*. I asked her why an eight-year-old girl wanted to watch four octogenarians talking about their eyesight going, but she ignored me.

I started cooking. Angry cooking. Crashing and banging around the kitchen like a cranky chef. The CCBs turned out well. I split one between me and the kids as a peace offering and they made all the right noises. I gave them a kiss and told them theirs were the only opinions I cared about.

We have to head off in a minute. The kids have made her home-made cards that they worked really hard on. I'm hoping that will take the heat off me. I hope.

Me again. Flash forward. Mum's wasn't too bad. I'm too tired to break it down for you. Mum made all the right noises when she tasted the CCB, which gave me more relief and pleasure than it should, but there it is. Mothers.

Be good to see you soon, dickhead. Let's make it happen.

Love you, mate.

S x

Lizzie

'I'm so sorry I didn't tell you about being a runaway bride and I'm really sorry I lied to you about not knowing who Rick was and I'm sorry I didn't give you the letter before Max did and it was stupid and cowardly of me and I'm so very sorry.'

Greg was standing at the open wardrobe about to choose a tie, and turned to stare at me, an incredulous look on his face. In a rare moment, we'd found ourselves alone in the same room for more than thirty seconds, and this was the moment I'd chosen to blurt out a garbled apology before losing my nerve. My timing could have been better. It was the morning of our niece Nessa's confirmation, and we needed to leave the house in twenty minutes, but I just couldn't stand it any longer. The tension, the silences, the cold politeness. I'd been a coward for long enough and when I saw the opportunity I took it.

My voice had sounded wobbly and I was expecting Greg to grunt that it was 'fine' and that we should 'probably just get going so we didn't miss the priest's opening monologue about how we were all going to burn in hell'. Greg wasn't big on confirmations or any of the other church-related events he'd been forced to attend since becoming part of the Abela family. But in typical Greg Barrett fashion, he didn't say or do anything I expected.

He stared at me for what felt like forever, then walked over and wrapped his arms around me without saying a word. I nuzzled into his chest, tears welling up in my freshly mascaraed eyes. God, I'd missed his smell close up (Fahrenheit), the feel of his firm chest against my cheek and those strong furry arms around my body.

'I'm so sorry,' I whispered.

'Took you long enough.'

'So, are we good?'

Greg pulled back and frowned. 'Yeah, you don't get off that easy, buddy.' He released me and walked back to the wardrobe, taking out his green polka-dot tie – my favourite. 'I want to hear the whole story – all of it – from your lips, not just reading it on a piece of paper.'

'Okay, how about we have lunch this week?' I suggested. 'We could have a picnic in Alma Park and I'll tell you everything.'

'Everything,' he said, his tone softening slightly. 'I want details.'

'Why can't you be a normal male?' I said, taking the risk of lightening the tone and praying like hell that he would match it. 'One with zero interest in specifics?'

He gave me a stern look and I froze. Too soon for me to be making jokes perhaps? But then his face relaxed into a half-smile. 'Ah, but then I wouldn't be the one-of-a-kind man you fell in love with.'

It felt as if Greg had reached out and hit a magic release valve. All that crushing pressure that'd been stifling me for so long had been released. 'No,' I said softly. 'You wouldn't.'

Taking another risk, I stepped forward and reached up to kiss him, just as Zara appeared in the doorway, looking way too old in her spaghetti-strapped Dotti dress for my liking.

'Get a room!'

'Get a *jacket*!' I shot back. 'It's freezing outside.'

'Ugh!' Zara groaned and headed back to her room.

I saw straight through the exasperated pre-teen act. Zara was thrilled to discover her mum and dad canoodling in the bedroom. Of all four kids, she'd been the most tuned in to the tension between us. It must have been a huge relief to see her parents acting 'gross' again.

She wasn't the only one who was relieved. 'How about Tuesday for the picnic?' I said.

'Sure.' Greg nodded. 'And don't even think about leaving anything out or I'll ask your brothers for their version of events. Or worse, Auntie Carmen.'

'Please don't!'

'I can't believe no one in your family has slipped up in fifteen years,' Greg said. 'Not exactly known for their discretion, the Abelas.'

'It's the shameful secret of the Abela family,' I said. 'Lizzie's dark day. The Day That Shall Not Be Named.'

'Curiouser and curiouser,' Greg said, pulling on his jacket. 'Life is full of surprises. Like Stella telling me that you're helping out with the school play, even though I believe your exact words when they started school were, "I'll join a school committee when you join the ballet."'

'Time for you to buy a tutu, my friend.' I smiled, grabbed my jacket and walked into the hall.

'Let's move it out, kids!' I shouted, feeling a million times lighter. 'Time to get our confirmation on!'

'Look how skinny Mum was!'

'Ta, Max,' I said, staring down at the open photo album in his lap.

Nessa's confirmation had gone off without a hitch, apart from Max farting during the Concluding Rites, which made his cousin Marcus laugh so hard that he fell off the pew and did a bit of wee in his pants. Once Nessa had been officially sealed with the gift of the Holy Spirit, we all headed to Dad's for a celebratory feast where the dining table was heaving with platters of kannoli, pizza, gbejna and pastizzis.

Two hours later, the adults were scattered all over the kitchen and lounge room. A bunch of kids were playing video games, while Zara, Scarlett and Nessa were out in the backyard, probably comparing Chatsnaps, or whatever it was the other girls had on their phones. Max was on Dad's knee, looking through an Abela family photo album.

'Your mother, she was the best soccer player in Australia!' Dad said, nudging Max. 'Fast, strong and best left foot you've ever seen.'

'I want to play soccer!' Max cried on cue. 'But Mum won't let me!'

'Why not?' Dad glared at me. 'What rubbish is this?'

'He's got enough on his plate with footy,' I said, taking an empty bowl out of Dad's hand. 'I am not over-scheduling a six year old.'

I walked into the kitchen to dump the dirty dishes in the sink and found Rosa scraping and stacking dirty plates.

'Oh, I'm going to put those in the dishwasher!' she cried. 'Leave it, I'll do it!'

From the look of sheer panic on her face you'd think I was about to pull the pin on a live grenade. God forbid I should deprive Rosa of her martyr status.

'It's fine.' I gave her the same smile I reserved for Stella when she went into meltdown over an unscheduled family excursion. 'I'll stack if you can get the boys to start clearing.' I'd be damned if my brothers got to sit on their fat arses and talk football while the women cleared around them. I'd had enough of that sexist shit growing up. But Rosa's supercilious expression didn't waver.

'I've already started stacking,' she said with a what-are-you-gonna-do shrug, 'and I have a system, so I'd rather ...'

As Rosa continued rattling off examples that proved she was kicking my arse in the Best Female Abela category, I glanced out the window and noticed the three cousins laughing as they swang back and forth in the hammock. Something about the look on Zara's face made my mum radar ping.

I walked out of the kitchen, leaving Rose mid-sentence and went to stand by the open window in the laundry so I could eavesdrop on their conversation.

'Yeah, well, she was all, like, "Oh, I'm having an anxiety attack!"'

Mocking laughter.

'I know, Martha is so full of it!' Zara said. 'She plays in my netball team and she's always trying to get attention!'

Martha? Martha was a lovely kid, and she did have anxiety issues. Zara knew that. Why was she agreeing with Nessa's nasty analysis of her? I wasn't even aware that Nessa and Zara knew the same girls.

Nessa sighed. 'She's such a drama queen!'

Um, pot kettle black, Nessa.

'She told me once that she can't eat dairy because it makes her ...' Zara froze as I stepped out of the laundry.

'Zara, can I talk to you, please?'

The blood drained from my daughter's face as she climbed out of the hammock and followed me into the laundry where I shut the door behind us and turned to face her.

'You know what sound I hate more than anything?' I said in a low voice. 'The sound of three girls lying in a hammock bitching about another girl.'

Zara's complexion was even paler than usual and she stared up at me with wide guilty eyes.

'I thought Martha was your friend.'

'She is.' My daughter was close to tears.

'Friends don't talk about each other behind their backs,' I said firmly but gently. I didn't want the kid to end up a sobbing mess at a family celebration.

Zara stared at the yellow and brown tiles under her feet. 'Sorry, Mum.'

'You're better than that, Zara,' I said. 'Now, go help Archie collect dirty plates, please.'

She scurried off and I looked out at Scarlett and Nessa who, by the looks of it, were still relishing in their bitchy conversation. There was no logic to the rules of female teenage friendships. I knew better than anyone that if you didn't at least try to follow them, you wouldn't fit in, and being frozen out was a fate worse than death. It was a tricky road to navigate and my heart felt heavy at the thought of my own girls having to go through it all, but I'd be damned if I'd stand by and watch them turn into narcissistic little bitches.

'Come on, Zara, lights out, please.'

Zara slapped her *Hunger Games* book down and rolled

her eyes. 'Why do I have to go to sleep at eight-thirty?' she complained. 'No one in grade six goes to bed earlier than nine-thirty.'

'I don't care about anyone else,' I said.

'Ruby Parnell goes to bed at eleven!' Stella announced from across the room.

'Stella, lights out.'

The last thing I needed was for Stella to start asking more logistical questions about animated Disney characters as she had earlier that night when she'd asked if I thought Rapunzel's social skills were too well developed for someone who'd spent her whole life alone in a tower. *Tangled* was one of our family's all-time faves. 'I See the Light' always made me weep, and Megan and I had discussed at length the validity of us being attracted to Flynn Rider, despite him being a cartoon character.

'Well, she had her chameleon and her fake mum to talk to, don't forget,' I'd replied.

'Yeah, but for a girl who'd never seen a man, she was pretty confident with Flynn Rider.'

Couldn't argue with that.

'Is she going on about Rapunzel's social skills again?' Archie had called out from his bedroom.

'Mind your business,' I'd called back, before turning to Stella. 'Maybe you can write a thesis on it when you're older?'

'Maybe I'll write it tomorrow.'

'Good idea,' I'd said. 'Better make sure you're well rested then. Goodnight.' That was an hour ago and I'd thought she was asleep. More fool me. I took the book out of Zara's hand, laid it on her bedside table and leant down to kiss her cheek. 'Goodnight, darling.'

She grabbed my wrist and looked up at me. 'Mum,' she whispered, 'can you sit with me?'

This wasn't like Zara. 'Sure, honey.' I sat on her bed. 'You okay?'

Zara glanced over to make sure Stella was facing away, then whispered so softly I had to lean over to hear her. 'I'm scared about next year, Mum,' she said, her voice shaky. 'What if I don't understand anything or if nobody likes me? What if the teachers are mean? I don't want to leave primary school.'

I looked at my beautiful girl and gently stroked her face. Zara might give everyone the impression that she was nailing this growing older thing, but she was still so young. 'I know it's scary, darling,' I said, 'but I promise I'll be there to help you through all the new stuff. There's nothing to worry about.'

'Thanks, Mum.' She squeezed my hand. 'And I'm sorry about today ... saying mean things about Martha. I don't know why I did that, but I promise I won't do it again.'

I could see how genuinely sorry she was and any fears I may have had about Zara transforming into the worst kind of teenage girl abated. 'I know, darling.' I kissed her and whispered in her ear. 'Everyone's going to love you. How could they not?'

Finally, everyone was in bed, including Greg who'd had one too many pastizzis and about four too many beers. I went straight to the computer and opened Facebook. I hadn't looked at it for months, and hadn't posted anything for years, so had to spend twenty minutes trying to remember my password, then resetting it, before finally logging in. Hearing the girls bitching in the hammock that day had brought memories of my own girlhood best friend flooding back. I'd been so lucky to have had Melissa by my side during those fragile, formative years.

I typed 'Melissa Morton' into the search bar and suddenly there she was, except that now she was Melissa Grange. So many photos of so many events and moments. Her husband was a nice-looking man with short grey hair and a kind smile, and her two little girls had fair hair and big green eyes like their mum. Just looking at their little pixie faces, so like Melissa's, immediately brought tears to my eyes. How was it possible that Melissa – my Melissa – had created two human beings and I didn't even know their names? Her most recent post was from last week and read: *Wrist bands for rides at the Williamstown Primary Fete are now available to purchase! Put November 15th in your diary! It's going to be the biggest and best yet!*

Dad's birthday lunch at Abelas was on November 15th. I'd be right around the corner.

Megan

Scrooge – Aiden Pictome
Bob Cratchit – Jiang Chau
Mrs Cratchit – Elyssa Rickards
Belinda Cratchit – Stella Barrett
Tiny Tim – Nazeer Furaha
Fred (Scrooge's Nephew) – Caleb Zisis
Jacob Marley – Rocco Bede
Ghost of Christmas Present – Sophia O'Shea
Ghost of Christmas Past – Lola Hatfield
Ghost of Christmas yet to come – Gemma Hall
Creepy Kids (Ignorance & Want) – Kyle McNamara & Myabi Saito
4 other Cratchit kids
Townspeople

Megan sat in the kitchen, tapping her brand-new, freshly sharpened HB pencil on her teeth and looking at the cast list she'd written down in her 'Baytree Primary Play' notebook in longhand. *Longhand!* Using an actual writing implement! Ellie told Megan a lot of theatre directors used pens and notebooks (although how she could know this was anyone's guess) so Megan had headed to Officeworks the day before the auditions and bought herself a black hardcover A4 notebook, two HB pencils, two highlighters and one Lamy fountain pen. Megan had never owned, or used, a fountain pen in her life, but she assumed Dickens would have approved. Just holding it in her hand made her feel clever and director-y. Plus, it was pretty.

After a week spent agonising over who-should-be-which-character, the main roles were finally locked in, and all she had to do now was fill in the smaller, background roles. Feeling very satisfied with herself, Megan got up to pour herself a nice big glass of red and was about to put pasta on for Oscar's dinner, when Lizzie rang.

'Stella might not want to be in the play now.'

'What?' Megan almost tipped the entire packet of penne into the saucepan. 'But her audition was great.'

'She was all right.'

Megan knew Lizzie would rather die than brag about her kids. She'd once told Megan that Archie came home crying one day because all his friends made the Districts team except him. Lizzie had cuddled her son, made him a hot chocolate, then suggested maybe he didn't make it because he was bad at running. When Archie said she was mean, Lizzie explained the difference between being 'mean' and 'facing facts'. 'You can't be good at everything,' she'd told her sniffling son. 'It's a disappointing fact of life, but a fact, nonetheless. I'm bad at maths, your dad is bad at every kind of sport, and you're not the best at running. But you're *really* good at drawing, so, y'know, every cloud!'

Megan usually applauded Lizzie's tough love approach to parenting, but she wasn't having it tonight. 'Stella was *great* in the auditions,' Megan repeated. 'What changed her mind? Did you tell her she wasn't any good?'

'No!' Lizzie cried, then lowered her voice. 'I think she got freaked thinking about an audience watching her.'

Megan was finding it hard to hear Lizzie over whatever was clattering around in the background.

'Max! Ball outside, now!'

'Can you talk her round?'

'I'll try,' Lizzie said. 'She's coming ... gotta go.'

Megan hung up, picked up her pencil and put a question mark beside Stella's name. Maybe Riley would be a good Belinda Cratchit? She had good volume and hair long enough to put up in an old-fashioned bun.

'Mum?' Oscar's voice echoed down the hallway. Megan ignored it.

'Mum?'

'Oscar Campbell, if you want to talk to me, come in here. You do not *shout*!' Megan shouted back, aware of the irony.

Oscar's feet pounded down the hallway as Megan stirred the pasta.

'Don't I have footy tonight?'

Megan froze mid-stir. Fuck! It was Thursday. She glanced at the clock on the wall. Five to six. Bryce would be here any second. Oscar hadn't eaten and was still in his school uniform. She'd completely forgotten.

'Yes!' she said, shooing him towards his room. 'Quick! Go get dressed!'

'But my footy gear isn't in my wardrobe,' Oscar cried. 'I already looked.'

Megan suddenly realised she hadn't done a load this week. It must still be in the dirty washing from last weekend's game. The doorbell rang.

'Dad!'

Oscar ran for the front door and Megan ran for the laundry to forage through the washing. Yep, there they were.

Filthy, smelly footy shorts, top and socks lying underneath wet towels and more filthy, smelly clothes.

'He's not dressed.'

Megan walked out to find Bryce walking down the hallway, dragging Oscar behind him with one hand. This was one of Oscar's favourite games with Dad. He'd clasp his little hands around Bryce's big one, then fall to the floor and yell at his father to 'Go, Daddy, go!' and Bryce would take off, dragging Oscar along the wooden floorboards.

'I haven't had a chance to wash his gear yet.' Megan was careful to remove any trace of an apology from her tone. She'd apologise to Oscar, but not to Bryce. 'He can train in his school uniform.'

Oscar leapt up, a look of fear on his face. 'The coach doesn't like that!' he cried. 'He gets angry if you're not in your footy stuff!'

'The coach can deal with it,' Megan snapped. Jesus, was it really the end of the world if a kid wasn't in his gear for training? He wasn't being paid three million dollars to play for the AFL, for God's sake.

'It's fine, mate.' Bryce smiled at Oscar reassuringly. 'I'll talk to him. Just get your footy boots on and we'll go.'

Oscar ran to his room and Bryce turned to Megan with *that* look on his face. She knew that look. It was the look that said he *really* wanted to have a go at her but knew it wouldn't be worth it. Megan hated that look. It represented everything that had happened between them. Bryce would be kind enough to bite his tongue and let her stuff-ups slide because he was in love and about to get married, so life for him was pretty fucking sweet. It was a look that reeked of smugness and pity.

'What?' Megan said, crossing her arms, raring for a fight.

'Nothing.' Bryce used his calm mindfulness voice, which she also hated. 'You obviously have a lot on your plate.'

'What's that supposed to mean?' Megan lowered her voice.

'He was late for Sunday's game too, which pissed off his coach, by the way,' Bryce said quietly, 'and now he's showing up without his kit, so I'm assuming you have a lot going on with work.'

'Sorry, but I don't have a partner to pick up the slack,' Megan hissed. 'And why do you assume it's work? Maybe I have other stuff going on.'

Bryce brightened. 'Do you?' he said. 'That's great!'

Christ, he thinks it's a man, Megan thought. Whatever. Let him think that.

'Let's go, Dad!' Oscar clomped down the hallway in his footy boots, grabbed Bryce's hand, and dragged Bryce down the hall.

'Have fun!' Megan called after them.

Bryce grinned before closing the front door. 'You too!'

Megan fumed as she took the boiling pasta off the stove. *He thinks I'm going to text my lover to come over for a quickie while my kid's at training. If only.* She glanced at *A Christmas Carol* on the bench, picturing Bryce's grinning face in her mind. Her newfound interest in Dickens was the closest she had – or wanted – to a man in her life. Twenty-first-century men were overrated.

The laptop pinged with a notification, reminding her for the third time that day to update her twenty thousand Chill subscribers on this month's latest news and stock. Megan sighed. Casting the school play was way more fun, but she couldn't avoid work any longer. She'd been warned about the dangers of lacklustre engagement with her subscribers by three different social media strategists, all of whom had a combined age of about fifty. Megan dragged the laptop across the bench towards her to find that she already had a blank Mail Chimp document open. She must have gone to start it last week before she got distracted with the play. Megan opened her inbox, copied the text she'd been tweaking and emailing to herself all week, and pasted it onto the blank document. She gave the copy a quick once over, made a couple of additions and pressed send.

Done! And in under five minutes! Megan shut the laptop, grabbed her fountain pen and opened her notebook. *Okay, let's cast the hell out of these background roles, Megsy*, she thought, flicking through the pile of audition notes. Next to the name Fletcher Castle, Lizzie had written 'Losing the will to live'. For the same kid, Sam had written 'Remember John Travolta in *Look Who's Talking*? This kid makes that performance look like Travolta's professional pinnacle'.

Megan wrote *Townsperson Number Four* next to Fletcher's name.

Five hours later, an exhausted but happy Oscar was sound asleep (his coach had been totally fine with him turning up in his uniform), two loads of washing (including Oscar's footy gear) were hanging on the clothes horse and Megan was typing up the last of her casting notes for Miss Mitchell. She was about to close the laptop and go to bed, when an email from a Chill subscriber, Jenna Christensen, slid across the top of the screen. The first line was visible in its shortened notification form: *I am shocked and disgusted at the callous and nasty …*

What the fuck? Megan frowned. This couldn't be for

her. Jenna Christensen must have sent it to the wrong address. Stupid woman. Still, Megan couldn't push down a rising sense of dread as she clicked on the email.

I am shocked and disgusted at the callous and nasty way you would describe a young innocent child modelling for your company! I, for one, will be unsubscribing from Chill emails, and certainly won't be ordering any items from your business in future.

It only took a few seconds for a grim possibility to dawn on Megan. But no, she couldn't have been so stupid. She scrolled down past the woman's furious reply to her original email, then kept scrolling past the copied and pasted section, and there, right at the bottom of her cheery, *Spring is Almost Here!* update announcing Chill's latest stock and a few choice photos of kids modelling the latest brands, right at the very bottom of the email, at least ten Return key spaces after Megan's signature Chill sign off… was one single incongruous line that read: *Never use that kid again – arrogant little shit and face like a smacked arse.*

There was a sickening thunk in her guts and Megan's blood ran cold as she remembered typing the personal note to herself on a blank document a week ago during a particularly stressful photo shoot; the same blank document she'd come across earlier tonight; the blank document that Megan had copied and pasted her update onto without first scrolling down to check what else might be on there. And now she'd sent this cruel assessment of a five year old (thank Christ she hadn't named the kid!) to every single one of her twenty thousand subscribers.

Ping! Ping! Ping!

As one outraged email after another began appearing in her inbox, Megan slammed her laptop shut and dropped her head in her hands.

Dad came over for a visit. Droning on about I don't know what, when I hear her name. Lizzie Abela. I asked him to tell me again. 'Joel Harkin bumped into Sally Farley at the markets, and she told 'im that Lizzie Abela had delivered her granddaughter a couple of weeks back. Said they saw each other in the hospital when Lizzie came to check on the baby and they had a hug and a catch up, y'know?'

I didn't know. I didn't know any of this. I didn't know hearing her name would make my eyes sting and my shoulders tense. I asked if Sally said how Lizzie's doing. Dad told me Sally said she looked fantastic and that she was really good at her job. Sally's daughter even said that they didn't know how they would've coped without Lizzie as their midwife. The best I could manage upon hearing this was, 'Good old Lizzie Abela.' And that's when Dad rediscovered his old sacks of venom. 'Ah yeah, but that's the thing, isn't it?' He paused. 'She's not Lizzie Abela any more, is she? She's married with a bunch of kids. Apparently, she's shacked up with a builder type who's got 'em a real nice place near her work.' Dad was taking so much pleasure in all these details it was like he was reading me a bedtime story. 'Yeah, looks like good old Lizzie Abela has made quite the life for herself. But I reckon she was always gonna do all right, y'know?' I said I supposed I did know that. 'Yeah, knew when to cut and run.'

I didn't bite. I had in the past. Dad had used the failure of that relationship as ammunition and fodder for a long time. My tolerance was high. I asked which hospital and he told me what Sally told him. I said it must've been such a happy day for Sally and her daughter and their family. I said what a special thing it must be to bring babies into the world and agreed again that Lizzie had done well for herself. And now I know where she works. Lizzie. My Lizzie.

Sam

To: jack_woz_here@hotmail.com
From: samhatfieldchef@bigpond.com
Subject: Cookie Monster

Jesus, calm your farm.

I'm well aware that I didn't treat Sasha – Market Lady, as you so fondly described her – very well. But I'm not a monster. Even if I am, I'm more of a Cookie Monster. HOWEVER, you can call off your dogs, because I went back today after drop-off and apologised. No excuses, just said that I'd been a shithead and was really sorry I'd taken my stress out on her.

She told me a story about a time she yelled at her regular barista after she found out she'd lost a big client – have I told you she used to be in advertising? The barista had asked, 'How's life?' as he often did, and Sasha launched into a tirade about invasive, entitled hipsters who expect everyone to lay their lives bare for all to see and maybe he should just make her fucking double shot macchiato. Later that day, she left work early and caught the barista flipping the *Closed* sign inside the door. Apparently, he looked really scared when he saw her, but Sasha mouthed 'I'm so sorry' through the glass door and the barista smiled, indicated for her to wait, popped behind the counter and brought her a little box of leftover pastries. Sasha was so grateful that she started crying. The barista told her to forget about it. He said it was obvious that she was a good person having a bad day.

Then I gave her one of my leftover coffee crème brûlées. She said thanks, then neither of us said anything. We started looking around and nodding for no reason until Sasha finally spotted something to talk about; a poster for the Baytree concert.

Quick tangent ... rehearsals for the end-of-year Christmas school concert are underway, and Megan's turned into a theatre diva. She's loving it but also seems kind of stressed, but I don't think that's just about the concert. I asked Lizzie and she said Megan had 'work issues'. Also, Megan and I talked briefly about this new teacher, Rick. Lizzie knows him from way back. Apparently, they went on a few dates when they were teenagers. He didn't seem like the kind of guy Lizzie would go for, but hey, maybe in her youth she found disconcertingly intense guys super-hot. Megan thinks he's okay, but I dunno.

Anyway, back to Sasha. She says the play looks like fun and I say something about our esteemed playwright, Megan, not having much experience, and that a bunch of kids told her the play was boring and that they don't know what 'fettered' means. (I told you she's picked Dickens' *A Christmas Carol*, yeah? For *eight year olds*!)

Sasha says she's worked on heaps of campaigns where she's written dialogue and that she'd be happy to help with the school concert script. She doesn't want to step on anyone's toes, but she likes the idea of being part of it.

Then I say that if she's serious I can make a quick call and she says go ahead, so I call Megan and ask if she wants help with the script, and Megan says *good God yes*, she would love Sasha's help!

I tell her about Sasha while Sasha's in front of me, which is the *perfect* way to compliment people to their face without it being weird. Genius move. I say, 'I've only met her a couple of times, but she seems really clever. And funny.' That one backfired, because I blushed and Sasha saw.

Megan says she could meet Sasha in the school hall now if she's free, so I ask Sasha and she says it's quiet and that she can close for an hour. Megan's like, 'Yes, Sam! You bring that clever, funny woman here immediately!'

I hang up and Sasha says she takes the tram to work so I say, 'I can drive you,' followed by, 'Not in an Ivan Milat way.'

Luckily, she laughs and says something about always 'packing heat' and then she closes up and there's a bag over her shoulder and we're walking to my car. It took all of three minutes to get to Baytree, which was good because I felt like I was driving like a fuckwit. I felt really . . . observed. I plugged my phone in and the stereo picked up my Spotify from where it left off, playing 'There She Goes' by The La's. Sasha started singing along, mid-second verse, word perfect. Then I was singing too. We're driving along singing together and the song ends just as we pull up to the school and we laugh at the timing of it, and maybe at the fact that we just had a singalong to some seminal Britpop.

Megan meets Sasha and instantly says she loves her, followed by a brief inquisition about Sasha's knowledge of Dickens. They talk more as they walk into the school hall where Lizzie and Miss Mitchell are flicking through scrapbooks and pinning things on Pinterest like nobody's business. I fade into the background as they discuss the elements of the show, talking about how Megan wants to give all the kids their 'moment' to appease all the parents. And I notice that I'm sitting there smiling. I caught my face in the act, dickhead.

Sasha is flicking through the script and starts suggesting ways to make it more engaging for the kids, all the while complimenting Megan on what a great job she's done. She's good, dickhead. It's easy to imagine her in a boardroom, pitching to some bigwigs for a multi-million-dollar account. Very impressive. At one point she asks how they're going to manage the transitions and how they're planning to break up the scenes.

'How about live music?' I ask out of nowhere.

Megan asks, 'Like what?' and I say I could write some tunes to fill the gaps.

Megan says, '*You* could write some songs?'

I then confess that before I trained to be a chef I played in a few bands. Then the inevitable question comes from Miss Mitchell: 'What was your band called?'

I'm too far gone now so I reel off the names of the bands I was in: *The Nervous Rex, Tequila Mockingbird* and *Your Neighbours' Wives*. That last one got quite the reaction, dickhead. Your idea. And it still gets a reaction.

They all love the idea of live music to accompany the show. I suggest it should be played by the kids, to which Lizzie replies, 'Fuck that noise', which receives applause, including from Miss Mitchell.

Then they agree to explore the idea further and Megan asks if I can write something for her to listen to in the next week. I say yes, neglecting to mention that I haven't picked up my guitar in – oooh – ten years.

At the end of the afternoon I gave Sasha a lift home. She talked about how cool Megan and Lizzie were, and how it's great we're so involved in the school community. I asked Sasha why she gave up advertising. She said it was a stressful, relentless life and she wanted something different.

She made good money so had enough to take a break. And during her break, she decided she'd never go back to advertising. She loved working at the market and getting to know her regulars. I dropped her back at the market, but when I pulled up, neither of us got out. First Aid Kit were still being achingly beautiful and refusing to provide the journey with the musical full stop it needed. Sasha eventually opened the car door and thanked me for getting her involved in the concert. She said it's going to be really fun and that the music was a great idea and she can't wait to hear my songs.

And I could tell she meant it.

On the way home I sang along with every song at full shower volume.

I'm gonna prep tonight's dinner now. I'm trying out this roasted carrot side dish with rose harissa and pomegranate seeds.

Shut up. You'd love it.

S x

To: jack_woz_here@hotmail.com
From: samhatfieldchef@bigpond.com
Subject: Mommie Dearest

Hey dickhead,

I took the kids to visit Mum over the weekend, because I'm a thoughtful son who absolutely doesn't hanker for his mum's long-overdue departure from this mortal coil. After Mum interrogated Lola and Tyler about their professional aspirations and the potential for future drug use in their respective friendship groups, I let the kids take my iPad out to Mum's chair swing on the front porch. It's far and away my favourite thing about visiting Mum: seeing those two smushed together in Mum's big old-fashioned wooden chair swing. With the kids gone, Mum turned the bright, unrelenting interrogation light on to me. I barely let her get three words out when I just let her have it. 'Bridget's gone. She's been cheating on me with the same guy for ages and now she's overseas for work for three months and we're separating. Then we'll get divorced and I'll have the kids most of the time; maybe all of the time. But yeah, she's gone.'

And oh, Jack, the first thing out of my dear mum's mouth was so perfectly her. I had no expectations. I knew I wasn't going to get a hug or a stroke of the hair or – God forbid – an 'Everything will be all right, my darling boy'. I might've still wanted and needed any of those options, but I knew I wasn't going to get them, so what I got was almost a pleasant surprise because it displayed some level of concern. Immediately after I'd told my mother my marriage was over and I would be a single parent, she said, 'But you don't make any money.'

BOOM! Take a bow, Mrs Hatfield. I am giving you a standing ovation for that immaculate piece of parenting. And I did! I literally stood up and started applauding. Mum was so confused and angry, it was beautiful. She kicked off down the 'I just don't know how to talk to you' route, and I suggested she start by trying to *talk* to me, which amplified her confusion and anger. Mostly her anger, which always seems to overtake every other emotion like the fucking Road Runner. Then what came out was that Mum believes that if I'd been 'more of a man' and 'contributed more to the household', Bridget would've had no reason to leave. I emphasised that Bridget left because she'd been having an affair for over a year. Mum's counter-argument to that was to raise her eyebrows and say, 'Maybe he's just more of a man.'

Jack, the only way I could've left any quicker is if I'd pulled the chair swing chains out of the porch roof, strapped it to the top of the car with the kids still in it and driven away. I opened the front door with such force that I gave the kids a fright. Two pairs of eyes darted up from the screen, looking at me like I was a wild pig. I sure as hell felt a bit razorback. Lola asked what was wrong as I marched towards the car and Mum appeared behind us in the doorway. I told Lola that I thought I'd left the oven on so we'd better hurry.

Tyler responded with suitable speed and jumped into the car as I unlocked it. Lola held my hand, which made me slow down a bit so I wouldn't drag her behind me. She put her other hand on my forearm as we reached the car and I looked down at her. She asked if I was okay in a way that proved she knew I wasn't. I diluted my lie just a bit and said I just wanted to get home.

You remember that cul-de-sac in Oakleigh where Mum lives? She's still in the same place, right at the end, so when I park, my car's always facing her front door. When I got in the car, listening to my kids click on their seatbelts and shift their small bodies in their seats to find their sweet spots, I looked up at Mum, framed in the doorway, her arms neatly folded in a victory pose, and I realised in that moment that I never wanted to see her again. Not her, not Bridget. Just my kids. My kids and my friends.

She's right though, the old bitch; I don't make any money. Best sort that out.

S x

PS: I will see Mum again, of course. Can't afford to lose a babysitter in my current single parent status.

Lizzie

'I've made my decision,' Stella announced. 'I want to be Angelica, not Eliza.'

I pulled my head out of the bathroom cabinet and looked up at my daughter. 'Is this like when you made your decision *not* to be in the school play, then decided you *did* want to be in it, after all?'

'No!' Stella was indignant. 'This is not like that! I definitely want to be Angelica.'

I did love that my daughter had decided to dress as a character from a contemporary hip-hop musical that most kids have never heard of for the Halloween parade.

'Good Lord!' I pulled the umpteenth packet of cotton buds from the back of the cabinet. 'We could build a life-sized mammoth skeleton with the number of cotton buds in this cupboard.'

'When can we go shopping?'

'What for?' I asked, dropping the cotton buds into the canvas bag I'd marked 'KEEP'.

Stella sighed the sigh of one who was forced to cohabit with morons. 'For my Angelica Schuyler costume!'

'Oh right, yep.' I had to stop myself from gagging as I pulled a mouldy Wet One out from behind a Codral packet with a 2015 use-by date. 'We'll go after school tomorrow.'

'Thanks, Mum.'

I glanced at the clock. It was just after five. There was no way I'd be finished this before the kids' bedtime. 'Can you bring my phone here so I can call Dad, please?' I said as Stella turned to go. 'He'll have to bring pizza home. I'm gonna be here for a while.'

I'd spent the past few days emptying out, wiping down and culling every single kitchen cupboard, and had now moved on to the over-cluttered bathroom cupboards. Some people go on safari in Africa, or travel around Australia in a Winnebago for their long service leave. Me? I spring clean. My hospital mates had given me a lovely surprise when I'd arrived for my final shift last weekend. Doctors, nurses, my fellow midwives and the admin staff were all waiting in the staffroom and gave a huge cheer as I walked in. When Aileen stepped forward holding a cake with 'Happy Long Service Leave' written on it I'd burst into tears. Damn pre-menstrual hormones.

'Ah, ya silly mare,' Aileen cooed, coming over to hug me. 'We're gonna miss you.'

'I'm gonna miss you too,' I said, even though I hadn't really believed it at the time.

But now, staring into the seedy abyss of a cluttered bathroom cupboard full of foot, face and bum creams that were at least two years past their use-by dates, I missed them all. At least Greg and I were back to normal. Over our picnic at Alma Park, I'd told him the whole truth and nothing but the truth about Rick and our past. Greg listened and made all the right noises in all the right places, and we'd slowly returned to the familiar zone of open communication, mutual trust, weekly love-making and daily piss-taking. The September school holidays had provided a much-needed break from seeing Rick at drop-off every day, and Greg and I had tag-teamed with the kids, with Greg taking the first week off and me working nights the second. During my week, I took the kids for lunches at Abelas a few times, where we'd had to endure long discussions on a potential theme for the Abela family's New Year's Eve celebrations.

'Why are we even talking about New Year's Eve?' I'd finally exploded one afternoon when the kids and I had dropped in for kannoli, only to be dragged into an argument between Dad and Auntie Carmen over whether it should be a Disco or First We Feast theme. 'It's September! And when is it *not* a First We Feast theme at an Abela event, by the way?'

'Never too early to start planning the family event of the year, Lizzie,' Dad said, wagging an icing-sugar-coated finger at me across the table.

My family was obsessed with New Year's Eve. The email trails on where it would be (always Dad's house), who was going to bring what, and what the weather might be that day began expanding in our inboxes by early June. Once upon a time, the Abela siblings had done their own thing on 31 December – the boys went partying, and I was either living overseas or hanging with mates – but we'd slowly begun gravitating back to the family home over the years and looked forward to seeing the new year in together. A barbecue in dad's spacious backyard, with a glass of red in my hand and the kids tucked up in the spare beds by 11 p.m. was far and away the most appealing New Year's Eve option these days. Maybe my resolution this year could be to fork out for a cleaner to deal with my mountain of cotton buds and old bum creams.

***

'Herr Director!' I said.

Megan jumped, dropping a bunch of scripts on the floor.

'Oops, sorry.'

'You're early,' Megan said, glancing at her phone. 'You're never early to rehearsals.'

'I am when I'm not working and in desperate need of escape from the *Hoarders* house I've created.'

Megan either didn't hear my hilarious *Hoarders* comment or chose to ignore it, so I put my bag down and surveyed the empty school hall. It felt wrong being in here without teacher supervision, like the time Melissa and I had snuck into our primary school's empty hall and stolen three bags of snakes from the lolly-drive crates. We ate all three bags between us in less than thirty minutes, then spent the rest of the afternoon in sick bay, wailing in agony, while our classmates sat in the sunshine eating a much more sensible number of snakes. I learnt a big lesson that day: never eat more than one bag of lollies per thirty minutes.

'Can you wait here in case the kids turn up?' Megan said, heading for the door. 'I have to drop Rebecca's costume notes into Penny, then I need to talk to the grade-three teachers about props.'

'Who's Rebecca?'

'Nate's mum.' Megan made a face as if I'd asked her who Madonna was. 'She's in charge of the set and costumes. I met her for coffee last week to talk about it.'

Since when did Megan meet *other* mums for coffee? I was her only school mum friend as far as I knew. 'Oh, cool,' I said, trying to hide my childish jealousy.

'And Sasha sent through a few more changes to the script last night,' Megan was saying now, 'so I'll go to the office and print them out and ask Karen in the office to email Lisa the new script.'

I'd almost forgotten Lisa Mitchell worked at the school

to be honest. Even when she did show up, she was distracted and all but useless. Sam and I had been helping out as much as we could – and I had to admit it, it was fun – but Megan was doing the lion's share and was obviously relishing her volunteer role. She was the one running lines with the kids and explaining what the story was about, while all Sam and I did was prompt them when they needed it, or help herd the background kids on and off. Sam also spent a bit of time mucking around on his guitar and jotting down chords, and whenever Sasha showed up his little face lit up like a Dickensian Christmas tree. It was good seeing him look so happy after all the shit he'd been through.

Megan picked up another bunch of scripts and added them to the growing pile under her arm. 'Lisa won't be here today or Friday, so I've told Penny I'll work out blocking for the middle section this week.'

I frowned at my flustered friend, standing in the school hall, surrounded by scripts and lists of kids' names and to-do tasks. 'Umm ... you are aware that you don't actually *work* for this school, aren't you?' I teased. 'Or are you giving up your business to move into the lucrative primary school theatre sector?'

Megan was instantly defensive. 'What?'

'I just mean ... well, you're pretty much doing everything and ...'

'Maybe I want to,' Megan shot back. 'Maybe I'm enjoying doing something for other people. If that makes me sad and pathetic then I'm sorry.'

'Hang on!' I held my hands up. 'I didn't say anything about sad or pathetic!'

'That's what you were implying,' Megan said, one eyebrow raised.

'What are you *talking* about?' How had the conversation taken this turn? 'You just seem a bit obsessive about it and really, who cares? It's only a school play. It's not like real work. You're overloaded – look what happened with that Chill subscriber email.'

'That was one mistake, and I dealt with it,' Megan snapped. 'I don't need your judgey opinions about this, Lizzie. I may not have four kids or do shift work, but I can handle more than one thing at a time! And I *like* being busy! Just because you don't want to do anything out of your comfort zone doesn't mean I don't!'

Megan stormed out of the hall and I stood there, my mouth hanging open and my heart racing. I hated confrontation, but especially with Megan – someone I never dreamt could be that furious with me. Had I been judgey? I know I'd been accused of it in the past. I should have just shut up for once and not pissed off one of my closest friends. All because of my own stupid issues around volunteering for the school. Melissa's fifteen-year-old face appeared in my mind as I remembered doing a similar thing with her – making fun of her when she offered to help the Sisters with their Saturday morning cake stall at the local market.

'Why does it matter to you if I help them?' she said after I'd laughed and called her a suck up. 'Does it make you feel cooler because you're not wasting your time with some daggy old nuns?'

I'd felt like a terrible person then, and an even more terrible one now that I was an adult and couldn't dismiss my actions as the folly of youth.

'Hey!'

Oh good. Another reminder of my impeccable track record of good behaviour.

'Hey Rick, I said.'

'Is Megan around?'

'She'll be back soon.' I suddenly felt uncomfortable alone in a big empty space with him. 'Can I give her a message?'

'Just wanted to let her know that I can help out with rehearsals from next week onwards,' he said. 'I've been flat out with this PD course but that finished yesterday. Penny thought it would be good to have another teacher around since Lisa is away so much at the moment.'

Of all the teachers in the school, Penny had to ask Rick Cooke to help with the bloody show. 'Okay, I'll tell her.'

'Should be fun,' Rick said with a grin. 'And I promise not to bust out any more Taylor Swift. Total professional from here on.'

I smiled, remembering his daggy dancing and wondered if this might be a good thing, after all. Maybe we could finally get past our awkwardness and just be a parent and a teacher who were working on a school production together. I might not tell Greg, though. There was no need. It wasn't as if I'd be keeping a secret from him or anything, it was just easier. *Yes, you just keep telling yourself that*, a little voice whispered in my ear. *Shut up*, I told the voice.

I nodded at Rick. 'Great!'

Megan

Megan closed her front door and sagged against it. All the anger was gone, and she just felt sad. *Why did I snap at Lizzie like that?* she thought. She was only making a joke, like she had a thousand times before. All I had to say was, 'Oh yeah, didn't I tell you? I'm an official Baytree employee now, on the payroll and everything!' Then Lizzie would have made another crack about nurses and teachers being underpaid, and everything would have been fine.

Instead, Megan had taken it seriously, and as a result, the rehearsal had been agonising. Sam hadn't been there to act as a buffer, and it was strained and awkward between them. They avoided eye contact with each other as they told the kids to 'stand there', 'walk there' and use their 'outside voices'. Finally, rehearsals were over, and Megan made a beeline for her car, unable to even glance in Lizzie's direction. Thank God Bryce was picking Oscar up from school and having him overnight. She clearly wasn't in any mental state to be dealing with a child tonight and would probably yell at her son for using the wrong coloured Lego.

As she wandered through the empty house and into the kitchen, Megan wondered if she was losing the plot, as Lizzie had inferred. Her life had definitely taken a turn for the bizarre ever since she'd responded to that bloody tweet and attended Henry's funeral. And despite what she'd told Lizzie, she had totally fucked things up on the work front lately. Ever since the copy and paste incident two months ago, Megan had been in full damage control with her Chill subscribers. She'd sent out a formal apology, making up some bullshit story about her 'six-year-old son getting to her computer and adding the offensive comments without her knowledge', but it hadn't made much of a difference and pinning the blame for her unprofessionalism on Oscar was not a huge step in the 'Good Person' direction she'd been trying to move in. Henry would be so proud.

Megan had lost more than five thousand subscribers after that email, and a chunk of Instagram followers too. She'd also forgotten to put in a large summer stock order last month, which put the delivery date back and guaranteed her customers wouldn't get their new funky bathers and summer dresses in time to hit the kiddie pools. So, not a great few weeks on the business front, which was why Lizzie's comment had touched a nerve. It had reminded Megan what a terrible person she was.

But helping out with the play and stepping up to fill Miss Mitchell's shoes ... surely those were good, worthwhile things that balanced the scales a bit? she wondered as she absentmindedly put the morning's dirty bowls and plates into the dishwasher. And although most of the kids were woeful in the play, some of them were good. Like Stella. Thank God she'd changed her mind and decided to do the play, after all. Lola was also fantastic, but then again, she *was* living out her fantasy – speaking nineteenth-century dialogue out loud and not getting teased for it. Lola had complained so much after Sasha had modernised the script that Megan had allowed her to continue saying her original lines instead of the twenty-first-century adaptation.

But Aiden was Megan's favourite. He was doing such

an awesome job as Scrooge that Megan felt real pride whenever she watched him stomp across the stage, shaking his tiny fist and barking at everyone. The first time he did it, she, Sam and Lizzie clutched each other in delight, then demanded that everyone give him a round of applause for his projection and characterisation. The look of delight on Aiden's freckled face had stayed with Megan for the rest of the day and, for the first time, she felt like she was making a difference. She'd never experienced that kind of gratification in her work, regardless of profit margins or social media profile.

That night she'd gone home and googled 'New Career Woman Mid-Thirties'. Out of the six million or so results, most just told her to 'Be Practical' and 'Have a mental picture of achieving your goal!' But Megan didn't know what her goal was. She knew she was ready to move on to something new, she just had no idea what that was. She had no qualifications, no degree and no passion for anything specific. It was the sort of conversation she might want to have with Lizzie, but obviously that wasn't going to be an option anytime soon.

The doorbell chimed. Probably Bryce because Oscar had forgotten his footy boots again. But when she pulled open the door it was Lizzie who greeted her instead.

'Glass of wine?' Lizzie said, holding up a bottle. 'Oh well if you insist ... Or do you still hate me?'

Lizzie banged her hand down on the arm of the couch in excitement. 'There are heaps of things you could do!' Megan had filled Lizzie in on her late-night Google searches, and was bemoaning the fact that there was nothing out there for a 35-year-old woman with no qualifications or experience in anything other than kids' fashion.

'Like what?' Megan asked, picking up her third dumpling and popping it in her mouth whole.

'High-class escort?'

Megan almost choked, then leant across the coffee table and whacked a grinning Lizzie on her outstretched leg. The night was turning out to be one of the best Megan could remember. Surprising when she considered how miserable she'd been feeling before Lizzie invited herself in two hours ago. Before she'd even crossed the threshold the two women were simultaneously apologising and forgiving each other. Soon after that they'd ordered dumplings, cracked open a bottle of Shiraz and settled in for a good old-fashioned deep and meaningful. Lizzie was now stretched out on the couch, while Megan sat cross-legged on the floor as they stuffed themselves with dumplings and fried rice.

'Will Greg mind you abandoning him on a week night?'

'Nah!' Lizzie said, soaking her dumpling in soy sauce. 'Technically, I'm on holidays, so he encourages this kind of behaviour. And it's Wednesday, which means no extra-curricular activities to juggle. He just has to feed them and get them into bed.'

It occurred to Megan that this was the first time since she'd been in this house that she'd had a friend over. No great surprise considering that she was sorely lacking in the friends department, but the thought stung.

'I can't believe we haven't done this before,' Lizzie said, reading Megan's mind. 'Wine and takeaway on a week night.'

'One of us is usually working,' Megan said and shrugged. 'Or driving our kids all over Melbourne.'

'True that,' Lizzie agreed. 'But we should make an effort to do this, like, once a month.'

'You're on!' They clinked glasses and warm tingles ran through Megan's body. It would be nice to do this on a regular basis. Really nice.

'Which means I have to be a bitch to you every month,' Lizzie said, 'so I have an excuse to come over and apologise.'

'I was the one being super-sensitive,' Megan said, leaning back against the armchair. 'And you were right, it's only a school play.'

'No!' Lizzie fixed Megan with a fierce look. 'I *wasn't* right. It was a stupid thing to say. What you're doing is amazing. We're all in awe of you.'

'Bullshit.'

'We are!' Lizzie cried. 'Sam and I say it all the time. Even Rick told me today how much the kids are loving it.'

Megan had been waiting for the right time to bring Rick up and this was the perfect opportunity. 'Is it weird being around him?' she asked tentatively. 'You know, because you dated when you were younger?'

Lizzie blushed and stared into her wine.

'I mean, I'd feel weird if an ex-boyfriend of mine suddenly showed up,' Megan continued, not wanting to upset her friend twice in one day. 'Even if it was only a couple of dates a million years ago. Especially a cutie like Rick.'

Lizzie looked up and sighed. 'You up for another bottle?'

Lying in bed that night, Megan couldn't stop thinking about what Lizzie had told her. Despite Lizzie's fears, Megan's opinion of her friend hadn't changed once she knew the truth. God no. The girl had only been twenty-two years old, for Christ's sake!

'Do you think less of me?' Lizzie covered her face and peeked out through her fingers.

'Not possible,' Megan said, shrugging. 'Never thought much of you to begin with.'

The only thing Megan felt for Lizzie was sympathy. It must have been so stressful when Rick turned up at school like that. No wonder she'd handled it so badly with Greg. Megan couldn't imagine having to confess to your husband of twelve years that you were once engaged and ran out on your 'Big Wog Wedding', as Lizzie had described it.

This was one of the many details Megan kept turning over in her mind as she lay listening to the late-night trams rattling along Carlisle Street. Imagine having to let all those people down? The courage it must have taken to run out on something that huge! *Jesus*, Megan thought, *you'd have to have been deeply unhappy to go to those lengths.*

'But you don't still have feelings for him now, do you?' Megan had asked, needing to know if her suspicions were right.

'What?' Lizzie baulked. 'Not at *all*!'

'It's just that I've seen you guys laughing and talking together at rehearsals.' Megan was treading carefully. 'I thought it might have been bringing up old feelings for you.'

'I guess that's guilt.' Lizzie looked ashamed all of a sudden. 'I did a terrible thing to him and now, well, I don't know ... I guess I'm just overcompensating. But maybe I should tone it down. I'd hate to give him the wrong idea.'

'I'm sure you're not,' Megan said, only half-convinced but feeling better knowing Lizzie was aware now. 'Plus, he's married with two kids himself! Anyway, he must have known, even back then, that you weren't ever really in love with him.'

'I did love him at first,' Lizzie said. 'But it was that all-consuming teenage love that fills you up and makes you crazy for a while, until it fizzles out and leaves you feeling more like mates. You remember those kind of teen romances.'

Megan had nodded as if she understood. But the truth was she'd never had that kind of love, and certainly not as a teenager. Boys were either intimidated by her, or acted like total sleazebags around her. And although there was a lot of sexual chemistry with Bryce in the early days, she wasn't sure she'd ever felt true, all-consuming love for him either.

Megan meant it when she said she didn't want a partner, but after tonight she couldn't help thinking how lucky Lizzie had been. Lizzie had known deep love at least twice, maybe even three times – if you counted the Durham arsehole – in her life. Yet, here Megan was, thirty-five years old with her heart never broken, perfectly intact. Maybe even untouched.

A week later, Megan walked into the school office to find a man talking to Karen, the receptionist. She could tell how insanely expensive his suit was, even from the back, and there was something familiar about his shaggy hairstyle.

'If Penny Guthrie isn't around, can I speak with a Megan Wylie?'

'I'm Megan.'

The man turned and Megan recognised him immediately. 'Hi, my name's Eddie Paterson, I'm ...'

'Henry's grandson.' How the hell had she remembered that?

Eddie looked equally as shocked. 'You knew my grandpa?'

'Not as well as I would have liked to,' Megan admitted.

Karen cleared her throat. 'Mr Paterson wanted to speak to you about ...'

'Yes, thank you.' Eddie gave Karen a tight smile. 'I can explain. Megan, can we talk outside?'

'Sure.'

Karen appeared to be having some kind of silent attack. Her eyes were wide, and she was jiggling her eyebrows up and down at Megan, mouthing something that looked like *not happy.* Or it could have been *no nappy*. It was hard to tell. Megan frowned and shook her head, making it clear she had absolutely no idea what the receptionist was trying to tell her, before following Eddie down the front steps of the school.

'So, what's up?' Megan asked Eddie's back. It really was a lovely suit.

Eddie turned on her, his eyes glinting angrily. 'What's "up" is that my grandfather dedicated years of his life to volunteering at this school,' he hissed at a startled Megan, 'and then my family finds out that you intend to repay him for that loyalty by portraying him as a selfish, uncaring miser! The exact opposite of who he was!'

Megan blinked.

'We all saw that post you wrote about Grandpa months ago,' Eddie continued, 'but now you go aligning him with a character like Ebenezer Scrooge?'

Megan finally found her voice. 'No, of course not!'

'That's what my sister heard.'

'Well, your sister needs to get her hearing checked!'

Eddie blanched. 'Excuse me?'

'I don't know where your sister got her information,' Megan said as calmly as she could, 'but we are *not* comparing your grandfather to Ebenezer Scrooge!'

'Then why ...?'

'We're dedicating the show to his *memory*,' Megan continued, 'and if you've ever read the play, you'll know that it's about community. Forgiveness, compassion, family ... those are the themes in *A Christmas Carol*, which is why I chose it, because they were all so important to Henry!'

Jesus, she sounded like an English lit teacher, but she was on a roll now. 'It's *us*, the Baytree community, that's Scrooge, not Henry! *We're* the selfish ones.' She was shaking. Actually shaking. Maybe Lizzie had been right about her becoming obsessive about this play. If Eddie's expression was anything to go by, she had. 'Sorry, I get a bit passionate about this whole thing.'

'I can see that,' Eddie said. 'Want to get a coffee?'

'Sorry?'

'I don't have to be at work for another hour or so,' he said, glancing at the phone in his hand. 'I thought maybe we could get a coffee and you could tell me a bit more about this concert you're so passionate about.'

Megan hesitated. She had to reply to a bunch of emails, unpack a stock delivery and speak to Penny about next week's rehearsal schedule.

'Let's go.'

He's just a normal bloke. No doubt that's how he's been described his whole adult life. He's probably always taken it as intended, as a compliment. But it's not. It's a friendly way of saying he's boring. He seems boring to me. A man of simple tastes. Boring. A meat-and-three-veg kind of guy. Boring. Knows his way around Bunnings. Boring. I'm being mean, but I'm not wrong.

He walked straight up to me before school this morning, shook my hand and introduced himself. He shook my hand for a bit too long. His grip was overly firm, but that's typical Australian male, so didn't bug me. He asked a couple of questions about the school and the job, then said something about the weather and how it could affect his current work. I had to swallow two yawns in the two minutes we spoke.

I just don't see how Greg could be a match for Lizzie. What does she get from him intellectually? I can't imagine good old reliable Greg chewing the fat about the deeper meaning of life or the nature of being. Poor guy's head might explode.

So, what does she get from him?

Loyalty, maybe. Stability? No fuss, almost certainly.

I never saw Lizzie as a woman who would settle. And she should never have had to.

Sam

To: jack_woz_here@hotmail.com
From: samhatfieldchef@bigpond.com
Subject: Avengers can blow me

Hey dickhead,

No, I haven't seen the latest *Avengers* movie, nor have I seen any of the previous 328 *Avengers* movies. I'm saving them for when I'm in palliative care.

Speaking of bad ideas, Lola has some corkers for her birthday party. She wants to do a bunch of weird nineteenth-century parlour games, inspired by the Brontë sisters. My favourite is a game called Puss Puss in the Corner. No, I'm not going to describe the rules to you. I'll just leave that game name in your capable hands and you can imagine what you will. I can't exactly tell my daughter that she may well be committing social suicide at her own party, and I want to encourage her ideas because it's her party, but holy shit. I'm going to have to get the attention of a bunch of eight-year-old girls and announce that 'It's time to play Puss Puss in the Corner!'

I can already see the tumbleweed rolling across the living-room floor.

But it's her birthday, so I'll make it work. If nothing else, we'll all laugh about it in ten years, during very expensive therapy.

I dropped the kids to Mum's for a couple of hours last night so I could do a big food shop, mainly because Mum's been guilting me about not getting to see them enough. I didn't want to deprive her of time with her only grandkids, and they love her because they're small, ignorant people. I don't think it's my job to tell them their granny is a toxic tsunami of negativity.

But I think they've now got their own inkling of that. When I arrived to pick them up, Mum answered the door, her head already shaking and her eyes full of disappointment. Lola was crying on the couch, and Tyler was sitting cross-legged in front of the TV staring at the floor. When I asked what happened, she said, 'Well, I thought they knew, so I just asked them how they were coping.'

'Coping with what?' I asked, hoping she hadn't done what I knew she'd done.

'Well, their mother leaving them, Samuel.'

I scooped Lola up off the couch. Her fingers dug into my ribs. I told Tyler we were going. He got up and walked to me, his eyes fixed to the floor. I looked at Mum, but I couldn't say anything because my kids were right there, needing me.

I know what you're going to say, and yes, I probably should have told them the whole truth earlier. They knew Bridget was overseas, I did tell them that, but I didn't say she wouldn't be coming back to live with us. I was still trying to find the words. Maybe I just wanted to delay their heartbreak for as long as possible.

I did okay in the car. Lola's crying had subsided, and she and Tyler were staring out their windows. I told them Granny is bonkers and doesn't know what she's talking about. I said their mum loves them more than anything.

Tyler asked, 'Is Mummy coming back?'

'Yes,' I said. 'Of course. You know what it's like with Mummy's work.'

Then Lola chimed in with, 'You're staying with us though, even if Mother isn't?'

We were only a couple of minutes from home, but I pulled over, killed the engine, took off my seatbelt and climbed into the backseat.

It was a very uncoordinated move and the kids got a kick out of it. I plonked myself between them and wrapped them in a double headlock. I told them that there's nothing in this universe that could take me away from them. I kissed their heads and told them they're well and truly stuck with me.

Lola asked if 'Mother' would be at her party. I told her she would try her best. Lola said, 'That means no.'

Then Tyler said, 'I need to wee.'

So, I clambered back into the driver's seat, clipped myself in and started the car, looking in the rear-view mirror at my kids, who were trying with all their might to be okay.

It struck me then that we're all in the same boat. And I have to be the captain and lead the way, back to okay.

S x

Lizzie

I wasn't lying. When Megan asked if I could meet her before drop-off to talk costumes and I said I was 'meeting a friend for coffee', *technically* I was.

Some people might dispute my use of the word 'friend' when referring to a person I'd once had a long-term relationship with and was, okay, engaged to for over a year, but *technically* I was telling the truth. Rick was sitting at a table in the front window of Follow the Leader. It was the closest café to school, and the first place I'd thought of when he asked if we could meet so I could bring him up to speed on the play. Guilt was the reason I'd said yes. Plain old guilt. Compensating because I wanted forgiveness and absolution. I didn't want to be the evil woman who broke his heart. It was ridiculous, really, because that's what I was. What was I expecting? Did I think that if I said yes to coffee, and laughed at his jokes, that he'd understand why I left him at the altar? That he'd forgive me? From what I'd seen, Rick was the more mature of us. He'd moved on, found a woman who wouldn't rip his heart out and had two perfect children (perfect in my mind as they were OPT – Other People's Children), yet here I was still acting like a nervous and needy teenager. *Please forgive me. Please say something to make me feel better about myself, because obviously it's all about me!*

'I don't want to hassle Megan,' he'd said. 'She's got a lot on her plate.'

I frowned when I noticed him looking at a menu. He'd said *coffee*. Everyone knew having coffee with someone was completely innocent and justified when discussing school matters. If we ate a meal together, did that make it less innocent?

'Hello!'

'Hey Rick.'

Ash appeared and nudged me with his bony hip. 'Morning, luv.'

'Good morning, young Ashley.'

Ash had owned and run Follow the Leader ever since I started drinking coffee there five years ago. A handsome thirty-something with spiky brown hair and smooth baby skin, he always wore a T-shirt and shorts, regardless of the weather, and was a gifted barista, even by Melbourne standards.

'This is my friend, Rick,' I said, gesturing across the table. 'He's a teacher at Baytree.'

Ash frowned and glanced at his watch. 'Shouldn't you be at work?' he asked Rick.

'The grade-five and -six kids have Districts this morning,' Rick said. 'So this falls under my term-planning time.'

'I hope you're whipping those slack-arse Baytree parents into shape,' Ash said, flicking my leg with his pad, 'including Lazy Lizzie here.'

Rick laughed. 'Doing my best!'

'I'll have you know,' I said, turning on Ash, 'that I'm now volunteering on the school concert.'

Ash scoffed. 'Bullshit.'

'I am!'

'What are they paying you?'

'Um, nothing ... hence the word *volunteer*.'

Ash shook his head. 'Someone must have something over you,' he said. 'There's no way you'd be doing it otherwise.'

I stared at him for a moment. 'I promised Stella,' I admitted.

Rick and Ash both laughed.

'Knew it,' Ash said smugly. 'So, flat white for you, Lizzie, and what can I get you, mate?'

'Soy latte, thanks.'

'Too easy.'

I cocked my head at Rick as Ash walked away. 'Soy?' I asked.

'Yep.' He nodded. 'Can't do cow's milk any more.'

'Well, look at you,' I teased. 'The boy who held the club record for drinking five banana milkshakes in a day is now lactose-intolerant.'

Rick shuddered. 'That kind of behaviour may well have been the reason I stopped drinking milk,' he said. 'Talk about a cast-iron teenage gut.'

'Actually, you were pretty sick.' I laughed. 'Spent the night with your head in a bucket in Abelas' kitchen.'

'Serves me right.'

'I remember Dad yelling at you, "You spew on my floor, you *out*!"'

He chuckled. 'I do remember that.' He shook his head. 'Your dad put up with a lot from us. Traipsing through Abelas with our muddy soccer boots after training.'

'He loved it.'

'He's a good man, Joseph.'

'Did you see him much? After ...' My voice trailed off and I stared at Rick, mortified. *Fuck!* Why would I bring that up? Here we were chatting happily about milkshakes and soccer, and I go and mention the unmentionable. But Rick didn't seem fazed in the slightest.

'A few times,' he said, nodding. 'Then I went to college and moved away so, y'know ...'

Our coffees landed on the table with perfect timing.

'Enjoy,' Ash said, before moving away to clear a table in the back.

'So, what does your wife do?' *Nice, Lizzie. Extremely smooth segue.*

'Marketing,' Rick said, going along with my abrupt change of subject.

'Oh, right.' Part of me was desperate to address the elephant in the café, but I couldn't bring myself to shatter the veneer we'd established with our first conversation all those months ago. Best to stick to a safe line of questioning.

'Where do your kids go?'

'A school over the other side.'

'In Williamstown?'

'No. Northside. Thornbury.' His voice seemed colder suddenly, and he avoided eye contact for the first time since I'd sat down. Clearly he had no desire to discuss his family with me. Fair enough.

A gust of cold air hit my bare neck as the door opened and someone came in behind me.

'Hey, should we order?' His voice sounded warm again and I was so relieved that I decided the least I could do was have a meal with the guy. It wasn't a candle-lit dinner for God's sake. Just breakfast.

'The Eggs Benny here is really good.'

'Bullshit!'

'I am!'

'What are they paying you?' Auntie Carmen said.

'You make me sound like some kind of mercenary arsehole,' I complained. 'You do know that I spend my life pulling babies out of women's vaginas and making sure all parties stay alive? I'm not selling blood diamonds for a living.'

'Calm down.' Auntie Carmen laughed. 'It's not that you're not a good person ...'

'Gee, thanks!'

It was Sunday afternoon, over a week since my breakfast meeting (not date) with Rick, and Auntie Carmen and I were in the kitchen, attempting to stick sixty-six candles into Dad's birthday cake, which was taking a lot longer than expected. The rest of the Abela clan were out in the restaurant, making the sort of noise usually reserved for European football finals. Joey and Lucas were leading the pack at the back table, shouting at each other and a handful of the kids as they played a rowdy card game of Speed. Luckily, Dad had closed the restaurant for the day as I couldn't imagine customers wanting to hear 'Such a cheat!' and 'I wasn't ready!' screamed across the room as they ate their lunch. Greg had gone off to quote a job, so was missing this week's Abela gathering.

'Oh damn, I'm working!' he'd said, throwing his hands up and groaning in mock dismay when he saw *Dad's Birthday Lunch* on the kitchen calendar.

'You sound devastated,' I said, glancing up from chopping veggies and giving him a wry stare.

He put his arms around me. 'Can you please photograph and video *every* moment for me?'

'Sure.' I wrapped my arms around his neck. 'I'll even get Rosa to tag you in the fifty thousand photos she shares to Facebook during the actual event.'

'Please don't. I am sorry I can't be there for your dad, though.'

'I know.' I'd given him a quick peck on the lips, which developed into a much longer peck, and we might have gotten a wee bit carried away if Stella hadn't walked into the kitchen at that moment.

'Don't mind me,' she'd said, grabbing an apple from the fruit bowl. 'I'm just going back to my room to throw up.'

Greg and I had been in a kind of honeymoon period ever since our Alma Park picnic, and it wasn't waning. Quick gropes as we passed each other in the hallway, long kisses on the couch after the kids went to bed, and better-than-ever sex, which was saying something. I hadn't told Greg I'd met Rick for coffee, or that we were hanging out at rehearsals, because there didn't seem any point. I hadn't told Auntie Carmen about reconnecting with Rick yet either. I wanted to ease her into it by mentioning my volunteer work on the school play first. The woman was in her late sixties and I didn't want to bring on a stroke.

Max and Marcus poked their heads into the kitchen. 'When are we having cake?'

'When it's ready!' Auntie Carmen shouted. 'Out!'

'You better not be wasting seven boxes of candles on that cake!' Dad called from the restaurant, where he was doing the old horsey-falling-through-the-legs bit on Alex, who was scream-giggling with delight. 'Those things not cheap!'

They really are, Dad.

'We're not!' I called back, trying to find room on the chocolate mud cake for the last few. 'Didn't Dad tell you not to put the exact number of candles on his cake?'

Auntie Carmen shrugged. 'Of course.'

'Evil woman.' I grinned.

'What's taking so long?' Christopher yelled. 'Dad's gonna be eighty soon!'

'You wanna come in here and do it?' I shouted back.

'She's ready!' Auntie Carmen said, sliding the final candle into the smooth shiny icing. 'Let's light her up!'

'You got a flame thrower?'

It took at least another four minutes to light all sixty-six candles, and by the time we were done, the entire family was chanting '*We want cake!*', which morphed into '*Happy birthday to you ...*' as we entered, carrying the cake between us.

There was the usual bedlam of bowls and spoons being passed around as Rosa sliced the cake and handed it out to everyone. I squeezed in beside Lucas and Poppy at the far end of the table and was reminded of my thirteenth birthday when I'd also had a chocolate mud cake (with way less candles). At least half the faces around the table were the same too. There was one face missing, though.

'You okay?' Lucas asked. 'You were on another planet there for a second.'

I dug my tiny fork into the cake. 'I was thinking about Melissa.'

'Melissa Morton?' Lucas said. 'I still see her down the shops or walking her dog around the park.'

'Yeah, I saw her there a few months ago too.'

'You say hi?'

'Nah,' I said, shrugging. 'Bit weird ... y'know.'

'Yeah, right.'

'Her kids go to our old school,' I said, watching Archie

take a second slice of cake. 'It's their fete today. I saw it on Facebook.'

'You should go.'

'Nah.'

He gave me a gentle nudge. 'You should go.'

And it suddenly felt as if Lucas had given me the permission I'd been seeking, so I finished my cake and informed the clan that I had 'a few errands to run over this side of town'. The kids stayed to play with their cousins, and I headed out the door and towards my old school with absolutely no plan whatsoever.

I could hear the tinny pop music blasting out of the grounds from a block away and slowed my pace. I comforted myself with the fact that it was mid-afternoon, so Melissa might've already left, and even if she was still there, the chances of finding her in the crowd were slim. I'd more than likely end up heading back to Abelas without a story for my little brother. Rounding the corner, I could see the grounds of my old primary school heaving with people, stalls, rides and food trucks. There was a stage set up at the far end of the playground where some kind of children's hip-hop dance group were busting some impressive moves. Not much had changed in thirty-something years: the red-brick wall with its white targets, where Melissa, the boys and I had played endless hours of downball; the low wooden log benches lining the oval where Melissa and I had shared numerous packets of salt-and-vinegar chips; even the portable classroom, where I'd murdered the *M*A*S*H* theme on recorder, was still standing. For someone who lived in a suburb that was forever being upgraded and 'reinvigorated', it was refreshing to see the structures of my childhood still very much intact.

'Lizzie?'

No fucking way.

'Oh my God,' I gasped.

Melissa was standing right in front of me, looking as shocked as I felt. Out of the hundreds – literally hundreds – of people at this fete, Melissa Morton – wearing jeans, white runners and an orange high-vis vest over a black hoodie and a badge that read: *Here to Help!* – had found me before I'd even taken five steps into the school.

Up close I could see there were more lines around her eyes, and grey flecks at the roots of her shoulder-length fair hair, but otherwise she looked almost exactly the same as when I'd last stood this close to her twenty years ago. That fair skin, the freckles across her nose and that one crooked bottom tooth that always looked to me like it was leaning over to tell the other tooth a secret.

I instinctively stepped forward to pull her in for a hug, but she stepped back and frowned. 'What are you doing here?'

My heart sank. This was worse than I'd imagined. She hated me. 'I was just at Dad's birthday lunch and I ...'

What should I say? That I'd been stalking her on Facebook and knew she'd be here?

'... I saw there was a fete so thought I'd check it out, maybe bring the kids down.'

'Oh, right.'

The silence between us seemed to drown out the surrounding din as I stared into her bright-green eyes. Eyes that seemed so cold and distant to me now.

'So, you have kids?'

'Yep, two.' She was looking around now, desperate for an excuse to escape this torturous and awkward encounter. 'You?'

'Four.'

She gave a short laugh, but her eyes stayed cold. 'Wow. You must be a fucking saint.'

'Well, you know that's not true.'

The sentence hung in the air for a moment too long. I couldn't stand it for a second longer. I had to make this right. 'Hey, can we go sit down and …?'

'*Melissa!*' A small blonde woman in an identical high-vis vest ran up looking distraught. 'The canteen has run out of gold coins,' she panted. 'Can you go and get some bags from the office and take them over there ASAP? The line is around the building!'

'Sure,' Melissa said, looking relieved.

The woman nodded frantically, then scuttled away to find something else to stress about.

'Gotta go.'

Don't go! I don't want to lose you again! I wanted to scream.

'Yeah, of course.'

She barely gave me another glance as she turned and hurried away to join her real friends.

Megan

Megan was stressing about the fact that it was less than a month until the concert as she pulled up for Wednesday's rehearsal. The days and weeks had been rushing by in a blur of rehearsals, drop-offs, pick-ups, footy training, footy games, Applewood visits and work, and she couldn't believe it was coming up so soon. *Tell the kids to know all their lines by next week*, Megan thought as she climbed out of the car and looked across the schoolyard – a sea of blue as the Baytree kids made the most of the last ten minutes of lunchtime. Rehearsals were usually held during lunch, but with the show only a few weeks away now, the teachers had added an extra rehearsal per week during class time. Megan was happy with how rehearsals were going, although there were still days when she had frequent urges to pull her hair out.

'You have to speak up!' she'd said at least a dozen times to at least a dozen kids. 'No one in the audience will hear you!'

'If they say the right words in the right order, we're all winners,' Lizzie frequently reminded her.

Sasha had turned out to be their saviour. The clever writer had managed to adapt Dickens' play into twenty-first-century contemporary dialogue, while maintaining the essence of the story.

'She's done such a fantastic job,' Megan whispered to Sam one day as they watched Sasha explaining pudding and chestnuts to the kid playing Tiny Tim.

'Yeah, she's pretty amazing,' Sam agreed, gazing adoringly at the pretty brunette as he strummed his guitar.

'You should ask her out for coffee.'

'I dunno,' Sam said.

Megan and Lizzie were desperate for Sam to ask Sasha out. It was obvious to both of them that Sam liked the writer, who reminded Megan of a young Jennifer Jason Leigh, without the *Single White Female* psycho tendencies.

They'd unanimously decided that Sam should provide musical accompaniment to selected scenes with his guitar, but Megan had noticed him jotting words down on a notepad as he strummed, and suspected he was writing songs too.

'Definitely the sign of a man in love,' she told Lizzie.

Lizzie was relishing her role as Dramaturg/Assistant Director, although she told Megan that even though she googled 'Dramaturg', she still didn't know what it meant. In typical Lizzie fashion, she'd taken to her new duties with vigour, often shouting directions at the kids in the middle of a scene.

'*Aiden!* You're supposed to look scared when you see Jacob Marley, not like you just bumped into your mates at the skate park! *Gemma!* I've seen scarier ghosts in Pac Man! *Kyle and Molly!* You're supposed to be creepy ghost kids; you're not auditioning for *Project Runway*! *STELLA!* If you keep twirling that plait, I'm going to cut it off!'

Far from being upset by Lizzie's manner, the kids seemed to love it.

'Stella's mum never shouts at me,' Megan overheard a mournful Rocco complaining to Gemma one afternoon. 'I want her to say funny things to me too.'

Megan loved the bi-weekly rehearsals. They gave her

a buzz she could never have imagined for doing a job she wasn't even being paid for. And Miss Mitchell was enormously grateful to have a smart, enthusiastic parent like Megan giving up her free time to do the job she *was* being paid for. The drama teacher spent most of the rehearsal time (when she was there) doing other work on her laptop or running off to take calls from her ailing father. This suited Megan, as her megalomania seemed to have gone into overdrive. She was revelling in her role and had confessed as much to Eddie in a text a few days ago.

M – Think I'm turning into a control freak monster director.

E – Well, at least you're not throwing fake birds at the kids' heads!

M – No birds in Christmas Carol. Just a dead goose on the Cratchit's dinner table.

E – Hitchcock! Throwing birds at Tippi Hedren!

M – WTF??

E – Jesus wept. I'm taking you to the Hitchcock marathon at the Astor next month.

M – I'll have to check my schedule.

E – My shout.

M – I'm in!

She wasn't quite sure how it had happened, but since their short coffee date, Megan and Eddie had become texting buddies. He travelled interstate for work a lot, so Megan hadn't seen him since they exchanged phone numbers outside the café, but they'd been texting on a regular basis.

Megan had told herself that the communication between Eddie and her was part of keeping Henry's family in the loop. However, in the last week she'd had to admit it had evolved. She got a kick out of their back and forth, especially the GIFs (Eddie was mad for them) and felt like Eddie understood her in the same way Lizzie and Sam did. Megan had been surprised to find herself telling this stranger the Chill email fuck-up story within a few minutes of that first coffee date. He'd thought it was hilarious.

'Saying a kid is ugly is pretty much certain death in my industry,' she groaned.

'Kind of in society in general, actually …' Eddie said, pulling in his cheeks to stop himself smiling.

'It's not funny.'

'It is a bit,' he said, allowing himself a wide smile that revealed a tiny dimple in his left cheek. 'Was the kid really that ugly?'

'Stop it.'

'No, but seriously, was he?'

Now Megan was trying not to smile. 'Yes,' she admitted. 'But his arrogance made him even uglier.'

'And that email went out to how many of your subscribers?'

'Twenty thousand.'

'Oof!' Eddie mimed taking a punch to the gut. 'That must have hurt.'

'I lost five thousand that *day*!' Megan's head ached at the memory. 'And another two thousand after I sent out an apology blaming it on my six-year-old son.'

'Harsh.'

'I know, right?'

'No, *you're* harsh,' he said, pointing at her. 'Blaming your kid.'

This was true, but the way Eddie smiled at her when he said it made the act seem less deplorable somehow.

He wasn't condoning her behaviour, but he wasn't horrified by it either. Megan and Eddie had discussed everything from the play, to family, to work – Eddie was the CEO of a big non-profit organisation – over the next hour, and the Vietnam trip Eddie had taken Henry on last year.

'Best holiday ever,' Eddie said, looking pensive for a moment before laughing. 'One of my favourite moments was when Grandpa ate the local cuisine of fried crickets, then tried to encourage a horrified Aussie tour group to "give them a go!"'

'Henry and my mum would have gotten on well.' Megan laughed. 'She's a thrill-seeker too. Mum was seventy-five when she bungee-jumped for the first time.'

'You don't seem old enough to have a mum Grandpa's age.'

'Mum was forty-three when she had me,' Megan explained. 'I hated school drop-off because everyone thought she was my nana. The boys used to call her Miss Daisy.'

Eddie shook his head. 'Boys are evil fuckers.'

'Not mine.' Megan placed her hand over her heart in mock sincerity. 'Oscar's an angel.'

'Of *course*,' Eddie said, matching her tone. 'My apologies.'

'Except for that time when he sent a nasty email to my subscribers,' Megan said. 'Other than that? Angel.'

'Why don't you get out of the kids' fashion business?'

'What?' Megan was thrown. Was her job dissatisfaction that obvious?

'Find a buyer for Chill, sell it and do something else,' Eddie said matter-of-factly. 'It doesn't sound like you're enjoying it any more.'

'Well, no, but …'

'I know someone who might be able to find you a buyer,' he said, pulling his phone out. 'I could ask her to start sniffing around, if you like?'

It had all felt a bit too sudden. Megan had become used to feeling discontented with her job over the past few months, and whining about it, but to consider letting it go was scary.

'I'm not sure that ...'

'No pressure,' Eddie said, picking up on Megan's vibe. 'I'll put out some feelers and if anything comes of it, I'll let you know.'

Since then, Eddie had sent her a few names of people who were looking to acquire a business or knew someone who was, but Megan hadn't contacted any of them. Despite the recent bumps in the road, Chill was still a successful business and one that had taken years to build. She couldn't just let it go when she had nothing else to go to. But Eddie had been right. The only part of Megan's life she wasn't enjoying right now was Chill. She'd always loved every aspect of running the business – scrolling through potential new stock, keeping up with the latest fashions on the market, organising photo shoots – but over the past few months, it had lost its shine. The passion she'd once had just wasn't there any more and it seemed like more of a chore these days. She only posted on the socials because she had to, and she just didn't care as much about what everyone else was buying or selling.

Megan crossed the playground, dodging balls and skipping ropes, and waved to a bunch of grade-three girls hanging upside down off the monkey bars.

'Hi Megan!'

It was Gemma and Molly from the play.

'Hi girls!'

In the two years she'd been there, Baytree kids had never said hello to Megan. Now she couldn't walk three feet without a small child running up to give her a hug or shouting a greeting at her from across the yard. It felt nice.

Megan found one of the activewear mums waiting in the hall for her, wearing her signature black leggings, black long-sleeved sweat top and gold sleeveless puffer.

'Hey Megan.'

'Hi ...' *Shit.* Megan had no idea what this woman's name was.

The woman smiled, not offended in the slightest. 'Nicola.'

'Hey Nicola.'

'So, there are a few of us wondering if you need any help with the concert?' Nicola said, looking over at the half-painted set pieces leaning against the wall and the half-empty box of props and costumes in the corner.

'Um, sure,' Megan said. 'We need help with the set, actually. I think Lisa started painting those over there, but it would be great to get a group together to finish them off. Maybe you could talk to Penny or Lisa about it?'

'I'll go ask Penny now,' Nicola said. She started to leave, then turned back. 'You're doing a fabulous job by the way. Everyone's saying how fantastic it is that you've given up your time for the kids.'

Megan blushed. 'Oh, it's not that much time, really.'

'Rubbish,' Nicola scoffed, waving her hand. 'You're a saint. And rehearsals are all Gemma can talk about at home. She's loving it.'

'Oh, you're Gemma's mum!' Megan instantly saw the resemblance.

'She wants to do acting classes now.' Nicola rolled her eyes. 'Can you recommend anywhere?'

'Sorry, no,' Megan said. 'Oscar's more of a footy and martial arts kid.'

'Oh, I just thought because of your background you might ...'

'My background?'

'Didn't you do acting and modelling?'

'That was a *long* time ago.' Megan laughed. 'I haven't done any of that for years.'

'Oh right.' Nicola nodded. 'Oh, here come the rest of your rehearsal gang!'

Megan looked over to see Lizzie and Rick walking across the schoolyard, laughing and talking. Sam lagged behind, scowling at his phone. Megan turned back to find Nicola with a strange expression on her face.

'So, Lizzie and Rick knew each other before he started here?'

The woman was clearly fishing, but there was no way Megan was going to gossip about Lizzie.

'It's just that I saw them having coffee together a few weeks ago,' Nicola said, raising one pencil-thin eyebrow. 'They seemed very familiar.'

'Yeah, they grew up together,' Megan said, trying to sound as casual as possible. 'Old friends.'

'Right.' Nicola looked out the window again. 'Cute, isn't he? Anyway, I'll go ask Penny about the sets. See you soon!'

'Happy' by Pharrell Williams began blaring through the schoolyard, signalling the end of lunchtime. Megan saw Rick veer off towards the school building and Lizzie drop back to give Sam shit about whatever he was doing on his phone. Megan knew that Lizzie and Rick's rapport was down to a shared history, just two old friends reconnecting. And it was clear to anyone who knew them how much Lizzie and Greg loved each other. Also, Lizzie had assured Megan that night over dumplings and Shiraz that she and Rick were ancient history, but still, Megan couldn't help wondering ...

'Herr Director!' Lizzie saluted Megan as she entered the hall. 'Ready for more mumbling and two left feet?'

No. Lizzie wouldn't do that to Greg. Nicola didn't know Lizzie at all. It was bullshit schoolyard gossip. 'You know it!' Megan said cheerily.

Sam looked up from his phone. 'Sasha's on her way.'

Lizzie grinned. 'Took eight texts to get that information, did it?'

Sam glared. 'Were you looking at my texts?'

'You know it, lover boy!'

Megan followed a bickering Sam and Lizzie over to the stage, hoping the Lizzie and Rick rumours would die away before they reached Greg's ears.

'Nana Clara!'

Oscar ran straight towards Bryce's mum who was standing at the zoo entrance, alongside her son and Adam.

'What the fuck?' Megan murmured.

'Oh Jesus,' Ellie murmured beside her. 'It's the zealot!'

'Mum, behave.'

'Did you know she was going to be here?'

'Nope.'

'Ugh,' Ellie groaned.

At least she had Lizzie, Megan thought. Oscar had only

wanted Max and Toby on his birthday outing in the end, which Megan was more than happy about. Supervising three young boys at the zoo, while dealing with her ex-husband, his partner and her ex-mother-in-law was more than enough. Megan saw Lizzie walking towards the entrance from the opposite direction, an excited Max and Toby skipping along by her side. Lizzie waved at Megan, then grimaced in Clara's direction, which made Megan laugh. Yep, she'd be fine.

'Good morning, everyone!' Ellie announced. 'Isn't this going to be fun!'

The only person oblivious to the slight note of sarcasm in Ellie's voice was Oscar. He beamed up at the people he loved, all together in the one place – a rare occasion – as if this was the best day of his life. Megan silently vowed to make this a fun, tension-free day, even if it gave her an ulcer. Megan was going to be 'Good Mother' today, and so she was. She didn't tell Clara to fuck off when she said it was insensitive to Christians to have lions on display. And when Bryce said he and Adam were thinking about using a surrogate to give Oscar a little brother or sister, Megan told them it was a great idea, when she'd actually wanted to feed *them* to the lions. When they all sat down for a picnic lunch and birthday cake near the reptile enclosure, Clara suggested they say grace before eating.

'Not bloody likely!' Lizzie snorted.

Clara's eyes bugged out of her head as Megan busied herself handing out sandwiches to the boys, trying not to laugh.

'I don't believe in that stuff any more,' Lizzie said, biting into a chicken sandwich. 'I grew up in a religious family, and I go along with it to keep my dad and auntie happy, but I've decided it's not for me.'

'That's unfortunate,' Clara said in her most sanctimonious voice.

'Each to their own, Mum.'

Megan heard the warning tone in Bryce's voice, and was surprised to see Clara immediately close her mouth. The old bat must have softened since the divorce, and Bryce was obviously speaking up more than he did when they were together. Megan felt strangely sorry for Clara Campbell. It must have been shattering for the woman, and her entire belief system, when her only son told her he was gay – a choice she'd never been allowed to respect or understand because of her faith.

'Hey Clara, how about we take the boys to see the giant tortoises?' Ellie suggested once the boys had wolfed down their sandwiches and juices.

Unlike Clara, who had needed Bryce's help to lower herself down onto the picnic rug, Ellie jumped up off the rug and wiped down her jeans with the agility of a thirty year old.

Clara shook her head. 'Oh, I don't ...'

But Ellie was having none of it. 'Come on, boys, let's help Nana up,' she said brightly. 'We old ladies get stiff legs when we sit for too long.'

The three boys giggled as they pulled Clara up off the rug, and Megan felt a surge of affection for her mother. Ellie had even thawed towards Adam as the day had gone on, laughing and joking with him as they watched the orangutans.

'Sorry, Bryce,' Lizzie said once the two older women were gone. 'I didn't mean to upset her with the whole "God is bullshit" thing.'

'It's fine,' Bryce said. 'She's learning that she can't force that stuff onto people.'

'Refused to make eye contact the first few times she met me.' Adam laughed.

'Awww, poor baby,' Bryce said.

'Hey, at least she still prays for me.'

Lizzie laughed and Megan shifted uncomfortably. As much as she'd wanted the we're-all-one-big-happy-family vibe for Oscar today, she wasn't exactly thrilled about her ex-husband and his fiancé flaunting their happiness in front of her. She wondered what Eddie was doing this weekend. Maybe she'd text him when she got home and tell him about Oscar's slightly strained birthday outing. Or maybe she'd save it for Monday when they were meeting up to talk about Chill. Just thinking about seeing him again improved Megan's mood immediately.

Two hours later, their little zoo posse began falling apart. Clara insisted on sitting down every ten minutes to catch her breath, and the boys were dragging their feet, shattered from walking the length of the zoo. Even Ellie had slowed to a stroll.

'I reckon it might be time to kick off the second part of your party, Oscy,' Bryce said, as they sat on large concrete steps watching seals flop about and slide off rocks into the water below. 'Whaddya reckon, boys? Ready for a sleepover?'

'YAY!' Oscar shouted, jumping in the air, startling a nearby ibis.

Megan was relieved. She was looking forward to a night at home after the exhausting affectation of today's outing. Maybe she'd invite Lizzie over for takeaway again.

'You've got Sam's address for Lola's party tomorrow, yeah?' she asked Bryce as they stood up.

'Yep, all good.'

Megan could see he was annoyed by the question. 'It starts at midday, remember,' she continued, 'and Lola's present is in Oscar's sleepover bag ...'

'Megan!' Bryce's voice was sharp. 'I've got it.'

The happy family vibe was melting faster than gelato in summer.

'Okay,' Megan said, smiling sweetly. 'Just confirming that everything is sorted, despite having "a lot on my plate".'

Bryce glared at her, before walking off to follow the boys.

'Touché,' Adam said, grinning at Megan.

A few minutes later, Megan, Ellie and Lizzie were farewelling the boys and Clara at the exit.

'Have fun tonight, champ!' Megan said, giving Oscar one last squeeze.

The moment they were gone, Megan let out a loud sigh. 'Jesus, I could use a drink.'

'Just the one?' Lizzie said, rubbing the back of her neck.

'You two wanna come back to mine?' Megan asked, getting out her keys.

Ellie shook her head. 'Think I'll head home.' She touched her forehead. 'Got a headache coming on.'

'You want a Panadol?' Lizzie asked, opening her huge tote bag and rummaging around. Sam called it her first-aid bag. Lizzie had everything from Elastoplast to Mercurochrome in there.

'Thanks, love,' Ellie said, 'but I should be okay till I get home.'

'Okay, let's go!' Megan said. 'I'll drop you straight home, Mum.'

But Ellie didn't move.

'Mum?'

Ellie swayed slightly and raised a hand to her head. Both Megan and Lizzie moved towards her as Ellie's eyes rolled back and she crumpled to the ground.

Sam

To: jack_woz_here@hotmail.com
From: samhatfieldchef@bigpond.com
Subject: Birthdays are Bullshit

Mate, it is now the end of what has been a long, weird day.

I *cannot* believe you came! That's quite the hike from your redneck backwater. Not that I'm suggesting you hiked, or even hitchhiked. It'd be a bold serial killer who'd pick you up on a long, lonesome highway. But I swear to God, I'm gonna pay you back your taxi fare! Tell me what it cost, damn you!

Before you rocked up like a knight in shining wheelchair, I was having a bit of a meltdown. I'm usually a machine when it comes to my kids' parties. But today was the first time I was flying solo as a – dun dun DUUUHHH – single dad.

So, I was desperate for it to go well, which was why I had a meltdown when I discovered that my hundreds and thousands were three years past their use-by date. Not that I believe those things are capable of going off, but the last thing you want at your nine year old's birthday party is a cheeky outbreak of food poisoning. Really kills the vibe.

Lola *loves* fairy bread. It's been a must-have at all her parties since she could shove food in her face. I prepped most of the other snacks last night, so I only had to pop them in the oven, or get them out of the fridge. You may have noticed I went a bit overboard on the food this year, but give a single dad – dun dun

DUUUHHH – a break. I wanted to impress my daughter and her friends and her friends' parents, and cooking is my party trick.

So off to the shops I went in search of hundreds and thousands. It was a blessedly uneventful trip. But when I arrived home and Lola came running out to the car, I thought, 'Oh, fuck, what now?'

But she was grinning and skipping, wearing her flowing, white *Pride and Prejudice* dress, and do you know what she said? You probably gave her the line, did you?

She said, 'I know it's *my* birthday, but I have a surprise for *you*.'

I followed her inside, confused and tense. Then I see you spinning around on the kitchen tiles! And you yelled something at me, but I was already laughing and hugging you.

The tears were probably a giveaway, but I was pretty happy to see you, dickhead. You made the whole day better. Especially towards the end of the party, I was *very* happy to have you there then.

I refuse to apologise yet again for the fact that you didn't get to meet Megan. Her mum is in the hospital, dickhead. Not about you, mm-kay? But you met Oscar, yeah? That adorable kid? Well, just imagine him as a six-foot-tall female. Anyway, it seemed to me that you were more than happy flirting with Lizzie; Megan might've cramped your style.

Lola's so happy. She had a great time and loved seeing you. She said everyone loved the food too. I asked what her favourite was.

Der. The fairy bread.

I did feel good about the food. I should've made triple the amount of guacamole (will I ever learn?), but reckon I nailed it overall. You were outside showing Tyler your wheelie skills when I brought out my veggie samosas and some kid's teen-ish sister/nanny who'd been there for about two minutes asked what they were, and I said, 'They're samosas. Indian.'

To which she replied, 'Um, racist.'

Yes, dickhead, my serving of Indian food was racist. Or maybe my use of the word 'Indian' to describe the cuisine was the culturally inappropriate part? Who knows? I was going to let it go but someone else heard; your favourite party friend, Lizzie.

To the best of my recollection, the conversation proceeded thusly:

> Lizzie: Pardon?
>
> Girl: That was racist.
>
> Lizzie: What was?
>
> Girl: He said 'Indian'. That's racist.
>
> Lizzie: No, that's the word he used to correctly describe the food he was serving.
>
> Girl: It was the way he said it.
>
> Lizzie: With a smile on his face?
>
> Girl: No, he just said, like, '*Indian*'.
>
> Lizzie: Do you go to school?
>
> Girl: Yeah.
>
> Lizzie: Do you do well?
>
> Girl: I do okay.
>
> Lizzie: Do better.

Then Lizzie selected a samosa and took a huge bite, all the while looking straight at the poor misguided teen as she made near-orgasmic sounds.

Once the food was out of the way, the rest of the party went pretty smoothly, don't you reckon? One kid cried, one spewed and one I wanted to throw in the oven. And Puss Puss in the Corner was a hit!

I'm still reeling a bit from Bridg's surprise appearance. I mean, we were halfway through 'Happy Birthday' for fuck's sake. The cake was out (that was orange zest you could taste, by the way) and the lolly bags were lined up by the front door ready for departure. Job was done.

Eat your cake, take your kids and let me have three quick beers.

But there she was. The song trailed off as Lola screamed, 'MOTHER!', and ran into her arms. You took control, instructing everyone to sing 'Happy Birthday' at twice the volume as before because we'd stopped before we'd finished and that's the rule when you stop singing 'Happy Birthday'. You always had a gift for bullshit.

Did you see what Bridg gave Lola for her birthday? Were you still there when Lola unwrapped that little number? I remember you appearing in front of Bridg as she approached me, engaging her in conversation while I retreated to the safety of the kitchen. I could hear you laughing and cajoling and saving me. But then you left. I think. I managed to squeeze in those three quick beers while I was cleaning up.

Bridg gave Lola a MacBook Pro. The fifteen-inch model. Apparently, it's been upgraded and pimped out as much as is possible. I looked it up just now before emailing you. Costs about six-and-a-half grand.

Lola's nine, dude. She doesn't need to hack NASA.

Lola was over the moon. She's old enough to know it's a damn good computer and, prior to today, was under the impression she wouldn't be getting her own laptop until high school. That's what I've been telling her for the last year. Bridg knows that. But hey, we're not a couple any more, so I guess all that 'united front' bullshit has gone in the bin right along with our marriage. Lola hugged her and cried and thanked her *so* much for the computer and then Bridg left. Job done.

I have to go to bed, dickhead. I feel . . . what do I feel?

Defeated.

I put lots of time and effort into today. I wanted it to be great. I love my kids and they deserve good parties. But right now, today feels like a battle lost.

Thanks again for coming. You're a soldier and I know you're on my side.

S x

I never expected there to be sparks of any kind. I thought we'd catch up, maybe put some old issues to bed with minimum fuss, make some small talk and go about the rest of our days. But there were sparks. She's definitely still attracted to me. She blushed when I said she looked great. She toyed with her teaspoon and couldn't look me in the eye. I made her laugh. More than once. And she laughed in that way that sounded like her own laugh took her by surprise. And every time I made her laugh, she looked at me with curiosity and surprise, as if she was discovering a new man inside the one she thought she knew.

It was worth the wait. These past few years, checking recruitment online and waiting for a job to come up at her school, getting in shape, working my charm on the principal. It was all worth it.

Because now I see her every day. And I still know her better than anyone, which is why I can make her blush and laugh. All that is left to discover is when and how we get back together. And I don't mind if it takes years. I understand she'll have to extricate herself from her current situation, and that won't be easy.

She loves her kids. But so will I.

Lizzie

'Is Sasha coming to rehearsals today?' Max asked.

Sam grinned. 'Yup!'

'Yay!'

My youngest bolted away from the bench towards a waiting Oscar and Toby to share this happy news.

'You've got some competition there,' I said, sitting next to Sam and handing him his coffee.

'Huh?'

'Max, Oscar and Toby all have a huge crush on your girlfriend,' I teased, nodding at the three unwise monkeys in the distance.

'Not my girlfriend.'

'Why not?' I persisted. 'What's wrong with her?'

'Nothing's wrong with her!' Sam looked genuinely insulted. 'She's smart and beautiful, and funny and ...' He clocked my victorious expression and slow blinked.

'Knew it!' If only Megan were here to share this childish victory with me, but she'd texted Sam and me last night to say she couldn't come to rehearsals today, asking if we could run them. Ellie was still in hospital.

'Shut up,' Sam said. 'How's Ellie?'

'Haven't heard from Megan today,' I said. 'How'd you pull up after all the excitement and drama of the Jane Austen extravaganza?'

'Fine.' Sam took a big slurp of his coffee.

He was lying, but I didn't want to push it. I still couldn't believe that wife of his showed up when and how she did. What a piece of work. Poor Sam seemed to go into shock when he saw her. Thank God his mate Jack was there to put the spotlight firmly back where it belonged. Now there's a story. Jack and Sam. Sam has never exactly been an over-sharer, but I thought he might have told me about a near-death experience in his youth. Mind you, I haven't been forthcoming with my own dramatic past.

'So, how do you know Sam?' I'd asked Jack as we hovered around Sam's to-die-for chicken sandwiches.

'We met when we were doing Little Aths together in primary school,' Jack said, wheeling closer to me so I could hear him over Ariana Grande. He must have clocked my confused expression because he laughed and gestured to the wheelchair. 'This came later, obviously. Sam and I played in a band together when we were eighteen and had a nasty car accident on the way to a gig one night.'

'Oh Jesus,' I said, horrified. 'Was Sam, I mean, were you ...?'

'Sam was driving, but it was the other guy's fault,' Jack said quickly. 'The idiot crossed double white lines.'

I glanced at Sam, who was trying to explain the rules of some old-fashioned game Lola wanted to play – Pussy's Corner or something weird and inappropriate like that – and my heart broke for him. Poor Sam.

'I'm so sorry,' I said, turning back to Jack.

'No apologies, all good,' Jack said, waving his hand. 'Life's there to be lived, and I am livin' large.'

I'd felt real tenderness for the smiley man and his amazing attitude. Thank God Sam had Jack in his life. Hearing about their long friendship had also been an uncomfortable reminder of my recent unsuccessful reconnection with

Melissa. I'd been carrying around the memory of her cold stare like a constant dull ache in my chest ever since.

'I liked your mate, Jack,' I said to Sam now. 'He's cool.'

'He's a dickhead,' Sam said with genuine affection. 'Caught a maxi cab from Ballarat to surprise me, for fuck's sake.'

'That's a good friend.'

'A best friend,' Sam said. 'I heard you were a pretty good friend yourself on Saturday. Snapping into action when Ellie collapsed.'

'Nah,' I scoffed. 'Just glad I was there.'

I could still remember the fear that washed over me when Ellie went limp, like a rag doll. Luckily her head had landed on soft grass, not the low iron railing a few inches to her left. Megan went into full panic mode, which was to be expected, so I went into full take-charge mode. I'd grabbed the nearest passerby and told them to call an ambulance, then I turned Ellie on her side, put my jacket under her head, checked her pulse and silently thanked her for waiting until the kids had left.

You're a good woman, Ellie Wylie, I thought, looking at her slack, tanned face. Megan squatted beside her mother, tears streaming down her cheeks, and I rubbed between Megan's shoulders; small circles, just like I do at work for women in pain. Megan wanted to go in the ambulance with her mum, who had regained consciousness by then but was groggy, so I told Megan I'd take her car home. As she climbed into the back of the ambulance, Megan tuned to me, white-faced. 'Could you let Applewood know too?'

'Of course.' I squeezed her hand. 'Text me if you need anything, okay?'

Then the ambulance was speeding away, lights flashing,

siren blaring, and I was standing at the entrance to a darkened zoo, wondering what the fuck had just happened. Was it a stroke? An aneurysm? Ellie was in better physical shape than me, for Christ's sake.

'How does a fit and healthy woman just collapse like that?' I'd asked Greg that night after the kids went to bed.

'It's terrible,' Greg said, shaking his head.

'It made me think about Auntie Carmen.'

Greg leant across the couch and pulled me to his chest. 'I know, buddy,' he said, kissing the top of my head. 'No one likes mortality slapping them in the face. We've just gotta make the most of our time with the people we love.'

'Says the guy who considers an annual visit with his parents overkill.'

'I said *the people we love*.'

Greg's parents moved to Coffs Harbour a few years ago, and it was a relief for Greg and his sister. Stewart and Dale Barrett were far-right-wing, sexist, racist, homophobic fifth generation Aussies, who believed that the Clive Palmers and Donald Trumps were finally telling it like it was, and that all Muslims were terrorists. Suffice to say they were not missed.

Sam nudged me now. 'Hey, speaking of boyfriends ...'

I followed his gaze to see Rick walking across the yard, holding an envelope. 'Yeah, he would be classified as an *ex*-boyfriend.'

'Hey guys!' Rick approached us, beaming. 'We on for lunchtime rehearsals today?'

'Yep!' we chorused.

'Found something I thought you might get a kick out of, Lizzie,' he said, opening the envelope and shaking some photos into his hand. 'Bit of a blast from the past.' He handed me the photos and I began to flick through.

- Me – big head of curly hair with gelled fringe, wearing high-waisted black jeans and a white frilly pirate shirt – standing next to Rick – black jeans, white T-shirt and black suede vest – out front of Abelas.
- Me in green tracksuit pants and my striped Felines soccer top, lying on Rick's bed reading *Misery*.
- Rick, Melissa and me on a Vinnies caramel-brown leather couch eating pizza.
- Rick and me sitting on the footpath outside a house party, beaming into the camera – my arms draped drunkenly around Rick's neck, a Santa hat on my head and red tinsel around my waist. Rick in red jeans and a white T-shirt looking deliriously happy.
- A group shot of our under-17s soccer team.

'Can I see?' Sam snatched the photos out of my hand and an expression of pure delight crossed his face as he flicked through them. 'This is *you*?'

'That's her,' Rick said.

'That *fringe*!' Sam chortled.

'Shut up!' I growled. 'It was the nineties.'

'I can't believe Megs is missing this,' Sam said, studying the photos as if they'd been recovered from a pharaoh's tomb. 'She's going to be furious!'

His expression suddenly changed. *Uh-oh*.

'So, you guys were, like, a proper couple, huh?' he said, frowning. 'I thought you just dated a few times?'

'We were a couple for a little while,' I said, avoiding Rick's eye. 'But we were part of the same big gang for a few years too.'

'Oh, right.'

Ah, men. Gotta love their lack of interest in details. If that had been Megan or Aileen, or any other woman over the age of twelve, they would have insisted on knowing every detail of my past relationship with Rick, including an annotated timeline of our entire relationship.

'Who's that?' Sam said, pointing at a photo.

'Melissa,' I said. 'She was my best friend.'

'Cute.' Sam nodded his approval.

'I saw her recently actually,' I said, looking at Rick.

His head jerked back slightly, and he frowned. 'Melissa Morton?'

'Yeah, saw her at the Willie Primary fete,' I said, eager to move the conversation away from our relationship. 'Looks exactly the same.'

'Does she?' Rick seemed thrown.

'Have you seen her lately?'

He looked away. 'Melissa? No. Not for years.'

Maybe they'd had a fight after I left. I wasn't going to dig. That would bring up the kind of reminiscing that wasn't going to do me any favours with Sam sitting right here. I'd tell him one day. Just not today. I looked back at the photo of us at the soccer club, with Rick looking super cute in his kit. I glanced up at the older version standing a few feet away and felt butterflies low in my belly. *What the hell?* All this nostalgia was affecting my brain cells.

'Gotta go,' I said, standing up. 'See you both at rehearsals.'

The butterflies spread in all directions as I hurried away.

Megan

How did Lizzie stand it? All that time in a hospital. Megan hated everything about them; the sterile, antiseptic smell, the sound of rubber-soled shoes padding up and down endless white hallways, the depressing decor. And the sickness; broken, diseased, decrepit bodies everywhere. From the young jaundiced-looking woman in a wheelchair Megan passed in the corridor to the old man she glimpsed through an open door, in bed with tubes coming out of his mouth. It was all so depressing and undignified.

The man in the bed looked at her and Megan realised she'd been staring. Ashamed, she quickly continued down the corridor, carrying coffee and three different types of chocolate back to her mum's room. She wasn't as good as she'd liked to believe she was. A truly good person wouldn't react with disgust to sick strangers. The nurses and doctors in this hospital were the good ones. They did good things all day every day. The only selfless act Megan had ever done was help out on a little school play. There she was, thinking she had it all going on with this good person bit, that she was the saviour of Baytree Primary and keeping Henry's spirit alive with her generosity of spirit, when it was all bullshit. Saviours didn't fall apart in the face of a crisis at the sight of their mothers prostrate on the ground. If it hadn't been for Lizzie ... Megan felt ill at the thought.

They'd whisked her mother off as soon as she arrived at the hospital. It seemed like hours before a doctor came out to talk to her. *'Bleeding on the brain … abnormal heart rhythm … not enough blood flow … pacemaker … ECG …'* Megan tried to process everything the doctor was saying, but all she wanted to know was, *Is my mum going to die?*

'Her heart rhythm slowed, which is what caused her to collapse,' the kind-faced doctor with short blonde hair and brown eyes told Megan. 'Inserting a pacemaker is a quick and easy procedure and your mum will be back home in a few days.'

'A pacemaker?'

'They're more common than you think,' she had continued, 'and your mum will be able to resume her normal, active lifestyle relatively quickly.'

Watching her mum sitting up in her hospital bed, texting concerned friends while complaining about the runny eggs she'd been served for breakfast that morning, Megan had to admit that Ellie seemed back to her normal self already. So much so that she'd sent Megan off to find her some chocolate to 'get the taste of that God-awful breakfast out of my mouth'.

'Megsy!'

Megan turned to see her brother jogging along the corridor behind her. 'Matt!'

He'd come. Thank God. She'd been so worried he wouldn't. She loved her brother, but he was a useless man-child. She gave him an awkward one-armed, coffee-and-chocolate-holding hug, then stood back to take him in. She hadn't seen him since last Christmas. He was wearing a grey T-shirt, ripped jeans, and apart from filling out around the belly and jowls, looked pretty much the same; short brown-blond wavy hair, full lips most women would kill for, a dimpled chin and shadowy moustache.

'You look ... healthy,' she said.

'You mean fat,' Matt said, grinning. 'I got fat.'

'You were too thin anyway.'

'Don't fall in love,' Matt warned, wagging a finger in his sister's face. 'This is what happens. Being content is overrated.'

'Who's the lucky man?'

'His name's Derek,' Matt said, beaming. 'He's a nurse at Randwick.' He shuddered. 'I don't know how he stands it. I fucking hate these places.'

'You and me both. Have you seen her yet?'

'Yep,' Matt said, glancing towards their mum's room. 'Just popped out for a fag. Doctor said it was slow heart rhythm or something? Needs a pacemaker?'

'Yeah, she had it put in yesterday,' Megan said. 'It was fucking scary, seeing her collapse like that.'

'I bet. Sorry I couldn't get here sooner.'

Useless.

Ellie's hospital room was wall-to-wall flowers, balloons, teddies, fruit and chocolate baskets and 'Get Well Soon' cards, all courtesy of her Applewood gang.

'Christ, it's like Mardi Gras in here,' Matt muttered as they entered the room.

'Yep, I'll be out today, Helen,' Ellie was saying into the phone, waving to Megan and gesturing for her to have something from the fruit basket. 'Oh, don't be ridiculous, I'm not using a bloody wheelchair! Tell Bob to put it back in the office!'

As if Ellie wasn't popular enough, this latest drama had guaranteed her superstar status at Applewood for the rest of her days. When Megan went to pick up toiletries and clothes yesterday, she'd been inundated by panicked residents before she'd even made it to the lifts.

'Why Ellie?' Carol had wailed, clutching at Megan's sleeve. 'Of all people! She's so full of *life*!'

'Still is, Carol,' Megan had assured her, patting the old woman's plump arm. 'She'll be back before you know it.'

'Gave us a hell of a bloody fright, she did,' Bert grumbled.

Megan rolled her eyes. 'Well, you know how she loves attention.'

That had them roaring with laughter and clutching their sides and Megan was worried another septuagenarian might collapse in front of her.

'She wants us to eat the fruit,' Matt said, passing Megan an overly ripe pear before peeling himself a banana.

Brother and sister sat on the end of their mother's bed as Ellie continued admonishing Helen for organising a welcome back party. Megan's phone pinged with a text from Eddie.

E – How's your mum?

M – Organising her social life from her hospital bed.

E – x-D

'Who's that?' Matt asked.

'Just a friend.'

She wasn't going to tell her gossipy brother anything about Eddie. Besides, there wasn't really anything to tell. He was just a friend checking in on her mum, same as Lizzie and Sam had been doing. Megan had actually been surprised by some of the messages she'd received over the past few days; at least five Baytree mums texted to ask if she needed help with Oscar or the play, there was a lovely email from Penny and a bunch of flowers on her doorstep from Dave and Kesh. Such kindness from people whose names she hadn't known six months ago. Would she have sent a text to a Baytree parent if their mum was sick?

'Good Lord!' Ellie said, finally hanging up. 'What a pack of panic merchants! You'd think I'd been gored by a rogue elephant. If they all just left me alone and stopped fussing, maybe I could get out of here before Christmas.'

Sam

To: jack_woz_here@hotmail.com
From: samhatfieldchef@bigpond.com
Subject: The Axe is BACK!

Ha ha. Yes, I do remember how to play the intro to 'Brown Eyed Girl', thank you very much. It took me a solid half hour to get it back in my fingers, but I got there.

No, I will not send you a video to prove it.

It's *fun* playing guitar again, dickhead, especially in front of people. Sure, the majority of them are aged between five and twelve years old, but they're an awesome audience. They love the stuff I've written. And Lizzie and Megan (and some other teachers and parents) have said really nice things. Well, Lizzie and Megan both said mean things that are compliments on the inside. And now, when the kids are in bed and I've done enough housework to feel like I can get up in the morning without hating myself, I play guitar. I sit on the couch and noodle around like I used to when I didn't know how precious time was. I'm also no longer scared of finding out that I haven't done something I was supposed to do, which is good.

I had to email Bridget to ask for money last night. She said she'd start a regular transfer as of Monday, but the account was still threadbare by Wednesday night. It took me an hour to write a two-line email that ended up reading:

Hey Bridg,

Just checking in to see if you've set up that transfer. It's probably the bank's fault but nothing's come through yet and there are a few bills sitting on the dresser.

S

Is that the wussiest email in the world? I was on the back foot for a reason. I've been feeling so good lately that it's led to feeling guilty.

I also had sex with Sasha last night. In her car. Turns out it's a good-sized car for good sex. I had sex, dickhead. With a great woman.

We saw each other outside the market, and she had a tonne of shopping, so I offered to carry some of the bags and she accepted because seriously, I think she had just shopped for the apocalypse. Maybe that's why she had sex with me, because life as we know it is about to end. I don't mind.

After playing boot Tetris with her shopping bags, Sasha asked if I needed a lift this time. I said yes, I did, even though I didn't because I'd been out for a walk and deliberately left the car at home. Lizzie had taken the kids to netball yesterday afternoon and offered to have them both for a sleepover last night. She could obviously see I needed a break. Good egg, that one.

So, Sasha and I got in the car, and she asked how it was going and I told her the concert was in a week and that I was nervous, but that I was having fun playing guitar and that it felt like I was reintroducing me to myself.

I think they were the exact words I used, dickhead. 'I feel like I'm reintroducing me to myself.'

What a cock.

She said she thought that was great, and that the school was lucky to have me involved because I'm obviously very talented. I asked how she would know if I'm talented and she reminded me that we'd sang together in my car.

I told her she had some pipes too, which made her laugh. Then she said, 'All right, let's see what's in store for our duo today,' and turned on the radio and cranked the volume.

The first thing we heard was a song neither of us knew, which made us laugh.

Sasha changed the station and HELLO Backstreet Boys.

Oh yeah, dickhead. 'I Want It That Way' was approaching its incomparable bridge. We jumped in within a nanosecond of hearing it, both hitting the same lyric mid-phrase, like we'd been listening to the whole damn song. Who knew that a man my age could find catharsis through the timeless music of the Backstreet Boys?

Then we parked. But not at my house. Sasha had pulled into a car park behind an oval nearby. There was no sport on, so the car park was empty. I started sweating because I'd figured out that perhaps we were 'parking' in the *Happy Days* sense of the word.

Sasha turned off the engine. The Backstreet Boys still had at least one more chorus to go so I gestured at the radio and made a disappointed noise. Then she took off her seatbelt, and I followed suit. It was so sexy that we both laughed, then we started kissing and etc. etc. Then she dropped me home and here I am.

Happy and post-coital. Post-CAR-coital. I've never done that before.

My email to Bridget should've read:

Hey Bridg,

Just had sex in a car. Checking in to see if you've set up that transfer. It's probably the bank's fault because I just had sex in a car, but nothing's come through yet and I just had sex in a car, and there are a few bills sitting on the dresser. Car sex.

S

P.S. Not in the backseat like the songs. Front seat, passenger side.

And before you ask, don't. I will not be providing a detailed description of the car sex.

S x

PS: There's still no money in the account. Don't care.

Lizzie

'Rocco isn't here, but I know all his lines so I can do his part!'

'All right, Eve Harrington,' I said, patting Charlie Walsh's shoulder. 'Let's just wait. The dress rehearsal doesn't start for half an hour.'

'Yeah, but what if he's late for the *actual* concert tomorrow?' Charlie said, frothing at the mouth with anxiety. 'And who's Eve Horrondon?'

'Never mind.' I looked at the rundown sheet Megan had given us all when we'd arrived for the dress rehearsal ten minutes ago. 'Go get your costume on.'

'The mouth on that kid!' Rick was beside me, shaking his head.

'Doesn't even know who Eve Harrington is,' I said. 'Loser.'

Rick adopted a Bette Davis-esque pose. *'Fasten your seatbelts. It's gonna be a bumpy night.'*

'Nice!'

'Thank you,' Rick said, bowing. 'Hey, can you help me look for more paper lanterns?' He held up a very crumpled paper lantern. 'Megs said there should be more in the storeroom.'

I glanced around the hall. Sam was singing through the closing song – 'Have Yourself A Merry Little Christmas' – with half the kids, and Megan and Sasha were doing a line run with the main cast. I was supposed to be checking props, which presumably included paper lanterns.

'Sure.'

Five minutes later, Karen was leading Rick and me into the storeroom behind the office, which looked as if it were inhabited by a hoarder with very eclectic taste. The room was littered with boxes of all shapes and sizes, with labels like *miscellaneous sport and art* and *FETE*. The shelves looked like a weird piece of installation art, displaying everything from piles of high-vis vests, to a glue gun that had seen better days.

'Good luck,' Karen said, giving us a wink and heading back to reception.

'Right,' I said, 'you start there, and I'll look over …' I turned and suddenly Rick's lips were on mine and he was pushing me back against the high-vis vest shelves. It took me a moment to register what was actually happening, but the second I regained my senses, I forced him off me with every bit of strength I possessed.

'RICK!' I cried. 'What the *fuck*?'

'Lizzie …'

I was furious. 'What made you think that was in *any* way okay?'

'I thought … I thought you …' He trailed off, looking genuinely confused.

Had he really thought something was going to happen between us? Had I given him that impression? Oh my God, what if I had! All those rehearsals when I'd chatted and laughed with him, the way I'd silently admired how sweet he was with the kids. But no. Being friendly didn't give him the right to force himself on me in a fucking primary school storeroom that smelt like dirty socks. I was ready to storm out, but then Rick slumped onto a milk crate and stared up at me, looking broken. Suddenly it was twenty years ago, and I was ripping his guts out all over again. I couldn't run away. Not this time.

'Rick, I'm sorry,' I said, squatting in front of him but keeping my distance. 'I'm sorry if you got the wrong idea, but it is. It's wrong.'

'Isn't there even the smallest part of you that still loves me, Liz?'

Jesus. The pain I'd caused this man, was still causing him. Tears filled my eyes.

'I did,' I said gently. 'Once. I did love you, back then, of course I did. I know I acted badly... *so* badly... when I ran away like that. There's nothing I can say to make up for it. It was unforgivable. I was a coward, and I should *never* have treated you like that. You didn't deserve it and I'm so sorry. But I'm married now, and I love my husband. And I want you to be happy too, but I'm not a part of that. I'm sorry.' Tears were streaming down my face now as I waited for him to say something. Anything. But he just stared at the floor, a weird, blank expression on his face.

'Rick?'

He turned towards me, his face stony and drained of colour. 'I went on the honeymoon, you know,' he said in a strained voice. 'When I got to the resort, they knew it was my honeymoon, so I told them you'd died.'

Jesus.

'I told them you'd died,' he repeated as he got to his feet and walked out.

To: lizabela19100@hotmail.com
From: melissamor@gmail.com
Subject: Hi

Hi Lizzie,

I got your email from Auntie Carmen.

I've been wanting to send this ever since I saw you that day at the fete, but I was struggling to think of what to say. It was a total shock seeing you like that. I guess that much was obvious. It's been such a long time, and you caused us all a lot of pain back then, but I've thought about you a lot over the years. Of course I have. We were best friends. And since seeing you at the fete, well, I've been thinking about you even more than usual.

I didn't know what to say to you when you showed up like that, but maybe we could try again one day? Life is short. I've only realised just how short recently when one of the mums at our school was diagnosed with terminal cancer. Forty-three years old, for fuck's sake. So, yeah. I'm up for a coffee if you are?

There's something else. I heard that Rick is teaching at your school now. I'm not sure what he's like these days, but I thought I should let you know that he went a bit weird after you left. He started getting into fights. Well, he started picking fights. A lot of fights. He'd sit on his own at Sails and get drunk, then he'd find the biggest guy (or guys) in the place and do whatever he needed to do to upset them enough to start throwing punches. He never came out of it well. I don't know if he was deliberately trying to hurt anyone, or himself, but it was as if he wanted something from it. Apparently, he was paying Eammon off (remember, the giant bouncer?) not to step in. It was pretty full on and it was almost as though Rick turned into a different person during that time. Then he disappeared for years. No one saw or heard from him. I was surprised to hear that he was working at your school and wondered if he seems okay now? Anyway, I'll wait to hear if you want to meet up.

Mel

Rick

What a fucking fool.

She's done nothing but make ruinous decisions her whole fucking life. She's dug herself into a shitty, pedestrian life that she wants to escape from. I give her the chance to do exactly that and she makes me feel like I'm the one doing something wrong. As if I'm the one who crossed the line when she's the one who left me. She left me broken. She knew that's what she'd leave behind, and she didn't care. She has no idea how that feels; how it still feels. How it's defined me and made every step forward in my life feel like I'm walking into a fucking hurricane.

I won't just be dismissed and disposed of. She doesn't get to fucking spurn me like that again and just slip back into her life. No fucking way. She needs to know what it's like to hit rock bottom in front of everyone you care about. That's what she did to me. Pity and shock and blundering attempts at sympathy and reassurance from every bastard. Me, silent, wanting to die. If I'd had a gun, I would've swallowed a bullet to give that wedding the finale it deserved. But I'd prepared no defence against the unthinkable thing she did to me.

I tried to fix it.

For years I've bullied myself into imagining better things, like forgiveness, new beginnings, atonement.

I'm fucking done.

Now I'm going to get what I need, for me. I need justice. On my terms and in my way. I'm done wasting time.

Concert Day

'Are you having a mental breakdown?'

It was Myabi, the girl who'd witnessed my BAM (Brownie Apocalypse Meltdown) months ago.

'No, why?' I asked.

'You were rubbing your head,' Myabi said. 'My mum does that when she's stressed.'

'Tell you what,' I said, 'if you go find Megan for me, I promise I won't have a breakdown today.'

Myabi ran from the dressing room where I'd been braiding one eight year old's hair after another for the past twenty minutes. I'd been rubbing my head because I thought I spied a nit behind Elyssa Rickard's ear, and now I had lice-paranoia. So, not exactly a mental breakdown. But I'd come close. Even though there were six teachers and five parents backstage, I was the person every kid ran to when the papier-mâché goose went missing – three grade-two boys were playing football with it – or when the Preps tied each other up with Jacob Marley's chains, or when Stella was suffering with performance anxiety. To be fair, I was Stella's mum, which was probably why they came to me about that. She was fine. Just needed a bit of a pep talk and a couple of red snakes and she was back in the game.

'Mum!' Zara poked her head in the door. 'One-hour call!'

'You look very cute in your headset.'

Zara had opted out of the Bullshit Bunyip grade-six play and put her hand up for backstage duties on both nights instead. She was loving her important role as ASM (Assistant Stage Manager).

'Thanks,' Zara said, glancing at the noisy backstage area. 'Your children are out of control, by the way. I saw Max swinging off one of the lamp posts and had to call Mr Hiney to take him back to his own area. Then I found Archie in the girls' dressing room.'

'Archie isn't even supposed to be back here!' I said, tying off a final braid. 'Tell him to help hand out programmes out front, please.'

'Yep.'

'And can you see if Dad is here yet? I need him to ...'

'Gotta go!'

'... duck home and grab Stella's apron!' I called, but Zara was gone.

'Don't think she heard you,' the girl under my hands said.

'I'll ask Megan,' I said. 'Right, you're done. Next!'

Despite the bedlam, and the possible case of nits I'd contracted, I was loving this. Best of all, I'd been so busy I hadn't spotted Rick Cooke, and hopefully could continue to avoid seeing him altogether. Although not knowing where he was made me more than a little nervous.

***

6.29 p.m.

S – Just rehearsed song. Feeling good! Everyone's amped!

J – lol

S – Inappropriate response

J – lololololololololololololololol

S – dickhead

★★★

'Zara, have you given the USB to Michael?'

'Yep, good to go.'

Megan thought Zara looked very grown up tonight in her black pants, black T-shirt and headset. 'Thanks, sweetie.'

'Do you think they'll like it?' Zara asked.

Megan looked up from the script, where she was making last-minute cue notes for herself. 'They'll love it.'

Zara and her friends had filmed a news segment to play during the show and it was brilliant. Lizzie had said Zara was a talented mimic, but Zara's impersonation of Tracy Grimshaw reporting on Scrooge's miraculous transformation was spot on.

'Zara, you're amazing!' she'd cried after watching it. 'Why didn't you audition for the grade-five and -six play?'

'I'm more of a screen performer,' Zara had said, looking as serious as a young De Niro. 'And that play was lame.'

Megan had to agree.

'Megan! Lizzie wants you!'

'Thanks, Myabi, but I don't think people in Adelaide needed to know that.'

Megan began walking across the crowded backstage area, and as she neared the dressing rooms she noticed three mums, Nicola, Rebecca and Farida, standing at the top of the steps that led outside. They looked upset and were gesturing madly to each other.

What's that about? Megan wondered.

★★★

6.35 p.m.

S – Something's going on.

J – What's going on?

S – Dunno. Doesn't sound good though

J – There's far too many of you crying

S – Who's crying? Wha?

J – There's far too many of you dying

S – dickhead

J – His dad shot him

S – You need to talk to someone

J – We don't need to escalate

S – I'm going now

★★★

'I can't believe she did that on school grounds!'

'She's been leading him on ever since he got here!'

'Breaking his heart once clearly wasn't enough.'

'What's this?'

Nicola, Rebecca and Farida froze, mortified, as Megan appeared behind them.

'We … we were just …'

'Talking bullshit about my best friend?' Megan finished Nicola's sentence.

The women's expressions flipped from guilty to defensive.

'We feel sorry for Rick, that's all,' Rebecca said, folding her arms across her chest.

'Why?'

'Lizzie made a move on him yesterday in the office storeroom,' Farida said, relishing the drama, 'but Rick wouldn't have a bar of it.'

Megan laughed. 'That's ridiculous.'

'Everyone knows,' Rebecca said, gesturing towards the groups of children spread out backstage with their teachers.

'The kids know?'

'Well, no. The adults.' Rebecca looked embarrassed. 'The receptionist, Karen, found Rick in a state afterwards. He told her everything.'

Fucking big-mouth Karen. But this couldn't be true. Lizzie would never ...

'We were just saying maybe it would be better if Lizzie wasn't backstage tonight,' Nicola said haughtily. 'It's awkward for everyone, especially poor Rick.'

★★★

I was working on my seventh head when I heard raised voices coming from outside the dressing room.

Oh Jesus, what now?

'Stella!' I called. 'Can you come and finish Gemma's hair, please?'

I transferred Gemma's thick strands of black hair into Stella's nimble fingers and walked out to investigate.

★★★

'We know she's your friend.' Farida's tone was so condescending it made Megan grit her teeth. 'But it's about the *kids* tonight, not Lizzie. We can't have her upsetting Rick and distracting him from his job.'

Blood pounded in Megan's ears. She knew she should keep her voice down, but she couldn't. 'I don't know where you heard this bullshit, but there is no way Lizzie would ...'

'Lizzie would what?'

The women turned to find Lizzie behind them.

***

Nicola shrugged. 'Nothing.'

She was lying. The woman's face went white the moment she saw me.

'Don't be a coward,' Megan hissed. 'Tell her.'

'Okay, fine,' Farida said. 'We think the way you've treated Rick Cooke is disgraceful!'

I nearly fell over. 'What?'

'Look, Lizzie,' Nicola said, a big fake smile on her face, 'we know you ran off and left him at the altar years ago, which is obviously your business ...'

'Is it?' My temper was rising by the second. 'Thank you for saying so.'

'... but he's part of this community so the way you treat him *now* is our business,' Nicola continued.

A community that didn't exist before Megan stepped in, I thought, finding it hard to form words.

'And we can't just stand by and watch you destroy a good man ... again,' Rebecca chimed in, 'so maybe you should just go home.'

Megan was saying something to them, but I couldn't focus on anything except the roaring in my ears and the bullfrog that seemed to be lodged in my throat. So, it was true, even if I'd tried to tell myself it wasn't. I'd made Rick, and everyone else, think I wanted to be with him again, to get him back. Not only that, but I'd been found out. The real Lizzie had finally been revealed. These stupid women's information might've been bogus, but the result was the same: they knew me now. They knew what a horrible coward I really was, just like Melissa and Rick had for years, and everything I'd spent years burying was crawling up out of the ground to reclaim me.

***

6.38 p.m.

S – Shit. Getting heated. Lizzie's in it too. Rick's gone to check it out.

J – You okay?

J – Oi!

S – soz

S – Bridg is here.

J – Did you know she was coming?

S – Nope, just spotted her in the audience

J – Do your thing, mate

S – What thing

J – Why are you there?

S – For the kids

J – and

S – And my friends

J – Correct!

***

Megan could sense the teachers looking in their direction, so she lowered her voice. 'The only people who are leaving this backstage area are you three,' she muttered. 'I'm running this show and I want you out!'

'Last time I checked, Penny Guthrie was still principal,'

Nicola spat back. 'If anyone's running this show, it's her!'

'Fair enough. Let's go find her,' Megan said. 'I'm sure she'd be very interested to hear what you have to say.'

'Hey ladies, everything okay?'

Rick Cooke, looking as innocent and harmless as Charlie Brown. *Well, this is awkward and inconvenient as fuck,* Megan thought. *We've got a show to put on here, people!*

'It's okay, Rick,' Nicola said sweetly. 'We're just … clearing the air.'

'Lizzie? You okay?'

Greg! Jesus, where had he come from? *Now* it was awkward as fuck.

'What are you doing back here?' Lizzie looked like she was about to vomit.

'Stella left this in the car,' he said and gestured to the beige apron in his hand. 'I thought she needed it for the play. Everything okay here?'

He looked pointedly at Rick when he spoke, but Megan couldn't decipher his expression. Greg's bottom lip was twitching slightly, and he was holding his arms at a small but unnatural distance from his sides, like he might take flight.

Rebecca decided she was the best person to tackle this little imbroglio. 'I think we all know the situation here, so let's just act like adults, okay?'

'Maybe you should take your own advice, Rebecca,' Megan said.

'There's no need to attack Rebecca, Megan,' said Farida.

Megan watched Rick's eyes dart from woman to woman. Greg's eyes stayed fixed on Rick. Megan felt like she was holding the pin in a grenade. 'Okay, Farida,' she said, making placating motions with her hands. 'Let's all remember why we're here.'

'We're here to let Rick know that he has the backing of the school community,' Nicola said, pulling the pin from the grenade.

'What does that mean?' Greg's tone was flat and low, a semi-tone away from a growl.

'Greg, I'm sorry if this is awkward for you and Lizzie,' Farida said, 'but let's call a spade a spade. Things have been done that can't be undone, and you two have to deal with that in your own way, but ...'

'What's been done?' asked Greg.

Rick stepped forward, holding his hand up to Farida. 'It's okay, Farida, there's no point going over it again.'

'What's been done?' This time, Greg directed the question at Rick, his voice calm but direct.

'Now, Greg,' Rebecca began, 'this is difficult for everyone ...'

'Sure,' Greg interrupted with an almost gentle smile, 'but it sounds like – from what you're saying – that it's mostly difficult for me and Lizzie. So, I wanna know *what's going on*?'

Megan couldn't stand it any more. She threw the grenade. 'These three are saying that Lizzie kissed Rick,' she announced, glaring at the women as she spoke, 'and that she's been leading him on, and has broken his heart all over again.'

Nicola, Rebecca and Farida stared, eyes wide, looking as if a judge had just pronounced a guilty verdict. Megan felt woozy as she checked her watch. They *had* to get ready for the concert. She looked up to find Greg nodding slowly. His bottom lip seemed to have disappeared altogether and Lizzie was looking at Greg, shaking her head in the same rhythm as Greg's nodding. Everyone stood very still.

Greg took a slow breath then turned to face Rick. 'That true?' There was no danger in his voice.

Rick held his gaze for a moment, raised his eyebrows and looked down at the floor, while the three gossipmongers cocked their heads and adopted their respective 'poor guy' expressions. Megan couldn't tell if this triptych of patronising pity faces were for Rick, Greg or both. But Rick had clearly indicated that the answer to Greg's question was a definitive yes. Greg turned back to Lizzie, whose head had become a perpetual-motion toy, shaking involuntarily, her mouth open and silent, then he looked at everyone in turn, in this circle of awkward, combustible controversy.

'Wow,' Greg said, then did something Megan wasn't expecting. He chuckled. Sort of a snorty scoff. Megan was worried he was about to snap, and that she'd have to call an ambulance while the three gossipmongers filmed every moment of whatever awful shit was about to go down on their phones.

'What a crock of shit,' Greg said the words as if he was teaching a crucial English sentence to international students.

Rick looked up, his brow creasing.

'Anything else I should know about my wife, ladies?' Greg asked Nicola, Rebecca and Farida.

They didn't so much shake their heads, as have a collective neck spasm.

'Okay, good,' Greg continued. 'My turn then.' Greg shifted his stance, so he was facing Rick. Megan suddenly lost all interest in what time it was. 'I know you kissed my wife,' Greg began. 'I know *you* kissed *her*. I know that because she told me less than twenty minutes after it happened. And she made me promise not to say or do anything because she's still messed up about what happened between you two – what she *did* to you – a lifetime ago.'

'Listen, mate.' Rick's voice cracked.

'I'm not your mate,' Greg said. 'I'm not your mate, Rick. You have a history with Lizzie, I know that. But her future is with me.'

Megan looked at Lizzie, but every cell of her friend was with her husband.

'You weren't there,' Rick said, his eyebrows still raised, supplicant.

'Come again?' Greg said.

Rick steeled himself, looking to his cheerleaders and reassuring them with a smile. 'I get why Lizzie lied about what happened, Greg,' he said in a condescending tone. 'But I was there. It happened.'

Lizzie blanched. 'You liar.'

'One of us is,' Rick replied in an even tone.

Greg moved to Lizzie and took her hand, their fingers interlocking, knuckles white. 'I believe my wife.'

'Cos you need to believe her,' Rick mocked.

'Don't need to. Just do,' said Greg. 'I've also found out a few more truths about you this week. You don't have a wife. And you don't have kids.'

'That's bullshit.' But Rick looked rattled, and even his cheer squad were suddenly looking like they'd just woken up in a strange place.

'You've never married, and you live alone,' Greg said. 'That's a fact.'

'What the *fuck*?' Lizzie looked from Greg, to Rick, then back to Greg again. 'How did you find ...?'

'It's a fucking lie!' Rick hissed. The wounded victim act had given way to seething anger and a heavy silence fell over the group.

'I'm sure we could all have a fascinating existential discussion about the nature of truth,' Megan said finally. 'But Greg says he knows what happened and he believes his wife, right?'

'Correct,' said Greg.

'And I believe Lizzie too. She's my best friend and I believe her,' Megan said. 'Which means I think you're lying, Rick. I think you're a liar.'

'That's your right,' Rick sneered, shooting Megan a disdainful look.

'I don't need you to tell me what I have the right to do, or not to do,' Megan said, darkening. 'Maybe tell these three what their rights are.' She gestured to Nicola, Rebecca and Farida. 'Because they seem to give half a shit about what you have to say. Mainly because they all imagine themselves sitting on your face while you try to whisper sweet nothings through a mouthful of punani.'

The three women gasped as if they'd just witnessed an awful act of violence. Megan briefly wondered if she'd gone too far, but then decided she was fine with that.

'Rick, listen,' Lizzie said tremulously, 'I told you I was sorry for what happened – for what I did to you ...'

'You're not sorry,' Rick snapped, his eyes flashing angrily.

'Hey.' Greg stepped forward, placing himself behind his wife's left shoulder.

'Guess what, *mate*,' Rick hissed, 'this has nothing to do with you.'

'Rick ...' Lizzie began, trying to diffuse him.

'No!' Rick was starting to shake. 'He doesn't get to be involved in this. This is about you and me. You and me! Not him, or anyone else. You should've been with me. You should be with *me*!'

'Stop!' said Greg.

'Rick, please!' Lizzie sounded desperate.

Nicola, Rebecca and Farida were no longer enjoying the show and were trying to back away slowly, to extricate themselves from the snowballing ugliness.

'*Rick, please!*' Rick mimicked. 'Jesus fucking Christ. I *tried* begging, Lizzie. I begged and begged, but you weren't even there. You didn't give a shit. You had another life to lead. A life without me. But you were wrong and you needed to know that, you needed to be kissed to be reminded of ...' Rick trailed off.

Nicola, Rebecca and Farida stopped dead in their tracks, and Greg's entire body seemed to grow by at least five per cent. Lizzie looked at Rick with a mixture of pity and anger. *It was time to put a full stop on this*, Megan thought. She spoke in a measured, even tone. 'Rick, you need to go.'

Rick's breathing was shaky, and blotches of red spread across his face and neck. He looked wild, and Greg looked like he might rip him in half.

'Megan! Mum!' Zara appeared, looking annoyed.

'You're supposed to be running a warm-up on stage in five minutes,' she said. 'Oh, hey Dad. What's ...?'

Zara furrowed her brow as she tried to read the situation in front of her, like she was trying to find the 3D image in a magic eye picture.

Rick shot Lizzie one final look, then walked down the stairs and out of the building.

'Jeez, this concert is making everyone freak out,' said Zara, throwing her hands up.

Nicola leant forward. 'Megan, look ...'

'OUT! Out out out out out out!' Megan barked at Nicola and her minions.

The three of them almost sprinted away towards the auditorium.

'Sooo, warm-up?' At least Zara still had her eye on the prize.

'We're coming now, darling,' Lizzie said, putting her arm around Greg's waist. 'Go get everyone together.'

Zara scrunched her face at her parents' public display of affection and left.

The three friends looked at each other and took a few collective deep breaths. Megan put her arms around Greg and Lizzie, and they shared a good, long, necessary hug. Megan pulled back and looked at Greg. 'I'm gonna need to borrow her.'

'Just don't pash her, okay?'

'No promises.' Megan took Lizzie's hand. 'Come on, let's go.'

Lizzie gave Greg another hug with her free arm. 'See you after.'

Greg smiled. 'You will.'

***

To: jack_woz_here@hotmail.com
From: samhatfieldchef@bigpond.com
Subject: Shit fight

Hey dickhead,

The school concert to end all school concerts is done and dusted. I feel like I've just run a marathon; or at least for a tram. I'm pretty unfit, so those two experiences aren't that far removed.

I thought I was going to drown my fretboard in sweat before I even started, before I even knew Bridget was there. The first half of the concert ran so smoothly, I think it took all of us by surprise. The kids were amazing, the audience was getting into it, and backstage was a well-oiled machine.

The second half was more along the lines of what you'd expect from a primary school concert. This sweet grade-four girl had been struggling with her early nineteenth-century peasant's costume, trying to discreetly adjust it on stage. But she wasn't discreet and looked like she was trying out a self-imposed exorcism technique. And the audience was loving it. Then her bonnet flew backwards off her head and she tried to catch it before it hit the ground but missed. She chose one of the best words I know: 'Shitballs.'

The crowd laughed harder than they had all night, and it seemed like that was the moment someone stuck a pin in our balloon. From there the show just careened in every possible direction. In the scene that was meant to have a projected image of a town, they projected an image of all the ghosts of Christmas instead. A couple of little kids started crying, which threw off the older kids who had lines. Lizzie was prompting from the wings so loudly that she may as well have come out and made it a one-woman show. Also, Lizzie was wearing a headset so she could communicate with Megan, who was operating the slides and sound cues and when Lizzie pulled the headphones off, Megan's colourful language was audible to all nearby.

At the end, when Scrooge is meant to give gifts to everyone, the kid didn't have enough gifts to go around. Lizzie grabbed her purse and slipped him some cash, so Scrooge started dishing out coins and notes, much to the delight of his fellow cast members, who clearly had no intention of returning their 'props'.

There was no sign of Rick after kiss-gate – I'll tell you about that later – which was a relief, especially for Lizzie who, although rock solid throughout the show, was a bit shaky nonetheless.

At the end of the show I got on stage and led the kids through a tear-jerking version of 'Have Yourself A Merry Little Christmas'.

Backstage after the show, Megan was mortified; she genuinely felt she'd failed. Lizzie was the first person to give her a hug. She held Megan's shoulders and told her she'd done an amazing thing, so I started playing Alex Lloyd's 'Amazing' (yes I still remember the chords, thank you very much), which earnt me a hug from both of them.

I felt so happy, dickhead.

Then Penny Guthrie was there looking like a proud den mother. Megan's mum, Ellie, was jumping up and down hugging her daughter, her new pacemaker working overtime. And all the kids were flapping around, peaking off their little heads. They accosted Megan and Lizzie in small groups, saying how much fun they'd had and how this was the best concert ever, and begging them to do it again next year, at which point Lizzie looked to Megan with an expression of distilled horror.

Then Megan beamed and hugged Lizzie again and all the kids cheered and whooped, and one Prep boy asked if they were gay.

Henry's grandson, Eddie, and what must've been his entire extended family, came backstage too. Megan started assaulting them with apologies, and Eddie finally told her to SHOOSH because they loved it. Mate, that family couldn't have been more touched by everything Megs did to honour Henry, including the piece she added to the programme with his photo on the back.

Megan started crying and hugged Eddie, and I think she realised she'd been hugging him for a bit too long because she suddenly broke away and hugged every member of that family for the same amount of time.

Then Sasha was in my arms, saying how great the music was and that the kids sounded so good and how cute I look when I'm nervous. And Lizzie and Megan were smiling at us.

I have some really good friends, my friend. And yes, you're fortunate enough to be included in my exclusive inner circle But tonight was for Lizzie and Megan, and they smashed it. I'm so fucking proud of them.

And me. I'm proud of myself, dickhead. I got up on stage in front of people and played guitar for the first time in nearly ten years. And it reminded me that music is a goddamn magic elixir. Did I mention I'm feeling really happy?

By the way, your texts were as unhelpful as they were hilarious, so thanks for nothing and everything. Were you listening to Marvin Gaye while you were texting me, or did that shit just pop into your disturbed mind? Honestly.

Oh, and something happened earlier that was – as Tyler would describe it – pretty epic. Bridget came backstage during the show. Yep. As soon as I saw her at the play I should've known she'd find a reason to get pissed off.

So, Bridget goes backstage and starts talking to Lizzie. I didn't hear what she said. The first discernible words I heard came from Lizzie: 'It's a *school play*.'

It was clear Lizzie was in a conversation she wasn't enjoying, so I go to investigate further and I spot Bridget, finger out, jabbing it too close to Lizzie's chest. Bridget's head sort of lolls back a bit when she sees me, like I've just dropped a TV spoiler. I walk over and ask what she's doing back there. She'd miss Lola's bit. Bridget then points out that Tyler's costume makes him look like a beggar. Lizzie says, 'He is a beggar. I would've thought the kneeling and holding out of the hands might've been a giveaway.'

Bridget asks if I approved Tyler being cast as a beggar, then said her son deserves more and shouldn't be made to pretend he's a homeless bum in front of his friends and the whole school community. Lizzie is looking at me, waiting for me to do something. So, guess what, dickhead?

I did something.

I said to Bridget that Tyler's had an absolute ball rehearsing for this, pretending to beg for every meal I've served him in the past couple of weeks, making me laugh like a drain because he's good at it and he's funny. Then I said I agreed that Tyler deserves more – but not when it comes to this concert. Tyler deserves more than a part-time mother. I said both our kids deserve more than a mother who can't name their best friends, and they deserve more than a father who lets himself be scared into submission by a wife who thrives on the fear of others. And I told her that's what the kids have now: an unafraid father who will do everything necessary to put them out into the world as fucking great people.

Bridget tried to jump in a few times, but that shit didn't happen this time. I just kept right on talking. Talking like I might never be able to again. I could feel Lizzie there with me. She didn't say anything, but I knew she was with me.

I told Bridget she was right to leave me, and that she and Conrad seem like a good fit. They love themselves more than anything or anyone else, and they can live in perfect parallel lines, filling the space between them with nice things and premium airport lounge access and platinum credit cards. I said it's good that she left, because I never would've had the guts, so she's done us both a favour. I said I know she loves the kids, even if she doesn't know how to show it, and that she'll always be a part of their lives because she's their mum and they need her.

By this stage I'd insulted her and thanked her so many times that she didn't know how to react. I paused to see if she had anything to say, and after a few seconds, she just told me that the direct debit was sorted now. I thanked her and asked if she was going to stick around for the song.

'What song?' she asked, which couldn't have surprised me any less. I told her I'd written a song for the concert and the kids were about to sing it with me backing them on guitar. She asked if I was singing too and when I said I wasn't she said that was 'probably for the best'. Then she left.

I felt hollow, but not in an empty way. I felt like a vessel ready for filling. Lizzie asked if I was okay and I told her I was. All I wanted was to get out there and help those bloody excellent kids do their thing.

I think I played well. Not too sure. But everyone clapped at the end and the kids beamed and gave me a thumbs-up or their 'rock on' gesture of choice. I watched them walk off stage, feeling proud and happy and relieved and a little fuller.

Today's been a shit fight, dickhead. But we all won our battles in the end.

S x

19 December

Review: A Christmas Carol *by Charles Dickens (adapted by Sasha Jeffares)*

So, last night, I left Daddy Dearest in front of the telly and took the girls to Baytree Primary's junior Christmas concert. I have to admit, I was slightly dubious when I heard it was an adaptation of Charles Dickens' A Christmas Carol, *especially with its outdated and politically incorrect representation of persons with physical disabilities. However, credit where credit is due. The concept was simple but effective, and it was obvious that the show had been clearly thought through – from costumes, to props, music, lighting and performance. There were a few bumps (I was horrified at one point to hear a curse word fly out of a child's mouth, not to mention from the show's director, Megan Wylie, when her expletives from backstage were amplified through the school hall) but overall the audience seemed to enjoy it. The students had plenty of time to shine, and the musical accompaniment, provided by Baytree parent Sam Hatfield, was a highlight, especially the final song – 'Have Yourself A Merry Little Christmas'.*

The show was dedicated to the memory of Baytree Primary's lollipop man, Henry, who passed away earlier this year, and I think he would have been very proud of the school he dedicated so much of his time to. Earlier this year, I expressed my dismay at the Baytree community's lack of compassion when Henry passed away, so I was pleased to see that they have pulled their socks up and gone some way to rebuilding their sense of responsibility, care and empathy. If this Christmas concert is anything to go by, they definitely seem to be on the right track. A great night out. Even without wine.

Cody Fletcher
Author of the Mother Unfolding Blog

Epilogue

It was past midnight. Officially Christmas. And even though I knew I'd regret it in the morning when Max jumped on our bed at 5 a.m. screaming, 'SANTA CAME!', I didn't want to go to bed yet.

The house was silent. Not a creature was stirring and all that, and the five most important people in my world were fast asleep, while I lay outside breathing in the warm night air, sipping my wine and enjoying the calm before the festive storm to come.

Greg and I had stayed up late, placing presents under the tree, chomping on biscuits and carrots, and pouring half the milk down the sink, as per our usual Christmas Eve routine. Then we had one last glass of wine together as we watched the runner-up of some TV talent show attempt to turn 'Silent Night' into a pop ballad on *Carols by Candlelight*.

'Merry Christmas, buddy,' Greg had said, leaning over to kiss me.

'Merry Christmas,' I said, kissing him back.

After Greg went to bed, I took my wine into the backyard, lay down on our striped banana lounge, stared up at the clear night sky and thanked the stars for my family, my friends and my life. After the past six months, I owed the universe a bit of gratitude. I thought about how much I was looking forward to seeing Melissa and her family. They were coming to our place for a Boxing Day barbecue. I was nervous about seeing her again, and meeting her family for the first time, but they were good nerves. Sam, Megan and the kids were coming too. I'd asked Sam if he wanted to bring Sasha, but he said he'd rather just bring Lola and Tyler.

'We've decided to just be mates,' he told me on the last day of school.

I was disappointed. Megan and I so wanted Sam to be happy and have someone ace like Sasha in his life. And sex. We both really wanted him to have loads of sex. That's friendship.

'It's cool,' Sam said. 'I'm just getting a handle on being single; a single dad. And I've developed a pretty big crush on my guitar again, so I reckon for now it'll just be me, my kids and a lot more music for all of us.'

Megan did a loud cough.

'And my friends,' Sam added. 'I'll squeeze my friends in there somewhere.'

'What about Eddie?' I'd asked Megan. 'Do you want to bring him?'

'Absolutely not,' Megan said. 'We haven't even had a proper date yet. I'm not bringing him to your house so you can fill him with beer and unleash the Spanish Inquisition!'

'I would never in a million ...'

Megan and Sam stared.

'Yeah, all right,' I said, shrugging. 'I totally would. I'd make the poor guy sing like a bird.'

'You're very scary,' Sam said.

'But would you hurry up and go on a date already?' I implored Megan.

Megan said she wanted to take it slow with Eddie. I knew that she was protecting herself, which was understandable, but any fool could see they were a good fit. Megan had agreed to let him help her sell Chill in the new year, so at least they were getting in bed together in a business sense. So, it would just be Sam, Megan and the kids coming along on Boxing Day to meet my oldest friend and her family, which was fine. Lola wanted to wear her costume from the play (she'd been grieving ever since it finished) so I'd made Stella promise to wear hers too, in solidarity.

No one had seen or heard from Rick since the night of the concert. Zara was devastated that her beloved Mr Cooke seemed to have vanished without warning.

'But why would he miss the last week of school without telling us?' she'd moaned every afternoon when yet another school day had passed with no sign of him.

'Maybe he had a family emergency,' I'd suggested, avoiding eye contact with my canny daughter, lest she notice the twitch in my left eye whenever he was mentioned.

I found out that it was Auntie Carmen who'd helped Greg dig the dirt on Rick. Apparently, Greg rang her the night Rick kissed me and asked her to find out whatever she could about my ex. Auntie Carmen had used her personal gossip hotline and fed the results back to my husband, all without my knowledge. Greg told me that Auntie Carmen had discovered that not only did Rick lie about having a family, but he'd apparently been trying to track me down for years. And now he was gone. I couldn't help feeling sorry for him, and slightly worried too.

'I've done it again,' I'd cried to Greg the day after the concert. 'I've broken his heart all over again.'

'You've done nothing,' Greg assured me. 'He's a grown man, and he has to work out how to deal with his own shit in his own way. You're not responsible for him, buddy.'

Since then, I'd promised myself that I'd let it go. The

past. All that pain, guilt and shame. I'd spent the better part of my life defining myself by that one event, that one thing I did when I was barely a grown-up. I've done a lot more since then. A lot. And I wanted to start redefining myself. Not just by all the things I'd done up until now that filled me with pride and happiness, but by the things I'd do today and tomorrow ... and on it goes.

All that mattered to me now was my family, my friends and my community.

Max got an early Christmas present that he was pretty happy with. A couple of nights ago we had pizza and watched *Bend It Like Beckham*. Max loved it, even though it was 'all girlie'. During the closing credits, I told him I'd enrolled him in the local soccer club, starting next year. My timing was off because he had just taken a huge bite of Margherita. When he tried to speak – his mouth full, his eyes wide and his little body convulsing with joy – he rained tomato down onto the rug. The other kids screamed at Max to stop, or pretended to vomit themselves – both excellent sibling responses to grossness – and Greg couldn't stop grinning. I told Max to calm down and finish his mouthful.

'Are you serious, Mum?' he asked, fixing me with a fierce stare.

'Dead serious,' I answered. 'I think I'm going to start you in the midfield.'

Greg turned to me, but I didn't take my eyes off Max, who was thinking hard about what I'd just said to him.

'The coach tells me where to play,' he said finally.

'Damn right I do,' I replied.

Poor Max looked as though his head might fall off. 'But ... but you don't even ...' he stammered.

'Don't worry, kiddo,' I said with supreme confidence. 'I know a thing or two.'

Greg started chuckling, quietly at first, as if in shock, then louder as I turned to him, raised my eyebrows and smiled proudly.

'It's in my blood,' I reassured my dumbstruck young son. 'Your nannu coached me, and now I'm gonna coach you. It's officially a family tradition.'

'Those poor kids,' Greg said.

'Those poor kids are gonna be bloody champions, my friend,' I said, my confidence unflappable.

'I don't doubt it, buddy,' Greg replied.

We looked at each other, happy. Greg pulled me back onto the couch, folded me in his arms and kissed me. The kids roared their disapproval then piled on top of us, all greasy pizza fingers and love, before we screamed as the couch toppled over backwards. Yep, it had been a great night.

I finished my wine, peeled myself off the banana lounge and went inside.

Acknowledgements

The Drop-off came into existence – first as a web series and now as a novel – because of the people we met while our two daughters attended Ripponlea Primary School in Melbourne.

In fact, we loved the experience so much, we bought the school.

That's obviously:

a) not true
b) a ridiculously dated reference to an electric shaver ad from 1979.

Moving on.

At a time in our lives when the desire to make new friends had diminished to the point where we actively avoided the human race, the community we discovered at this small school forced us to rethink our curmudgeonly ways. We now have a full, boxed set of new best friends, all of whom come with many special features and behind-the-scenes extras. (But not in an *Ice Storm* way, which is only a 27-year-old movie reference. Nailing it.) These are folks we regularly dine with, drink with, laugh with, cry with, cry-laugh with and holiday with.

We found so much love and spirit in this place, we were inspired to try to capture it as best we could using the skills at our disposal. We wanted to create something that provided a fictionalised tribute to this place and these people who taught us the true value of community. A better bunch of dickheads you will never find. However, it takes more than a bunch of dickheads to make a book. There are a lot of other amazing people we need to thank too.

We have been endlessly surprised, challenged, encouraged and energised by the enthusiasm, expertise (#alliterationftw) and passion of the wonderful people at Echo Publishing. Angela Meyer was the first person to suggest we adapt and develop *The Drop Off* web series into a novel, and for that we are forever in her debt. Mainly due to a late-night visit to a whiskey bar, but also for her vision, her ardour and her brilliant brain.

Also, to the other awesome ladies at Echo Publishing: Benny Agius, Liz Robinson and Justine Taylor, thank you for your constant and unflappable support. You have been true champions of this book every step of the way. Thanks also to our publicist, Debbie McInnes, for making us appear to be more interesting than we are.

To our dear, trusted peers and friends who took the time to read the book at various stages of (in)completion, your unnervingly undiluted opinions and suggestions were invaluable. (Except for the thing about the zombies. Maybe next time.) So, to Kylie Jeffares, Sonja Ebbels, Leanne Gianchino, Sally Rippin, Jane Clifton, Karen Harris, Bec Howard, Toni Jordan, Adam Fawcett, Helen Macdonald, Rose Jost, William McInnes, Danny Katz and Pia Miranda, we extend our arms and wrap you in the awkwardly long hug of gratitude. THANK YOU!

Thanks also to Katie Brannaghan, Yvonne Hogg and Thomas Rechnitzer, who lent their expertise and professional experience to ensure we looked like we'd engaged in gruelling, in-depth research. We are so grateful for your time, your notes, your patience and your ability to tell us just how wrong we were without laughing in our faces.

To Seahaven Village in Barwon Heads, and Ash Wilson at Follow the Leader café in Ripponlea, thank you for providing two very different, but equally ace, creative sanctums.

Finally, to the team who helped create *The Drop Off* web series, it bears repeating to the lot of you that there would be no novel without the audiovisual piece of entertainment that we made together. You all own a part of this. Not in any way legally, though, we're just being nice. Christie Whelan Browne played the character of Megan in the original web series, and imbued Megan with humour, subtlety and grace. It made the writing of the book that much easier, already having a vivid image of the character she created. Thank you, CWB. The same can be said of Scott Edgar, who played Dave. Although without the grace thing. But that was obviously a very clear character choice. So nice one, Scott. We love you both dearly. Thanks to Screen Australia for giving us the funding to bring our show, characters and stories to life, and to Paul Walton – our mentor, our friend and the stick of dynamite up our bottoms – who has been instrumental in *The Drop Off*'s creation and ongoing success. We owe him so much gratitude, and at least a dollar thirty-five. Thanks for everything, Paul. We're organising a payment plan, we promise.

Finally, thank you to the two human beings who inspire everything we do in this life. Finn and Abbie, we love you both so much. If you think we're embarrassing now, wait until you read this ... once you're old enough.

The Drop Off web series

This novel's first incarnation was as a short-form comedy web series. We've always wanted to make good things with good people, and *The Drop Off* – particularly the second series, which received principal funding from Screen Australia – was the epitome of that ideal. The web series explores that strange bubble of time, also known as 'school drop-off', that parents know all too well. It's a show about inappropriate conversations, unexpected encounters and accidental friendships. Left to their own devices, Lizzie, Sam, Megan and Dave would never have become friends. But, due to a short list of life choices, both deliberate

L-R: Scott Edgar as Dave, Christie Whelan Browne as Megan, Fiona Harris as Lizzie and Mike McLeish as Sam.

and accidental (i.e. when they had kids, where they live and where their kids go to school), they are friends. They gravitated toward each other and found safety and solace in their ability to share in the joy of a good takeaway coffee and, more importantly, a laugh. Yes, laughter is more important than coffee. There's a meme somewhere that says so. If the mood takes you and you'd like to explore this novel's origin story (no spider bites or gamma rays involved), you can find all existing episodes of the web series by following any of these links:

http://kissandgo.com.au/project/the-drop-off/

https://www.facebook.com/thedropoffshow/

https://www.youtube.com/channel/UCAcDg9Rv7cPTGN2Z0-S_N9g/

The three best friends and the rest of the Baytree Primary community are back.

THE PICK-UP

Nothing ever goes wrong on school camp, right?

Lizzie, Sam and Megan are very different people who became best friends over good coffee and even better laughs at school drop-off.

Midwife Lizzie is flat out juggling four kids and an absent husband. Newly divorced Sam is navigating the 'delights' of online dating. And single-mum Megan is contemplating a slightly scandalous relationship.

As if that wasn't enough, this year the trio have decided to embrace their inner parent helper and volunteer for the annual school camp. If they think their personal lives are chaotic, this camp's going to teach them what chaos really means . . .

'Hilariously relevant, disturbingly relatable. It's real life, but way funnier.' SAMMY J

Read on for a sneak peek . . .

'Wait, what?'

'I said, they're gone!'

'They can't be *gone*. Where would they go?' Megan looked panicked. 'Maybe they're just hiding somewhere?'

'The girls have searched the whole camp.' My voice sounded shaky. 'They ... are ... gone.'

I was trying desperately to stay on point, but another part of my brain was still reeling over my second shock of the night.

'Shit!' All the colour drained out of Sam's face as he ran his hands through his hair.

Megan took a step forward. 'Are you sure? They're probably just ...'

'I told you!' I roared. 'Are you listening to me, or are you still too wrapped up in ...?'

'Hey, hey, come on, guys,' Dave said, stepping forward. 'We're not going to get anywhere by attacking each other.'

'Shut up, Dave!' I snapped. 'You don't know what I saw when —'

'Don't!' Megan glared at me before her face crumpled. 'Jesus, this is all my fault.'

'It's *our* fault!' I hissed. 'I'm to blame, too!'

'Come on!' Sam stood up. 'We have to find them.'

Dave nodded, then looked back at me. 'And we have to tell the others,' he said.

A strange feeling of calm washed over me. 'No. We're not telling anyone. Not yet.'

Chapter One
Lizzie

Seven weeks earlier . . .

'Who's that?'

'She's familiar,' Sam said, handing us our coffees.

'She's babelicious,' Megan added.

I agreed with both sentiments. In fact, the first time I laid eyes on Rania Jalali, I thought that Meghan Markle had mistaken our school for a crisis centre.

We all stared at the gorgeous woman creating a stir at Baytree Primary on this warm February morning. Excited Grade Six girls (and some equally excited parents) zeroed in on the mystery woman, acting like ... well, like paparazzi with Meghan Markle.

Huge sunglasses covered the upper half of her face, but even so, it was clear that this woman was exquisitely beautiful. The kind of beautiful you don't expect to see in real life, let alone a school playground. Her burnt-orange wrap dress highlighted toned legs and slim brown arms, and long, freshly tonged dark hair bounced around her shoulders. A tiny boy, with equally thick dark hair and dressed in the Baytree uniform of navy-blue shorts and light-blue polo top, hid behind her impossibly long legs. He was staring at a phone and seemed oblivious to the hysteria caused by his mother's presence.

'Maybe she's one of those YouTubers who talks to kids

about following your influencer dreams,' Sam suggested, joining us on the bench.

'Maybe.' Megan's smooth brow creased. 'But Penny didn't mention anything. I would've put it in the newsletter.'

Sam and I shared a look. Ever since her official coronation as 'Best School Mum and Community Member', my best friend Megan prided herself on being across *everything* that happened at Baytree Primary. Prior to that, she wouldn't have been able to pick her son's teacher out of a line-up.

But Megan Wylie had won the admiration and respect of the entire community after masterminding the school Christmas concert two years ago. Since then, her involvement with Baytree Primary had significantly increased. She was now in charge of compiling the weekly newsletter (rebranded *The Baytree Buzz*) and was on the committee for the Grade Five/Six Camp, which she would also be attending. Sam and I found this gobsmacking for two reasons:

1. Oscar was in Grade Four, so Megan had no parental obligation to be involved.
2. Megan wasn't the camping type. Her idea of roughing it was staying in a three-star hotel.

There were few things I could think of that would be worse than spending three days with forty pre-pubescent children who didn't belong to me, but Megan seemed excited by the prospect.

'Hey, did you see?'

Dave's voice was even more manic than usual. The forty-something dad was jogging on the spot at the end of our bench, like a man in desperate need of a loo. Dave

Podanski was a scruffy-faced Robin Gibb lookalike, who usually wore an ensemble of skinny jeans, maroon Converse and some kind of geek-branded T-shirt. Today's shirt was emblazoned with a large mathematical pi symbol. He always wore a goofy grin on his bearded face, but this morning's had an unnerving intensity, and his eyes were wide behind his Buddy Holly frames. It was difficult to tell if he was excited, horrified or having an aneurysm.

'You mean Miss Hotness over there?' I nodded at the woman now posing for selfies with a succession of girls and their mums. 'Did she recently marry a prince?'

'You don't know her?' He sounded as though we were all looking at Oprah.

Megan raised a hand to shield her eyes from the bright morning sun. 'No idea, but I'd kill for her sunnies. Oscar rushed me out the door for band practice and I left mine at home.'

'Here.' Sam offered his bright blue-and-green-framed polarised sunglasses.

Megan recoiled. 'Yeah, nah, I'm good.'

'Rude.' Sam scowled and put them back on.

Baytree's queen of style wouldn't be seen dead in Sam's daggy dad sunglasses. Megan was one of those infuriating women who always looked amazing, even if she was wearing something as basic as a T-shirt and leggings. Although, now it appeared as if she could lose her throne to the sleek new mum on the block.

'Wow.' Dave looked at us each in turn. 'I can't believe you don't know who she ...'

'Dave!' I cried. 'Just put us out of our misery!'

'That is Rania Jalali!' Dave held out his hands, like a priest reciting the prayers of the faithful.

A noisy game of four square going on nearby became more audible in the long pause that followed this announcement.

'Who?'

Dave shook his head. 'Rania Jalali!'

'Saying it twice doesn't help.' Sam scratched at his stubble in frustration. 'Actor? Singer? Influencer?'

'Rania! From *The Rebound*!' Dave held his Astonished Man pose – shoulders up, arms out, eyes bulging, mouth agape – for at least three seconds. 'How can you not know this?'

Megan screwed up her face. 'The *reality TV* show?'

'Thank you!' Dave released the tension in his body with grand relief.

I'd never watched *The Rebound* but had overheard many conversations about it at work. Even if you hated those types of shows where women degrade themselves for the attention of a muscly dude who made millions selling protein supplements to bullied kids, you'd have to have been living under a rock not to have heard of the TV juggernaut Aussies loved to hate. My hospital co-workers had spent weeks dissecting the personalities of the unfortunate contestants, as each one was humiliated in cruelly creative ways. They'd speculate about who would sleep with whom, or who was the biggest bitch-slash-bastard. From what I could glean, the premise of *The Rebound* was something along the lines of: recently single, attractive Aussies (with rock-bottom self-esteem) looking for – you guessed it – a rebound. Classy. I mostly tuned out when these discussions started up, but I did recall often hearing the name Rania.

Even my fourteen-year-old daughter had got caught

up in the tawdry frenzy when it first aired last November.

'Please, Mum?' Zara begged at dinner one night. '*Everyone* is watching it!'

'I'm not.' I'd then proceeded to point one by one at her siblings around the table. 'Archie's not ... neither is Stella, and Max definitely isn't watching it, so ...'

'You know what I mean!' Zara hadn't appreciated my hilarious pedantry. '*Everyone* in Year Eight is watching it!'

'Well,' I waved my fork in the air, as though gesturing towards Zara's invisible classmates, '*everyone* in Year Eight can look forward to rewarding careers stacking supermarket shelves.'

For a moment, it seemed as if Zara was considering flipping the table, but instead settled for her signature eye roll. That was the last time *The Rebound* was mentioned in the Barrett household.

'Some of the guys at work watched it,' Sam said. 'Apparently, the "hot Pakistani chick" was everyone's fave.'

'Aren't men great?' Megan asked derisively.

'So, what's she doing here?' I watched as a small collection of dads started sidling their way into Rania's orbit. 'Shouldn't she and her new life partner be walking the red carpet at the opening of an envelope somewhere?'

'They broke up,' Dave said, bereft. 'A week after the last episode aired.'

'Aw, mate, you okay?' Sam said. 'Did the reality stars shatter your dreams when they consciously uncoupled?'

Sam's wife, Bridget, had left him for another man two years ago, significantly diminishing his romantic streak. These days, he was living his best life on Tinder and having lots of sex. Lots. We could always tell when Sam had got lucky the night before because he'd take an unnaturally long breath the moment he sat on our bench at drop-off. This was our cue to ask how the date went, which we always did. Megan and I were happy for Sam and his sexcapades. He deserved it after putting up with Bridget for so long.

'Rania has a five-year-old son.' Dave sat down, eager to fill us in. 'He must be starting here.'

'Gotta say, wouldn't have picked you for a reality fan, Dave,' I told him.

As a self-confessed uber geek, comic-book aficionado and talented graphic novelist, Dave was the unlikeliest viewer of reality-TV trash.

'Oh, Keshini *loves* it,' Dave said, slapping his hands on his thighs. 'I wasn't into it at first, but it sucked me in. I mean, if you start breaking it down, there are some great archetypal characters there.'

'You do realise these are actual human beings with actual feelings, don't you, Dave?' Megan snapped.

Oblivious to the warning tone in Megan's voice, Dave continued, 'Well yeah, of course, but these shows have been around long enough for people to know what they're signing up for.'

I had to agree with him there. Had people learned nothing from the litany of fallen and faded reality TV stars over the years?

Rania was still smiling and posing, but her gigantic sunglasses made it hard to tell if she was genuinely loving the attention or simply going through the motions. Either way, I suddenly resented this D-grade celebrity's intrusion. Megan wasn't the only parent who had unearthed her community spirit at Baytree Primary. Everyone contributed more these days, including me. The most recent working bee had broken all records for attendance (a meagre record to break, in fairness) and Megan, Sam and I were now the official organisers of the annual junior school Christmas concert. Last year, the kids performed Hans Christian Andersen's *The Little Match Girl* (not a dry eye in the house), and this year Megan and the drama teacher, Miss Mitchell, were planning an ambitious production of Leo Tolstoy's *Papa Panov's Special Christmas*. If anyone could pull it off, it was my bestie. Christmas was still a while away, so Sam and I had told Megan she wasn't even allowed to say the word 'concert' until term three.

There'd been a fair shifting of sands in my personal life over the last couple of years, too, including the fact that I now had two kids in secondary school. This was something I still found difficult to wrap my head around. There had been the whole private-versus-public discussion with every friend, co-worker and family member during Zara and Archie's last year of primary school. Greg and I couldn't afford private school, so two years ago we'd sent our twins off to Baytree Secondary, and hadn't regretted it for a moment.

Sam slung his charcoal Crumpler over his head and stood up. 'Gotta go.'

Megan frowned. 'I thought you started at ten?'

It was still weird to see Sam in his new work get-up. Up until a few months ago, he'd lived in jeans and a hoodie, but now that he was a respectable working man, a shirt (ironed), slacks and sensible shoes was the new look. He had a job in the next suburb over selling food-processing equipment. He didn't exactly love it, but he didn't hate it, either.

'Who could ask for anything more?' he'd said.

With his updated wardrobe, brown/grey stubble, short,

dark hair and rosy cheeks (probably from all the sex), Sam was happier, healthier and more handsome. He'd had a 'glow up' as my teenagers would say. Amazing what ridding yourself of a toxic wife could do for a man's libido and complexion.

'He wants me in at nine-thirty from now on,' Sam said. 'Early bird catches the mega-boring sales data and all that.'

'I'll walk with you!' Dave jumped up. 'Maybe I can sneak a selfie with Rania.'

'Please don't,' Sam groaned as he turned towards the gate.

Up until a year ago, Dave had only hung around on the periphery of our trio, but three had slowly become four and Dave was now one of us. He and Sam had even started an acoustic duo that played at last year's Mum's Night. They still didn't have an official name, although Megan and I had suggested many. Our top three were The Dad Jokes, The Baytree Bangers and Nana Nap, but the duo had chosen to ignore our inspired ideas and remained nameless. Actually, Remain Nameless was a pretty good name too, come to think of it.

'Yeah, okay,' Dave said, trotting after Sam like an obedient puppy. 'Probably best if I wait to get her alone.'

'Wow, that doesn't sound creepy at all.' Megan stood up, too. 'I have to talk to Penny about the newsletter. Bloody Nicola wants two full pages spruiking her Therapy Kitchen Hamper business.' Nicola McGinty was a school mum with a PhD in passive aggression.

'Okay, see ya tomorrow.'

'Not this arvo?'

'Nah, working.' I made a work-dread face. 'Aunty Carmen's doing pick-up.'

'Well, let me know if you need me to get them any other days this week,' Megan said. 'Us single mums gotta help each other out!'

Single mums. Ouch.